SLIPPERY

Liam Carroll

CONTENTS

For Peter,
who taught me to think clearly and laugh loudly,
Always

Author's Preface

Towards your final years of secondary schooling, you will most likely be forced to take a seat opposite a careers counsellor. Staring across the table at you, an earnest man or woman, well groomed and ill informed, covered in cheap fragrant enhancers and even cheaper clothing, will politely guide you through the world that exists beyond the school's perimeter - a frightening world where you have to earn a living.

What do you want to do with your life? What do you want to be?

The usual worn out paths will no doubt be considered. Medicine, law, engineering, building, accounting, even teaching may earn a mention. The phrase, a hard day's work for a fair day's pay, will likely fill your eardrums with misdirected anticipation of how the outside world functions.

It's rare a student will see straight through the well-intended farcical conversation and be brazen enough to say hey listen, I just want to make fuckloads of cash! In a world where cash is King, a student with the clarity of thought to ponder such a query is well on the road to righteousness.

Slippery

I was not that kid. I was bright eyed, freckle covered and cursed with adolescent notions of compassionate purpose. I chose physiotherapy, completing the requisite academic hoops and jump ropes to receive a piece of paper signed by a dean and stamped with University of Sydney insignia. Well done.

I continued on to endure a few years of having my good nature beaten out of me, my life consumed with endless thirty-minute appointments of pure misery. Patients would stare longingly into my eyes, believing I could somehow touch them like Jesus and wipe their pain clear. Meanwhile, men and women with dollar signs in their eyes and vacuums between their ears were banking bonuses that made my hip pocket weep and my heart fill with spiteful fury.

What were these people doing all day in those investment banks and trading firms anyway? The careers counsellor never laid out what exactly was going on at the top of the corporate ladder in those flashy office buildings.

I would have to work it out on my own.

Liam Carroll

1/ Thrown a Lifeline to Escape the Mundane

The problem with money is, you need it

It's Friday, midnight. I'm riding home from the Steyne Hotel, Manly Beach, grogged out of my mind after an evening at the Round Bar, smashing pints, yelling at footy games. The usual. Pedaling my BMX (with pegs) along Manly beachfront, to my right, whitewater bounces in the moonlight, to my left, heavily sea-salted air is misting around street lamps and infiltrating car engines. My mobile rings, more numbers on the screen than the screen can hold. Who the hell is this?

"Hello" I stammer, pulling the thrasher to a stop.

"Hi, am I speaking with Flynn James?" The razor sharp voice of some Englishman barks down the line. Sober up Flynn. Fast.

"Yes, Flynn here. How can I help you?" That was fairly convincing. I hope.

"Great, great. OK, I'm Steve Pemberton, head of recruitment at Scion Commodities. I received your CV, excellent stuff mate. Listen, I need you in Singapore next Saturday for an interview. I will send you an email, reply to my assistant cc'd and she will arrange the flights." These words travel down the phone line as if it is the most normal, matter of fact, mundane conversation ever.

"Yes, OK. No problem…thanks." I mean seriously, what the fuck?

"Good night." He was gone. That was that.

I continue the short ride home, sporting the unmistakable glazed expression a dumb-fucker sports when he has no idea what is going on, but thinks he can work it all out if he just holds that feeble stare long enough. Sit in an exam hall and watch the vacant gazes of all the poor battlers who inhabit the lion's share of the bell curve. This stare is unavoidable.

I'd sent a CV off merely a week earlier to a Swiss commodities company advertising for junior trading positions in their oil and metals trading arms. I'd sent plenty of CV's around the financial world juggernaut, usually to receive no answer or, occasionally, be sent some pithy reply, often months later, at best, about lowering headcounts, keeping ears to the ground, fingers on pulses, things in loops, synergies, blah, blah, total unrequited blah.

I had previously worked in an investment bank for three years trading precious metals derivatives, whatever the hell they are, sneaking my way on to the trading floor via a global markets traineeship. I was eventually turfed via the joys of international banking mega mergers and was now back doing what I hated…physiotherapy. Don't get me started. I'll come back to that little topic some other time if I'm completely bereft of ideas and want you to stop reading. Suffice to say, when you're 18 years young, wide eyed, simple minded and commercially useless, it is no time to be choosing career paths.

Although studying physiotherapy at Sydney University was a great way to see and touch scantily clad young ladies in the noble pursuit of mastering anatomy.

I wake up Saturday morning to Steve's email outlining various flight options Sydney to Singapore. This hadn't been some drunken reverie on the ride home. I reply with option number 3; Take off 8am Saturday from Sydney, land in Singapore at 2pm, head to a 3pm interview, wrap that up by 4.30pm and be taking to the skies on the 10pm flight home, straight to Sunday brunch. Seriously.

Only yesterday I was tooling around being a physiotherapist, pretending to give a flog about ruptured tendons, torn muscles, arthritic joints and how much they can hurt when the right person decides to crank up the pain perception volumes in their misery-focused thoughts and grace me with their half naked presence. My destiny was never supposed to comprise being subjected daily to these whining, brain-dead, pain worshippers looking at me for answers, some sympathy at the very least. Listen, I don't care! Shut up. Toughen up. Piss off. Surely there was a better way to fill the years between graduation and retirement than this.

But, to fulfill life's two certainties, death and taxes, an obvious requirement is the need to make a buck. 'No mun, no fun'. No taxes though, that is compelling. No food either, dammit. The cursed swings and roundabouts. But if you're put on this Earth to make money, why settle for a pittance by feeling up old ladies when you could be making shitloads playing with someone else's hard earned? Greed is good, a modern necessity really. And when you're university qualified with postgraduate icing on the supposed money making cake, it's soul destroying that simply paying for rent, food and a few alcoholic refreshments is enough to clear the bank balance.

Trading is the quickest way I know to become flush with cash and now I have a chance to get back in the trading game. You fucking beauty! I have to nail this. Where is the CV I sent them? What garbage have I spewed in their direction that they think is so excellent?

Yes, of course, derivatives, I basically invented the things. Ahem, naturally, corporate strategy, I am a master strategist, especially strategy as it pertains to the corporate realm. I mean come on, what other realms are there? Team player, no question, I live to work in teams and bind together for successful execution of strategic initiatives. Who wouldn't? Why would you possibly rather be surfing off some remote, tropical island when you could be team building? And bam, effective communication, it is kind of a hobby of mine, an area I take particular relish in exploring, discovering, perfecting the *art*, if you will. Fluent in German, French, Spanish and Indonesian, currently studying Mandarin, you know, because the future is, of course, China and I want to be able to communicate effectively with this vast nation of forward thinkers and dog connoisseurs.

Yes, indeed, all total, utter and complete horse shit. Of course they love it. How could they not? Well they should have, though I'm certain they probably didn't read it too closely. These smart bastards also made you answer four questions; why do you think you would make a successful trader, what trading positions do you currently have, what trades and initiatives would you undertake at Scion to increase profits while maintaining minimal risk profile, what do you like doing in your free-time? Savvy.

Any fool can steal a bunch of fancy sounding convoluted corporate hogwash buzzwords and phrases, spoof that onto a CV with a suitable couple of friends who can masquerade as references and off you scoot to an interview in your new suit past smoking hot receptionists into rarely used meeting rooms with impressive mahogany tables. But, to have a meaningful and well thought out trading idea, a profitable way to turn a little money into a lot, with minimal risk…now *that* is tough. Do you have any thoughts there champ? Come on. Don't be shy. Let me hear 'em.

No, you get some of those ideas, well thought out trading ideas with the backbone strength to put them on the chopping block, along with your balls, cock and jugular, and don't skimp on the white knuckle psychopathic commitment to hold on for the ride and, hey presto, you have real corporate value beyond your wildest dreams. And free time…you don't have any. You're too busy making money. Come on.

Thankfully, I had researched the company thoroughly and put together a response that they should use their existing logistics expertise to expand into agribusiness pursuits, levering their expert oil know-how to deliver improved pricing to the predominantly diesel based fuel requirements of agriculture and thus ensure an increased likelihood of success in entering the new market. A market which, on the whole, is currently grossly undervalued and will take on greater significance in the very near future. It's important to clarify, I have no idea if any of what I've just said is remotely near accurate, but it sounded good, didn't it? And seems as plausible as anything an *economist* has ever said. Anyway, who fucking cares, it worked.

Now, they're looking for *talented young professionals*. Instantly those three words should, by any logic, automatically exclude me. With *ambition*…now we're getting there. I may fit the mould. *Ambition*. Yep, tick. What do we want? Cash. When do we want it? Now! Do we care how we get it? What, you having a laugh? They need these talented young professionals to join their oil and metals trading teams and be fast tracked to become a commercially successful component of their global commodities trading business.

I have next to no idea about oil trading and it's nearing twelve months since I've worked in precious metals derivatives trading, a field in which I never for one moment had a clue as to what I was doing anyway. I have to refresh the memory banks on the metals side, and I better learn something about the no doubt extraordinarily nefarious world of oil trading.

I spend the entire weekend studying like a man possessed. Then, Monday to Friday at work, I think and breathe oil and metals trading, while successfully pretending to give a flying fuck about the patients' ailments. "Yes, Cheryl, you're really improving, no need to worry about that persistent nerve pain."

Returning home in the evening, I immediately resume my studies. I read and re-read every past scribble I've maintained regarding metals trading and financial markets. I scan every available piece of information on oil trading and anything at all on the current state of commodities, equities, interest rate and currency markets, global politics and interview tips.

In a blur it's Friday night. I'm lounging on the couch, having dinner, trying to relax, sipping a Heineken, watching Chelsea Lately. The next moment it's Saturday morning, I'm seated in business class plush soft brown leather aboard Singapore Airlines flight SQ 417, ravaging my notes and preparing for the full repertoire of questions to be flown my way. Steve had explained the format of the interview in his email: Two 40-minute interviews with two senior traders in each, the traders being from a variety of backgrounds and products.

For the uninitiated, here's what you must know about traders, they're cunts. Plain and simple, checkmate. This is not being rude. This is a fact. If they weren't, they wouldn't be traders. Not successful traders at least. They'd be off playing golf, scratching together their two brain cells while being paid to be a superannuation fund manager or some floozy well paid excuse for a job like that. You know the sort. Played rugby at a posh school or some shit. Their dad knew their dad, fucked their mum sort of routine. Or they somehow managed to snap nude photos of a CEO in a debauched gay orgy with little boys, a get-out-of-meaningful-labour-free-card, one of those Godsent Kodaks. No, not all cunts are traders, some sit in parliament, scalp concert tickets, sing in church choirs or function in some other equally slimy way that a perfect world wouldn't require. But the fact remains, while not every cunt is a trader, every trader is a cunt.

So here I am in the Changi airport toilets, straightening my tie, squirming in my suit, looking at the ambitious spastic in the mirror, giving myself the pump up speech, about to cab into a skyscraper; a modern day corporate Gladiator den to face four definite and seasoned cunts, all the while praying like hell they invite me into their beautiful world of well-paid-cuntiness.

I step through the airport doors only to be slapped in the face with inhumane levels of humidity. Sweat beads instantly engulf my temples. It is early afternoon in monsoonal Singapore. The sky is a charcoal grey. Standing undercover doesn't prevent horizontal raindrops from slamming straight into my eyeballs. A few minutes pass before the octogenarian in official garb directs me to a waiting taxi. The driver recognizes the address I'm heading to and we're off. Mercifully, the air-conditioning is blasting full bore.

Singapore is widely regarded as the Switzerland of Asia; clean, efficient, free of personality. But, it's refreshing to see the taxi drivers here are equally as insane as their counterparts in Jakarta, Bangkok and Ho Chi Minh. This beaten up vehicle is capable of going from zero to 100km/h in seven seconds and there must be a local law against staying in the same lane over that same magical seven-second mark too. My focus shifts from interview preparation to the more immediate need for repentance and the embedded hope for survival.

Within twenty minutes, we're at Raffles Place. Mr. Schumacher informs me this is the building I asked for. I pay the lunatic, give my tie a final adjustment and walk in. Like most modern day corporate Gladiator dens, the foyer is lavish, decorated with abstract art works, decadent chandeliers and middle-aged spectacled men in cheap suits behind immense reception desks.

"Excuse me sir, I have a 3pm appointment with Scion Commodities. Would you be able to direct me to the appropriate floor?"

"Yes sir, please use the lifts in the far corner, you need to go to floor 25. I will press the button to allow you access once you reach the lift."

"Thank you."

I'm whisked skyward and once again fidgeting with my tie. The elevator doors open and a stunning Singaporean woman in a figure hugging white dress is smiling almost violently at me through glass doors as I exit the lift. I walk reluctantly towards her. It's the sort of smile reserved for Cuckoo's nest dwellers. She presses a button to open the doors.

"Hello, I'm Angela Fong, I'm the HR manager for Scion's Singapore office. You must be Flynn." Angela's pleasantly self-assured voice belies her borderline insane smile.

"Yes, indeed, hello Angela." We shake hands. Her smile somehow intensifies while her eyes disappear.

"Please, follow me. Would you like water, coffee?"

"No thanks, I'm fine."

We reach a boardroom and two gents are already there waiting. They look impeccably smart, mind-numbingly serious and deeply, deeply Asian.

"Flynn, please meet Jason, he is from Beijing, and Calvin, from Singapore. They are also waiting for their interviews this afternoon. I will come back soon and let you know when the interviews are ready to start." With that, Angela's out the door.

"Hi guys, how are you?"

"I'm well, fank you, Fwynn." Could Jason be any more stereotypically Chinese?

"Nice to meet you, Flynn, hope you're well. Where are you from?" Calvin looks like Jason's twin, but he has somehow managed to steal Barack Obama's voice.

"I'm from Sydney actually, was quite a flight to get here. Feeling fine though. Good luck with your interviews guys."

Before I get the chance to settle into Saturday afternoon high tea with Jason and Calvin, Angela's back. "Flynn, please walk to the very end of the corridor. Your interview is in the 'Newton' room. When your interview is finished, please just come back to this room and wait for the following interview here. Good luck."

Here goes. I check my watch, 2.59pm, and follow Angela's directions through the corridor to the Newton room.

"Helloooo, you are Flynn nyess? Pleeease, take seeat." I'm thrown from the outset. This eastern European gent has greeted me so warmly despite looking about as welcoming as a Siberian wolf. His eyes are jet-black, menacing and ice cold. His plain white shirt is unbuttoned halfway down his chest, sleeves rolled up to the elbows. There is also a young Indian guy seated in the room, though he's busy scrolling through emails on his Blackberry as I enter.

"Good afternoon, yes, I'm Flynn, nice to meet you."

"I'm Artem and this is Pranav."

"Great to meet you both." We shake hands. I take a seat. Pranav seems irritated at having to lose eye contact with his phone for the briefest of introductions.

"So, why you think you will be good trader?" Artem is the Usain Bolt of interviewers, no foreplay here, straight to business. I feel my hands quivering a little and make sure they're out of sight under the table.

"Well, I…"fuck, get it together…"Well, I want to be in a position to make critical decisions. Decisions which can prove highly profitable and which carry significant risks. I want to be able to incorporate all the factors which have driven a commodity's price to where it's trading now and take a view as to where it will move in the future, and put trades on accordingly which have the best probability of making money."

"Nyess, nyess, I hear aenswer like thiss all day. Sound very nyice nyess, of course. But why will you be good trader? Why you?" Bloody hell Artem, just give me the job, ya bastard, I'm a good bloke.

"OK, I hear you. I...I will be a good trader because I live and breathe markets..."

"Huuhhhhh," a lengthy, exasperated sigh evaporates from Artem's lungs, "I hear this too many times already, tell me why. Why you good trader? Why?" This Artem bloke sure is a cunt. But I already knew that before I came here, didn't I.

"Will you let me finish mate?"

"Nyess. Plaeese, continue."

Whatever is next to come out of my mouth better be sen-fucking-sational.

"I will be a good trader because I'm not afraid to trade against prevailing market sentiment, to take a view and put my trade on, even when current market commentary may be contrary to my opinion. But, far more importantly, I will be an excellent trader because I am certain I will often be wrong and, for that reason, enter every trade with the disciplined approach and defined plan of exactly when, where and why to take profits, or to stop out and take a loss. There is no emotional attachment involved. I do not delude myself with the misplaced confidence that I am always right or that markets come close to something which makes logical sense. The trading world is thought of as a world for men with big balls and swinging dicks. Fortune favours the brave apparently. I don't believe in this mantra or fit that mould. My mind is broad, my balls are small and I'll definitely require some lengthening surgery to allow my dick to ever swing on anything but a hot summer's day. But all that aside, I will most certainly be an excellent trader for your firm because I work tirelessly to research every factor pushing prices, while trading with discipline and shrewdness, rather than big balls or chest-beating charades of alpha male attempts at courage, bravery, or success." Cop that, ya fucking Slav cunt.

"OK, nyess, I think I've heard enough."

"Umm, OK." Have I flown from Sydney to Singapore for the quickest interview in history?

"Thank you for coming, Flynn. You have another interview at 3.45pm, please wait in the conference room for that." Wow, Pranav, nice of you to join us.

"Thanks. Good afternoon gents."

What the hell just happened? I'm back in the original waiting room and it's 3.05pm. Such a short interview cannot be good. Or can it? Angela walks in. There doesn't appear too much surprise in her eyes that my interview lasted no longer than a movie preview. I decide I do need some caffeine.

"Angela, is there still a possibility of getting a coffee?"

"Yes, of course, one moment."

I replay the preceding six minutes in my head. I can't really think of anything I could have done differently. I could have asked some questions of the company I suppose, but they didn't really give me the chance. And who was that snotty Indian kid?

There's no sign of the other two candidates when Angela arrives back with a coffee. I ask her about the two that interviewed me. She tells me Artem is a Serbian scrap metal trader. Scrap. Seriously. Fuck my luck. Scrap metal trading is reserved purely for Mafioso's who have killed a minimum of three family members to even be admitted to the trade. Wretched Serb. And Pranav is an Indian genius whiz kid who trades naphtha, whatever the fuck that is. Pair of cunts.

She leaves the room and I stare out at the incessant rain bucketing in, sipping my coffee. This is not looking promising.

3.44pm, Jason and Calvin return simultaneously, waxing lyrical about their interviews. Fuck. Angela advises me to take the first door on the left for the next interview, the 'Galileo' room this time.

"Flynn, good afternoon. I'm Joel and this is Andrew." Joel stands about 5'10, speaks with a subtle Kiwi twang and, like most New Zealanders, sports the physique of an ex rugby union star; bulky neck, powerful chest, mauled up cauliflower ears.

"Good afternoon, Joel. Hi, Andrew. Thanks for having me."

"Please, take a seat, Flynn." Andrew's voice box is sculpted with a South African brush. His physique also sporty and he can't be taller than 5'6, bang on the mark of a healthy Napoleon complex.

Joel gets things started, "I like this resume, Flynn, I especially like the references to where you've studied and worked. Pray tell, is this the first time you've ever left Sydney?" He and Andrew burst into hysterics. He holds my CV up and I realize that on the right margin there is a recurrent 'Sydney, Australia' written almost continually, beside each job I've had and where I studied at university and school. Ah, yep, I feel the intense thudding pain of the bullet I've so astutely shot into my own foot.

This is the last interview of the day and once the initial chortling subsides, Joel and Andrew launch into the more usual interview proceedings. They ask me some trading questions, I smash it back over the umpire's head, over the boundary fence, maybe I do know what a derivative is. Andrew asks how the first interview went earlier. I don't hold any punches, saying I'm fairly certain Artem thinks I'm less useful that tits on a bull and that's probably many shades higher than the esteem the Pranav bloke would hold me in. Joel and Andrew again start laughing, "Noone likes those pricks anyway mate. Don't sweat it."

They test the linguistic mastery I have over-inflated on the CV. With Baby Jesus by my side, Joel picks the only language of the five that I can actually speak, German. He asks, *auf Deutsch,* my opinion of Angela Merkel. I reply in fluent German straight out of my arse, my mouth no longer required, that she has a very difficult job convincing the German *Volk* to bear the burden of the Greek debt crisis, but she should take a leaf out of history's book and grow a set of balls like Hitler, well one ball at least. Joel fucking loves it! Andrew doesn't speak German, *wie schade.*

These two are clearly good friends. They talk up the company and the opportunities that are there for me. Joel then looks me in the eye, "So, Flynn, why do you want to be a trader?"

I had a prepared answer to this precise question, more in keeping with the usual corporate-speak filled mantra of hard-work, dedication, that sort of total and utter crap, which millions of CV's are filled with and interviewers are subjected to each and every day. Ah, the humanity. I had already answered Artem's question of why I would be a good trader, but why did I actually want to be a trader in the first place? Money, obviously, but there is more to it. I sense the camaraderie already in the room and get the feeling to be personal in response, to a point perhaps considered almost corporate suicide in any other scenario.

"I am so bored with physiotherapy. Bored out of my brain. I fucking hate these old ducks whingeing garbage about their decrepit old bodies. I know I can trade. I know I can spot bull-shitters and loopholes. I know I have the smarts to see an opportunity and the backbone to push the button and put the trade on. I want to come to work pumped, every day, and take big but calculated risks with huge sums of money and endless opportunities to win and lose. This is the world I want to be in."

Joel and Andrew turn to each other and smile, look back at me, Joel says, "that is the greatest answer I have ever heard. We would have also accepted, 'I want to make shitloads of money', but let's just assume that's a given hey."

With that, we shake hands and I'm off. It's 4.10pm. Angela stands from the reception desk, walks me to the elevator and wishes me good luck and a safe trip home. I don't see my dear pals Jason and Calvin. The lift doors open on the ground floor. I undo my tie, take off my jacket and step outside into the overwhelming humidity. My brief encounter with Scion is complete and I'm walking the streets of Singapore to find a bar and kill some time before flying home.

There is no doubt I nailed the second interview, no doubt, three cunts in perfect harmony. The first interview was disastrous. But I get the impression Joel is the big cheese, the individual who reigns supreme inside the boardroom when decisions are ultimately made.

I walk a few hundred aimless metres before settling in a bar on Club St, order a pint of tiger beer, take a hearty first sip and start watching rugby league. It's barely fifteen minutes since the interview and that glazed stare following Steve's initial phone call only a week earlier is back with a vengeance. I look beyond retarded, attempting to piece together the afternoon's events. The phone rings, the requisite dizzying amount of numbers on the screen once more alert me to who will likely be on the end of the line.

"Hello, Flynn James speaking."

"Flynn, it's Steve from Scion. Listen, fantastic interviews, fantastic. The traders loved you. We need you in Geneva in a fortnight. I'll send you an email, reply to Luciana with the preferred travel arrangements. Now, in Geneva, we will run a simulation-trading day. It will run from 9am to 4pm, three separate games to test your trading and negotiation skills and general teamwork, decision making, that sort of thing. It's easy mate, stressful, but you'll smash it. Joel Ryan will be in charge. You met him today yeah?"

The big cheese, I knew it.

"Yes, he interviewed me this afternoon."

"Great, yes, of course. Then after the simulation day, it's dinner with the board, senior staff and traders. A kind of musical chairs set up. Basically, seven-course dinner and each course you stay seated, the Scion guys will move round the table and get to meet all of the candidates. We're just finishing up all the interviews today in our Geneva and Houston offices as well. It will be quite the United Nations on the day mate. Any questions?"

"No, no. Ah well, anyway to prepare that you recommend?"

"Be yourself mate, you're smart, you'll be fine."

"OK."

"See you in Geneva, Flynn."

I immediately call Dad, "Super Dad, mate, I fooled them! They're sending me on to Geneva in a fortnight for something called 'Simulation Day'. I get through that little chestnut and I'll have the gig."

"Good on ya, Dumb Kid! Bloody ripper mate."

Arriving home Sunday to a clear, crisp Sydney morning, having slept like a log in the full lay-down chairs of Singapore Airlines' Business Class, I'm immediately preparing for Geneva, reading financial news and researching 'negotiation' books that I will have to read and master in the next fortnight. Steve said you cannot prepare for the Geneva 'Simulation'. Yeah right mate. You can always prepare. You always have to.

I start feverishly doing maths problems, not overly complicated formulae or pointless shit like that, no, just the quick thinking arithmetic and probability understanding required to be a bookie, trader or drug dealer. 21 times 52, 112 divided by 4, 1kg is equal to how many troy ounces of platinum, if I buy a call option on me successfully nailing this simulation day, what delta would I expect to pay? Every moment is absorbed with this mind play.

Oil trading is a truly global business. I survey each dark corner of Google maps, learning every major city name, every country, every river and mountain from Vladivostok to the Panama Canal. I read, for the first time with real interest, the global affairs component of the news, always a bit of a joke in an Australian 'news'paper. I resort to online outlets for this. What the fuck is the Gaza Strip? Who's in charge of Saudi Arabia? Which companies control oil pipelines in the USA? Which African nations are the Chinese heavily investing in? Just what the hell are all these eastern European nations with –stans at the end and gorgeous women throughout? My mind is racing with all this and I become engaged in learning like never before. Here for the first time, the chance, potentially, to apply knowledge in a meaningful way - meaningful being, obviously, to make fucking shitloads of cash.

The logistics of flying from Sydney to Geneva for an interview requires some swift thinking and necessary truth-bending in order to reasonably explain to my current employer why I can possibly require a whole week off in less than a fortnight for, of all reasons, to fly to

Europe. Luckily I can once again pull out the German trump card, having lived there as an exchange student when I was a teenager.

"You'll never believe it, my host brother back in Germany is getting married, it's all very sudden and they were so sorry that they hadn't given me a decent amount of time to prepare flights that they would pay for me to fly to the ceremony in Switzerland, if only I can get the time off with such short notice. Can you believe it? My host-brother, Jens, is getting married. It would be amazing if you could let me take that week off, it would mean so much." I'm a fairly poor liar at the best of times, but it's so critical to success in life, I'm doing my best to improve quickly. ·

"Of course, of course. That sounds amazing! Wow, I've never been to Europe. That will be fantastic. You have a great time OK."

I thank my boss, Amanda, and pray for success in Geneva so I will never have to work another day in this cesspit of mediocrity and forced smiles.

2/ The Geneva Simulator

You have two choices, go big or fuck off

I put my suitcase into Dad's boot with an autumn drizzle bidding me farewell. We set off for the Emirates flight waiting to jet me to a Geneva Simulator Interview. Dad presses play on his usual mix of Leonard Cohen, Lou Reed, Talking Heads and Dire Straits.

"I don't know too many people who are flown business class around the world for job interviews. You must have a pretty spectacular Dad."

"Yeah, he's not too bad."

"He's probably a total stud with the ladies too, you'd have to think."

"He goes alright."

We pull into Kingsford Smith. Talking Heads' 'Road to Nowhere' is blasting.

"Now, I may not have any words of wisdom for you, Dumb Kid, but I do know this, if I could bet on anyone excelling in any situation, any situation at all, I'd put the house on you, mate. And I'd win every

29

time."

"Cheers Super Dad."

"Oh, and if they ask any really tricky questions, just remember, look at it this way…" Dad looks me in the eye then tilts his head to the side, holding me in a confused, constipated stare.

"I'll definitely remember that one."

"Safe travels mate, I'll be thinking of you."

"Thanks SD."

"Wouldn't be dead for quids aye."

"Not a chance."

I grab my suitcase and hold my head side on as I wave Dad goodbye. I walk on in to complete all the usual checking-in, scanning-thru, form-filling sort of rigmarole that's required to board a plane. My business class ticket does entitle me to wait for my flight in the business class lounge. Air travel, the true bastion of class division and social inequality. So civilized. Regardless of how much money I could ever make, there will never come a point where I could justify forking out the cash required to fly any other way but in the cramped confines of cattle class. But when someone else wants to foot the bill, then please, pass the caviar.

I arrive in Geneva on Monday afternoon, feeling a million bucks. Anyone with the audacity to whinge about business class travel can fuck right off. Once I'm checked in at the hotel, I set off walking through town, around the lake, Geneva on a Monday afternoon in late spring, gorgeous. To be perfectly honest, it's a pretty odd place. Signs everywhere for ridiculously overpriced watches and handbags, serious looking people carrying briefcases, baguettes and stern faces. 17 francs for a ham and cheese croissant, that seems a bit pricey.

Groups of peeved looking black youths abound on street corners, looking menacing, freestyle rapping in French. I hesitate a moment, assessing the pedestrian tunnel ahead, Nigerians hanging out all around it. CNN-pre-programmed-racism is powerful stuff. Ah fuck it, I may as well, live a little.

"G'day fellas".

"Alo".

I loosen the grip on my wallet as I stroll through and off down the street, Mont Blanc smiling down in the distance.

Tuesday morning, 9am, I'm seated in a large boardroom with 17 other candidates. It's safe to assume the table is mahogany. Steve wasn't kidding, the UN would be proud to see such diversity in a room. I'm scared shitless, mega-litres out of my depth, certain to vomit any moment. Yeah, I'm ready. Along the walls stand a group of maybe a dozen Scion staff, all gents, one steps forward to the end of the table.

"Welcome, everyone. We're delighted to have you here. I'm Steve Pemberton, head of global recruitment and in charge of our junior trader program. I've spoken with all of you over the phone and will be sure to meet each of you today. Firstly, congratulations on being here, we received close to 5,000 applications, no easy task assessing all of those, but much more difficult to stand out in such a big crowd, so, well done. Secondly, I want you to enjoy today. It will be stressful, no question. We will be assessing every single thing you do, which is obviously awful. Please, be yourselves, and just enjoy the challenge. And finally, if successful, we want you to slot straight into a trading desk, learn the ropes in the shortest time possible and be trading metals, oil or both in a commercial role in the very near future. I will now hand over to Mr. Joel Ryan, our Head of Far East Trading and Senior Director."

"Thanks Steve. Welcome once more everyone. You are all obviously tremendously gifted and smart. Today, we want to see how you react to situations, which we deem critical in the successful day-to-day functioning of a physical commodities trader. There are 18 of you here today. If you are all exceptional, we will hire all of you, if you are all atrocious, we will hire no one. There is no quota. So please, you are not in competition with each other. Do your best, have fun. Myself and a whole bunch of other senior traders and members of Scion will be asking you questions and assessing your every move throughout the three tasks we've arranged for today. As Steve said, this is awful for you. Sorry. It's critical in assessing you. I will now pass over to David Simmons. He is in charge of the nitty-gritty of how today will work. Listen closely. Enjoy. Good luck."

David steps forward and outlines 'Simulation Day'. Game one is an individual task, lasting 84 minutes, divided into twelve 7-minute trading windows, each window designed to represent one trading week, twelve windows designed to replicate a 3-month trading period. We will receive an email at the start of each window containing information about all manner of events and will have until the 6:59 mark of that window to ring one of the brokers (i.e. one of the Scion people seated in the room, manning the phones) and buy or sell January or February crude oil futures contracts or January or December gasoline futures contracts. The email will contain the opening price of the crude and gasoline futures, as well as various other pieces of market information. Prices may shift throughout the 7-minute window. Markets rely on prices moving otherwise traders face extinction.

Each candidate will have two computer screens to work with, one with an email account to receive the 7-minute-ly updates, the other with an excel spreadsheet to use as a trading blotter. We will also have a notebook, pencil, calculator and a phone to call the brokers. At all times, a Scion trader will be seated next to each candidate, asking questions and assessing, while other Scion staff will be roaming the room, asking questions if they want to, and assessing from afar.

David finishes his outline of the next 84 minutes with, "it's not necessarily about making money, it is about being able to articulate your strategic reasons for the trades you make and reacting to the news and price movements throughout and placing new trades accordingly. Taking profits, stopping losses, increasing or decreasing exposures."

Despite this pep talk, I'm sure if you do make a lot of *imaginary* money that has to help your well-paid-cuntiness prospects.

The fourth trading window pushes into the third minute. The emails firing out every seven minutes are usually four to five paragraphs long, essentially in the format a newsreader delivers to the nation each night, only there are no wooden smiles or flirting with weather ladies here. Like most news, the emails contain all manner of information, mostly useless:

'A new iPad has been released. It is anticipated to be the fastest selling Apple product in history. The UK is considering implementing new measures to decrease welfare dependence. There are reports of evacuations at the Norwegian county of Hordaland, as Statoil's Mongstad refinery explosion causes havoc for local rescue officers. The Mongstad refinery is Norway's largest. President Obama has declared the continued resistance to his planned Medicare changes is against the best interests of all Americans."

Three weeks ago, I would have been absorbed in wondering about what this latest iPad might look like, how much did the UK spend on welfare, what were the specific details of Obama's Medicare changes? Not now though, those details are speed read through and determined, without hesitation, to be fluff standing in the way of meaningful, market-moving information. I'm loading up a short position in crude oil, length in gasoline.

"Why do you have that position, Flynn?" Joel asks politely over my shoulder.

"Large refinery outage, decreased need for input, crude, market short refined product, gasoline." Seems straightforward enough.

"Exactly. Now why are you being such a fucking pussy, short 50 lots crude, long 30 lots gasoline? You're nowhere near your risk limit with those pathetic trades, mate."

"Umm" I am a pussy, no intestinal fortitude to back myself, just a pair of delectable beef curtains.

"Strap it on, Flynn. Strap it fucking on, son!" Joel's towering over me at my seat as I tremble with fear, quivering like the pussy I am, about to be royally fucked.

"Yep, yep, gotchya." I mean, what are you supposed to reply? Nod, smile and strap it the fuck on.

"It's the right trade so either go big or fuck off!"

With that he thunders off, his shirt half tucked in, his sleeves rolled up, stalking the room for prey, victims to abuse, vilify, generally make sure that if they get through today without falling in a heap, crying for their creator and pleading for mummy, then maybe, just maybe, they are indeed top notch material for a role in the commodities trading business.

As he storms off I ring the broker, "Where's your bid? 400 lots Jan crude? Yours. Cheers. And offer in 300 lots Jan gasoline? Mine.

Thanks." I update my blotter and steal a glance over my shoulder, "Kenneth, what the fuck are you doing, you stupid fucking retard? I told you already, that is a bad trade. Fuck it off! Why do you still have it on? Why? Why the fuck! You sure are one dumb cunt, Kenneth."

Mr. Joel Ryan, hopefully my future boss, has just decimated Kenneth, a fellow candidate. I met Kenneth last night at the hotel. A pleasant enough lad from Korea, he talked a big game about having a degree in pure mathematics and trading electricity futures in London or some shit. It's probably a lie he tells his mates, parents and, naturally, chicks. He is more likely some shit-kicker in a bank or trading firm, who thinks by sitting near a trader, he is one. Asians, on the whole, like to think they're good at maths. Maybe they are. Who cares? It's maths, maths fucking sucks. Trading isn't maths. Accounting, physics, mathematics, that's maths. Go do that if you're so good at maths and love it so much. Get your rocks off on Microsoft excel, you deranged weirdo. Kenneth's day is, so far, not going well. Fantastic.

This is not your typical interview process and it's becoming clear, this is not your typical, modern, castrated sort of company. I smile, starting to feel right at home and try to swiftly piece together what Kenneth has indeed so supremely fucked up and how to do the opposite immediately - and in size.

The final trading window closes; 84 minutes elapsed in an arrhythmic heartbeat. 12 seven-minute slices of pain and glory, brow rubbing and phone calls, questions and bullshit-stained answers, now behind me. I'm told to save my spreadsheet blotter and email it to the assessor's address. I've amassed close to ten million imaginary dollars. There are scribbles and notes all over my desk. My direct assessor who's been seated next to me for the duration, asking questions and being fat, John, a rotund cockney Englishman with thick glasses and a thicker neck scribbles some final notes on his pad and says, "Nice work geezer." He rises out of his chair with clear difficulty and waddles away, I assume to the mens' to unleash hell.

There's a fifteen-minute recess. I'm standing in a smallish room by the side of the trading floor with the international assortment of fellow wannabe-cunts, having a biscuit and black coffee. I've traveled the furthest to be here today, but I'm impressed with the breadth of geographical bases Scion has scoured in its search for talent. There's obviously Kenneth from Korea. He's a broken man. I hear him tell someone he lost 15 million in the game. I'm euphoric. There's Dan from Canada, a nice fella and rock-climbing fanatic, Andrea from Cape Town, legs from heaven complimented by a divine rack, definitely would, Fred from Belgium, which unsurprisingly reminds me of Dr Evil's webbed-feet-prostitute-mother.

I don't have time to meet everyone. Ravi from Mumbai is fascinated with me. He thinks, quite incorrectly, that based on my Australian-ness, I give something of a toss about cricket. I hate cricket. He rattles on about some test match that went on for five days in the searing heat of some Hindu forsaken scorched oval in Calcutta. It ended in a draw, for fuck's sake. Cricket-lovers, and sports-fans in general, can waffle through nonesense conversations like this for eternity. Do they not understand the whole exercise is a farce? The Ravi's of the world, and there are billions of them, can't see the whole charade of professional sports for what it really is; the ultimate showground for bookmakers to fix the lot and make trillions, while shoe salesmen, grog peddlers and tobacco pushers seize the opportunity to entice you into superfluous consumables while your life disappears in a damp seat at some stadium or on a soft couch in a suburban home. Come on. Get with the program.

We remain gathered in the glass bubble, a room of coffees, biscuits and nervous tension. All of us are looking into the vacant trading floor of computer screens and keyboards. Along the walls are sporadic windows dreary and dull with Geneva's attempt at muzzled spring sunshine failing to provide any meaningful light. David passes each of us a piece of paper outlining the rules of 'Game 2'.

"There will be four trading windows, each lasting twenty minutes. You have been placed into pairs for this exercise. Please check the board behind you now, find your partner and introduce yourself."

Despite the high probability that each of the candidates in this room is extremely intelligent, human-herd-stupidity prevails. 17 university qualified morons race for the board simultaneously. I grow in confidence, watching these fools scurry as though it's first to see their name wins. I stand back and wait. David notices and gives a nod.

"You're Flynn, yes?" I come back to the moment at hand, a middle-eastern looking young woman with an American accent introduces herself, shakes my hand, smiling.

"Hi, yes, nice to meet you, Sira." Thankfully, we're all wearing nametags.

"Where are you from Flynn?"

"I'm from Sydney. You?"

"Lebanon originally. But I've lived in America since I was ten. I actually have relatives in Sydney, though I've never had the chance to visit them."

"Cool. So we're a team then yeah? I haven't checked the board."

"Yep, you and I, dynamic duo. Let's smash this shit."

Based on first impressions, this Lebanese Yankee is one cool chick. I feel we've got a shot in this next game. David allows the group a minute for introductions.

"OK, hopefully for all your sakes, your partner is smarter than you. Now, this game is concerned with freight markets. At the beginning of each window, you will be given an update on the price of copper in various ports throughout the globe and the quoted freight rates to ship goods from these ports to Shanghai and San Francisco where your clients await shipment. You will also receive a news report of prevailing market conditions for copper and other commodities, financial instruments such as foreign exchange and currencies and general news. Your sole requirement is to deliver a minimum of 25,000 tonnes of copper to Shanghai or San Francisco, and up to a maximum of 100,000 tonnes. Along with that requirement, you want the shipment to be profitable. Prices will fluctuate, opportunities will present themselves, larger shipments may carry cost benefits, but with added risks, you will again receive all this information via email at the outset of each twenty-minute window. You are entitled to completely lock down your cargo, costs, profits or losses within the first trading window. That would obviously be a little silly, we didn't create the four windows for that purpose, but you can do that if you think it's a good option. Again, trades are to be executed via calls to the brokers and documented on your trading blotters, which will again be emailed to the assessors at the end. You may lock in a price in an earlier window and then look to unwind it and start again in later windows. That is perfectly fine and may well prove to be a profitable strategy. This game will require more analysis than game one, calculating freight costs will require some thought and consideration. As per game one, your direct assessor seated next to you will be questioning you about your decisions, but now they will also serve as a resource for you to ask questions of, as you deem necessary. Good luck. Decide at which desk of your pair you want to set up shop and we will commence in three minutes."

Sira is an excel superstar. In less than five minutes, she absorbs each parameter of the game into a spreadsheet to calculate ideal freight rates at which we can maximize tonnage and profits. It provides a clear and concise comparison of San Francisco versus Shanghai margins and costs and is complete with color coding and shading.

Chicks, they really are too smart. It's scary. If not for hormonal volcanoes wreaking havoc on the day-to-day reliability of such amazing clarity of thought, men would be obsolete.

I manage to hide how impressed I am, and offer advice on how to coordinate the spreadsheet, tailor it to our needs. *Improve* it. I have no idea what I'm saying, but she seems to be nodding and making the adjustments. I have actually assisted, though I would not have been able to produce this spreadsheet alone. The assessor looks suitably impressed and asks few questions. When we ask his advice, he is neutral or in simple agreement with the approach we have taken. Beautiful.

The third trading window is nearing a close and we've locked in a $3 million profit on a cargo totaling 70,000 tonnes. We have reservations about committing to the final pricing before the fourth window, but together draw the same conclusion that, in the near term, prices in supplier ports look set to rise, while end users face likely supply gluts, freight rates should inevitably drop with this imbalance and may provide profitable opportunities, however we mutually decide copper price fluctuations are a greater downside risk to our profitable position than the upside of falling freight.

Adrian, our assessor, another Englishman, agrees with our analysis and concurs it is sound commercial reasoning to lock trades in and be safely money-making rather than risk waiting and become loss-producing.

The fourth window email arrives. Primo. Our $3 million profit would have been eroded to $500k had we not crystallized the trades and locked in our positions. We are able to sit back and watch the other pairs scramble. Adrian shakes our hands and wanders off. Sira and I talk about boxing kangaroos, crocodile hunter manslaughter, and kebabs.

It's 12.30pm. We're breaking for lunch, seated once more in the original large boardroom where the day began. I'm refueling on an ethnically diverse variety of foods in keeping with the many nationalities in the room. There's some couscous and Moroccan lamb, a vegetarian samosa and some buttered chicken, a slice of pizza and more black coffee. I'm no *foodie*. If I was having a bowl of Weet Bix and vegemite on toast I would be right at home. Nothing would change. I would still be munching away and mulling over my strategy for how to approach the remainder of simulation day.

A phenomenally fit looking bloke next to me says hello. "Hi, I'm Sebastian. I'm from Madrid. That was an intense morning, yeah? I can't wait to get back to the hotel later, do some yoga, run the bath and chill." Who/what are you? Sebastian looks to be fresh from a swimming session with Michael Phelps, a human V, in preparation for Olympic glory. And he seems to have confused Simulation Day with some sort of anti-gluten, meditation course.

"Yeah, hi mate, I'm Flynn, from Sydney. Yeah, intense is an understatement. I'm not sure about the yoga and bath mate, but I'll definitely be having a beer and a chill as soon as the next simulation is over."

Lunch winds to a close and I'm cursing the array of foodstuffs I walloped down. The mixed ethnicities have declared Jihad on each other in my stomach. The 6 mugs of black coffee throughout the morning are serving as abdominal kerosene to fuel the racial tension. The fighting will inevitably end in an inverted, almond-tinged, mushroom explosion straight to the core of some unfortunate Genevan porcelain. I can't wait. The number two is far and away my favourite.

David begins his explanation of 'Game 3'. I can only hope he isn't drowned out by my grumbling guts.

"How's everyone going so far? Great. Well, you're almost finished. For the final game, you will be in groups of three. There are 18 of you here today and you have been divided into three groups of six and two groups of three within each. There will be three members playing the role of buyers, three members as sellers. You are working in teams to either buy or sell an iPhone-type widget with various parameters, which will be explained to you in the instructions we will soon hand out.

The aim of the game is to strike a deal. For the initial 45 minutes, you will be in a room in your group of three to work out the best possible strategy for the product you're trying to buy or sell, what terms of the deal you require to make a profit. You will have two assessors in the room with you, watching and assessing. For this game they are not a resource to ask questions of. Pretend they are not there.

After 45 minutes of strategy, you will have a 5-minute recess. Then, the final 45 minutes of the day will involve each of the three groups of buyers and sellers facing off in a boardroom, negotiating price and quantity for an allocation of these widgets. There, you will have a total of four assessors, the two from the buyer and seller sides, making assessments of the negotiation and taking note of how your boardroom antics match with your strategy ideas.

There are more rules and specifics to the game, which are outlined in the instructions and I will let you work these out in your strategy session. Remember, we want you to strike a deal and ideally, that deal is to your benefit as buyer or seller. As always, good luck."

Game 3 is a tricky bugger. My brief, along with my partners, David from Luxembourg and Peter from Germany, is to sell as many iPhone widgets as possible. There are four widget colours: black, red, green and blue. Every other detail of widgetdom is identical, aside from the fact that our imaginary warehouse is stocked with 7,000 black and 3,000 green widgets, which we apparently didn't sell last year. If we can sell these, it is pure profit, the sweetest kind. To manufacture a red or blue widget will cost $20, black and green widgets only cost $15. Racism and inequality are rife in imaginary widget manufacturing. Our sales target is 15,000 widgets, colour unimportant, and a minimum of $100,000 profit. Profit doesn't discriminate.

Two very similar looking men sit in the shadows of our room at the far end of another mahogany table. They look to be in their early 40's, both wearing crisp white business shirts and navy blue ties, and each sport long hair slicked back like European love children of Gordon Gekko. For their sins they are watching David, Peter and my good self, *strategizing*. You have to feel for them. It must be torturous.

Games 1 and 2 were a dream, smashing the lights out in the individual game and then blessed with a perfect partner for the pairs performance. Now I'm shunted with two complete nonces, useless fodder who simply must have known someone high up in the company to have been ushered through this far in to the selection process. They waffle and pontificate about our best approach as sellers of these imaginary widgets and give no thought to a specific number with which we can turn a profit, based on the information we have been given.

I've spent half an hour with David and Peter and I hate them intensely. Not because they're totally useless, most people are, but because they are wasting my precious time at a point in my one and only existence when time is well and truly of the fucking essence. While they've been wanking on about God knows what, Wimbledon, castles along the Rhine, fuck knows and I, especially, don't care, I'm busy scribbling away trying to work out the combinations and permutations of different coloured widgets that will be ideal to smash the $100,000 profit target and shift some damn widgets.

I try to invite them in to this line of gaming, "David, you mind passing that calculator? Cheers, let's work out some formula for widget colours, quantities, profit or loss numbers, final sales prices for each." I mean fuck, it's not rocket science, but you do want a number in your head of where you profitably sell your damn product before entering a meeting with the purchasers.

David passes the calculator over and he and Peter continue talking *strategy* with each other, *how to sell* sort of bollocks. I am grateful the two men in the shadows can see that I'm the brains behind this outfit, because there is no doubt once I tell my pals from Luxembourg and Germany the perfect combination of colours and quantities to nail this game, they will have no hesitation in claiming my commercial thinking is something to be shared equally three ways.

It's time to negotiate. Opposite the united colours of Luxembourg, Germany and Australia, sit Jean from France, Henry from the UK and Xia from China. Honestly, 'Xia', a good sort too, though I'm not convinced she was born a woman. We are joined by two further assessors who have spent the previous 45 minutes surveying Jean, Henry and Xia in the throes of strategizing next door. The assessors look impressive and ominous, as though they just walked out of a Gillette commercial. Razor sharp.

Henry is the definition of fine British breeding, no doubt he attended Eton or somewhere similar, played rugby with Prince Harry and can trace his lineage back to one of the many King Henry's. I am pleasantly enjoying watching his posh English accent tear apart some of the confused tangents my Luxembourgean simulator colleague has tried to float across the table.

"David, we are not interested in financing arrangements. As already discussed, we are prepared to pay the full price on delivery. That is not the issue. We need simply to agree a price, a delivery date and a quantity for each colour, not a sliding scale of prices and cascading dates with various interest repayment options against myriad colour schemes." Go Henry! I love it. Myriad. Nice word.

Here's what you need to understand about David, he is a waste of space, opening the 45-minute negotiations with the delivery of an impromptu ten minute gambit, a very much non-agreed to or even mentioned sales pitch during our 45-minute strategy session. Henry is now decimating him in a way that I only wish I could if I'd known precisely what a liability David would turn out to be in a boardroom.

Henry, Jean and, to a lesser extent Xia, have torn holes in David. Impervious to the onslaught, a further 25-minutes has now gone by and Peter and I have been unable to get a word in as David digs us deeper. He has waffled through 35-minutes of blubber Free Willy would be envious of and has not followed any of the strategic ideas he, Peter and I had concurred on at the conclusion of the initial 45-minutes together. Prick.

Scion deals in a highly lucrative, gritty business, where decisions must be made in heartbeats and delivering impromptu nonesense is anything but tolerated. The assessors know this. I know this. Thankfully, having had the two crisp shadows in the strategy session ensures they are well aware that after today, David is heading straight back to whatever chocolate factory he came from. But my opportunity has just presented itself perfectly to salvage a deal, impress the judges and head to dinner with the Board still holding half a chance of being catapulted into the exulted realm of well-paid-cuntiness.

"Henry, as you're aware, the cost involved in the manufacture of specific iPhone colours is not uniform. With that in mind however, we appreciate you would prefer a single price per unit. It you are prepared to accept 7,000 black, and 3,000 apiece of green, red and blue, 16,000 in total, we can deliver by the 15th of next month at a price of $14.50 per unit." I use my big-boy voice, channeling Morgan Freeman as best I can.

Having filtered out Peter and David's 45-minute *strategic* wank-fest and run the numbers on profit and loss realities against various colour and quantity combination possibilities, I know perfectly well that if the buyers agree to this, it equates to $117,500 profit for my *team*. It also has the buyers suitably impressed, as it has become clear throughout the negotiations that they are aware it costs a minimum of $15 simply to manufacture these imaginary things.

"Excellent, thanks Flynn. Please allow us a 5-minute recess to discuss this."

As part of the rules, each side is allowed one 5-minute recess during the negotiation. The 5 minutes is still included in the overall 45, so if they come back in and want to talk further details, a deal is unlikely. Time, as always, is precious.

I feel somewhat bad for Peter. He seems a fairly nice chap but has not had an opportunity to contribute anything. Blame your Luxe neighbour though sport, it's not my fault. Xia, Jean and Henry re-enter the room.

"Yes, those terms will be fine. We agree. Where do we sign?"

We sign our names, shake hands and leave the room. One of the assessors pulls me aside in the hallway, "like your style mate, good job." Simulation Day is complete. Musical chairs with the Board awaits.

I've ditched the tie, undone a couple of buttons of my overpriced power-blue business shirt and am soaking up afternoon rays on the shores of Lake Geneva. I'm still wearing the suit I hadn't graced since my cousin's wedding almost six months ago and am enjoying a plastic stein of Heineken in a waterfront café. Mont Blanc is twinkling away high above, the lake is shimmering a pristine turquoise and a group of garcons are skimming through the water in 12-feet laser sailing boats. The disgruntled Nigerians are yet to unleash their freestyle rapping. The weather is far too picturesque to mesh properly with their tortured franco-file rhymes.

Dinner will kick off at 6.30pm. Steve informed the group at the conclusion of Simulation Day that dinner was by no means an interview. Instead it served as an opportunity to mingle in a more relaxed setting. Was he serious? Not an interview, an opportunity to *mingle*? Get fucked! Here you are, sharing a seven-course meal with a group of money-hungry corporate psychopaths and you're telling me they just want to mingle. Human Resources *professionals* are certainly excellent comic relief value.

The fact is, tonight's dinner will be the biggest interview I may ever have. I've done well today, I'm certain, but tonight is show time. You can be as smart as you like, but there's not necessarily a lucrative job at the end of that rainbow. No, you must be likeable; a character that people want to be around for a minimum of 12 hours a day for the duration of their working life. I drain the stein and stroll back to the hotel, dodging trams and trying to spot one smile on the countless grim faces in this nation of neutrality.

The third course is almost complete. I hope I'm using the correct cutlery for some of these exotic dishes - I feel a little like Julia Roberts in Pretty Woman, only I'm endowed with less of a horse face, but blessed with an equally scintillating pair of legs that were sculpted perfectly to reside in thigh-high-fuck-me-boots. Steve was partly correct. This is definitely a relaxed setting, candidates and Scion staff alike, all giving the vino a solid nudge. I'm disciplined and ensuring a healthy gulp of Evian between sips of French wine.

Good fortune is being ladled my way in completely undeserved quantities. Two of Scion's senior members are fellow Australians. Gary Fraser, Global Head of Trading is a cricket nut. I am now, of course, also tragically infatuated with cricket, the game of long whites, grassy wickets, high teas and endless maidens. Thank you,

Ravi for earlier reminding me of some cricket jargon. And there's Ian Halliday, sporting a cartoon super hero's chiseled jaw line. He's from Tasmania, a place best known for incest and apple plantations, two of my favourite topics. Our conversation has instead revolved completely around surfing, his role in the company, no doubt of extreme importance, seeming totally irrelevant to the discussion. Unlike cricket, I don't have to pretend for this, I love surfing, but, if anything, I talk down my love affair with the ocean. The connotation with a passion for surfing and a devout bong-worshipping bent is a prevailing train of thought I'm keen to sidestep.

There is a Dr Evil look-a-like, Rickhart, from Poland. He says very little, but appears sanguine enough as he devours wine and polishes his pinky signet ring. His eyes light up on his bowling ball head when talking about the joys of risk-taking. The final course arrives and the wine is starting to take effect. I'm now seated with Adrian, my game two assessor, on my right, and have the big cheese, Joel, to my left. They are giving it to me.

"How's this stupid Aussie, bloody physiotherapist? He thinks he can come over here and trade commodities." Joel's reveling.

"Yeah, I mean, I've seen some bollocks before, but this is trollop of the highest order." Adrian, also loving heaping shit on me.

"You reckon we send him on his way? Tell him to continue touching up old ladies."

"May as well. Have a look at him, he probably loves it."

"Not as much as when he's touching up the fellas."

They are crying with laughter and guzzling champagne.

"Yeah, I'm not too bad with the old ladies, I guess that's why both your mums like to fake groin injuries and fly to Sydney to feel my tender touch." Too far?

"Hahaha! You're a good fucking sport Flynn! Now, get properly drinking you pussy!!" Joel fills my glass to the brim. His attitude to drinking bearing the hallmarks of his approach to trading, *go big or fuck off!*

Dinner winds up shortly after 10pm. I'm jetlagged and hyper-simulated, confidence sky high after being forced to drain champagne for the past quarter of an hour. Steve thanks us for attending the day and assures us that decisions will be made within the next few days as to whether or not we have gained a place on the junior trader program. He then invites us to join a farewell party with some other Scion staff at a nearby bar for a metals trader whose last day was today. The metals trader is retiring. He's 33.

Some of the senior Scion guys choose to head home for the evening at the conclusion of dinner. I shake countless hands, wish them well and hope these members of the top brass remember me with the fondness required to give me the thumbs up when decisions are made as to who deserves a role. The majority of candidates and about half of the Scion dinner party are now trudging through light rain and the brisk Swiss night air to the bar nearby.

Slippery

Entering the bar, the Gillette shadow men from game three of today's simulation define the *look* of basically everyone here. Black or navy suit, matching black or navy tie, crisp white shirt, clean shaven, slick hair – must be the uniform. There are a handful of stunning women too, sophistication and sexuality wrapped perfectly in physique-compressing black dresses.

Ravi tries to hound me again. The cricket topic has hopefully been bludgeoned to death earlier in the day, but now he wants to know all about what I thought of today's events. With the precision of a seasoned socialite, I beg his pardon and escape to the toilet. Seriously, fuck off Ravi. I deftly avoid him as I return from the gents.

Joel is camped at the edge of the bar with a dozen others, gulping whatever drink makes its way into his vicinity. He sees me waiting to order, swoops a drink from the table next to him, hands it to me, "grab this Flynn, all yours, come out front for a chat, I need a smoke."

I follow the big cheese through the crowd to the front balcony. We're standing under the cover of an awning, almost stationary raindrops glow in car headlights on the street in front.

"So how'd you like today?" He squeezes the words out through one side of his mouth as he lights up a cigarette.

"I was nervous at first, but I think I settled in fairly quickly. Loved it."

"Yes, indeed, a nervous little pussy you certainly were. I gave you a good rev up, though. Great. Excellent. Listen, you did incredibly well mate. I expected you to be total shit, thought it would be a good laugh to get you over here. Great effort, but listen…"

"Joel, oh my God! How are you?!" A sex goddess hidden beneath corporate clothing constraints screeches straight into the conversation…the timing! Piss off, you gorgeous skank! Please.

"Ah, Rose, my dear. I'm great. It's so good to see you. How have you been?" Rose, curse her, has just ruined whatever piece of wisdom the big cheese was about to impart. But, bless her, she is one amazing creature, clad in a tight black dress, which any grown man with flesh and fury would simply love to tear straight off and admire the glory of her curves naked and unleashed, bobbing up and down.

Joel is polite enough to introduce me to this stunning interruption, but his attention is obviously now focused on breasts rather than junior trader recruitment. Can't blame him. What a rack. Our beers are nearly empty. I tell him I'll grab him another, but I won't. I hope he cops a nice blowie in the toilets and associates his last images of me with good times and a beautiful cunt.

I return towards the bar. My fellow candidates are conspicuous through a combination of nervous unease and a need to impress, while the Scion proper are easily recognisable through raucous laughter and a sense of complete ownership over the place. I look out to the front balcony, no sign of Rose and Joel. I steal a quick glance of the room. The Scion heavyweights are gone. Fuck this, I'm exhausted, time for a smoke bomb. I pretend to go off to the toilet and make a beeline for the exit, racing off through the steady rain and straight back to the hotel.

I walk into my room fully drenched, throw my soaked clothes on the bedside couch, jump in the shower, relive the day, dry off and look once more at the spastic in the mirror. "Good job retard". I set my alarm for the morning, crack a Heineken from the mini-bar and fall asleep watching CNN. Simulation complete.

I land home from Geneva, my mum and step dad pick me up from the airport to take me home. Five minutes into the journey, the mobile screen lights up with the dizzying array of numbers I've now grown used to. Mum's a nervous wreck as I let her know this is probably Geneva calling and my step dad pulls over. I step out of the car to take the call.

"Hello, Flynn speaking."

"Flynn. Steve here. Make it home OK?"

"Yes, great flight. I just landed."

"Brilliant. Well I have some excellent news. Everyone was very impressed with you in Geneva. Of the 18 candidates, we felt there were only 5 with the calibre we require. We'd like to offer you a position." You fucking beauty! My calibre is delighted for the recognition.

I let a smile break and mum immediately goes mental a few metres away from me. It is not easy to maintain the façade of coolness when your mum is having a rather noisy motherly fit. Decibels of maternal hysterics are no doubt flying down the phone line. Covering the receiver, I swiftly walk away down the street.

"That's great, Steve. Thank you very much."

"We would like to start you in Singapore, on oil, spend the initial six months there. And then, given your experience in metals and fluency in Mandarin, send you to Shanghai, our hub of Asian metals trading. You'll be employed via the Singapore office, paid in Singapore Dollars. We will start you on a $200,000 SGD salary." Umm, yeah, that seems about right seeing as I have no talent, no ability, no training. And let's not focus on that little Mandarin piece of misinformation...I'll get some beginner textbooks tomorrow to rectify that in no time.

"I will email the contract now. We can sort out the exact start date as soon as you read and sign the contract. Once again, Flynn, we are very impressed with you and can't wait to get you trading. If you are as good as we think you will be, you should expect to be earning in excess of a million dollars a year in the very near future." Let me just clarify I am very glad you feel that way.

"That's great news Steve. I can't wait to join. I will read the contract immediately and let you know if there are any concerns. I'm sure it will be fine. Look forward to seeing you again soon."

"Welcome aboard, Flynn."

3/ Treading Water in the Deals Lane

Welcome to Singapore, the land that fun forgot

Scion has graciously decided to not only completely overpay me, they're also stumping up for my accommodation in one of Singapore's swankiest bachelor pads. I now dwell on the 17th floor of the *Abode*. My apartment complex is literally called the Abode, in the inner city suburb of Somerset. From the balcony I look out through the heat to the monstrosity of Marina Bay Sands – a concrete boat, 56 floors above Singapore's Marina Bay, held aloft by three individual hotel-room-filled towers.

I would love to meet the person who pitched the idea of this airborne, serpentine, rudderless eyesore of a ship to the ultra-conservative Singaporean government officials and held a straight face, rambling corporate-speak nonesense, clicking through a slideshow of illustrations demonstrating just how thoroughly you can render your country a laughing stock - simply place a boat a few hundred metres into the 110% humidity air.

I'm told it is a very popular place to jump from, at least one suicide per week. Presumably the Einstein who commissioned the project was the first to plummet to his voluntary death, though this airborne atrocity is precariously close to the casino, one of the few legal gambling facilities in a part of the world immensely rich with degenerate punters. Splat Jack Extra-Ordinaires must surely flat-line the Marina Bay walkway pavement in the early hours of most mornings.

I jump in the shower, shave carefully and put on the suit and tie outfit of all modern day heroes. I take off out the door after one last look in the mirror, "smash it, killer." My sweat glands are already preparing for a full-scale assault before the elevator even reaches the ground floor. I walk out of the Abode and, less than ten metres into my journey, I take off the suit jacket. It's so stinking hot here.

I'm waiting for the train at Somerset station, sweat glistening on my temples and lathering incessantly down my back and chest. It cannot be healthy to be losing this much fluid while doing nothing more than standing still, though there must be a sizeable dose of first day nerves synapsing through me. Those will be under control soon. One more hour, I'll be so confused and out of my depth, I won't have a spare brain cell to occupy itself with worry.

The train arrives and I cram in with an ethnically diverse assortment of fellow corporate go-getters, all of us overheating in business attire completely inappropriate for a near zero latitude CBD. We set off and air conditioning jets through the cabin, allowing the flow of sweat to pause momentarily and the soggy waft of b.o to permeate.

It's a short journey, three stops. Destination - Raffles Place – an aptly named location for Singapore's epicenter of trading and finance. I somehow plucked my raffle ticket through a combination of a hyper-inflated resume, fortuitous interviewer selections and a timely knack for laying my best wares on show when it's time to simulate. I'm hoping my raffle ticket is a winner.

I shoot skyward in the same elevator I traveled in only weeks earlier, bright-eyed after the Saturday morning flight here from Sydney for an interview. I'm still spinning from the chain of events leading me back here. Delusions of my own grandeur keep me grounded. I reason that maybe, just maybe, I am as smart as the big swingers at my new firm seem to think I am.

The elevator opens to the Scion lobby. Two yellow fever inducing Singaporean women sit with perfect posture behind the reception desk, divided from me by the security of the access-card-automated sliding glass doors. I step towards the glass, my Anglo appearance, smart suit and short back-and-sides haircut allows the receptionists to assess me as no threat to security. Silly girls. The truth is, if my deranged trading *skills* are afforded a large enough line of credit and access to the appropriate buttons, I could blow this place up with ease, financially speaking of course.

Any terrorist wannabe can tuck explosives in his pants, walk into an innocent crowd, preach the usual compost regarding a human-formulated-God and ignite a genocide bomb. Well done. Rookie. But if you sincerely want to inflict hell on civilized western society, invest a few years in a degree like *financial* engineering, snake yourself high in the ranks of a bank, insurance company or ratings agency and unleash the fury. These financial engineering terrorist masterminds in tan slacks and short sleeve button up shirts, cloaked in standard deviations and swimming with black swans, lounging in the comfort of ergonomic chairs high up in the revered offices of triple A rated organizations must look at Bin Laden, et al and laugh. What amateurs?

The moderately less attractive of the two receptionists, body from heaven, face from purgatory, clothing from Prada, steps forwards with remarkable ease, considering the height of her heels must be in excess of half the length of her shin. She pushes the green button on the wall, opening the doors and the scent of my first moment in well-paid-cuntiness is enriched by her tang of freshly waxed office ho.

"Hello, I'm Flynn James. I'm starting today on the junior trader program."

"Of course. Please take a seat. I will call Angela to let her know you've arrived. Would you like a coffee, tea, bottle of water?" This Southeast Asian beauty speaks with a refined, almost British accent. How majestic? Stealing another glance of her Victoria's Secret physique however, I'm sure the accent isn't the driving reason for her employment.

"No, thanks. I'm fine."

Angela is the HR manager whose psychotically enthusiastic smile formed my first impression of my new employer. She greets me once more with that terrifyingly cheerful face. Within 45 minutes, she explains all the policies on any number of matters I pay no attention to and could not care less about. Sick leave, gym memberships, family health care insurance plans. I don't give a fuck. Just pay me my salary. I'll sort out the rest.

If everyone thought like me, the world would obviously be in hedonistic shambles, but at least all these human resources *professionals* would be in the dole queue where they belong. Mercifully, the orientation is finally complete. It's time to get a seat and a phone, a computer and a boss, and work out what the hell the physical commodities trading caper is really all about, as well as find an answer to the burning question; just how much of my soul am I expected to sell to justify the salary I'm being paid? I'm assuming the lot, and then some.

Angela hands me my security access pass complete with my pretty little photo in the middle. Hello, handsome. We take the lift down a level to the core of Scion's Singapore office. Exiting the elevator on the 24th floor, I look past the countless rows of desks, busy bodies and endless computers, through the floor to ceiling glass windows and I immediately notice my serpentine comrade across the harbour, looking his usual shade of ridiculous atop Marina Bay Sands. The welcome tour begins.

"To your right is the finance and credit department," appearing as you'd expect. Dull.

"Gotchya." I look forward to seeing their antics after a few drinks. Never trust the quiet ones. On we go. Angela walks with speed and purpose, her finely formed legs distracting me slightly as she continues down the room.

"These are our ferrous and coal traders." A group of ten portly gents look me over. They each bear a striking resemblance to the sort of man a circus reserves for dressing in leather and firing cannonballs into. They don't appear overly chummy, obviously jealous of the clear gap between my chin and chest, medically referred to as a neck. Theirs are distant memories covered in jowls of pelican gullet impersonations. I recognize John, my round one assessor in Geneva.

"Hi there geeze! Flynn, right? Pleasure to welcome you aboard son." John's cockney accent diverts my attention from the bratwurst fingers protruding from his puffer fish hand as his grasp engulfs mine in a bone-rattling handshake.

"Yeah, John, thanks mate, great to be here." I won't be able to type for a few hours. My hand is numb.

"Anyffing you need, you just shout out alright, geeze?"

"You betchya, thanks."

The tour continues.

"This is our metals trading team; copper, zinc, lead, aluminium, scrap." Even before Angela finishes her sentence the Serbian scrap metal human personification of infuriated is on the approach. Is he smiling?

"Flynn! Helllooo! Welcome! Why you say to Joel I don't like you? I like you, nyeess, it is great to have you here." This is a welcome contradiction to the kneecapping I was preparing for as he approached.

"Artem, how are you? Hawh, sorry about that, I thought I didn't have a good interview with you, that's all. But I like you! Sorry for the confusion." Artem shakes my hand and takes it a step further - we hug it out in a bromantic eastern European embrace.

Angela continues down the room. The big cheese smirks in his chair, seeing Angela and I on the approach.

"Whoa whoa, what's this about then, Angela? I mean, really, what the bloody hell is going on here?" Joel, a born shit-stirrer, I hope.

"Mr. Ryan, I'm sorry, is there a problem?" Angela's voice is quivering.

"Why'd you let this bloody fool in here? Let me guess, he's Australian I presume. Please call security and have him removed immediately. Good day." Joel turns around, walks away.

"Umm, Flynn, please come with me." Well, that was a speedy stint in commodities trading, easy come, easy go, I guess.

Joel turns back, "wait, wait, I changed my mind, he can stay. Smile Angela. It's Monday morning. Smile. Five full uninterrupted days of adding value to look forward to. Flynn, mate, how are you then sir, alright?"

"Well thanks. How are you?"

"Look at me, look at me, I feel almost as terrible as I look. Now, that's enough about me. Go meet Jannah over there. You're on her team now. She'll whip you into shape boy, literally, wait till you see her whip. You'll love it, you filthy bugger."

Joel grabs his ringing Blackberry from his pocket, "how the fuck are you then, cunt-face?" and saunters away down the room, radiating the aura of complete command. Angela leads me the final steps of the welcoming tour to Jannah's desk, three down from Joel's, while Andrew, the South African from my original interview with Joel, makes eye contact from a few rows away. He gives me a nod, a wink, and a peculiar sort of Colonel Jessup salute.

"Hi Jannah, please meet Flynn. He is starting today on the junior trader program and will be in your deals desk team." Jannah turns in her seat and we shake hands. She can't be over thirty years old, but the bags under her eyes carry plenty of excess luggage.

"Hi Flynn. We will chat tomorrow. I'm very busy today. See the geek over there with his thick glasses. That's Kristian. There is a spare seat next to him, all set up with computer, phone, you sit with him today. He will teach you some things." She immediately turns back to her screen once these words are delivered, sneezing as she scrolls across a manic looking spreadsheet.

"No problem, Jannah, speak tomorrow, thanks." As I say this she is already on the phone to someone, "this makes no sense retard, you better explain this garbage clearly. You've got ten seconds. One, two…"

Angela's tour has one final stop. As we round another row of desks, I catch a glimpse of Sebastian, Michael Phelps' Spanish swim-training buddy. He looks up from his computer, smiling hello as I walk past. He is one of the five to simulate into a role as well. Maybe yoga is the answer.

"Kristian, good morning. Please meet Flynn, he is starting on the junior trader program today."

"Of course, the Australian, yes." Kristian's eyes seem to light up, though it's hard to tell, they are essentially unreadable beneath his almost-translucent specs. Is he blind? The lenses are so substantial, when trying to make eye contact with him I feel I'm peering into another dimension.

"Good morning, Kristian." He stands to shake hands, I notice some sort of friendship band on his wrist, the type all German backpackers sport when they've successfully hiked through Thailand without ruining their Birkenstocks or befriending a soul.

"Please, call me Kris. Take a seat mate." He hams up the 'maate'. Only Australians can say mate properly, mate.

"Thanks."

"OK, Flynn, IT will be along soon to set up your computer and arrange your Blackberry. If there are any problems, please contact me."

"No problem, Angela, thank you."

"Here comes the IT guy now, Flynn. This will take half an hour to sort your shit. Let's get started as soon as you're ready, maaate." Kristian seems nice enough I guess, cunt-ish, of course, but I suppose that's normal.

The IT fella, Erwin, sets about doing all manner of things to the phone and three computer screens infront of me. I sit back and peruse the room. There look to be about 150 people here. The majority appears to be of Asian descent. The remaining Caucasians all seem to be recognizable to me already from the various stages of the interview process. Obviously the top brass is imported. Imperialism is alive and well.

"OK, Fwynn, please contact me any problem, fink all OK."

"Cheers Erwin. Thanks."

Kristian leans across and takes the reigns, handing me a notebook and a pen as he domineers the keyboard and mouse, flying through all sorts of programs, spreadsheets, systems, etc which coordinate every facet of the business from a chaotic rabble into Microsoft dependent utopia. At some stage I feel on the edge of passing out in an information overload induced coma. Three hours pass in a wink.

"OK, that's enough for the time being. Let's grab some lunch, Flynn."

"Sounds good to me."

Kristian's barely see-through glasses have not prevented him from concisely introducing me to every aspect of my role for the next six months. It's called *Deals Desk*. In the physical commodities trading world, unlike an investment bank, there is no back, middle, and front office division of labour, class, equality and salary.

An investment bank likes to have a 'back' office, a place where all the nitty-gritty of trade reconciliation and such tasks are completed. These chores are now routinely outsourced to India where a willing population provides abundant cheap labour with an unnerving pursuit to not waste precious time thinking in their job, rather an adoration of following orders and flowcharts signifies the foundation of a meaningful career.

Then there is the 'middle' office, filled with those irritating accountant, lawyer and risk management types. The sort of highly educated retards who like to think they're entitled to hefty paychecks even though their contribution to the wealth creation component of entrepreneurship is non-existent. They stitch designer labels onto their cheap suits, buy the highest quality fake Rolex's, visit art galleries, watch foreign films, spend the majority of their work day planning trips to Cinque Terre, frowning at their share portfolio as it inevitably plummets, or a return to university to study something *meaningful*. Most assuredly, these fine folk always turn up to work functions with their drinking shoes on if, and only if, the tab is to be footed by a Director. Real 'salt of the earth' types in the 'middle' office.

Then you have the 'front' office with the analysts, brokers, traders and dealmakers. The 5% of the bank's population tasked with feeding fat profits to the remaining 95% through a combination of front-running and colluding, blatant lying and reckless punting, clever manipulating and occasional brown paper bag filled inducement levering to the regulation controllers of officialdom. You know, the typical foundations of successful capitalism and the ruthless upholding of the best interests of the shareholders. What would the world come to if concern ever veered from the best interests of those noble shareholders?

And let's not forget the other defining characteristic of an investment bank; that most aptly named 'Chinese Wall'. A wondrous wall designed to keep all those filthy Mongolians out and never let traders talk shop with the merger and acquisition folk. There's a conflict of interests apparently, though their collective salaries and bonuses are drawn from the same dollar mine, interestingly enough. No, the Wall is insurmountable, of course it is. It must be. Just google any random graph of a company's stock price against the 'news release' parameter. You'll find a remarkably unavoidable trend. A stock price's sharp rise or drastic fall always, every single time, always precedes the release of news. Precedes it. Always. How strange? What a coincidence. It wouldn't be like the Chinese to build a faulty wall, would it?

The commodities trading world is an entirely different beast. There is no peculiar division of labour into front, middle, back, sideways, diagonal, or oblique office environments. Not here. There are traders. Unsurprisingly, they trade; buy something, sell something, buy something else, sell it, hopefully, for them, at a profit, if not, adios Amigo. They don't sit in some ornate 'front' office with Greek gods, crystal balls and polished knobs. They are here in the same corporate den as everyone else, overwhelmed by enough computer screens to ensure Bill Gates' pension fund remains in strong shape and saddled with the expectation of alchemy every single day…turn nothing into something, make wads of profit appear from thin air. How hard can it be?

The traders seem predominantly to sit right next to their *operator*. An operator appears to be a logistics expert, sleeves rolled up, pencil in the ear, belly overhanging the belt. They're tasked with knowing precisely when and where a vessel is due to arrive, whether all the correct paperwork is dotted and crossed with i's and t's, and, most importantly, is the oil or metal, or whatever the commodity is meant to be, is it precisely what has been agreed to in the contract. If the assay is indeed of a higher grade than anticipated and contractually agreed, button the lip, pray the counterparty doesn't notice and report the profit. Alchemy complete. Gainful employment ensured for another day. If the assay report shows an inferior spec of material, shout loud, shout fucking loud and make sure the counterparty stumps up a fortune to compensate, or simply refuse to accept the off-spec shit, let them know you have good friends in low places who aren't afraid to get the message across in medieval terms of communication.

Owing to the fact that physical commodities on the whole are shipped around the world, there's a large chartering team. Some commodities are obviously transported by rail, truck, wheelbarrow, whatever pleb device you can put wheels on, but we're big boys here, big swingers, we ship shit, ship it global, so we need a group of drastically overpaid taxi-booking agents for giant tankers filled with oil, copper, iron ore, coal, etc. For some reason I'm unaware of, chartering is an empire almost entirely full of Danish natives. The Great Danes have some affinity with shipping, like Australians with barbecues, Brazilians with waxing and Colombians with cartels.

Enough about them, let's focus on me. I'm three hours deep into my deal desk career. The deals desk role involves overseeing every aspect of a trader's specific portfolio of deals. This comprises trade reconciliation, risk reporting, costs forecasting of all aspects associated with each trade, ensuring trade contracts are water-tight, creating and executing the appropriate hedging plan to offset any pricing risk throughout the trade's life from agreement to delivery, and, most critically, being able to answer any question a trader may have regarding his cargoes within nanoseconds.

If this were an investment bank, I would be tiptoeing between the front, middle and back offices like a financial vigilante ballerina by performing all these tasks from the one desk. Here though, noone blinks. The conflict of being able to complete the hedging trades for a deal, while also filing risk reports and making costs forecasts does not appear to bother anyone in this office, so I can only assume it bothers noone in other commodities trading firms and multi-national oil behemoths. Fair enough. Investment banks employ far too many people anyway. I'm happy to see a dozen roles absorbed into one.

Jannah is in charge of the deals desk team. The bags under her eyes now make a lot more sense. Her team comprises eight super bright young people overseeing every trade completed across all components of the oil barrel from crude to gasoline to naphtha. Naphtha, that realm my interviewer Pranav is apparently so gifted at. Where is that little prick, anyway? Kristian tells me there are 30 oil traders in the Singapore office, meaning there's no shortage of work for the deals desk team to fuck up and Jannah to be responsible for.

Essentially, a trader will try to swiftly double check the likely profitability of a deal with his allotted deals desk member before executing it and will then proceed, or not, with the deal, usually with the counterparty simultaneously on the end of the phone or some on-line messenger device. It's important to clarify these aren't insignificant sums involved. To charter a tanker, fill it up with some form of oil, insure the lot, hedge the pricing risk, yada yada yada, the usual dollar commitment can range from ten to one hundred million dollars. And this isn't a foreign exchange dealing desk. It's very unlikely you've got a phone in each hand with a willing buyer on one line and a keen seller on the other, simply quote each party a tidy little spread, seal the deal, clip the profit and head off to lunch, clicking your heels together while singing along to Tina Turner's *Simply the Best*. No, your chartered tanker full of purchased oil with borrowed cash is most likely going to be sitting in the watery abyss of the Atlantic, Pacific or Indian for a short while before knowing exactly where the (with any fucking luck) profitable delivery destination is. With all this at stake, a deals desk role carries with it the high probability of being physically beaten to a pulp if you report incorrectly to the trader. Fuck him, he'll fuck you, eye for an eye, fuck for a fuck.

As a member of the junior trader program, I'm expected to absolutely master this deals desk role within six months and then complete a further six months in operations, master that little chestnut too, naturally, in Shanghai no less, home of the revered dragon and the succulent dog, and then be a trading superstar before I blink. No pressure. I won't let the pulsing headache from this morning's crash course bother me. My future is laid out.

"There's a hawker market around the corner. Great food. You like Asian food?"

"Of course."

"Let's go then."

We ride the lift back down to the perpetual humidity of ground level Singapore. The hawker market is two blocks away. Any further and I would not be able to wear this shirt again. I can already feel sweat congealing around the collar of my fresh white shirt into a putrid smoker's-teeth stained yellow. We arrive at Lau Pa Sat, a circus shaped arena of Asian cuisine, the hazy air infused with kaffir lime, peanut oil and MSG.

"My favourite is this Korean BBQ, but feel free to have a walk around and just grab whatever. All the stalls are excellent. Meet back here in five."

Lau Pa Sat is filling rapidly. The lunchtime rush of corporate mouths is drooling and set to pounce. I decide to leave the stall exploring for another time and join the line at the Korean place with Kristian. I'm not too familiar with the menu, I order some sort of Kow Well Hung chicken noodle soup dish with mild chili and we take a seat.

"How do you like it so far then Flynn?"

"Umm, not too sure about this food mate. I sweat enough here already without adding chili to the system."

"Not the food, you idiot, this morning, at work. How's it feeling?"

"Ah, right. Yeah, I'm pretty confused but it's really interesting. Thanks for all your help. I feel like I've learnt so much already"

"No problem. I am on the junior trader program too, you know. I completed the trader exam last week in Geneva."

"The exam?"

"Yes, haven't they told you? At the conclusion of your twelve months on deals desk and operations, you have to be nominated by one of the senior traders to actually sit a final exam before becoming a trader."

"OK, I wasn't aware of that."

"Yes, Joel nominated me, of course. The exam is spread over four days. Each day is filled with all those simulation type trading exercises and negotiation tasks. Then most evenings, they try to get you really drunk, so that you will struggle the following day. Smart arses! It's fun though. I found it very easy, of course. I've already traded oil at Goldman Sachs. I only took this downgrade for 12 months because I wanted to trade in a commodities firm. The bonuses at the banks are pitiful nowadays, since the whole GFC shit show."

"Yeah, right."

"I'm actually from Germany, so a move back to that part of the world would be nice. I can trade anything. I have a feel for it. It just comes so easily to me, so naturally. Joel should be able to tell me where I'm starting my trading role this week."

"Good news then mate. You'll smash it, I'm sure." Kristian has now graduated from cunt-ish to a herpes-riddled gash with this little chat. 'So naturally', please, spare me.

The Kow Well Hung was only doused in mild chili, but that's more than sufficient to send my sweat glands into orbit. We walk back the mere two blocks to the office. I feel heat exhaustion lurking nearby. This is ridiculous. The blissful, arctic wall of air-conditioning in the office foyer is messianic. I feel my shirt instantly unglue itself from each sweat-filled pore of my torso. We continue on to the lift.

Joel emerges from the elevator well, "Flynn, let's grab a coffee. Alright with you Kris?"

"Sure."

"Cheers Kris, I'll have him back to you in a jiffy. He's been behaving himself this morning I hope."

"Yes, of course, very well behaved."

The big cheese and I turn and head back out into the sauna briefly before settling in a coffee shop, air-conned, thank Christ.

"What you drinking then mate? It better not be too faggy, you fucking homo."

"A flat white, no sugar. Is that hetero enough?"

"Barely. Two flat whites please, my dear, to have here. We'll grab a seat over there. Cheers. Keep the change."

We take a seat. Joel looks me in the eye for an extended glance. I barely know this bloke, but I get the feeling the one thing he may love almost as much as making shitloads of cash is mind-fucking people, for no real reason, other than for the pure pleasure of seeing confused faces staring blankly back at him. His wish is certainly being granted. I stare back with a mishmash of confusion, fear and awe.

"First day, big man. How is it?"

"Ah…"

"Oh fuck, I don't care, don't bore me with answering that. Tell me, has Kristian taught you all you need to know to be able to fill in for his role now?"

"I guess so. I mean…"

"Great."

The coffees arrive. Joel wallops his down in one gulp as though he's drinking water during a marathon.

"OK, let's go then, back to work."

Huh? OK. What the fuck? My coffee is full minus one small sip. We walk out and straight back to the lifts, not saying a word. Joel taps out an email on his Blackberry as he joins me all the way to my desk. Kristian is seated, facing his computer but looking down at his friendship band.

"Kris, the super teacher, Flynn says great things about you. Nothing I didn't already know, of course. I've got some news for you and I need another coffee, you free for five minutes?" It's safe to assume when Joel asks a question he is being politely coy. It's not a question.

"Yes, sure. Flynn, just carry on with preparing the hedging plan for the July cargoes."

"No problem."

Kris and Joel walk away. I nurse a headache trying to recall how it was you hedged any cargoes, let alone the July ones. Kris' explanation given to me before lunch must be among the pages upon pages of notes I scribbled this morning. My attention is drawn away from my notes as Kris' three computer screens suddenly black out. Angela arrives moments later and begins going through his filing cabinet, her deranged smile still plastered ear to ear.

"Hi Angela, are you looking for Kristian? He has just stepped out for a moment."

"No, that's fine. I'm just clearing his desk."

"What?"

"He's fired, he did very poorly in the trader exam. It's OK. You will do all his work now. We like you much more."

"Huh…OK…cheers."

An email pops up on my screen. 'Kristian Kaufmehl has left Scion with immediate effect…'

Joel walks back as I attempt to process the rapid-fire nature of my employer and search my notes for a scrawled explanation on how to hedge these cargoes.

"Flynn, you're the man now OK. Kris is gone. Fucking cocky little kraut cunt he was. You're now the deals desk guy looking after the crude oil team, as well as the oil derivatives trader. Got it? You met all those fellas this morning yeah? Don't fuck it up. Let's grab a pint tonight too, welcome you to Scion properly."

"Yeah, perfect. Yeah, I've met the crude and derivs guys. That's great, I've got it covered."

"It wasn't a question little man. I will grab you on the way out. Get your work done ASAP. I'm thirsty, can't miss happy hour. Not that I give a fuck, I'm fucking loaded, it's gonna be your shout is all, you poor fucker."

"Rightoh. Cheers. You're quite the philanthropist mate."

"I am aren't I? Well said."

Joel walks back to his desk, eyes focused on his Blackberry. I'm part chuffed, part frightened, and completely clueless as to what I'm doing or what I'm meant to do. Three hours with a 'fucking cocky little kraut cunt' was a delightful welcome to the company and I certainly learnt an awful lot, but it wasn't exactly the ideal training I anticipated to enlighten my senses to the nuances of physical commodities trading. I squirm in my seat, straighten my tie and tap my fingers. I doubt it's worthwhile ever trying to get too comfy in a place like this. One blink, head off to a meeting with an executive and you'll likely find yourself back behind the security glass doors, minus the access pass and swollen salary. I spend the afternoon trying to look inconspicuous and not get fired.

"Cheers to the new boy, Flynn." Joel raises his glass.

"Cheers." I join the chorus with my new workmates from crude oil and derivatives trading. And why not, cheers to me. I've arsed my way through yet another day, have not fucked anything up too severely, even the July hedges were apparently without error. I'm still on track for trading greatness and now have a pint of tiger to lubricate any grave thoughts regarding the churn and burn nature of the industry I'm now a part of.

We're gathered around a bench in the early evening happy hour glow of an Irish pub overlooking the sullied, steamy waters of Boat Quay. There's an ice cold, air-conditioned bar inside, completely empty of customers. My drinking buddies couldn't possibly enjoy the indoor comforts. Their nicotine addictions render the great outdoors the only viable location for downing alcohol.

The Singapore crude trading team comprises Keith Wang and Huan Lee. I hope that I don't spend too many hours chuckling at Keith's surname. Obviously it's hilarious, Wang, gold, but Keith is one fucking serious looking fella. He is Singaporean, but as I'm quickly realizing, being Singaporean can mean just about anything. Most likely, it means you're of a Chinese, Malaysian, Indian and English combination of descents. He seems reasonably calm with a pint of tiger in his grasp, but I've watched him through the afternoon inflicting certain ulcers on his gastric lining, and brokers' alike, as he yelled orders and spat instructions down his broker box. My sympathy is with the brokers who mixed up his orders. When Keith speaks, it is incomprehensible unless you are fluent in English and Mandarin, which I guess I am. According to my CV at least.

Meanwhile, Huan Lee is the picture of cool. Sure, he's been dealt a poor hand in the looks department. To a Lord of the Rings fan, Huan resembles a less malnourished Asian version of Gollum. A modeling career was never on the cards, my precious, but he is a silky smooth character, swigging on his tiger, drawing on his Marlboro, chatting with the sort of polished international accent gained from an English college tertiary education mixed with a youth dedicated to US gangster rap.

My original interviewer Andrew is here too. He trades fuel oil, not crude or derivatives, but felt compelled to pop along for a few pints, having met me at ground zero when I was in the interview stages, as well as to feed his alcohol dependence. He's from Durban, is a rugby fanatic and alarmingly racist considering the two crude traders are quite obviously Asian and standing right next to him.

A fellow Australian, Paul Maher, is the oil derivatives trader for whom I'll be deals desking. He is a no-nonesense kind of bloke, heart on the sleeve, beer in the hand, ciggie in the ear, fists of fury in dispute resolution sort of man. I like him. Within moments of shaking hands and about to wallow in the obligatory small talk requisite when meeting new people, he instead launches into a merciless diatribe of the debacle which is the Mumbai office.

They routinely cost him small fortunes by managing to 'lose' his trades… yeah, his trades just 'go missing' between being executed on the exchange and traveling through cyber space to the world's second most populous nation for settlement and reconciliation. These David Copperfield trades then usually 'turn up' moments before expiry or when they've become heavy losses. Fucking beauty. I will now be taking care of all his trades, risk reporting, positions management, etc and he makes it clear that it will be impossible to be worse than the Mumbai-ans, but his shouting will be far more intense face-to-face as opposed to over the phone, "so don't fuck anything up, mate".

Joel takes charge after the fourth tiger pint and says we should dine at a Japanese place nearby, Kinki's. Noone argues. Kinki's raunchy title doesn't quite match the sumo wrestler on the restaurant's signage. No funny business or pole dancing here, this is a *Japanese with an urban attitude'* restaurant overlooking Marina Bay. We're seated at a table for the six of us by the window. It's now 8.45pm. The Marina

Bay light show sprays neon through the night sky and across the harbour as Joel orders a combination of dishes for the group as well as six Asahi's, two jugs of sake and asks for the wine menu. Before I have a chance to feign marvel at the light show, plates of sushi, bottles of beer and ceramic cups of sake arrive.

"Gents, grab your sake. To Flynn, welcome." Joel leads the way and we each shot our sake in unison. As my first hit of sake makes its way south, Joel is already refilling everyone's ceramics. "One more to Paul." Swig. Refill. "To Keith." You get the picture, six sake shots in sixty seconds. Nicolas Cage lost in Fukushima. I'm wasted, but the drinks keep coming. Joel is now in possession of three bottles of red, pouring us all hefty glasses in between ordering us to shot more Sakes and to eat more 'faggy' sushi.

I'm thumped to life by the blaring of my 6.30am alarm on the Blackberry drumming bedside. Piss off. I fling my arm and magically hit the snooze button. Bullseye. I'm lying prostrate, palms by my side facing the ceiling while my neck is jammed at ninety degrees, peering out from my pillow through the window to the glares of the waking sun next to that fucked up floating serpentine. Hangovers like this shouldn't be possible on a Tuesday morning.

"Mmm, good morning." I roll over. There is a blonde with flawless fake breasts, zero clothing and crystal blue eyes, "I have very fun night. You very nice, crazy man. I had such a fun." Who the hell is this chick? And where did she learn English? Her language teacher should be ashamed.

"That's great. Listen, I have to get to work. I got your number yeah?"

"You don't want fuck?"

"Umm."

She rolls my aching body over and straddles me, rubs her cement bolt-ons in my face and with both hands violently pulls her blonde hair towards the ceiling as she arches her back and grinds me. My hangover vanishes as I search alcohol-fortified memory banks for any idea of who this girl is. She starts screaming, loud, licking her fingers and telling me to fuck her harder. I try my best, that's all anyone can ask of you right, and down her in my morning glory with impressive speed. You're welcome. I roll away a load lighter, oddly well prepped for day two on the path to international commodities trading superstardom, and walk to the shower.

I try in vain to wash myself. I doubt a liberal dose of nivea visage exfoliant over the loins will clean me sufficiently. I hop out, dry off, shave and head back to the kitchen for some breakfast. The blonde, name unknown, is sitting by the kitchen bench in a little black dress and pink stilettos, brushing her head of sex hair and looking extremely whorish.

"So, you pay me now, yes?" Ah, for fuck's sake.

The five-minute walk to the train platform is more than a tad discomforting. I suppose that's inevitable. It's not customary for my journey to work to include being mistaken for a pimp. There's a Citibank ATM at the station, $300 SGD and this debacle can be over. It's a blessing barely a soul in Singapore actually knows me. Imagine dear Nan was part of the throng of public transporters walking past right now. Sure, I'm copping plenty of raised eyebrows of curious approval from male gawkers, and even though Jesus was praised for associating with prostitutes, I'm fairly certain none of the horrified women walking past will be following me to Galilee.

I hand the blonde the cash, not bothering to ask her name, how rude, though she mustn't care too much for such etiquette, she kisses my cheek and asks me to marry her. I politely decline. Shame, she might have been the one. I escape through the turnstiles and continue solo down to the train platform.

I walk up the stairs at Raffles Place station with the balance of a new born giraffe thanks to a resurgent hangover beating drums through my temples while images of bouncing silicone play on repeat in the front, centre and rear of my thoughts. Day two, I'm ready. It takes more than a hangover and the need for an urgent STD test to sour my mood.

It's shortly after 8am and the 24th floor is almost empty. Singaporeans like their beauty sleep it would seem. Kristian's seat has been taken by Sebastian. He smiles as I approach and take my seat next to him.

"Good morning Flynn, good to see you again."

"Hi mate, sorry, was going to pop over and say hello yesterday, how you doing?"

"Well thanks. I started last week. Jannah told me to sit over here with you now. She's going to take that seat on the other side of you today and start teaching us stuff."

"Well that's lucky, I've got no idea what's going on."

"Me neither."

"Wanna grab a coffee? There's no one here, we may as well sneak out quickly."

"Sounds good."

Sebastian is a week ahead of me on the learning curve, but more important than imparting any newly attained knowledge regarding commodities trading, he leads me straight to where the best coffee in Raffles Place is to be found. We arrive at the Dimbulah coffee shop, which not only serves up half decent flat whites, there are also vegemite and cheese toasties, as well as chockie lamingtons on offer. My hangover will wash clean with the first munch of some vegemite toast.

With the revelation of Dimbulah, Sebastian has successfully crossed the yoga divide, which I previously thought might prevent us from any chance of a meaningful friendship. Don't get me wrong, yoga is a phenomenal way to view slender women engaged in all manner of leg spreading, down dogging and sweaty chanting, but it's no religion, it doesn't offer some divine gateway to the soul, nor should it allow the participant carte blanche to laud their instructor's *oneness* or pollute bookstores with ever more yoga tomes. It's stretching. That's it. I like stretching. Sebastian is now granted immunity from my hatred if he decides to spit some yoga propaganda my way. You can't grow angry when a man has led you to the promised Lamington Land.

"How have you settled in over your first week mate?"

"Oh, it's not easy. I am deals desk for the fuel oil traders. I'm very lost. I have experience with trading foreign exchange, bonds, credit default swaps, stuff like that. I wanted to get this job because there seems something special about physical commodities. You feel like you can touch them or something like that, you know. It's real. But, it seems to be a real nightmare so far. Things are always going wrong."

"Yeah, I bet. Financial instruments are just numbers on a screen at the core of it. Oil is in a barrel or a tanker or squished in some underground lair somewhere. Not so easy."

"These guys are ruthless too. Most days someone gets fired. There seems at least one email each day of someone's 'immediate departure' somewhere in all our offices globally. I'm told that is just code for 'fired'."

"Wow. Yeah, the guy who was supposed to be teaching me got fired yesterday afternoon."

"I know, I know."

"Ah well, what can you do? Ready to head back?"

"Sure."

We arrive back to level 24 right on 8.30am. The room is still predominantly empty, though Jannah is now seated to the immediate left of my spot and is feverishly going about whatever it is she is going about. Sebastian and I continue to our seats, mesmerized by Jannah's keyboard-tapping, staccato concerto and screen-focused tunnel vision.

"Flynn, good morning, apologies for not being able to spend some time with you yesterday. In five minutes, we will have a chat OK and I can outline to you all the things expected and what I want you to learn." She refuses to allow this chat to interfere with her concerto or tunnel vision.

"Great."

"And Sebastian, I am just fixing all the mistakes you've made on the July storage and blending analysis. I will email it back to you now, please note the changes. Do not make those same mistakes again, ever, and send me the same analysis for August. It better be perfect."

"Oh, sorry. Yes, of course."

The stream of arrivals is increasing. 9am is the Singapore office official starting time. When Angela yesterday completed her HR summary she outlined claptrap information such as official starting and ending times, lunch hours and the rest of the blah blah theme song. I assumed it was wise to pay no attention. You can't expect to successfully navigate your way through this world if you think being handed the opportunity to earn millions of dollars will be coupled with a time punch card.

"Flynn, here's a notebook, come with me to a meeting room. Pay attention. Take lots of notes. This run down is a one off affair. You got it?"

"Got it."

Half an hour with Jannah in the glass-bubble corner office meeting room is more than ample for scribbling my way through an entire notebook and sweating off my hangover. Despite being a 'cocky little kraut cunt', in all fairness to Kristian's teaching credentials, he did cover the majority of Jannah's material yesterday in an easy to understand manner. Where is that bloke now I wonder? A mere 24 hours ago he was a self-ordained trading *natural*. I suppose he still is, only the 'self' component of the ordaining now carries a bit of a delusion-crushing sting. One crucial and now rather telling piece of advice missing from Kristian's lesson is Jannah's emphasis on corporate culture.

"Flynn, this work is difficult, there is no doubt about that. You need to be fully absorbed with every aspect of every aspect of every fucking aspect of the trader's cargoes, the pricing risks, the potential cost blowouts, the hedging dynamics, the never ending changes to all the assumptions once the vessel is actually underway, and many more things which will become apparent over time. This is very difficult. Sure. But the true hurdle for you is this; the traders must love you. I once thought I would like to be a trader. It sounds impressive. Like being a surgeon or a rock star. And often I know more than the traders. And they like me, sure, but they don't love me. They don't trust me to go into a meeting or to know how to create opportunities

"That's a bit stupid."

"It's fucking retarded. So, imagine you're locked in to buy a huge physical cargo, its price based on the settlement quote average over five trading days. Each day of those five, you bury the paper market, selling, selling, selling, pushing the price down so that the eventual price for the cargo you have to buy is artificially tanked thanks to the way the system works."

"Fuck yeah."

"This trading game mate, it's a nightmare and a dream. It's as complicated as you want to make it, or as easy. The true genius, the gift that will always ensure you stay alive in this game, is knowing faster than anyone else in the market, where is the squeeze?"
"The squeeze?"

"The squeeze, the only thing that matters to a trader. You figure out who to squeeze, how to squeeze, what's gonna make 'em squeeze, then you act on that. And you act aggressively once you know the squeeze is on. So, today, I reckon the stupid ChinoPet cunts have bitten off way more than they can chew. They've been out buying fucking everything in paper and physical lately, the price hasn't skyrocketed as they planned, I've been in contact with as many other traders as I can, noone has been dealing with them direct as far as I can tell. They're long and they're about to be fucking wrong. As soon as some decent selling comes in, they're gonna race for the exit and there's not gonna be a bid for 'em to escape. Fucking little Chinese cunts. They're gonna cop a squeeze today."

or think clearly once all that risk exposure is on my plate. If you don't want to end up like Kristian, you need to be sure the traders love you. Kristian was incredibly smart. But, he thought he was better than everyone, including the traders. If something went wrong with their trades, he would smirk and try to advise them on how to avoid that scenario in the future. What an idiot! No street-smarts! Listen OK, brains, immense intelligence, that's just expected around here. That is why you are here, but it takes more than that to progress. You understand?"

"Yes, thanks so much for the insight, I really appreciate it."

"OK, good. Any questions, you ask me. But, ask me twice, I won't answer, ask me three times, I can fire you. Got it?"

"Got it."

I head back to my desk with Jannah's morose attempt of a pep talk behind me. It's 9.15am and the 24th floor is now free of empty seats. The Scion corporate juggernaut is free to launch at full capacity. Joel looks reasonably dusty as I proceed past his desk. I arrive back to my seat and the internal messenger lights up at the bottom right corner of one of my three computer screens.

It's the big cheese, 'What you end up paying for that blonde piece of tart?'

'300 Sing.'

'Hahahah! I must be paying you too much'

'Well I don't remember bartering, I just woke up and she was in my bed.'

'Hello morning glory! Good deal I reckon, she was tasty, you reprobate!'

'What a night, no idea what happened.'

'I love it! Right, get busy, enjoy day 2, any questions just work it out yourself you fucking retard.'

'OK, sounds easy enough.'

. . . .

I jolt to life with the misplaced dread that I've slept through my alarm and am now late for work. The sun's well and truly risen, the day clearly in full swing. I check my Blackberry, a few hundred new emails received through the night, fairly standard, but more relevant and noteworthy, it's Saturday. I slide back under the covers in my ice-cold abode. My apartment may be encased in glass, not a wise architectural move when designing equatorial real estate, but the electricity bill is footed by my employer and the air conditioning unit has not been afforded a moment of reprieve since I moved in three months ago.

I could easily keep snoozing for another couple of days or more and still be far from adequately rested. This new gig is no picnic. Yesterday marked the completion of my official probation period, not that such an achievement bears a particularly large amount of relevance. Firings are part and parcel of every workday. It's so entrenched in the culture, that anytime someone heads off for a meeting, someone else will always joke, 'make sure to take your wallet and keys with you…just in case.' It's not overly side-splitting how often these meetings do indeed culminate in a company-wide email informing those remaining that another someone has left the company with immediate effect and that we wish them well in their future endeavours. Do we? I suppose so.

My longing to stay cozy under the covers is overcome by millions of decibels of construction sound effects. There is no such thing as a slowing economy in Singapore. Buildings upon buildings are being erected in every possible direction. This is a nation infatuated with property. Thanks to borderline slave wages for manual labour and an evergreen flight of wealth from Southeast Asia into the relatively safe enclave of the Singaporean property market, no alarms are necessary on a Saturday morning. Bangladeshi men are jack hammering their little hearts out with sweaty abandon as yet another skyscraper begins its ascent to the heavens.

I'm lying on my side and bracing to discard the comfort of bed when I become acutely aware of a lump. It's an overwhelming lump of pure lard where my lat muscles are supposed to be. My wings? What's happened to them? I've become the fattest of fat bastards with such effortless disgrace. I walk naked to the bathroom and look horrified at the image staring back in the mirror. I am a splotchy plastic bag, filled with expired milk and covered in pubes. I resist the urge to jump on the spot. I won't have time to wait for the jiggling to subside. Enough is enough. Today, I am joining the damn gym.

I hop in the shower quickly, no point completing the full beautifying regime. With a little luck and an even smaller amount of exertion, I'll be doused in perspiration in the very near future and on track to regaining some form to my once mighty lat muscles. I lace up my sneakers, covered in dust from hiding away in the closet for far too long. Even my ankles look podgy.

A few blocks from home is the *Pure* gymnasium. I waddle on in. The anorexic, praying mantis, leotarded reception woman looks me over on the approach and prepares a new membership form before I even open my mouth. I complete the paperwork. She then offers a gym tour by one of the trainers. Before I can decline, a trainer emerges. You know the sort; glass half full, brain wholly washed, skin completely waxed. Brad steps forward, dressed in a patronizing grin and the usual hoop-lah of short shorts, a muscle tee and the vascular-preserving accoutrement of every devoted gym junky, *skins*. Please. I compose my thoughts of wanting to choke Brad with a heavily laden bench press bar and focus instead on reliving the horror of seeing myself in the mirror this morning. Stay cool. He's trying to help.

Brad embarks on a tour of the gym. It's a gym, mate, not the Museum of Natural History. I think he maybe even imagines he has assisted me by pointing out the leg press, the chin up bar, the various settings on the treadmill. Good tour mate. Thanks *Brad*. How about you show me the two-way mirror looking into the ladies' change-rooms so this isn't a complete waste of time? Just when I think the tour is over, he says I'm entitled to a free personal training session with the new membership. I am poised to refuse, obviously, but decide against my better instincts, fuck it, why not?

Always trust your instincts. Always. Having neglected the instinctual urge to boycott Brad's gift of a free training session, I now find myself strapped upside down to a chin up bar via some NASA moon boots with blood flushing my cerebellum and Brad yelling at me to give him one more, one more, one fucking more. The 'one more' Brad is referring to is the gravity conquering act of reaching my fingers to the bar for the 30th time. Fuck this and fuck you, Brad. I'm stuck upside down to a fucking bar. Who's the moron here hey? I give him the one more his life is so desperately lacking and then endure the dignity destruction of allowing Brad to undo the moon boots and cradle me in his arms back to an upright posture. Please, someone kill me.

With my plunge towards insanity complete, and 45 minutes of voluntarily entered into fitness-based torment behind me, I am able to finally leave the gym, my free session over. Brad shakes my hand and tells me how well I did today. Just fuck off and die, buddy. I leave the *Pure* gym and head straight to the New Zealand Ice Creamery at the mall right next to my place. I order a super max sized chocolate thick-shake. I suck with all the suction I can muster and the shake's thickness is tantamount to icey, chocolate cement, pure, diabetic ecstasy. Cop that, Brad.

I return home shortly before midday, throw the sneakers deep in the closet, never to be spoken of, or worn, again, and take a long, well earned shower. Saturday is not really a rest day. Not entirely. Owing to the fact that oil trading is potentially the most overly complicated career path I could ever hope to find myself on, a large chunk of every Saturday is spent back at the office reviewing everything learnt in the past week, reading all the market dynamics and commentary articles that I have not had time to explore throughout the week and continue to plow on through the volumes of material, textbooks, and manuals Jannah never ceases to throw my way regarding the oil trading world. She is one nightmarishly tough taskmaster. For someone of such small stature, she is in the highest of my regard, a person who has transformed my understanding of what hard work actually is.

My physique may be bloated, but nothing's swelling as rapidly as my bank account. Without any free time or friends to engage in a social life, with rent paid by Scion and no hint of a girlfriend to wine and dine in overpriced restaurants and bars, there is nigh on $60,000 SGD in my Citibank account. Three months of hard yakka has been well worth it. I brush my teeth, leave the A/C running, lock the door and head in to the office for a studious Saturday afternoon well aware that all is fine in the world of Flynn James.

The office is empty and after an hour of reading through my personal notes scrawled down through the week, I grab one of the texts Jannah has lent me and decide to study up on the underlying chemistry of oil. With the passing of another hour I think I may finally have some idea what naphtha is. This word that sounds like a speech impediment is the equivalent of Evian in the world of the Hydrocarbon Man. It's a distant, distilled, refined relative of the crude oil extracted from the earth which causes me endless headaches on a daily basis.

The early evening shimmer of the imminent Marina Bay light show is in the air when my mobile rings.

"Slip, how are ya?"

"Yeah, well thanks. Sorry, who's this?"

"It's Strop, mate. Your dear old mate, Strop."

"Hawh, fuck off! Strop! What's cracking?"

"Mate, one of the boys told me you lived in Singas now. I'm here for a mate's bucks party. The sad cunt knows fuck all people here in Singas buddy. Come along for a booze-up tonight. We're heading to some Bungy Bar at Clarke Quay now. Then no plans mate, just get flogged. Would be good to see ya. Come along. I'm off home to Oz in the morning."

"Yeah, yeah, rightoh, listen, I'm just in the office now. I'll meet ya at that Bungy Bar. I know where that is. I will be a couple hours though, alright?"

"No worries, Slip."

"Cool, be down soon bro."

"Beauty."

I hang up and continue on with the crash course in self-tutored carbon chemistry. I make sure to add plenty of very basic notes to my reading. My memory is sure to be far from its best after a night with Strop. I'll have to rely on some well-scribbled notes so this studious afternoon is not a waste of time. How the hell did Strop get my number anyway?

For those unfamiliar with Singapore, there is a continuation of 'Quays', which snake their way inland from Marina Bay. The putrid water of these quays looks like a suitable altar to baptize the anti-Christ. It is hideous. Another one of the sick jokes some Singaporean Satan worshipper plays on citizens and tourists alike is running 'River Cruises' through these filthy waters and for some bizarre reason, the 'Cruises' always appear full. What are those people doing? Paying money to cruise the sludge? I might start running tours of the sewer. It would be of equal aesthetic appeal. I'm grateful that my employment is all consuming. If I were to find myself regularly lumbered with more than a few consecutive hours of free time in Singapore, I would certainly kill myself. This place is one fucking shit hole.

Boat Quay is nearest to Marina Bay and closest to my office. At each day's close of business, or earlier, you'll find Boat Quay's many Irish bars full of plump expats chugging Marlboro's, downing ales, watching the English Premier League and talking about how fit they were before they moved to Singapore. Clarke Quay is the next stop, a frenzied sort of more tourist-oriented continuation of Boat Quay. The Irish pubs and well-fed, overpaid expats become replaced with themed restaurants, flashy nightclubs and Singaporean youths struggling to find an identity.

The Bungy Bar marks the beginning of Clarke Quay. You can smash a few pints then indulge in some reverse bungy jumping, i.e. you can pay to be flung at Mach 10 speed into the sky, I'll pass. My cab pulls up and I walk on in to see good old Strop.

"Slip, you fucking shyt for sore eyes! Give me a hug." Strop is such a sweet talker. I haven't seen him for a few years, which suits me fine. He is a reckless unit. This was a big mistake coming here. I've got immediate regrets.

"Strop, good to see you mate. What the hell are you doing here?"

"Meet Geoff. Geoff, this is Slip, Slip, Geoff." Geoff is one monster of a man, huge. And he is swaying like a freshly stun-gunned hippo.

"G'day, Slip. Nice name for a homo. I'm getting married next week. Stupid bitch finally wore me down." From first impressions, I can definitely concur that said girl is indeed a stupid bitch.

"Right, that sounds romantic."

"Just fucking with ya mate, she's my soul mate. Fuckin love the tramp more than heroin." I hope I get an invite to the wedding. The speeches would be a treat.

"Yeah gotchya. OK, I need a drink."

"Let me Slip, I'll call over our little bar wench, she fucking wants me so bad man. Only human." Just so you understand how misplaced

Strop's confidence with the ladies is, be aware his physical characteristics can best be described as forming the brainchild for the Michelin Man advertising campaign.

"Only human indeed mate."

The next two hours involve me binge drinking to the extreme to insure the conversation doesn't entice me to jump into the waters of Clarke Quay with lead glued to my shoes. Along with Strop and Mr. Head over Heels, Geoff, are another two fuckwits. Like wolves, fuckwits travel in packs. There's Russell from Perth, he looks like a Hells Angel lieutenant and I'm yet to figure out what he's actually doing for a crust in Singapore. He's not what you'd call a big talker and sporting a lengthy, jagged scar on his cheek, he's not the sort of bloke I'm keen to probe too intently for information. And then there's Jason, a tubby Greek guy, sweating profusely and joining Strop in the delusions of desire he assumes the waitresses have for him. Between gulps of tiger, I'm eyeing my opportunity to smoke bomb out of this bucks party at the first clear chance.

"Well fuck this, let's get some fucking chicks hey." Geoff, his adoration for his chosen 'tramp' is questionable, I've gotta say.

"There's a good karaoke bar nearby mate, full of little fucking flippers bro." Strop pipes in. He seems to know Singapore better than me. And what the hell is a flipper?

"Well let's go then aye. Finish your drinks lads."

We each neck the remainders of our drinks and walk to the taxi rank about 50m away. There are five of us, one too many for a single cab. Thank you, Lord. I sense my smoke bomb prospect and immediately pretend to take a phone call. With my Blackberry to my ear, I look flustered and yell out to Strop, "I'll just see you there mate, I have to take this call sorry bro."

"Nonesense, I'll wait with you and we can go together."

"Ah, great. Good idea." Fucking Strop.

Strop opens the cab door for the others, tells the driver where this 'flipper' place is and then stands by my side as I speak earnestly to thin air before hanging up, "OK, let's go then mate. Fuck it's good to see you." I really wish he would hurry up and just piss off.

Strop hails down the next cab. It's nearing 11pm. I resign myself to the reality that I'm locked in to at least another hour before I can escape home. Strop tells the driver to take us to Circular Rd. Huh? Circular Rd is right next to work and a street where I often grab lunch, phenomenal noodles.

The cab pulls in to Circular Rd and I hop out to see Geoff, Russ and Jason being led into a bar by a dozen barely legal Filipino girls. This is the same bar that serves up noodles by day. What the fuck? We start walking towards the bar. I realise just how pissed I am. Each step is accompanied by a wobbling balance re-adjustment.

"This is an awesome karaoke bar, Slip, you drunk enough to have a sing yet?"

"Umm, yeah, I guess. These girls look pretty damn skanky mate."

"Yeah, don't sweat it. Geoff loves his flippers."

"What are flippers?"

"Filipino girls mate, Circular rd is flipper central."

As we arrive at the entrance, a couple of flippers grab me by the hand and lead me inside. It's freezing in here, the air con is spectacular. The window to the street is completely fogged from floor to ceiling. The girls, sorry, the flippers, are giggling away as they lead me to the bar, looking like they should probably be at home studying for school exams, rather than parading on Circular Rd in skimpy black dresses. One asks me what I would like to drink. I order a tiger and take a seat with the others at a bench, expecting to see some microphone and the usual karaoke paraphernalia. No stage is visible. Maybe they just bring the microphone to you if you pick a song you want to ruin by singing. The little flipper returns with a tiger.

"That will be twenty dollars."

"Twenty dollars? Shit. Rightoh, here you go."

"And you wann tequila?"

"No thanks."

"You sure? Tequila very good."

"Nah, I'm fine. Cheers."

"And which one of us you like?"

"Huh?"

"Which one better for you, big boy? Me or my sister?"

"Umm, you're nice."

"Hawwhh, you really mean it big boy? You like me?"

"Well, I guess so."

"Awwhhh, ffanks honey bunny."

"Sure."

My chosen girl now sits on my lap, not easy as I'm perched fairly high up on a bar stool, while the sister walks off in a huff. The selection of this girl was based on her teeth being a few degrees less fucked up than her sister's. There's obviously not a big affection for dentists in flipper land. I notice for the first time that each of the other lads has a flipper on their lap too. Mine puts her hand straight between my legs and starts grabbing for my dick. OK, I know I'm a real dreamboat, but this is ridiculous, what the hell is going on?

I turn to Strop, "mate, what's the go? What sort of karaoke joint is this?"

"How long have you been living here in Singas, Slip?"

"Three months mate."

"And you've never been to Circular Rd before?"

"I get lunch here a fair bit."

"You crack me up mate."

"This chick's giving me a fucking handy."

"Hell yeah, that's the point."

"The point? Isn't this a karaoke bar?"

"Karaoke. Hahaha! Nah mate, that's just what we tell our wives and shit. These girls will suck you off mate. It's fucking awesome. Order a round of tequilas and see what happens. Or don't see. You'll understand soon buddy."

I continue sipping on my beer, balancing this flipper on my thigh and trying not to lose a load as she frantically rubs away on my crotch like a cavewoman trying to start a fire. The five of us are sitting at a bar bench, each being tossed off under the table, all the while continuing to talk rubbish banter and sip our grogs.

"Let's get a few rounds of tequilas hey." Strop takes charge and the flippers all squeal with excitement.

"Fuck yeah!" Geoff's thirsty.

"Rightoh." My enthusiasm is somewhat muted relatively.

The barman fills up a few dozen plastic shot glasses of tequila while some old duck of a flipper appears from a back room and wheels a canister towards our table. The shots arrive and we all tuck in, flippers included.

My flipper unzips my fly and looks into my eyes, giving me a crazed smile, "You have nice dick. I wann suck." As she says this, the old lady cranks a button on the canister. Within moments the room is full from floor to ceiling with smoke. I can't see beyond a few inches, visibility is non-existent. As I try to accustom myself to this newly formed Operation Desert Storm, I feel this flipper's lips sucking away on my cock. I grope through the smoke for another shot of tequila on the table and smash it down, trying to induce a coma so I can forget that this girl's teeth look like they belong to an angry guard dog. This head job is far from relaxing. The smoke settles to a level about chest height. There is enough clear air to see across the bench and witness each of the others' blow-job-receiving faces. This is so fucked up. From chest level down, it's a sea of haunted house smoke and tequila-laced suction.

I pull the girl away from my groin, zip myself up and tell her I have to go to the toilet. This whole scenario is just way too heavy. She points to the corner of the room and asks if she can join me. What is wrong with this flipper? It's nice to be wanted but I need some solo reflection time and quickly dash through the smoke. I splash litres of water in my face. I can never eat noodles here again. I splash more water in my face for another minute and try to un-experience the past five minutes. No luck.

I return towards the bar. The smoke is starting to fully subside. Geoff is now standing and facing the bench. As the smoke fades completely, I see his bare arse thrusting back and forth, his pants round his ankles, a pair of red high heels bouncing up and down on his shoulders as he throttles the flipper now seated on the bar stool. The other blokes watch on, cheering. To hell with this karaoke bar, I walk past the bucks-party-flipper-fuck-fest-smoke-show into the street and hail a passing cab. As I open the cab door Strop rushes into the street, zipping up his fly, "Slip, where ya going?" I shut the door without replying and tell the driver to floor it to the Abode.

I'm out of bed shortly before my Monday morning alarm, having slept my way almost through the entirety of Sunday. The only waking moments for the Sabbath involved an ice cold shower, ravaging the fridge, and ringing family and friends at home for a healthy dose of wholesome reality. I'm up and bouncing. This week is no ordinary week. This week, for the first time in my Scion life, the Singapore office will be graced by God.

God, not that floozy pretender who created Man in his own image or promised Abraham as many offspring as there are stars in the sky, as dire a proposal as that may sound, no the true God to my universe, Scion's CEO and Founder, Giovani Farina. I've garnered only scant snippets of information about this force of nature. Staff members, traders included, speak of him in hushed tones while persistently glancing over their shoulders, worried Giovani might wondrously appear from his Geneva HQ.

Scion is not a publicly listed company with its shares listed on stock markets, hung out to flourish or flounder at the behest of investors or its books open to pesky invasions from would be corporate raiders. No, this is a fiercely private company where commercial decisions are made on strictly revenue-producing grounds of reason, free of ethical considerations to cloud capitalist streams of consciousness. I cannot wait to meet my Maker, Mr. Farina, in the flesh, but am well aware one wrong move could spell the end of my tenure here in this company, if not Earth.

Our Creator is in town for the busiest week on the Asian oil trading calendar; APPEC - the Asia Pacific Petroleum Conference. I'm told this is a dedicated week of meetings, presentations, back room negotiations, an opportunity for anyone and everyone in the mug's game of oil trading to get together and figure out how best to profitably spread hydrocarbon molecules through the planet.

For the first time in three months, I decide to start the day with some stretching, not yoga, just stretching. After five minutes, all major muscle groups are reasonably supple despite still being well camouflaged beneath layers of flab. Air conditioning floods the room, but some light exercise sets the sweat glands racing, my face has a rosy glow; healthy body, healthy mind, healthy lather.

I head to the bathroom, scrub thoroughly in the shower, then pay close attention to shave precisely before generously splashing my face with the Issey Miyake *Eau de Toilette* reserved for special occasions. I even don a suit jacket and tie for the first time since my opening day. It's impossible to overdress when an encounter with God awaits.

Slippery

I arrive to Dimbulah in unison with Sebastian, grab my vegemite toast and flat white while he gets some sort of herbal tea laced with the semen of a Bengal Tiger. Bestial sicko. I have absolutely nothing in common with Sebastian, nothing whatsoever, apart from the obvious fact we are both hanging on for dear life to the same ladder leading to the pinnacle of well-paid-cuntiness. We're now a mere few rungs from the trader culmination, although each day is filled with cold sweats in those milliseconds before submitting a piece of work. One minor mistake and any grip on that ladder will simply vanish, with or without a farewell song from some fat bitch songstress, a genuinely insincere 'Flynn has left the company with immediate effect' email to bid me adieu.

On leaving the café, we run into Paul, the Aussie derivatives trader, also en route to fuel up on vegemite toast and a full cream flat white, "best behaviour today boys, big Giovani's in town." He smiles and continues on his way. As we enter the office shortly after 8am, it's clear we are not the only God worshippers at Scion. Every other morning of my three months here, aside from the presence of myself, Jannah and Sebastian, the office is empty until at least 8.45am. This morning there are people in all directions well before the decreed 9am official start time, all furrowing their brows, looking agitated, partaking in a staged semblance of corporate contribution. What a pack of phony cunts, God won't be fooled by these crawlers.

My probationary ninety days has enlightened my awareness to the Singaporean psyche and general way of life. To call Singaporeans superficial would be to undermine the concept of superficiality. Being superficial implies there is something of substance beneath the surface. No assumption of substance seems fitting for Singaporeans. In a country devoid of sporting heroes, cultural icons, or anything remotely worth being patriotically proud of, Singaporeans have fully embraced the notion of inhabiting nothing more than a Material World.

In this financially prosperous nation whose geography resembles a pimple on the tip of the Malay Peninsula, the twin cornerstones of its population are fear and greed. Singaporeans are fearful of everything, be it chewing gum, freedom of speech, or merely finding themselves amongst the native *savages* in one of their neighbouring Asian countries. You literally need to hold a gun to a Singaporean's head to convince them to drive the Johor-Singapore bridge into Malaysia. They are certain they will instantaneously perish if they set foot there. And you'll have even less joy trying to convince them to post something politically controversial on their Facebook page…they are right to be fearful here though, people have a habit of 'going missing' shortly after their Facebook posts make mention of any perceived social shortcoming in this so-called democracy. And chewing gum, well that probably has germs or AIDS wrapped up in it, yuck, get rid of it.

Now, as for greed, this pillar of Singaporean modus operandi is far from unique. Greed plagues humanity as a whole. I mean, fuck, it's the reason I am here in this job in the first place, purely because I want to make as much money as possible. But Asians, in general, appear nauseatingly consumed with the value of material wealth, the only difference being, Singaporeans are endowed with enough financial freedom to waste it willingly on watches, handbags, and cars in the steadfast manner their Asian neighbours can only dream of.

I resist the urge to continue bad mouthing Singaporeans in my thoughts. It can't be healthy having this much pent up anger. I settle instead on my morning tasks after quickly destroying the vegemite toast and slowly sipping away on the flat white. I update the cost forecasts for Huan and Keith's latest cargoes, ring the credit department to ask for an explanation as to why they're rheeming Keith with financing fees, *Fees!* This isn't retail banking. We're all in the same firm here. I then proceed to adjust the hedges on one of Keith's cargoes for an outturn gain.

Outturn is the actual quantity of oil discharged at the terminal. Usually there will be an outturn loss, where the quantity discharged at the terminal is less than the loaded amount quoted on the bill of lading. The boffins like to reason this is due to evaporation, or temperature and pressure anomalies at each port or maybe some oil is just stuck to the tanks. General shit like that, which sounds plausible enough, I guess. This is *physical* commodities trading after all. Nothing is straightforward or precise. At the end of the day, we're dealing with filthy, greasy, slippery oil.

But to have an outturn gain? Apparently the 596,000 barrels of oil loaded in Oman has now expanded to 599,000 barrels upon delivery in South Korea. Huh? There may certainly be temperature, pressure, and many more differences between Muscat and Seoul, but an outturn gain of 3,000 barrels doesn't necessarily pass the Flynn

James' sniff test, regardless of what any boffin wants to tell me. The vessel this oil has traveled on must have been throwing regular crude oil swinger parties in the storage tanks during the voyage and didn't provide appropriate prophylactics. Or someone's playing funny business at loading or discharge when reporting barrel quantities.

Either way, fuck it, Keith isn't worried and why should he be, 3,000 barrels at $100 per barrel, hello $300,000 of, most possibly, adulterated alchemy into the Scion coffers, under Wang's ledger. I continue on with deals desking my way through the morning, grateful I didn't have to be the messenger for reporting an outturn loss. Keith and his frequent autistic outbursts scare the fucking shit out of me. Every afternoon when he's engaged in a trading frenzy down his broker box, yelling instructions in some kind of Pigeon Singlish language he's invented, if you ever walk past and can see through the spit flying from his mouth to focus on his facial expressions, you'd think he's auditioning for an Asian adaptation of the Exorcist.

I re-read the contract for Huan's first ever transaction with a Russian counterparty to ensure he won't be sending Scion into bankruptcy. Seems OK to me, but what the fuck would I know? I'm a qualified physiotherapist who's also got a few years precious metals derivatives trading experience under the belt. I'm no lawyer, although if I were, I'd probably be the sort to sink my un-losable case by asking OJ to try on a glove. Anyway, it's time to focus on the worst part of each day, reporting the 'PNL' (profit-and-loss) for each of the traders' positions as of yesterday's close-of-business.

Jannah's boss, some narcissist I've never met who sits in Geneva, makes it a requirement for deals desk to provide a *commentary* of each trader's PNL performance. This is a nightmare for all concerned, especially me. Remember, I want the traders to not only like and respect me. I want them to LOVE me. Meanwhile, I am tasked with critiquing their trading decisions. Every day! It's like the ball boy telling Roger Federer how to hold his racket, not at the end of the match either, as infuriating as that would be for the most composed tennis player the world has ever known, no, tell him after every single point.

This hellish tight rope walk is a daily balancing act which saps every shred of my linguistic capacity. There's a requirement to stroke egos, provide commercial insight, and ensure the PNL evaluation is perfectly correct, whether it is flattering to the trader or not. I complete my assessments then email them to Keith, Huan and Paul, cc'ing the Milky Way galaxy of Scion busy bodies who deem their awareness of such results imperative to their corporate existence. I remain glued to my screen for the next two minutes, awaiting an abusive tirade from any of the three traders for having misreported anything.

Once this two-minute stay of execution is complete, I hop on the phone to Mumbai to ensure they haven't *lost* any of Paul's overnight trades. It's option expiry in two days and, as Paul originally promised on day one, the Mumbai trade reconciliation specialists are experts at covering their tracks and *misplacing* trades, only to find them moments before the futures contracts expire and the market is about as liquid as ice, the very exchange at which the trades are executed on in the first place. The "ICE", the Intercontinental Exchange, must be growing sick of my panicked calls in the hours before contract expiration, trying to channel Sherlock Holmes and piece together what indeed some curry enthusiast in Mumbai has managed to cock up so royally.

Huan sits four places to my right. He stands slowly, stretching his arms over his head and holding the pose for a few seconds before heading my direction. He doesn't look upset, which would usually be the disposition on his face if coming to chat shortly after I send him the PNL report. In my three months so far, it is rare I am able to report any P in Huan's PNL report. He has a healthy knack for losing money. Each day I'm amazed when he returns from meetings and I haven't received one of the 'immediate departure…' emails with his name featured.

"Jannah, you mind if Flynn joins me for a meeting with the ChinoPet traders?" Huan wants me to join him for a trader meeting. This is a first. I'm kicking goals nice and early on this fine Monday morning.

"No, of course not, that's fine Huan."

"Alright with you, Flynn?"

"Yeah, sure. Now?"

"Yep, let's roll mate."

Huan leads the way as we walk out of the office and to the elevators. I've kept the tie on, as uncomfortable as that may be against my newly evolved double chin. I'm not planning on removing the blasted slither of silk as long as a chance encounter with God is on the cards. We hop in the lift and walk straight out of the building into a waiting taxi.

"Paterson Rd, thank you." Huan gives the driver instructions as he busily scrolls away on his Blackberry.

"Yes sir."

"Sorry for the stitch up Flynn, but there's no meeting to head to."

"Sorry, what do you mean?"

"This APPEC week gets properly underway for the traders on the Sunday evening. All the big swingers arrive from all round the world in one heap on the Sunday afternoon. They're gagging to make the most of time away from the rugrats and the missus, all fucking sweating for a hit of some Asian brass."

"Brass?"

"You know, hookers, pro's, ostros. I saw that juicy little blonde you put away a few months back last night, she was having her temperature felt through her panties by the sweaty mitts of some fat Texan fucker, right in the middle of Bricks."

Despite being of strikingly obvious Asian descent, Huan's demeanour is part Pommy geezer, part American gangster. The words coming from his mouth simply don't match the Gollum-esque face they're spouting from.

"Huh, well…"

"Nah, see I just need your help, I'm in a fucking pickle. My girlfriend is Dutch. She has been back home for the past fortnight for her mum's birthday or some shit and she gets back to Singas tomorrow. Well, I've been going proper bonkers on the whores this last week mate. And I keep ending up with the stupid fucking desperate bitches who are on their fucking periods."

"What?"

"Well, I fucked this one bitch, she bled everywhere, ah well, fuck it, I pay her to get the fuck out of my pad and just turn the mattress over. Result."

"Makes sense."

"And then, I get all razzed up last night, heat off the scale, flogged and raging, find myself off tits in Bricks once again."

"Wait, what's Bricks?"

"You're shitting me cunt?"

"Umm, no. What is it?"

"It? It's a nightclub full of whores. The place we took you that first night a few months back. You know, the place where they kicked you out for pashing on with that little blonde. You're supposed to pay 'em and fuck 'em mate, not kiss 'em like you're sleepless in fucking Seattle."

"Oh…"

"Anyway, I'm all razzed last night, take another bird home, give her a good pummeling and then lose my shit, there's blood fucking everywhere."

"Jesus."

"Too right fucking Jesus. This bitch has just completely bled out on the other side of the mattress now. Ah well, what can you do? I was so fucked I managed to fall asleep without thinking too much about the pool of blood I was in."

"Holy shit man, you're a sick bastard."

"Yeah, yeah, save it, I just want you to help me carry the mattress out of the place and down to the garbage pile in the basement. Already ordered a new one to be delivered this afternoon."

"Of course, that's fine."

"Oh, and I'm a bit worried about stray hairs and that sort of thing man. My girl is a blonde haired Dutchy. All these whores I've been pumping, they're all dark haired Filipinos. So once we've dumped the mattress, I need you to help me give the place the full white glove once over. My girl barely trusts me. I know she'll be giving the place the CSI treatment, searching for stray hairs, used condoms, that sort of thing. You gotta help me make sure the place is pristine man. The place has to be spotless. Can't miss one black hair, if she finds one, I am fucked."

"Yeah, yeah, no worries."

We hop out, Huan paying the driver while never losing sight or touch of his Blackberry.

"This way Flynn, just cross here. You recognize that place over there?"

"The Hyatt? I've been there, once, to the international food buffet."

"Yeah, you mean the international brass buffet?"

"Nah, not really. Food."

"Shut up, would ya, Bricks is just down those stairs there, you daft prick. Just my luck I live right next door to the fucking place isn't it. Every time I walk past here with the missus I keep my head down in case one of the girls or the bouncers shouts out to me."

We continue on to Huan's pad, 15 stories above Paterson Rd and spend the next hour removing a mattress that looks like evidence in a homicide case and crawl around with white surgeon gloves on our hands and cave-diving torches strapped to our foreheads eradicating the place of musty stains and prostitute hair extensions.

We cab it back to the office. I feel grimy. Huan can't be too racked with guilt. He's already bragging that some whore is texting him, saying how much she wants to suck his cock tonight. The content of the message is nice, I suppose, the context could be better. I'm not looking forward to meeting his Dutch girlfriend someday, being forced to play the whole happy relationship charades game, what a pain.

The cab pulls up in front of the office and I open the door to head in. Huan says he'll catch me later in the afternoon and to tell Jannah I did really well in the meeting. I proceed into the office, watching the taxi shoot off with my partner in mattress disposal busily texting prostitutes from the passenger seat. Fuck knows where he's off to now.

The elevator is empty so I do what you always have to in such a situation, check myself out in the mirror. I straighten my tie and double check there's no menstrual flipper residue on my shirt, while at all times maintaining one disapproving eye on the pasty, podgy man staring back. I really should persevere with the gym. Even the almost insignificant jolting stop of the elevator at the 24th floor is enough to elicit a little bounce in my rapidly developing man mammaries.

Most people are out for lunch. Having God in the office may be sufficient to warrant an early arrival to the office, but it won't prevent a lunch break. Jannah is obviously at her desk. Lunch is for the weak and occupies no significance in her working day. If you're going to be addicted to anything, it may as well be work. Being seated next to Jannah has rendered any hope of lazing a distinct impossibility, but the volume of knowledge now circulating through my gray matter is almost exclusively thanks to the influence of this incredible little lady.

"How was the meeting?"

"It was good. I learned a lot."

"Excellent. Listen, I'm sorry if you have some other things on, but I need you to quickly help me with something?"

"Yeah sure, what do you need?"

"My boyfriend is from Chile, his English is not so great, neither is mine, can you help me with his CV?"

"Of course."

"Great, thanks. I will email it through. Please read and change as you think is necessary. He is trying to get a marketing role, that is the degree he completed in Santiago, but he is not having much luck so far. I'm no sugar mama, he needs a fucking job."

"No problem, I will see what I can do."

"Thanks. I have a conference call. I will be back in an hour."

I open the attachment with Marcelo's resume and, using my very own CV as a proven benchmark of obtaining a job I don't deserve. I quickly dismantle Marcelo's well intentioned attempt at gainful employment door opening into a one page, bullet pointed compilation of alluring spiv and unavoidable overachievement. I think back to my interview with Joel and Andrew and make sure to leave out repetitive mentions of geographical locations.

"Already on the hunt for a new job then?" Andrew has snuck up out of nowhere.

"Ha, nah mate, just helping out Jannah."

"What? She's outta here too? Taking the whole team hey?"

"Not at all, it's for her boyfriend. His sugar mama funded days are over."

"Ah, that's a shame. Marcelo, yes, top fella that one. Make sure you help him out."

"For sure."

"Now, when you're done arranging everyone's careers, you want to sit with me this afternoon during the window? I've noticed Keith and Huan don't really include you in the crude window. If you're going to be our next superstar trader, you need to see how the window works."

"Of course, that would be awesome."

"Pop round to my desk around 3.30pm, will show you how we get ready, what positions I'm running, and then the window proper starts at 4pm for half an hour. You probably don't know too much about the fuel oil trading world, that's fine, won't bore you with the details, it's more about seeing how the market works."

"Really appreciate that mate. See you at 3.30."

Andrew strolls off spinning a cricket ball in his fingers and I focus back on a re-read of Marcelo's updated CV. Once I'm happy it's sufficiently radiant to help him break free of Jannah's sugar mama gripes, I decide to run out quickly and grab some lunch, pumped with thoughts of sitting in to watch the window this afternoon. I walk down the corridor with a clear spring in my step, swipe my access card, open the door into the elevator well and walk hurriedly straight into a plump, bushy eye-browed, Mediterranean old man, God. I recognize him immediately, having spent many hours on the staff intranet checking out his profile.

"I am so sorry." The words pass my lips in a quivering plea sort of way. I'm already in the lift well. He may as well just fire me now.

"Please, please, that is fine." God's Italian accent is subtle. His hand gestures appear forgiving. He is God after all. Joel is standing directly behind him, about to burst into hysterics, but instead steps forward.

"Giovani, please meet Flynn, he is one of our rising stars on the junior trader program."

"Ah, of course, Flynn, it is a pleasure to meet you, young man. Please, no need to rush, save your speed for fast thinking."

"Absolutely."

God continues into the 24th floor with Joel holding the door for him. I jump straight into a waiting elevator. Mercifully it's empty. I hit the button for the ground floor, exhale deeply, and feel the reassuring sensation of blood rushing away from my colon. I'll happily wait till my next celestial encounter before I shit myself.

I walk out through the foyer and feel the instantaneous discomfort of Raffles Place heat. There's no shortage of amazing food options here. Lunch could easily consist of Peking duck, Mongolian lamb or finely diced sashimi. I dodge all those options and head straight to Dimbulah for a ham and cheese roll and another flat white.

Wiping breadcrumbs from my shirt as I leave I notice an old school barbershop across the alleyway. A frail old man stands alone, sweeping the floor in his starched, white coat. I feel the ever-present sweat drenching my hair and decide, fuck it, a number one chop is long overdue. I arrive at the black and white square tiled floor of the barber's and motion for the buzz cut. The first clean swipe with the clippers is heavenly, I'm five degrees cooler by the time the haircut is complete. Function over form is my new mantra. It has to be. I look fucking horrible.

Returning to the 24th floor with my glistening, freshly shorn, white noggin, the room is humming. God's presence ensures there is plenty of faux hum in the mix. He is walking the length of the room back and forth, a hands free phone piece in his ear, busily conversing in multiple languages while getting a quality dose of exercise and ensuring everyone on his walk path is more conscientious than could ever be possible without a godly presence in the room, peering over their shoulder. Traders scurry back and forth between their level 24 desks and the formal APPEC meetings booked on level 25. They meticulously put on ties and straighten their suit jackets as they head up to schmooze clients, removing them just as fast as they return to their desks to ensure all is well on whatever information they follow on their five or more computer screens.

The hotter of the two yellow fever inducing receptionists enters the floor for the afternoon mail delivery, laden with envelopes, but weighed down far more rigorously by the immoral thoughts of every man in this room, watching her with precision as she makes the rounds. Anytime she bends over a table, an audible sigh fills the room, each man exhaling in unison. She walks past God. Even He turns in his stride for a follow up view, raising an eyebrow, pouting his lips and nodding approval.

"Flynn, thank you so much for helping with Marcelo's CV. This looks much better. I emailed it to him. He's really happy."

"No problem, Jannah, it's the least I can do."

"And Andrew wants you to sit with him for the window."

"Yeah, he asked me earlier."
"That's great. Keith and Huan…they're not very good teachers. It's good Andrew likes you."

"Definitely."

I watch God with one eye, never too sure where in the room he's going to pop up with this office walking program he goes through so thoroughly. My other eye focuses on completing the hedging plan for Keith's October cargoes. Keith likes to have a plan in place early so that he can proceed to not follow it at all. Instead he uses it as a template for elaborately complex futures contract trades which usually end up losing money rather than making any, while also causing me endless headaches in trying to graphically illustrate to senior management just what the hell the Far East crude trader is so busy doing. As I hit send on the hedge summary email for Keith,

Huan pops up by my right shoulder and gives me his unique version of the Dirty Sanchez, rubbing his right index and middle finger across my upper lip, the fresh whiff of rank puss goes straight up my nostrils.

"Fucking hell mate, you right?"

"Calm down, thought you'd like a bit of rotting fish stench to get you through the afternoon."

"What the hell?"

"I just saw your little blonde tart again, gave her a rub down for you."

"Fuck me mate, you're an animal."

"Bit of brass at the business lunch, sensational. Sorry you couldn't make it along. Thanks again for helping out this morning though champ, appreciate that."

"Yeah, of course, no worries."

"You want another smell of your missus?"

"Nah, all good mate. Enjoy."

Huan walks away with his fingers to his nose, giving an Oscar winning performance of a man who may actually be prudently deliberating over a profitable trading strategy in his mind, eyes closed, breathing in deeply. It's almost 3.30pm, I bring up an Outlook folder with all the fuel oil related emails I've saved over my three months here and start quickly reading through every bit of information I can on whatever the hell fuel oil is.

"Flynn, let's go mate, bring a notebook with you." Andrew yells out from his seat in the row opposite.

"Yep, beauty, one sec."

To Andrew's right is Sebastian and to his left is Rudy, his operator. I'm still sporting my tie, no small feat considering the lack of blood reaching my brain thanks to the plump in my neck being gained post buying this shirt. I'm grateful for my tie wearing perseverance though, I round the row of desks and cross paths with Giovani, he gives me a heartening wink of what I hope is encouraging endorsement.

"OK, have a seat here mate." Andrew has a spare seat waiting for me. He's biting into an apple and poring through his notebook of impeccably neat writing and rather artistic flow charts. There are six computer screens infront of him, three on the desk level, two above those and one directly to his right, opposite which I'm now seated. Flashes are going off absolutely everywhere, none of which is causing Andrew any real concern.

"Right, let's give you the run down hey," he pulls up a live price chart of the November Brent crude oil futures contract, "now, which way do you think Brent's going to move?"

"What time frame?"

"Good man, excellent question. In one hour, where will Nov Brent be trading and why?"

"May I?" I motion to the mouse. Andrew nods. I check the time component of his chart, 1-minute intervals. I hit the axis and check the 5, 30 and 60-minute charts, as well as a daily which has price movements over the past 18 months.

"So, what's your call, big man?"

"Well, Nov Brent's now $102.65, having opened this morning at $102.03/barrel and shooting straight to $103 on minimal volume after closing last Friday at $101.50, following a week of steadily climbing from a mere $95/barrel last Monday. I reckon some Asian muppets have got into work this morning and updated their quant formulae or whatever algorithm they think will make them rich and able to speak ahh da English. Idiots. Their little buying flurry created some short covering to push the price higher, but European traders will see this push higher as weak and sell the fucker. There is no reason for Brent to be trading over $100/barrel. Buzzard maintenance has been postponed again, while everyone knows the new Chinese data about better than expected construction figures is bullshit. Euro zone traders are going to sell Brent, I'd sell now."

"Fair enough. Here you are, just click on the bid here, how many lots you want to sell? Or, you want to put an offer up there?" Andrew's mouse is on Scion's internal order screen, where traders can send through their orders to our designated trade execution team.

"Sell 100 lots."

"Lovely. So, just adjust the lots amount to 100. Price, 'at market'. Done." Andrew clicks the order. It's in the system, my first trade. We're off. A confirmation email comes through on Andrew's screen. Short 100 lots Nov Brent at $102.61.

"Stop out at $103.10 OK. Can you place that order in the system as well?"

"Yep, good call too, Flynn. And where you want to take profits?"

"$101.52."

"Done. OK, forget about that chart now, time for fuel oil 101 and the window. Pen and paper ready?"

"Yep, all good."

It's now 3.37pm. Andrew tosses his apple core in the bin, grabs the mouse, faces his wall of computer screens and begins his express clarification of the imminent 'window'. It is the only time each day when this room does actually come remotely close to a Hollywood depiction of what a *trading floor* looks like. Martin Scorsese, Oliver Stone and many more would have you believe that a dealing room is some sort of hot bed of nonstop frenzy, a showground of theatrics, men screaming at each other, ripping up deal tickets, smashing phones on desks. Maybe that world does exist somewhere, with 'wolves' fucking whores in their leather chairs and snorting coke straight off their desks, all the while making millions upon millions of dollars, cause, let's face it, they're just that fucking clever. I very much doubt that world exists, no matter what Hollywood's finest directors and grossly overpaid actors want to put on a silver screen.

Andrew may be a short, racist South African, but there's no hiding it, he is one incredibly smart man. As has been quickly and deftly explained, the window, on the surface, is the thirty-minutes of trading fury and mayhem which ultimately decrees the daily settlement price of oil, the price of energy, capitalism at its barbaric best. But, far more importantly to the cunning eyes, ears and nuclei of the very best traders, this window gives the only real insight into what your fellow traders at the opposing firms are thinking, at what pricing levels they're getting involved, and how much or how little they're willing to chase oil or offload it.

"So, these are your buyers showing their bids for what price and during which dates they're willing to purchase oil, physical fuel oil. And here's the same for the sellers."

"OK."

"And here, this is the paper market, these are your derivative products. There are no specific dates like the physical market, obviously, there is no actual delivery required."

"Cool."

"The feature that you'll notice is you can actually see which counterparties are putting their bids and offers up in the physical window. Business doesn't need to be transacted through this window. We can call up any firm we like and do business direct, but this window does two things, you see who's dealing and at what price they want to trade, but we can also see who's not active in the window. Now, this may seem trivial, but we know that the big multinationals and other large trading houses have big storage facilities in Singapore and Malaysia. We know just how many tonnes of storage they have and can figure out what sort of cost outlay they're choking themselves with by holding on to those terminals. They need to get oil from somewhere, they need to turn the tanks, get some return on the outlay. So, if they're not active in the window, where are they being active, and who with? We can figure that out just as well from who's absent as from who's present."

"Aha."

"In the paper market, we can't see immediately who is on the bid of the offer, but each night I get a recap of who bought or sold what and at what level. Each night, I update all the transactions to try and figure out the market position of the other traders. Sometimes, they'll intentionally haemorrhage money on the physical market to make a bonanza on the paper market, 'game' the window, so to speak."

"Right."

"The other stitch up is, the final price at 4.30pm becomes the benchmark settlement price for the whole day. Lots of contracts stipulate the final price for a cargo is the average of the settlement prices over the course of a few days around the delivery time. The prices move all over the shop all day long, but wherever that price settles at 4.30pm for the number of pricing days for a certain cargo, then that average will ultimately determine the cargo's final price."

"Awesome! Squeeze away."

"OK mate, it's about to kick off, I've gotta get busy, just write down any questions as they come into your head and we'll go through it all afterwards."

"Good luck mate."

The window is flying past. Andrew is completely in his element, oozing cool, instructing brokers down the lines to work his orders and politely thanking them when the orders are filled, updating his own series of spreadsheets as activity takes place in the window, typing away at light speed in online chat rooms with all and sundry of the oil trading universe, tossing the cricket ball in his hands when trades go his way and it becomes obvious ChinoPet is being squeezed, pointing out various aspects of window action I would otherwise not have noticed, and writing notes and more flow charts in his notebook, and constantly in conversation with Rudy regarding all the specifics of incoming and outgoing shipments. All the while, I can hear Keith over my shoulder back in my row, spitting out his usual incomprehensible abuse at the brokers, crying foul of anything and everything transpiring in the crude oil window and smashing his desk and/or calculator in his daily autistic window outburst.

4.30pm, the decibels in the room immediately drop. I read over the notes I've taken down in silent awe as Andrew has shown his trading superstardom qualities.

"So, look at that hey, not sure if it's beginner's luck or maybe you really are the chosen one."

"What's that, Andrew?"

"November Brent, $101.53 on the offer. You want to buy back the short 100 lots?"

"Yeah, lock in the profit."

"$108,000 minus some brokerage. Not bad for sixty minutes work mate."

"Nailed it."

"I have to run to a meeting with the biggest of big cheeses now mate, got to give Giovani the fuel oil team's game plan for the next six months. You save those questions, I've got 108,000 reasons to answer anything you like."

"Thanks heaps."

. . . .

I walk out of Somerset train station and through the automatic doors of the FairPrice supermarket shortly before the 10pm closing time. I've lasted five months in Singapore without cooking one single meal at the Abode. It is largely due to the sushi platters I discovered here at FairPrice. Some other lazy bastard has clearly moved into the neighbourhood recently, obviously with the same fetish for raw fish wrapped in rice and seaweed. That's fine, but it means the late night sushi journeys to the supermarket on the way home from work have become a bit of a jackpot. Thankfully, there's a primo pack in the fridge. I grab that and some milk for the morning cereal binge, pay the frazzled old lady behind the counter who looks like she'd definitely vote in favour of legalizing euthanasia and continue home on the short sweaty stroll to my building.

I arrive home, crank the air con to Christmas in the snow temperatures and switch the TV on to watch Charles Barkley, Shaquille O'Neal and Reggie Miller talking smack about shooting hoops on the NBA channel. I replace my work attire with boardshorts and a wife beater singlet. I take a seat on my beloved couch and get busy on the sushi straight off the plastic tray. I've done this so many times, you'd think I might have worked out how to open the soy sauce packaging cleanly, but if there's one thing I do know how to make squirt, it's soy sauce. Another stain on the wife beater is something I can happily live with.

I finish off the sushi, no need for the chopsticks, grab a beer from the fridge and settle in properly on the couch with a can of Heineken and Morgan Downey's *Oil 101*, the oil trading Bible. I read back through pages of the Bible I've scoured many, many times already. Mr. Downey's tome has been my steadfast companion since moving here. In between paragraphs, I steal glimpses of the NBA channel's coverage of the epic 1992 Bulls vs Knicks Game 7 playoff game. Michael Jordan is putting nails in the Knicks' coffin with 42 points, while Patrick Ewing makes me feel better about my prolific sweat glands, I mean fucking hell, he must be covered in gasoline.

Three beers pass by. It's now midnight in Singapore, which equates to 6pm in Geneva. It's around this time each evening the Blackberry goes absolutely mental with all manner of emails. I like to place the digital device of voluntary slave labour enforcement on the coffee table and watch the unread email quota tick up frantically like one of those real time US debt clocks.

Way back on my first day, Kristian managed to include me on every email distribution list in the Scion network. Fucking cunt. I decided it was wise to proceed with the overflow of information though. It seemed the best way to become rapidly acquainted with the firm. But, sitting here on the couch, reading confusedly through *Oil 101*, listening to Magic Johnson's silky smooth HIV conquering commentary and wondering how much longer till the unread emails reach four figures, my attitude towards information is well and truly that more is less and less just has to be more.

I do notice an email from Marcelo, Jannah's man. He says he has passed the one-month probation period in his new marketing role with Revlon and wants to buy me dinner for helping with his resume. Bravo Marcelo! I save reading any of the other emails for the morning and go to bed.

I'm up at 6am to start the day with my pitiful attempt at exercise. A few push ups, a dozen sit ups, some lateral lunges and lots and lots and lots of supine lying on the wooden floor, completing deep breathing exercises. It's a fitness regimen suitable for an elderly emphysema patient, but it's doing something. My initial ballooning weight gain since arriving in Singapore has plateau'd. I can't face the gym. Spending any time whatsoever with Brad and the rest of the muscle bound, brainless *skins* brigade carries too great a risk of a Michael Douglas *Falling Down* scenario.

I shower, shave and watch the Bloomberg channel as I slurp my cereal and set about deleting the endless emails unrelated to anything concerning me. Steve Pemberton, the man who called me several months ago as I rode home from the pub in Manly on my BMX is in Singapore today. He has asked if I can assist with the interviews for the graduate program. Unlike the junior trader program I'm being fast tracked on, the graduate program is for candidates straight out of university. These grads aren't weighed down with trading superstardom expectations like their junior trader counterparts. Their program is designed to see them develop over a two-year grace period into a useful member of the operations or credit teams or something similar. I'm told we are looking for intelligent, disciplined, effective communicators with a bent towards lateral thinking aptitude rather than purely academic prowess. I'm not too sure how exactly I'll pinpoint those qualities, but I'm keen to know what specific characteristics they were looking for when they hired me.

Things move fast in Scion. Five months ago I was the new kid on the chopping block, now I'm part of the hiring squad. I'm flattered, but wise enough to know I'll be found out sooner not later. I've developed a reasonable understanding about how the cogs in the physical commodities trading machine turn, but I can't keep fluking my way through each day forever. Sebastian was far smarter and more capable than myself, but he was tinned only last month. He incorrectly hedged a cargo, mistakenly calculated a blend or asked the same question twice. I don't know what exactly, but can assume it was something rudimentary, which anywhere else in the corporate world would result in further training and some comforting words from a supervisor. Not at Scion, just hit the bricks, pal, you're out.

My days are numbered, I'm certain. I spend a final five minutes watching Bloomberg and reading through *Oil 101*, positive that some new piece of information from the Bible will invariably save my arse today, as it has every other day that I've spent here. Finally, I switch off the TV and throw Morgan's masterpiece in my brown leather, Indiana Jones man satchel and head to the office.

I'm nearing the end of my morning flat white and seriously concerned that Huan may commit suicide today. I've decided to update his PNL immediately upon arrival at work and send it to him ASAP. It's looking well beyond bleak. He managed to squeeze some profit out of his initial foray into crude oil dealings with the Russians last month. Lovely. But, silly fucker he is, he got carried away in a deranged, overexcited frenzy and bought a million barrels from the sneaky bastards for December loading. He thought the price was too good to be true, but went through regardless. Trading 101's cardinal sin, even I know that.

Their usual sales schedule is somewhere in the region of 1.5 million barrels per month. But, coming into the winter deep freeze, they've decided to offload 8 million barrels from the beautiful port of Vladivostok. That's fair enough, may as well clear stock before the ice sets in and everyone hides indoors through the harshness of winter to watch the gaps between their chattering front teeth grow wider each day.

Huan bought his million barrels at the princely sum of a $7 discount to the December expiring Brent oil benchmark. It seemed a winner. The deal was confirmed five days ago, at a time in human history when the crude oil trading world wasn't aware of the looming flow of plentiful Russian oil about to flood the market. Huan's November cargo of a more sanguine 300,000 barrels was purchased at a $5 discount and sold to one of his Asian trader-by-day, karaoke-enthusiast-by-night buddies at parity. $1.5 million revenue, lovely, but all the costs involved and general rigmarole sees you flick about $3 per barrel. Still, $600k clear, almost enough to temper a Naomi Campbell hissy fit, perhaps even cop a cheeky suck. Not this December cargo though, this is proving to be a rampant, coke-deprived, supermodel meltdown.

The final drips of the 8 million December loading barrels reportedly traded last night at a $25 discount. A Chinese refinery has apparently scooped up around 5 million barrels at this price. A trader there will be having a very merry Christmas. Where another 2 million barrels will be calling home is unknown, but it's safe to assume the buyer didn't stump up a price anywhere near the lofty heights of Huan's purchase.

I send him a personal email with the PNL, no need to cc the entire busy body galaxy just yet. Assuming Huan can sell out at the hideous current market discount of $25, he's spunked over $20 million in a week. Yep, that's a royal thumping up the ring piece, no lube, a career in tatters, rectal fissures the least of your concerns. He replies almost instantly, 'agree the position, right to send out, thanks mate.'

He is so nonchalant to the mammoth L where only P is expected and accepted, I figure he must still be drunk from a Wednesday night binge. I complete the PNL and commentaries for Keith and Paul as well, email the Milky Way and decide to jump out quickly to pick up a second coffee for the morning before joining Steve for a few hours of graduate interviews.

As I exit the building into the mid morning heat and commence the walk to Dimbulah, Keith is standing in the middle of Raffles Place sucking down a cigarette. His trading of late has been stellar, having made $3.5 million this week alone. It's only Thursday. With strong profits has come a softening of his venomous style of communication. I'm three weeks from the completion of the six months of this deals desk jaunt, but it has only really been over the past fortnight that Keith has begun to treat me something like a fellow human.

"Good morning, Keith."

"Really? What's fucking good about it then?"

"Umm, you OK?"
"Sorry, just that fucking Huan. Oh boy, he's a piece of shit, man."

"Not looking good with that Russian cargo."

"Fuck him. I just got call from Joel. Fucking Huan just quit."

"What? Not fired?"

"No, Flynn. He quit. He will start with ChinoPet after his gardening leave is finished."

"No?"

"You guess his sign on? Guess!"

"No idea."
"$2 million! Now I'm stuck with his fucking shit cargoes mate. Fuck!"

"Holy shit. Two Mill?"

"Unbelievable. He must interview well because he trades like dog shit."

"Too right. Keith, I'm just grabbing a coffee, you want anything?"

"I want Huan dead."

Keith stubs out his cigarette, motions me away and continues pacing as he lights up another. I continue on to Dimbulah. I'm certain of one thing; if there is anyone I know that could potentially be a worse trader than Huan, it's me. And he just made a two million dollar personal sign on bonus after losing 20 million Scion dollars in a single week! That's good work if you can get it.

Returning to the office carrying flat white number two, Angela is unwavering in the maintenance of her crazed smile while busily clearing away the various items from what was yesterday Huan's desk. Keith remains absent from his seat, he must still be pacing in Raffles Place, draining cigarettes and calling hit men. But that's all completely irrelevant, there's a spicy Latino woman standing at my desk, cradling an impressive leather compendium to her even more impressive rack. Five months in Singapore has not seen me fall victim to the yellow fever plague, rather, the rare sight of a woman with Nordic cheekbones, curvaceous salsa hips, and fully visible irises sends me into immediate tent pitching mode.

"Good morning, Flynn. I'm Steve's assistant, Luciana."

"Luciana, hi. How are you?"

"Excellent, now sorry, I hope you weren't looking forward to the Graduate interviews too much. We've managed to already complete all our selections, so you don't need to sit in with Steve and I today."
"Really? I think I can cope with that."

"Great. Also, are you free at some stage to catch up with Steve and I? We'd like to see how you've settled in and how everything's going."

"Sure, anytime before 3pm or after 5pm is fine. The window at 4pm can be a little hectic is all."

"OK, I'll double check a time with Steve and let you know."

As Luciana walks away I realise I'm not the only man in the office transfixed with every feature of her luscious femininity in high heel propelled motion. The chartering Great Danes each have their jowls on the floor. The metals traders are all indulging in a creepy gawk.

Team ferrous and coal would surely be jacking off in their seats if only their cocks weren't buried beneath substantial layers of fat and cellulite.

I take my seat, no longer blessed with Jannah by my side. As soon as I showed some proficiency in the role, she quickly relocated to whip someone else into shape. In her seat now is Darryl Hong, Knob Jockey Extraordinaire. He's a lifer deals desk member, but seems to think he runs this place. He is also a rare purebred Singaporean with both parents actually born here. Darryl's skull is molded from lego, a hollow, square head the canvas for a featureless face. His eyes are closer to his ears than his nose and his forehead stretches on for days, it's hard to say it culminates at all really. His wispy attempt at a comb over evokes more tears of sadness than laughter. If you were the last female alive and the fate of humanity rested on you spreading your legs for Darryl, you'd swiftly kill yourself and mankind with nil remorse before enduring another moment in his presence.

"Flynn, who was that? She is one sexy bitch. Get her back here. I think she smiled at me."

"She works with Steve in recruitment. I've never met her before, only spoken via email. She's gorgeous hey."

"Get her back here. Come on. What, you scared?"

"Fuck off, Darryl."

"You do know I'm your boss, yeah?"

"I do know you're an ugly, useless cunt."

"Fuck off."

"And you're not my boss. I don't know where you got that idea from, but like everything else in your head, it's complete garbage."

"You stupid Australian. You wanker."

Luciana sends through a thirty-minute meeting request for 11am, a quarter of an hour away. No problem. But cc'd is not only Steve, had assumed he'd be there, there's also Paul Maher, the Aussie derivatives trader, Artem Presenko, the Serbian maestro of scrap metal, and Joel Ryan, the biggest of big cheese. This is a fairly substantial who's who gathering of the people most instrumental and influential in my existence at this firm.

Ten minutes pass with Darryl attempting to explain some mathematical concept to me about option pricing. I never asked. He just leant across with his notebook and pencil, after he heard me chatting away with Paul in the opposite row about what to do with his current heavily in the money position for an option strategy still three months from expiry. Darryl piled in and started scribbling numbers all over the page, spit flying all over my desk as he rattled on at a million miles per hour, seeming to suffer a minor seizure towards the overdue, incorrect conclusion, his eyes rolling back in his head as he tapped several times on the bottom right of the page where the supposed answer to his masterpiece of risk free profit lay in scrawled Braille beneath a few litres of saliva. What a deadshit.

Option pricing is a little like counting cards in blackjack, every unhinged Asian male virgin seems to think he is the rare ace who's outsmarted the system. I take Darryl's sheet of paper, stand up, look him in the eye, rip the page to pieces, scrunch it in my fist and blow it all into his face. I make sure to take my phone, wallet and keys, and head off to my meeting. There's no option pricing formula necessary to be adequately cognisant that an impromptu meeting with not one, but multiple bosses, and two HR staff members, carries a strong probability of imminent unemployment.

Steve and Luciana are already seated as I walk in to the 'Copernicus' meeting room. Who the fuck named these rooms? I have not seen Steve since he invited all the junior trader candidates along to a bar in Geneva after a big day of simulating and a musical chairs dinner of schmoozing. We shake hands and I take a seat next to him as Paul, Artem and Joel enter the room.

"Your mate Huan has really fucked us now hasn't he?" Joel kicks things off.

"Yeah, top form, throw $20 million down the gurgler then quit." Sure, I helped him remove evidence of infidelity or murder from his apartment, but he's not my fucking mate.

"It's not your fault, Flynn, just revving you up as usual. Listen, your deals desk time is almost up and the original plan was to send you to Shanghai to complete an operations rotation, in metals, not oil, but Paul has run an idea by me." Joel finishes by motioning to Paul to carry forward with whatever this plan is.

"Yeah, Flynn, I asked Joel if he would approve you joining me on the derivatives trading desk. You'd sort of be my assistant originally, make sure you're fully up to speed with everything, and then gradually take on more of your own positions and risk exposure over the next 12 months."

"Now Flynn, Paul isn't the only one with a rather sickening man crush on you. Artem doesn't like this plan one bit." Joel is delighting in his compere role. Steve and Luciana do what HR do, sit and watch real people make decisions and earnestly nod along in tacit agreement.

"Nyess, I ffink this veery silly plaeen. Shanghai, big metals teeem. I want you spaend time there, maybe come back after few months, work with my teeem."

"Huh, OK." Five months of shouldering the weight each day of a pending firing lifts instantaneously. "What would you recommend? I want to be trading as soon as possible, but if there is an opportunity to spend another few months to make sure I am more knowledgeable with the operations component of the physical trading, that can't hurt."

"Nyesss, exaeeckly."

"That is a reasonable point mate." Paul's down-to-earth expression makes me confident he sees my point of view for the logical career enhancing pragmatism behind it and not as any sort of a rejection to his proposal.

"OK, I think it's best we persevere with the plan to complete at least a few months of the operations rotation. Artem has told me that one of the Shanghai operators on the copper concentrates team goes on maternity leave as of tomorrow. Flynn, you right to go home now, pack your shit, fly out tonight or tomorrow and join the Shanghai copper concentrates team by Monday?" Joel does not fuck around and it would seem he doesn't expect me to, either.

"Umm, yeah, no problem."

"Good. Learn all you can. We will reassess the situation if you absolutely fall in love with physical metals trading, but plan on having you back here in Singapore working hand in hand with Paul on the derivatives desk by April next year."

"Awesome. And what about the trader exam I've heard about?" Why would I mention that? That damn Kristian's voice is still twerping around in my thoughts for some reason.

"Oh that? Fuck that mate. We save that for the stupid cunts we want to fire. They all think if they pass the exam they get a trader role. Fucking morons. No, you've shown all you need to show. The role is waiting for you in a few months. Learn as much as you can in the meantime and don't eat too much dog over there."

"No promises."

"Luciana will help you sort out travel plans and arrange accommodation for you in Shanghai. Best of luck, will be in touch and see you back here in Singapore, the land that fun forgot, next year."

"OK, great."

"Oh, and Flynn," Steve can actually speak, "here's a $50,000 bonus cheque. Well done. Look forward to many more of these." Our head of HR isn't completely useless.

I smile at my group of very generous well-wishers and place the cheque in my pocket as I walk out. I shut down all the computers and throw a stack of my information gold mine notebooks in the man satchel without speaking a single word to Darryl. He's ecstatic, assuming I've been fired. I walk out, bank the cheque in the Citibank branch on Church St.

I've got $137,000 SGD to my name within five months. Amazing. Tax rates are minimal in Singapore and the actual bill is payable retrospectively. Like all overpaid cunts, I'm already thinking of ways to minimize the eventual bill, a wonderful problem to have.

Liam Carroll

4/ Operations 101 in the People's Republic
Communist China, Capitalist Paradise

I emerge from the international arrivals of Shanghai's Pudong airport on Saturday around 6pm. Friday was spent in a manic rush arranging the required visas and paperwork to gain entry to the People's Republic with such short notice. It didn't leave any time to stock up on some decent winter clothing. After five months in the Singapore sweat cauldron, Shanghai is absolutely freezing. A squat man dressed in black is carrying an A4 piece of paper with Flynn James written on it. Hello driver.

"Hi, I'm Flynn."

"Hello. Thank you. Thank you. Hello. Mister."

This fella seems to have been informed of my over inflated Mandarin proficiency. He watches me patiently as though I'm actually about to say something of importance or that he can at least understand.

"So, you can drive me home?"

"Yes. Please. Hello."

"Umm, let's go. Drive home. Vroom vroom. Beep beep. Home."

"Yes. Please. Hello."

I resort to some Driving Miss Daisy charades gestures and, before enduring too many more 'Yes. Please. Hello's.' my smiling little communist comrade leads me through to his minivan in the airport car park. He shows me some more writing at the base of the paper with my name on it. There is a number next to some Mandarin symbols that look more like frightened cats and pensive grasshoppers than anything of linguistic significance. I think it's my new address.

Anyway, we're off, heading away from the airport, vroom vrooming and beep beeping. Luciana arranged a studio apartment for me only yesterday. It is located in Shanghai's *French Concession* and is what is locally termed a *lane house*. I have no idea what to expect. I had intended to be speaking fluent Mandarin and have this bustling city of 25 million dwellers fully researched before my arrival. That grand plan fell victim to the lure of catching up on missed sleep or watching ever more NBA TV.

The major highway leading from the airport in to the city is futuristic and bleak. Every so often there is a low enough break in the cement walls lining the twelve-lanes of bitumen, allowing a quick view of never ending Chinese suburbia on the flattest of plains. There doesn't appear to be a single hill in Shanghai. Whenever the maps were drawn up for this city, the topographers went hungry.

We must be nearing the city centre. Sky-rise buildings are becoming more prevalent. The only landmark of Shanghai I'm aware of is the Oriental Pearl Tower, though the chances of spotting that are slim.

Each building's visible height is capped at around ten storeys, the level where the city's pollution blankets in comfortably, blocking any view higher.

The driver takes an exit ramp off the highway, leading us down to ground level, central Shanghai. Within a few moments we are locked in my first ever Shanghai traffic jam. Time stands still, I'm in voyeuristic overdrive. This is literally Chinatown stretched out forever. I really am in China. Horns blare incessantly. The road is barely one lane wide, but that hasn't prevented cars, scooters and horse-drawn carts somehow being parked on each side. Bike riders dart between non-existent gaps carrying crates of deceased ducks, fresh flowers, or mountains of recycled cardboard. Parents push their young ones in strollers through the Saturday evening with SARS masks covering their precocious faces. Groups of elderly tai chi aficionados complete their exercise regime in choreographed perfection on street corners. Overhead, the streets are covered with nonstop, amber-shaded, candlelit vigils and people's washing hung out to dry. Any tree somehow able to grow through the concrete footpath is being used as a surrogate telegraph pole with excess power lines wrapped around tree branches like fishing line on a hand reel.

There is eventually some flow to the traffic and we take a left. Beneath the Chinese hieroglyphics on the street signs, there is English writing as well. We've just turned on to West Nanjing Road. The candlelit vigils have given way to all the modern necessities; McDonald's, Citibank, H&M, Sephora, Starbucks, Tiffany's, a string of behemoth western conglomerates have gracefully penetrated the communist regime.

We turn left again onto Maoming Road. I notice signs for West Nanjing Road Train Station and look through the window to see a stream of people walking out of an underground tunnel and through a courtyard area. One out of every few is stirred by the crisp, chill air and proceeds to spit all over the footpath. I'm so cultured right now. The driver continues on for a short while longer before pulling over to the right.

"Mister. Hello. House." As he says house, he points out the window and there is a statuesque Chinese woman wearing a full-length beige trench coat and a Siberian Husky-furred head warmer. She steps towards the mini-van.

"Hello, Flynn?"

"Hi there."

"Good evening, I'm Monica. Luciana called yesterday and I arranged this place for you. Please, grab your things and I will show you inside."

"Great, thanks."

Monica and the driver engage in some vigorous conversation, God only knows what they're talking about. The discussion lasts almost five minutes and includes all sorts of hand movements and tones of voice. I stand on the Maoming Rd footpath, freezing to death as a snowstorm sets in.

"Eric will help you with your cases. Come, let's get inside."

We are standing infront of a locked metal gate, which leads down a laneway between two shops. The gate would not seem out of place in a prison. The shop to the left sells skateboards, shoes, t-shirts, all the usual designer punk gear pitch perfect for deluded youths holding on to daydreams of rebellion while waiting patiently for mum to cook dinner and check their homework. The shop to the right is a wedding store, the front window adorned with a vestal mannequin dressed in an ornate dove white wedding frock. Some poor fucker will have to mortgage his soul in the name of true love to afford that beautiful dress some day soon.

"OK, Flynn, the security code is 4-2-2-1." Monica punches in the numbers and Eric opens the laneway gate.

"OK, got it."

Monica leads the way down the shady alley. There are no lights, but the general radioactive effervescence bouncing off the clouds of smog in the night sky and the falling ashen snow lights the way.

"You will love this place, Flynn. The French Concession is the best part of Shanghai, especially for young people like yourself."

We've now passed three separate two-storey buildings and are at least 100m deep into this laneway. Monica stops at a door. There are no numbers anywhere. How she knows this is the correct one is beyond me. She steps forward and opens the lock, turning the key as a small pile of snow forms on her glove. We climb three steps into a decrepit hallway as she flicks a light switch. There is a timber staircase that simply cannot be younger than one hundred years old. The first step is essentially on the floor, having been worn in so thoroughly over the preceding century. The only possible way this stairwell is held together is thanks to the frozen lumber molecules throughout. It is arctic in here. When the spring thaw arrives, this stairwell will simply wash away. Monica leads the way up to the first floor. The stairs allow exasperated groans and creaks to escape with each step.

"Here we are, Flynn, your new home."

Monica opens another locked door on the landing of the first storey. She steps through and switches on a light. I'm prepared for the worst, but there's no need. Infront of me is a huge open space of polished timber flooring, fresh white painted walls, a three-seat leather couch, a modern kitchen, oversized TV, shabby chic bookshelf, mirrored built-in wardrobes and a king size bed. Next to the kitchen is a small bathroom and washing machine. This is unexpectedly homely.

Eric helps me place my suitcases on the bed, shakes my hand and walks straight out the door, out of my life and off into the night. Monica hands me the keys and a piece of paper with people to call if needed, the real estate agent, an electrician, a plumber, they each have the same number, hmmm, wait, what?

"Thank you so much Monica. The place looks great."

"No problem. I will see you on Monday."

"Monday?"

"Yes, I will see you at the office."

"You work at Scion?"

"Yes, of course, see you Monday."

"OK then, thanks again for your help."

Monica looks the place over one last time before walking out. I take a seat on the couch and unsuccessfully try to find an English-speaking channel on the television. I open up my laptop instead and hit play on the 'Easy Peasy Chinese' file I grabbed off iTunes many months ago. "Nee How…Hello….Shay Shay…Thank you." I give up instantly and crank up some Biggy Smalls to make sure the gangster rap is thumping while I unpack my clothes into the wardrobe. There are bay windows next to the bed looking down into the lane and directly across into someone's kitchen. I close the blinds when I notice a toothless Chinese granny staring straight at me from her kitchen sink.

In the corner of the room is a ginormous heater, a home appliance fusion of R2D2 and C3PO. The remote control is on top and, seeing as my teeth won't stop chattering, I figure I should work out how to utilize the device. The buttons all have Chinese writing indicating what the actual function of them is. There is one clear major button to turn the beast on, but the remaining knobs are a Mandarin mystery. I get agitated and start randomly pressing everything, hoping for the best. I astutely activate the air conditioning function, dropping the room temperature even lower. I decide to unplug the missing Star Wars character from the wall for the time being and wear two beanies while I unpack.

It's nearing 8pm. The wardrobe is filling nicely. I'll need to stock up on bed linen, warm clothing and some basic cutlery tomorrow. I'm sure my home cooking exploits in Shanghai will be very similar to Singapore, no need to get too carried away with any kitchen utensils. I decide to christen the toilet. I unleash on the dun bowl and stand up to admire my work before flushing. As I begin washing my hands at the adjacent sink, I notice the unavoidable rising waters of a clogged dunny.

I'm looking at the floaters near the toilet rim, trying to figure out if it's worth calling the plumber/electrician/real estate agent or giving this a nudge myself, getting in there and setting my Bondi cigars free to roam the Shanghai sewers, the way nature intended. There is a cupboard in the kitchen with a broom, dustpan and brush, no plunger. I decide I'll have a tinker with the broom handle and walk back towards the bathroom trying to amp myself up for the looming hideousness only for all the lights to go out. OK, what the fuck? I check a few light switches, all not working. Black out, day one, cheers Shanghai.

I switch on the torch of my phone and walk to the door. The hallway light is working. The busted fuse must be solely affecting my pad. On the other side of the first storey landing I see what look like electricity boxes. Underneath the boxes are several blue buckets covered with dinner plates and two empty birdcages. What the hell? I walk across the landing and shine the phone torch into the first box. It's definitely a fuse box, but once again, the writing is incomprehensible Mandarin. For a nation of close to 1.5 BILLION people, where is one in this damn hallway when I need 'em?

As I try to piece together some understanding of which fuse may be the culprit, I'm certain the blue buckets are moving. I refocus on the fuse box and decide there is one clear button flicked down which should be up. I reach my right index finger up to turn it on. A million volts fly straight through my arm and fry me to the core. I'm hurled into the wall behind me, collapsing to the ground.

I'm unsure how long passes before the gentle prodding of a Chinese boy wakes me. He's smiling. A pure smile only an infant is capable of. He's wearing *Toy Story* pajamas and mumbling soothing words I don't understand. I pull myself up bit by bit to now be slouched on the floor and can see the boy's parents, also in their pajamas and speaking incomprehensible words. I gingerly stand fully up and motion to the electricity box then point at my studio's door, trying to explain that the power is off. The three of them look understandably perplexed so I take the few steps back to my new pad and turn the switch back and forth a few times. The electricity failure becomes obvious, as does the aggressive stench of the clogged toilet.

The mother gives me a look of clear disgust and leads her little boy away, covering his nose as she does so. The man walks back to the electricity boxes, pressing a few things I can't properly see from my doorway before returning. He turns my light switch and it works fine. Hero. I foresee this whole fiasco happening again in the very near future so ask him if he can show me what buttons he pressed. Using words obviously doesn't work so I walk back to the electricity boxes and start talking again. He smiles so warmly I feel almost honoured. He hands me one of the blue buckets and says, "Welcome. Please." And then walks away down the hallway.

I shut the door and take a seat on the couch. I place the bucket on the floor infront of me and remove the plate lid. Staring up at me in water a few inches deep is a petrified little turtle, a fittingly bizarre welcome to the community. I place the lid back on, put the bucket in the corner, lock the door, turn off the lights and head to bed, fully clothed, still sporting two beanies. The gentle grazing of my reptilian housemate in the blue bucket sends me off to sleep.

In the early hours of Sunday morning I'm woken by a local catfight. Two felines clearly have a bone to pick. Their high-pitched screeches carry on in a nearby laneway while I wipe sleet from my eyes and head to the shower. That fucking floater, I forgot all about it and assumed the smell was merely Shanghai's morning stench. I grab the broom and skewer the toilet with the handle for a few minutes before the clogging finally resolves with a clockwise flushing kick-start. I grab some spray on deodorant and douse the bathroom in the Lynx Effect before hopping in the shower.

The water pressure is dire, steaming hot water dribbles down my skin while well-intended deodorant particles join forces with the stale colonic aftermath to fuse into a truly heinous tang. I race out of the bathroom before I dry reach, open the bay window fully, who gives a fuck if it's minus five degrees. I dress in the warmest clothes available and head straight for the door to escape this lane house of stink.

It's 7am. The Maoming Rd traffic jam of last night has disappeared, fresh white snow lines the footpath and a lunar looking round dot is rising in between two buildings on the horizon where the sun is supposed to be. I set off in the direction of the train station I saw last night. No shops have yet opened and I'm overcome with a piercing sense of isolation as I continue walking in the glacial morning air. This is a rare moment where I'm not consumed with thoughts of work or being imminently fired. What the fuck am I doing here? The realization that I haven't seen my family, friends or the ocean in many, many months hits in one stabbing breath. I feel my eyes well with tears and come back to earth in a heartbeat. 'Get it together you fucking weak cunt.' I'm here to make shitloads of cash, nothing more, nothing less. And with over one hundred grand to my name, I've got no right to be miserable.

I arrive at the courtyard leading into the train station and see a French patisserie, not necessarily the cultural awakening breakfast appropriate for my first morning in China. I walk towards Patisserie de France, dodging puddles of saliva. I order a hot chocolate and a croissant, pretending for a moment I'm in Basque country and write a list of the various household items I need to acquire today before stage two of the junior trader program takes flight tomorrow.

Through the window, across the courtyard, a stunning young Chinese woman speaks on her phone, radiating a gorgeous aura I've never seen in an Asian female. She pulls the phone a few inches from her mouth, arches her head up, holding the pose a moment before thrusting her upper body towards the ground, lining the pavement with a spitball so huge and mucus laden I almost cough up my hot chocolate. Yellow fever…yeah, that's no concern whatsoever.

The alarm isn't needed. Those pesky cats in the laneway must be running a dawn patrol feline fight club down there, screeching and scratching their way through the early morning. I hop out of the Dutch oven warmth beneath my newly acquired doona, put on my spanking new purple velour tracksuit after removing the dockets and go about my morning exercise regime with the curtains fully open so the toothless old bag across the lane can have a healthy squiz at a podgy white man draped in velvet while she sips her boiling green tea.

I finish off the fitness regimen with 30 push-ups, the most I've done consecutively in a very long time and jump in the shower. I'll have to do something about this feeble water pressure, but for the moment I don't let the feeling of being pissed on bother me. I hop out, dry off and suit up. There was not a single moment in Singapore where I felt comfortable in a suit, but here in the colder climes, if it weren't for the several kilograms of extra flab pushing outwardly at the waistline, I'd be feeling sensational in the full corporate garb. My hair seems all of a sudden quite long. I grab some product from my metro-sexual bag of tricks and slick the follicles down tight and greasy.

As I lock the door behind me, I notice my blue bucket ninja turtle has escaped. The bucket in the corner of the room is on its side and empty. Ah well, I'm late, leave him be. He can have the bachelor pad to himself today. I almost fall down the stairs. Just as the step closest to the ground is essentially at ground level thanks to a century of stair climbing, so too is the top step more like a two step drop. Not this time Shanghai, I'm wising up to your tricks.

It's 7.30am and Maoming Rd is starting to bustle. A taxi driver beeps his horn at a bike rider who proceeds to spit on the cab. It's unclear whether this is due to unrest or is something the cyclist would have done anyway. A woman across the street takes a break from pushing her stroller. She walks round to the front of the pram, picks out her baby, undoes some fabric on the back of the kid's onesie and pulls it forward through the child's legs to reveal a bare bottom in the morning chill. She then cradles the tiny baby by its feet in one hand, back of the head in the other and watches casually as the little fucker shits all over the footpath. Jesus Christ! Noone cares. The mother redoes the onesie, places the child back in the pram and continues on her merry way, dodging the excrement and singing a lullaby.

The footpath is wide enough for one and a half people. This means the two block walk to the station requires relentless body weaving and contortionism to avoid shoulder charging one of these overconfident, midget fuckwits, more commonly referred to as a Chinese person. The oncoming pedestrian traffic doesn't seem too interested in weaving or contorting. Little bastards. The left side of the footpath I'm on is closest to the oncoming flow of engine-powered traffic, not especially well known for their weaving or contorting prowess. Fuck this. By the time I've almost reached the station, I've had a gutful. I line up a particularly cunty looking little fucker and let rip with a shoulder charge. Cop that. As I turn into the much wider train station entrance I turn back to see the little shunt nursing his shoulder. Good. I'll see you again tomorrow, mate.

The footpath wars do precious little to prepare me for the carnage waiting for me on the train. I get my ticket from one of the automated machines, easy enough with instructions having an English option. I then continue through the turnstiles and down the stairs to the platform. Queues of five or more people are lined up perpendicular to the platform every couple of metres. I'm halfway down the stairs when a train pulls in. A few people hop off, having to shove the waiting queue members out of the way as they do so. Once that initial confrontation is complete, the queue members go berserk, cramming their way into the carriage like rugby players plowing into a ruck.

I continue down the stairs and take a spot in one of the waiting queues behind five others. I'm last in line for the briefest of moments, two people ram in behind me almost instantaneously. Over the hum of overcrowded humans on the platform, a faint, shrill whistle is accompanied in the tunnel by the slowly increasing ECG rhythm of thumping train tracks. My weight is completely on the balls of my feet and every muscle of my back is fully extended against the imminent crush of impatience. The bracing wind of the arriving train roars through the platform. I breathe in deeply and try to relax by reliving memories of first learning about the Doppler effect in high school Physics.

From the perspective of an Australian accustomed to wide-open spaces, the train already looks full beyond the brim as it arrives. Some passengers begin to disembark and the crush behind me builds quickly. It takes all my force to hold back from crumbling into the poor lady in front. As soon as it's apparent that there will be no one else disembarking, the sardine mayhem crush begins with zero mercy. I quickly throw away any notion of trying to resist the mob and succumb to whatever fate the public transport Gods have destined for me. My limp body is crushed and magically guided into the carriage, while my etheric body has buggered off elsewhere. There's no room for the etheric plane in the Shanghai underground.

My six-foot height allows an uninterrupted view of the carriage multitude. This predicament to a pickpocket must be pure heaven. My body is crushed from every direction from the chest down. If I'd forgotten to zip my fly I could probably have sex with a dozen people in this one short journey. While I can definitely feel the tender breasts of some lady pushing into my ribs, I can also taste whatever dumplings the man breathing over my right shoulder had for breakfast.

Hopping on the train is merely an entrée. The main course involves surviving the driver's antics. He is wreaking havoc on us all, accelerating wildly, slamming on the brakes, re-accelerating, jolting in a series of stop-start-stop-start-stops to mark the arrival at each station. The innocent commuters have no option but to collectively soak up the aftershocks of the driver's woeful propulsion. I've not activated a single muscle, but thanks to the crowds' communal shock absorbing dexterity, I'm moved in a radius of at least a metre with each attempt by the driver to run the train off the tracks. Unfortunately they haven't factored in my height relative to the 'overhead' metal handhold bar. Each wave of crowd movement involves me closing my eyes as my head crashes into this ice-cold metal rod. I would reach my arms up to deflect the blows, but they're locked to my side by the straitjacket press of commuters.

I'm mentally exhausted, potentially physically raped and will have to check a mirror later to see if one of the involuntary headbutts with the overhead bar has left me with a black eye. The train arrives at Lujiazui, pronounced Loo Jazz Way. I've made it, sort of. Dessert involves somehow getting off this fucking train. Hmm. The three-stop journey has seen me move from initially being near the doorway to now being stuck in the no man's land separating each carriage. I'm as far as you can ever possibly find yourself from an exit door. Rookie. The doors open and I prepare to channel my inner T-1000 and morph my way to the door via the snow slush covered linoleum flooring. Instead, this seems to be everyone's stop, the train empties in a single contraction, thousands of commuters escape to the rest of their day.

I walk off the train a born-again man. I see the empty few metres around me as an irrefutable sign of hope and freedom. I breathe in deeply, cherishing the fact that there are at least a few hundred atoms of oxygen amongst the pungent millions of fumes and rat poison. I bask in the post journey glow for a whole minute before the whistling and wind of an arriving train brings me back to reality. The imminent flood of arriving humanity is best avoided. I walk hurriedly away and up the stairs. How on earth would an elderly or handicapped person have survived that?

I complete the underground labyrinth through the turnstiles and hallways of the station and climb a few flights of stairs, following the signs to the Super Brand Mall. The Scion office building is apparently near that somewhere. As I exit the train station a frosty rush of air makes me sneeze. I don't bother cupping my mouth. I let snot, mucus and saliva coat the sidewalk, rude not to. The main intersection at Lujiazui is a gigantic roundabout hexagon with traffic darting every which way and large barricades preventing pedestrian traffic reaching the road. Above, there is an equally huge overpass walkway. I follow the herd to an outdoor escalator leading up to the elevated pathway.

I'm wearing immaculate leather soled shoes, a pair of finely crafted Italian tootsie decorations. The Milan catwalk is a distant relative to this snow covered, black ice path of death. I hum the South Park classic, 'what would Brian Boitano do' and homo-erotically glide across the 200m pedestrian bridge skating rink in homage to *Blades of Glory*. I make it safely over and descend the escalator down to the street while holding on for grim death to the warm black rubber of the handgrip, the metal grill of the escalator steps look sharper than frozen razor blades. A slip here would shred my suit and flesh like shark's teeth.

With the pending black eye starting to properly ache in my left temple, I check my Blackberry for the address and specific floor that Scion Shanghai inhabits. I walk the final steps along the Lujiazui Ring Road footpath and into the building. I cross the foyer and go through a sense of crowd crush déjà vu all over again. The queue for the elevators is manic. Why are there so many fucking people in this country? The etiquette here is marginally more refined than the subway, but I still wait for a few rounds of elevator comings and goings before I can actually infiltrate one and shoot up to my new corporate home. The lifts open and I walk out to see Monica seated behind the reception desk.

"Good morning, Flynn. Great to see you."

"Hi Monica. Good weekend?"

"Yes, thank you, very nice. How do you like your place?"

"It's perfect. Thanks so much again for organizing."

"No problem. Glad you like it. Can you please wait in the meeting room over there? There are seven other people starting today, so I will go through the orientation with you all at once when everyone arrives."

"Sure."

"There are no other junior trader people though. No one special like you."

"Ha, thanks."

I take a seat in a meeting room. I don't notice the name of an adventurer or highly lauded Renaissance scientist on the door. I stare out the window towards the Bund, the world-renowned river that flows directly through the middle of Shanghai. Flow is a strong word. There's nothing flowing in this body of sickly, grim, unholy water. Even on a clear blue sky day like today, light doesn't reflect off the Bund's waters in a way anywhere close to resembling the shimmer of radiant luminosity bouncing off Sydney harbour 365 days a year. No, light, like most things I imagine, dies in the Bund. Its actual name is Huangpu River, Huang Pu indeed.

Monica opens the door and waves in three other starters. I'm not really 'starting' and I can sense their unease at being in the nascent stage of a new job. I'm standing relaxed at the window looking out at the Bund, while the newly arrived trio immediately takes a seat, hide their hands in their laps and intently focus their attention on the mahogany table grain. Barely a moment passes and Monica returns with the final four of the orientation group. The seven starters and Monica are clearly Chinese, but my presence means the orientation is given in English. I grin with thoughts of bogan Aussies telling flamin' tourists to speak fuckin' English if they wanna travel to 'Straya.

Monica's orientation takes on the form of Angela's mind numbing speech delivered back in Singapore on day one. It's a shame for the others that she's chosen to speak in English, I am not paying the least bit of attention, though I do catch the moment where she mentions we can get gym passes for the Shangri-la Hotel next door, this includes use of the gym and lap pool. Lap pool hey? I picture James

Bond swimming laps on the Shanghai rooftop while waiting for the go ahead to kill some bad guys in *Skyfall*. Thirty to forty minutes pass before the orientation is complete and Monica makes the others wait behind while she takes me into the world requiring card-automated access.

"Your access card from Singapore should work, Flynn. Please try."

"Hmm, cool."

The red light on the wall mounted pad for card swiping turns green and Monica pushes open the glass door. As in Singapore, there are flawless floor to ceiling glass windows, giving way to a sweeping view. The Bund still looks hideous. I focus instead on the elaborate architecture of the heritage buildings, the ultramodern skyscrapers in the greater distance, and the humbling feeling of seeing the expanse of Shanghai stretch out for miles upon miles of flat, urban, overpopulated sprawl.

"This is one of the clearest days we've had in many months. Normally you will not be able to see so far into the distance. There is a lot of smog in this city. Sometimes it is better to not go outside. I will email you the website to check air quality."

"Yeah, that would be great."

"No problem. Please, follow me."

I know I'm supposedly in a flash corporate office, working for a multinational enterprise at the cutting edge of reaping bumper profits, but, walking past rows of people in this Shanghai office, I feel like I've walked in to the Chinese equivalent of a Tafe college's work for the dole delinquent class. What are these people wearing? Here I stand in my slick suit, with my slick hair and my slick leather soled shoes, personifying every cliché of how Hugo Boss imagines a global businessman, Master of the Universe, should look. These ladies and gents can't possibly think it's commercially acceptable to be wearing ugg boots, trackie dacks and smiley face jumpers at work. One in every three people seems to have caught the memo that this is gainful employment and not your bong-head buddy's crack den living room, and is wearing something of suitable corporate attire, but two thirds of the office better be un-fucking-believable at their jobs in order to think they can be swanning around like this.

"Good morning, Li Ming. Here is Flynn, he will start with you on the copper concentrates team today."

"Yes, hello, Flynn. Welcome." Li Ming belongs to the one third wearing business attire, sporting an elegant, black woolen dress, grey suede boots and librarian specs.

"Good morning, Li Ming. Pleasure to meet you." Li Ming stands to shake hands.

"Can you speak any Chinese?" I've been dreading this question for many months. Fingers crossed she hasn't checked the dubiously questionable fine print of my CV.

"A little, I'm learning." Nee How Maa is about as much as I've learned, and I only picked that up yesterday.

"That's OK, everyone on my team can speak English very well. How about Spanish?"

"I know a few basics, I traveled to South America many years ago."

"Great. Most of our copper comes from Peru or Chile so a little Spanish will help."

"OK, I will leave you now. Flynn, any questions just ask."

"Thanks Monica."

"It's great timing. Yan went on maternity leave last week."

"Yes, I heard that from Artem."

"Artem, that creepy man. He is strange."

"Yeah, I don't know him well, that seems pretty accurate though."

"OK, Flynn, just take Yan's seat here next to me and we can get you set up."

"No problem."

I walk past Li Ming to my new seat as she introduces me to the copper concentrates team, "Everyone, this is Flynn, please make him feel welcome and come say hello when you get a chance."

"Hello."

"Welcome."

"Hi, Mr. Fwynn."

I blush a little with all the attention, give the requisite "G'day" and place my suit jacket round my chair as I take my seat. Yan is clearly intending to return to this job when her maternity leave is finished and wasn't expecting anyone to be taking her place in the meantime. The desk is covered in notebooks, files, baby clothing catalogues and a Hello Kitty collection of pen, mousepad and humidifier. That will come in handy and add a nice touch of 21st century Asian femininity to my desk.

Li Ming leans across, "Just turn on the computer and see if you can log on with your Singapore passwords. Sorry for all Yan's crap. All her Hello Kitty garbage really shits me. A few cargoes have had troubles over the weekend, so give me half an hour to sort through some things OK."

"Sure, no worries, as soon as you're ready."

"Won't be too long."

I busy myself with trying to make some order of the files on the desk and booting up the computer. I take a moment to watch Li Ming in action. She bears many similarities to Jannah, typing away with total relaxation through her shoulders while her fingers complete the task in a nonchalant tapping frenzy, scrolling through multiple documents, spreadsheets and programs on her three screens while making a series of phone calls with no regard for niceties, all regard for problem solving and business continuity, speaking Chinese, English and Spanish, never skipping a beat.

My passwords from the Singapore office work fine. I log in and un-cc myself from the countless email groups which are of absolutely no importance to me now I'm on the metals team and in Shanghai. I look up for a moment. My new colleagues are all making phone calls and carrying about their daily business. There are two unmistakable syllables each person in this office seems to be articulating down the phone lines with reckless abandon, 'Nig-ger'. I've got no idea what they're all rattling on about, but a conversation seems to go like this, 'haawh nigger, ching chong chii huan chiin chin nigger, chi nigger, chong nigger, nigger ching. Nigger nigger nigger.'

As I listen to these racist bastards chit-chatting away, I see a youngish, super fit looking man, who may or may not be Bruce Lee, walking straight towards me. He's got a purposeful stride to match his sharp Triad black suit, shirt and overcoat and is definitely on his way to see me.

"You're Flynn yeah?" His accent is untainted Denzel Washington American Gangster, *either you're somebody or you're nobody.*

"Yeah, I'm Flynn." My accent is untainted Bryan Brown Australian gangster, *that's a lovely pterodactyl.*

"I'm Rob. Artem told me you were arriving today. Listen, can you drink?"

"Drink?"

"Drink. Alcohol. Can you drink?"

"Well yeah, I guess."

"Heavily?"

"I don't see why not."

"Good, put your coat on, you're coming with me."

"Umm."

"Don't be a fucking pussy. Come on. Chop, chop."

Rob starts laughing and chatting with Li Ming, dropping plenty of 'niggers' among the incomprehensible Chinese.

"Come on Flynn, let's go. Start with Li Ming tomorrow."

"It's fine Flynn. I will see you tomorrow."

"OK."

Ctrl+Alt+Delete. I lock my computer, grab my jacket and follow this overly assertive mystery man. He leads me back out to the lifts and hits the button for the basement car park.

"Artem, he's one sick fucker yeah?"

"I don't really know him, to be honest."

"That's lucky for you then."

The elevator doors open and Rob leads the way to a spanking brand new black Range Rover.

"Hop in."

"Nice car."

"Yeah, I like it. If I wasn't married, I'd be pulling so much arse with this puss mobile."

Rob puts the Rover in neutral and revs the living hell out of it. I make sure my seat belt is fastened. Tight. Rob doesn't bother to click clack and starts racing through the car park at a dementedly absurd pace to the exit.

"In a bit of a rush buddy? Where we off to?"

"I've got a meeting, a really fucking big meeting, with some sick puppies from a smelter. You're Aussie yeah?"

"Yeah."

Rob lowers his driver-side window and swipes his card at the exit. The red light flashes green, the boom gate journeys skyward. Rob beeps his horn as he drives the accelerator through the floor and sends a cluster of sidewalk pedestrians scurrying for their lives as we shoot past, fishtailing onto Lujiazui Ring Road.

"Fuck man! What's the hurry?"

"What? You want me to pick your husband up?"

"Ha, no, that's fine, he's busy with your wife."

"Hahah, good. I hope someone's fucking her, it's sure not me. OK, so, this meeting, the guys are like from the outback. Know what I mean? Rednecks. Backward. Sheep shaggers. Cousin fuckers. You dig?"

"Yeah, gotchya."

I'm holding the door handle so tight I feel it might rip off in my hand. The Asian drivers at home are shocking, but it's usually through an inability to merge or smoothly go around a corner. That would be a damn welcome change from this nutcase. As Rob carries on chewing the fat, preparing me for the upcoming meeting with a bunch of cousin fuckers, he avoids the gridlock created by a red light up ahead by straddling the median strip, beeping at oncoming traffic rightfully put off by a black Range Rover taking up the outside of their lane and continues on to drive straight through the red lit intersection.

"Holy shit man."

"You see, in China, people from Shanghai hate people from Beijing, people from Beijing hate people from Shanghai, that's fine. But these people we are meeting today, they are metal smelters from some disgusting place in southwest China, horrible, they hate everyone, everyone hates them. All they do is look fucking ugly, smelt metal, and drink."

"OK, so what do you need me for?"

We are now overtaking a truck, driving in the wrong lane at about 150km/h around a blind corner through a tunnel. This is it for me.

Today is surely my last.

"Well, this is good for you to see a proper Chinese business meeting. Artem says you will be a trader soon."

We fly out of the tunnel. The car actually gets airborne, and not for a nanosecond. No, my balls and the car have been in mid air for a good few seconds. Fuck me. Rob doesn't seem too put off. We're now on an empty, open road at least. If we do die a gruesome death on this stretch then we probably won't be taking any innocent people with us. The snow on the side of the road and the high chance of black ice on the actual road certainly doesn't induce Rob to slow down at all. It's hard to tell precisely from my angle, but my view of the speedometer tells me we're closing in on 180km/h.

"These meetings, these aren't what you'd call 'professional'," as he says 'professional', he turns to look me in the eyes and takes both hands off the wheel to raise them over his head and fully gesticulate the inverted commas. Yeah, I get it, eyes on the road when you're breaking the sound barrier hey and stick with ten and two on the wheel maybe. "You see, with these sorts of guys, if you can drink, they respect you. My other copper trader is on his honeymoon for a month. A whole fucking month! I may as well sort out the divorce paperwork for his return. I mean shit, a whole month with your wife. Fuck that! But, anyway, all the other operators, they're fucking pussy man. You saw them yeah, wearing their fucking ugg boots. What the fuck?! I'm from Shanghai, but I went to the University of New South Wales. You Australians…Holy fuck, you can drink. I saw the email from Artem that some Aussie was starting today, fucking beauty

172

mate."

"Glad to help." His 'fucking beauty mate' accent is spot on.

"So, in this meeting, we will be having lunch, and drinking. These guys don't speak English, don't worry, you don't have to say anything, but they will drink lots of baijiu."

"Baijiu?"

"It's like Chinese tequila. It's what we drink to celebrate, when we have a baby, get married, you know, things like that. Anyway, these smelter guys, they know that all the trading houses make big money. We need to show these guys a good time, make them feel happy. They live in a shithole, their wives never suck their dick, not that you'd want one of their pig wives sucking your dick mind you. Fuck, you'd rather rub melted cheese on your knob and dangle it in the sewer for a rat to have a lick of. Anyway, you get the idea yeah, their life is shit, they make chump change compared to us. They come to the big city, all the trading houses want their business, they know this, so they choose who they will buy their copper concentrate from based on who they have the most fun with. They're all basically government employees, so even if they do a great job, they won't really get paid like they would in a western company. So, we have to buy them. It's not a bribe. It's just welfare payment, you know. You don't have a problem with welfare now do you?"

"Of course not."

We're now in some sort of outer district of Shanghai and Rob starts to slow down to a more safety conscious 100km/h.

"So just come in, shake hands, smile, and when I tell you to drink, you drink."

"Got it."

"Oh, also, we will be eating some strange food mate. I know my Australian friends find Chinese food, not *fly lice and shwee sour pork*', no the real McCoy, I know they find it awful. Pig's tongue, sheep brains, duck vagina, all so tasty. Just eat what you can and drink everything. If you vomit or whatever, that's great. These guys will find it hilarious."

"So you want me to approach this business lunch like it's my 21st birthday?"

"Exactly."

We pull into a car park. Rob parks and we hop out. I ready myself to do Scion proud with the KPI of vomiting infront of the clients something I feel confident I can fulfill. The car park is empty aside from one bus. I notice a woman in a yellow one-piece ski suit pushing a stroller in the far corner of the car park. A black cat walks behind her. The whole bizarre experience has a very Matrix-esque feel about it. Rob leads the way inside the doors, along a red carpet and through a pair of golden arches, not McDonald's arches, this looks like actual pure gold plating.

As we pass through the arches, a stunning woman stands in a

sleeveless, full length, red silk dress behind an antique chest that was surely crafted during the Ming Dynasty. Her cartoon Astro Boy face, milk white newborn skin, and butter soft, slender shoulders look fresh from another world. Without saying a word she presses a button on the chest before leading us through a vacant hall of round tables, lazy Susans, and enough fish, eel and crab stacked aquariums to fill the East China Sea. We continue to the far end of this main hall to an inconspicuous door. Before we enter, she says something to Rob, sending him into fits of boyish giggles.

Rob gives me a wink as he opens the door. We step inside, five seriously overweight, middle-aged Chinese men are seated at yet another lazy Susan'd table. They look startled and breathless, but manage to cheers Rob as we enter the room, each of them raising their goblet looking Chinese pewter mug equivalents. They briefly look me over with suspicion before returning their full attention to the white tablecloth. Rob circles the room, saying hello, beaming the silky slime smile of a seasoned outperforming salesman as he completes the lap.

I motion to take one of the remaining two seats at the table before Rob reaches his arm across my chest, halting me effortlessly. One of the men thumps his right fist into the table and exhales deeply, slouching back in his chair. The others complete similar bouts of peculiar behaviour. A young lady, almost the identical twin to the concierge woman, pops her head out from beneath the hem of the immaculate silk tablecloth. The one woman under the table is followed by four more. The quintuplet gobby sisters scoot out from under the cloth and proceed out of the room, straightening their red silk dresses, wiping their chins and adjusting the chopsticks through their hair buns.

The gents all look far more welcoming now, freshly noshed off by undercover Goddesses. Rob picks out a packet of cigars from his coat pocket and hands them around the room and we take a seat. The room fills with smoke. My mind is choked with Circular Rd 'karaoke' flashbacks. My cheeks are bloated with bum puff drags. The original hostess wheels in a tray filled with ornate bottles, it must be the famous baijiu, and a massive silver teapot. She passes around menus and fills everyone's goblets with tea.

Rob hands the menus back to the girl and must be saying in Chinese what the order is. I assume he doesn't need my advice that another round of blowjobs would be great, thanks mate. He speaks with the woman for another minute or so. One of the smelter guys starts to drink his tea so I assume it won't be rude to try mine. Fucking hell, it is rancid. It tastes like reheated water direct from the Bund. I need a few litres of Evian, Colgate and a lengthy visit to the dentist to rid the filth from my gums.

The most repulsive of the smelter team grabs a bottle of baijiu from the tray and is filling up shot glasses for each of us. Before we can all toast and consume, Rob delivers a reverential sounding speech in Chinese, but finishes by addressing me in English, "Flynn, please take the honours to commemorate the occasion." All the guys place their shot glasses on the lazy Susan and Rob swings them all around to be now infront of me.

"Please, Flynn, as you know, the number seven holds great importance, it symbolizes togetherness. Together in business, together in life, together we grow stronger. Please stand now and finish the seven shots and we will see not only your strength, but can look forward to continued strength and prosperity together."

What a fucking stitch up. I look at each of the faces around the table. I've somehow found myself in an Oriental Knights Templar. Fuck it. I bring the first shot glass to my lips and take a final glance around the table. They're all smiles. I down it. Urgh, fuck that! The guys cheer. I grab two more of the glasses, one in each hand, up and down the hatch. My throat is fire, my temples about to burst. The boys cheer louder. I see Rob with tears on his cheeks, a smile ear to ear.

I grab another two, down. Fuck. I falter, briefly blacking out, almost collapsing on the table taking my body weight wholly through my arms. The guys are all in hysterics. Rob starts cheering, "Two more! Two more!" The others join in and scream with him. Before I can crumple back in my chair, I grab the final two. Done. Hideous. I sink in my seat. The men all stand and cheer. My throat is an exhaust pipe. My stomach churns. The pressure behind my forehead feels like it will escape through my eyeballs. I'm covered in sweat.

I grab my goblet filled with lukewarm tea, memories of its unique taste of wretchedness already forgotten in a baijiu hallucination, and scull it. The horrid Bund runoff fills my mouth as Rob slaps me on the left shoulder, I hunch forward, vomiting all over the floor. The room explodes in laughter. I continue to yak pure baijiu and Huangpu tea. The carpet is covered. I sit back up, vomit residue glued to my chin. Rob refills everyone's glasses. With my hands on my knees and more spew looming, I look up from my chair through a daze, six men are standing to raise their glasses, "Cheers, Mr. Fwynn!" I check my phone, 11.47am.

I excuse myself to the bathroom, asking Rob for directions. The main room of the restaurant now has a few more patrons, families, young children, noone too likely to order the sub-table services. I follow the directions to the restrooms, seeing the universal 'gents' stick figure signage in the far corner. As I walk in, there is a wall mirror atop one elongated hand basin housing five taps. The opposing wall is lined with a series of stalls, no urinals anywhere. None of the stalls have doors, no matter, I walk to the second of the row, stopping in my tracks with a grown man hunched naked over the squat toilet, pushing both arms out for leverage against the sides of the open cubicle, face squished into a heavily constipated emoji. "Sorry buddy." Fucking hell, this place is rough.

I've lost any desire to piss, shit, breathe or live. I park at the washbasin, splashing water in my face, staring down the drain, hands over my ears no match for a room filled with the sound bytes of a grown man's tireless efforts to take a dump. I splash my face a final time, clearing all the vomit, and walk back out, catching a second glimpse of the poor fella, squatting and sweating. I wish him the best. He doesn't notice. I continue out. Across the room, two of the waitresses are wheeling large, empty trolleys as they exit Scion's business lunch private room.

Rob welcomes me back to the table, now filled with steaming pots, hotplates and all manner of intensely foreign dishes. The two centerpieces are elaborate gold trays, filled with ice, oysters, eels and live lobsters. Their claws are clicking, antennae darting through the air, black eyes staring straight at me. Rob motions me to a dish, "start with this one, Flynn, it's your favourite mate, shrimp." There is a large bowl, filled with tiny brown prawn impersonators. They're all definitely still alive too, their tails wagging slowly. I'm certain it's not a baijiu hallucination. These shrimp are a little too fresh for my liking.

"Here Flynn, have some shrimp, they're so fresh here, the best in China." Rob grabs my plate, first filling the shrimp bowl with a long splash of baijiu then loading my plate. I look down at the drunk shrimp as I grab my chopsticks, picking out the most dead looking of the bunch. I feel it wriggling on my tongue, its tail brushing my palate. I crunch down, swallowing my first kill, reluctantly washing it down with some tea, absolutely atrocious. I smash down some more baijiu.

Rob is chatting busily with the smelters, their sleeves all rolled to the elbows, bibs covering their shirts, one man taking the seafood scissors to a live lobster's claw, cracking it open and munching away, fitting in gulps of tea and baijiu between speaking through a full mouth, never taking a breath. I finish my shrimp. Rob fills my soup bowl with something I can only hope is pumpkin soup, it's probably a duck vagina stew though. My only chance to get through this is to drink. I fill up on baijiu and pray my memory of this whole experience will at least be hazy.

Waitresses return to clear the plates and refill the drinks. Most of the gents pinch the girls' arses, laughing to each other and spitting on the floor. If China takes over the world, we really are fucked. The table is fully cleared and Rob asks me to move my chair to the side so they can set up the main course. Please be blowjobs, I've definitely earned one. The original hostess removes the lazy Susan and reveals a small circular open portion in the middle of the table. Rob whispers in my ear, "just stay cool."

Two women return with an empty trolley. They close the door behind them as I swig another baijiu hit. The men are dead quiet, the distinctive yelp of an evolutionary forefather shutting them up. The women remove the linen trolley cloth. It's a fucking monkey! The men cheer and smile, the monkey looks horrific, arms tied around its back, feet also tied together, seated on the base of the trolley. The top of the trolley is removed and the women push the monkey-loaded contraption past me and underneath the table.

The constipated bloke from the toilets enters the room wearing a white butcher's apron, carrying a huge cleaver. He walks to the tableside as the monkey's head pops through the gap. The ladies pop back out from beneath the tablecloth. The cleaver toting constipee leans to the middle of the table, pressing some magic button that causes a wood panel to close over the hole, locking the monkey's head, guillotined and crying. This is fucked. The monkey is still alive as this man cleavers directly through the skull of the poor, defenseless animal. Rob presses down firmly on my shoulder. I watch on numb, the others continue cheering, looks of delight fill their eyes as the skull pops open.

Rob motions to the man who must be the head smelter to take the first bite. The chef cuts out a slice of brain, blood filled and inches from its owner's eyes, placing it on the smelter fella's plate. The men watch on as he chews for a few moments before swallowing. The room erupts, tears of laughter and joy, the monkey's eyes now closed, please, please, I can only hope he's dead. I swig baijiu direct from the bottle. Piece by piece, the brain is consumed and the men's bond grows stronger. I'm the last to be included, swigging a hospitalizing serving of baijiu as the cortex lies on my plate. I look at Rob and the men in the room, one more swig, bring the fork to my mouth and swallow it whole.

You'd think I just walked on water. Everyone stands and applauds. I'm certain to vomit. I swallowed so fast I will thankfully never know the taste. The senior member of the smelting party commands everyone's attention, bringing his palms together with fingers outstretched and grasps his fingers through each other, saying the same few words over and over as he rocks his clenched fist solemnly back and forth in the middle of his chest.

Everyone shakes hands, beaming and embracing. Rob whispers in my ear, "he just said, 'together we do much business this year, next year, and forever more,' good work, you fucking crazy Aussie." I meet the other's smiling faces at the round table. I do my best to fake a heartfelt grin and raise the baijiu bottle to the ceiling. Everyone watches me closely while I look down at the monkey's empty skull and feel tears about to flow from my eyes. I tip baijiu down my throat until the bottle's empty and I'm deafened by the smelting applause.

. . . .

It's 7am on Christmas morning in Shanghai. I'm lying in bed, toasty warm, having finally solved the Star Wars heater button puzzle. Through the bay window I'm looking out at a slowly falling blanket of snow, my first white Christmas since I was an exchange student in Germany fifteen years ago. The bucketing snow has caused the cats to cancel their morning fight club and celebrate the birth of Jesus in laneway harmony. I grab my phone and send texts de noël to family and friends sweltering back in Sydney.

There is no public holiday for Christmas in China. I hop out of bed and don the velour tracksuit for my morning exercise routine, more appropriately measured in seconds than minutes, though my once taut body is trying to make a comeback. When I'm not invited to business lunch meetings as the consultant alcoholic westerner, I'm spending at least an hour every midday swimming laps in the Shangri-la indoor rooftop pool. James. Flynn James. Between the lap swimming, the morning home fitness work out, and rediscovering the joys of walking unaccompanied by torrents of Singapore sweat, I'm almost looking respectable with a shirt off. Almost. I throw the velour to the floor, jump in the shower, and get busy with the tried and tested shit, shave, spruce routine.

I close the door behind me and set off, I never did find that turtle again. I trudge with ease through the laneway snow thanks to a new pair of Columbia winter boots. I'm sure they're counterfeit

Columbians, but they were reasonably expensive so at least they're a good fake, the best you can hope for when making a purchase in China. I keep the Italian leather soled death traps at work, there's only so many times you want to skate to work over the black ice, or have fellow train commuters scuff the overpriced gloss off your fancy shoes.

My footpath pedestrian management program has blossomed. Before exiting the gate of my lane house complex each morning, I thump my left palm into my right shoulder four times and sing to myself, 'Kamma Tay, Kamma Tay, Faarrrk Youuu'. It's my Australian abroad Kiwi Haka tribute to rev me up for the ensuing two blocks of shoulder charging my way to the station. It works. I've made no friends in this French Concession so far, but I've definitely created some respectful enemies by refusing to play ball with their footpath hogging game plan. Playing chicken on the way to work is fine when you're weighing in about 30kgs heavier and a foot taller than your opposing roosters.

The subway commute still haunts me. There's no way possible to shoulder charge your way to comfort on a dangerously overcrowded train. I blame Pavlov for the immediate shudder that engulfs me each day as I pass through the turnstiles and down the stairs leading to the platform. The three-stop journey always ends with mixed feelings of physical violation and psychological torment. Christmas morning is no different. I'm my usual momentary wreck of frazzled synapses as I step off the train onto the Lujiazui platform and enjoy the relief of an entire 1m radius of free space to call my own.

I delve deep into my winter clothing cocoon and fish out my wallet, multiple layers from the outer jacket shell. Any wannabe pickpocket will have a better chance of giving me a covert prostate examination than pinching my wallet. I walk the final few metres of Lujiazui Ring Road to the office through a rapidly intensifying snowstorm. Sweeping gusts of wind whip falling snow into horizontal ice pellets. I slit my eyes for protection from the storm in a gesture of survival and assimilation. I continue inside to the elevator's warmth, once more cramped in with too many people in too small a space. I swipe my card and grab my seat. It's 8.26am. The office is empty. I start reading back through my notes and write down what details I need to chase up today.

I'm not at all bothered that I have to work on the holiest of holy days. I've got no friends here nor do I have anything of any real joy or value to do that doesn't involve learning the ropes of copper concentrates trading, drinking baijiu til I vomit or swimming laps in the chlorinated heat of the Shangri-la's pool. My first three weeks in the People's Republic have been intense, accompanying Rob to meetings all over the country and repeating the performance of my first day over and over again, winning him plenty of business for next year after making sure the company health insurance plan included generous compensation for premature liver necrosis.

When not evading death in Rob's Range Rover, I am thoroughly put through my paces by Li Ming, her crash course in copper concentrate operations is not helped by my being perpetually hungover or simply outright drunk. Regardless Li Ming carries on, emailing me hundreds of pages of files and manuals as I take my seat in the morning, then testing my knowledge meticulously before she heads home around 7pm. In much the same way Jannah's seat next to me in Singapore ensured I couldn't possibly slacken off, I'm grateful for Li Ming's oversight. She knows Rob well and is fully aware of the alcohol filled torture he is putting me through on an almost daily basis. She doesn't give a fuck. She plows on with her teachings with even greater intensity.

In the course of what untrained eyes could view as a three-week booze bender, I've proven to myself I am a highly functioning alcoholic. I force my way through whatever hangover Rob has stitched me up with and take my seat each morning next to Li Ming, certain she is about to impart some priceless knowledge and doubly certain to write everything down no matter how obvious it may seem at the time of scribbling.

In three weeks of Operations 101, I'm now blessed with a comprehensive awareness of the intricacies of obtaining financing for cargoes, the shipping paperwork and coordination required to ensure a cargo can be ferried around the globe, how to ensure an assay is verifiable and able to be legally challenged if a cargo arrives with off-spec material, and finally, how best to piece together a purchase or sales contract depending on the likely nature of the copper concentrate being purchased and the eventual end destination to sell it to.

As God would be well aware, the Devil is in the detail, and where the Devil is lurking, easy profits and capitalist utopia are sure to be hiding. Satan is without question a lawyer, and he has racked up hefty consultation fees through assisting Scion in drawing up our contracts.

Copper concentrates are the middle ground in the earth pillaging to retail distribution non-circle of life. There is copper in the ground all over the globe, usually bonded tightly to dirt, gold, silver, and many more subgroups of buried treasure and lethal carcinogens. Thanks to mining monoliths, this mishmash collection of subterranean bedfellows will eventually find their way onto shovels of varying magnitudes and face initial processing after a quick truck or travelator ride. The initial processing, milling, will turn a body of dirt which may have contained one or two parts per hundred of copper, into a concentrate of fifteen to forty parts per hundred.

The hallowed brown earth of South America, home to Incan Cities of Gold and arid meadows laced with marching powder, is also home to ore bodies rich in copper. Our Spanish speaking ore mongers, located primarily in Santiago and Lima, source an endless bevy of copper concentrate to ship across the Pacific Ocean and fill Chinese smelters with. Once Rob has greased the capitalist wheels of communism with blowjobs, baijiu and monkey brains, Scion is paid handsomely and the cousin-fucking smelters refine our concentrate into copper blister and then, eventually, 99.99% refined copper cathode is ready to glisten and glean in almost every manner of 21st century application.

The true kicker to turn this reputable business of questionable morality into a more refined corporate juggernaut of sickening profitability comes with the combination of fine print, a reasoned understanding of probability and the enduring lure of gold. Life is risky, that's why actuaries are always so lonely, noone wants to face the truth. But there seems little upside in placing all that probability know-how to use on life insurance premium calculations when you could be lining purchase and sales contracts in all sorts of embedded options and pricing triggers.

The game is rigged something like this. Each concentrate body of material will have its own unique combination of good, great, and bad things. Copper is good, obviously, the hint's in the name, this is the copper concentrates department. Gold and silver are great; precious metals of unquestioned divinity, especially glowing when bundled in bullion. Bad things, well, you're bound to have sulfur, arsenic, and plenty of other nasty bits and pieces which are costly to extract away from your good and great things and even more costly to dispose safely of. That disposal cost is not something I think too many Chinese businessmen or regulators are overly concerned with.

So, to place a monetary value on the concentrate, you need a pro's and con's ledger. It's fairly straightforward, there are live, exchange-listed prices for copper, gold and silver, so, take the assay reported content of these metals in the concentrate and multiply that by the price on the exchange. That was easy. Now, you'll have a cost involved in ridding your material of the nasty's, no worries, impose a penalty, let's say $100 per tonne or something. The number isn't important for the moment. The concept is all that matters. Good things balanced with bad things and don't forget all the other usual costs like shipping, insurance, etc, etc to give a final dollar value.

OK, now if you are a retarded, non-threatening, rarely-thinking member of society and are happy to transact business as above, that's fine, you'll be happily employed in a governmental role somewhere. You'll praise God for the food on your table, think there's true honour in working nine to five for the better part of a lifetime, and probably cry tears of genuine joy when your child receives a participation ribbon at the local school swimming carnival. There's nothing wrong with that. You're right in the meaty heart of honourable civilisation and you've got plenty of company. But when the chief requirement of your bloated paycheck is to create money from thin air, you need to be a little more thoughtful than simply taking a quantity of metal and multiplying it by a price on an exchange to think you deserve to be anything but fired.

So, what's a poor, aspiring capitalist to do? Create a potential trough of dizzying profits for the client's greedy snout, that's what. Rather than simply assign a dollar value to an amount of metal, let's have a cascade of pricing premiums and discounts assigned to the specific amount of metal in a concentrate. For instance, the overwhelming majority of copper concentrates will have a copper content of 25% to 35%. If you're selling concentrate, you'll get a higher price if the material has a higher content of copper. That makes sense. 5,000 tonnes of copper concentrate times 30% copper assay times listed copper price of $7,000 per tonne. $10.5 million. Done.

But what if the concentrate you've worked so hard to pilfer from the earth's crust has a low percentage of copper. Ah, the humanity, the whole process was a waste of time, why do bad things happen to good people? Never mind, our purchasing contract pays a small premium for concentrates with 20%-25%. What? Why? Well, this guarantees we get the lion's share of business, most other companies will refuse to buy the stuff with a content lower than 25%, so we can be certain the miners are happy to deal and prevent their downside risk, a risk which is always far bigger and more imminent than its upside twin. But, how can we offer this? God won't like this one bit.

Well, the fine print, inked, as always, at Satan's brothel, instigates a zero payment for all gold and silver in the event of a sub 25% copper quota in the concentrate. No biggie, the Julio's, Javier's, Jose's and Jesus's of Latin America aren't overly in love with the precious metal, they dutifully see the certainty of profitable copper dealing for what it is; good business. But, copper is priced in thousands of dollars per tonne, gold is priced in thousands per ounce, and our Chinese end users are enamoured with gold's lustre. The copper component of the concentrate may be borderline but we can sell them a lower content of copper at an unbeatable price because we will only charge a modest amount for any gold and silver ready to be unleashed via the refining of the concentrate. That's easy when we paid zilch for it to begin with.

Li Ming arrives as I'm reading back through one of my countless notebooks. "It's Christmas! Take the day off, Flynn! It's fine. Quick, go now, before anyone else sees you."

"Wow, thanks so much. Are you sure?"

"Of course, go home, Merry Christmas!"

I take off out the door, down the elevator and straight back into the grips of a late December snowstorm. I decide to escape the cold and spend the rest of Christmas morning at the Shangri-la, not swimming laps though, I think I'll have a sauna and a spa. Baby Jesus would like that.

. . . .

I'm welcomed to the opening day of Chinese New Year celebrations with a sparkling blue sky shining through my bay windows while Baghdad-imitating explosives and children's laughing reverberate through the lane way. 2013. Year of the Snake. The Chinese do indeed love a New Year's firecracker. The snow and Siberian cold of my initial month here are a distant memory. From all reports, December was one of the coldest on record. January was gorgeous, clear blue skies at perfect, manageably freezing temperatures. The sky's clarity was not overly endearing to this great nation though, it meant simply that the view from the office included more precise vision of the endless power plants burning plumes of toxic gas into the already contamination saturated air.

It's Saturday morning, February 9. I've got eight days of public holidays to properly celebrate the wonder of the Snake. I'd originally planned a trip home to Australia, but had to forego that idea through a nightmare cavalcade of paperwork which had to be filled if I were to ever regain entry back into this overpopulated land mass. Fuck it, I'll be outta here soon enough, will leave the current visa untouched. No, I've settled on eight days of sleep, DVD's and walking the city. I jump in for a leisurely thirty-minute shower, towel off and throw on my jeans and a jumper.

The French Concession is a ghost town this morning. Workmates have told me the Chinese New Year week long party is the only time of year that Shanghai is ever quiet. The city's population halves, most residents use the opportunity to return home to see their families in the countless small villages throughout this vast country. The majority of shops have their windows boarded up. The only spit on the sidewalk is stale and resilient, not fresh and fluid. The walkway is all mine, there are no shoulder charging heroics to be achieved in order to move freely. I see one lone car driving away about 500m down the street. There's nothing but frail sun shining on my back and a peaceful sense of Armageddon tranquility shattered every few moments by laneway firecrackers and children's laughter.

I turn solo down into the West Nanjing Road train station entrance. Not a soul. I check the timetable. Trains are still running. I hear the rattling tracks signaling one on the approach. I race down the stairs and across an empty platform to take a seat on the train. A seat!! This is civilized. I am on the same line as would normally take me to work. As there is no crush of humankind to prevent me, I hop out at the first stop, the People's Square station. I complete the underground labyrinth to find the surface and commence my walking tour with a Starbucks coffee. The caffeine bastion of 24/7 civilization is open.

The People's Park is breathtaking. Literally. My first view of outstretched, lush green grass in months causes me instinctively to breathe in deeply only for the noxious air to meet stiff opposition in the unblemished lining of my lungs. Even on a clear day in Shanghai, the air pollution index rarely drops below 'unhealthy' levels. Oxygen 'hits' are all the rage in Beijing apparently. Pure oxygen is selling like hotcakes. Fuck humanity. I can see the future and I'm scared shitless. There aren't any O2 dealers in this park, so I persevere with my morning stroll coughing and sputtering like a beaten up Holden Kingswood, shallow breathing a must.

I make my way through the park. My thoughts are consumed with the firm knowledge the world, as a whole, and China, more specifically, would be greatly improved if the one child policy were reduced to zero. But, all that rational thinking aside, there is a unique charisma to the gritty grandeur of Shanghai, the New York of Asia, the true Gotham City that Batman has chosen to shun.

I continue walking for over three hours, or four cappuccinos, whichever measuring tool suits you best is fine with me. The cold air is best staved off by holding onto warm styrofoam filled with arabica. I'm not too sure exactly where I am, but I've arrived at a three way intersection and a large group of Anglo looking blokes are standing infront of the 'Camel Sports Bar'.

"Hey mate, you here for footy today?" One of the guys yells across the street to me with a clear Aussie twang.

"Umm." A rickety bus wobbles towards the Camel. All the blokes grab their sports bags lying on the footpath.

"Come on, you're in the right spot, first game today, doesn't matter if you haven't been to training yet. I'm Tom, did you get an email from me about joining the club?" I walk across the street and join the group of 16 to 50 year old blokes.

"G'day Tom. Sorry, I'm not sure, footy?" It's been two months since I've spoken English face to face with a westerner. The words feel awkward and strained. It's taken me this long to feel like I truly don't belong in this completely foreign city and speaking to an Australian is the trigger to make me realize I am indeed light years from home.

"Yeah mate, the Shanghai Tigers Aussie Rules Footy Club. Sorry, what's your name?"

"Flynn."

"I can't see you on my list. You wanna play though? Where you from?"

"Sydney."

"Ever played Aussie Rules before?"

"Never."

"Perfect, you'll be fine, we're all shit. You look like you can play."

"Thanks. I don't have any gear mate."

"No worries, we've got spare stuff, it's more just training today anyway. If you like it, then join up properly. Hop on buddy."

"Cool. Cheers Tom."

"All good. Flynn right? I'll put your name down on the sheet. What's your surname?"

"James." I throw my empty coffee in a bin and take a seat on the bus.

Within a few minutes the others have loaded their bags in the undercarriage and we're making our way out of the city centre aboard the decrepit bus. The streets are looking more like usual now, a halving of the population still leaves a lonely 12.5 million people in the immediate vicinity. Newborns dangle from maternal arms, letting fly with gutter-filling shits. Oldies complete their osteoarthritis mitigating tai chi in any open space they can find. Bike-riding firecracker vendors cycle the streets, spruiking explosives available to purchase direct from their highly flammable wicker baskets. Tom takes centre stage, standing at the front of the bus with a clipboard and a 'Shanghai Tigers' hat.

"Welcome lads. Good to see some old faces and plenty of new ones. There are close to 30 of us here so we'll split into three teams of ten and have a round robin, nothing too serious. Our first proper game isn't for over a month. Today will just be a good chance to blow out the cobwebs. It's still nice and cold at the moment so won't be sweating too heavily out there, which will be good. I'll come through the bus on the way and make sure to get everyone's emails and phone numbers and give you a member card. And remember, just add Shanghai Tigers on Facebook and we'll always update that with game schedules and embarrassing photos of your attempts at sportsmanship. After a few games this arvo, we'll jump back on the bus and head straight back to the Camel, just show your member card and you'll get 50% off beers and food. Should be a good day.

Happy Chinese New Year boys."

I'm seated halfway down the bus. I introduce myself to a short haired, fit looking Irish fella next to me, Sean. He has been in Shanghai for the past two years after a decade in London, but has strangely developed a love affair with Aussie Rules after sharing a flat with an Australian back in the UK. He runs through various amazing Aussie Rules historical moments and quickly realizes I have no idea what he's talking about. Smart lad though, he settles on his other passion, Chinese women, and runs me through the endless dating Apps on his phone. The pictures he's showing me are of his 'dream girls'. I find most of them look more like malnourished young boys cross dressing in slutty outfits than a 'dream girl', but I'm not afflicted with yellow fever, so I choose not to judge the questionable beauty in the eye of this Irish beholder.

In the row behind me there is a legitimate global citizen, Ben. He is 17, sporting a neck tattoo that has effectively replaced his Adam's apple with an inked clock. He speaks eight languages. His Dad is Egyptian, his Mum Venezuelan. He's supposed to be at home studying for next week's *International Baccalaureate* exams at the French School of Shanghai but he just wants to run off his hangover after drinking all night then snorting coke till 7am this morning off the bare arses of Russian whores. Excuse me? He shows me some pictures on his phone that look far more appetizing than those on Sean's. Is this child pornography? Ben is living in a parallel universe in which the study routine I undertook before my high school exams would look even more teacher pet friendly than it already does.

We arrive at a collection of sports grounds consisting of the customary assortment of soccer fields, tennis courts and an oval running track. Not so ordinary though, is the eyesore of a power station behind barbed wire fencing at the end of the soccer oval. Sky scraping, plump grey chimneys reach up to the heavens and spew forth clouds of electricity generation run off. The morning sunshine has given way to an overcast afternoon and we walk towards the end oval, closest to the power station, and reconvene to sort out teams for a round robin.

"Flynn, jump on the Eagles team. Here's a jersey and you'll find a pair of boots and some shorts in that kit over there." Tom hands me my jersey and, much to my amazement, in the kit there is a pair of boots which fit better than any shoes I've ever had. I see my 'Eagles' teammates all grouped together and Sean leads us through a warm up. A light jog around the oval has transformed my virgin lungs into desperate skanks. Every particle of contaminated air is smashing its way through my once pristine lung tissue in a debauched orgy, leaving me coughing, breathless, and certain I will never again be playing Aussie Rules footy in Shanghai after today.

We finish the lap and start kicking a few balls between each other. It's been many, many years since I've played any organized sport, but my youth was spent with a constant foot, soccer, tennis or basket ball in my grip, and it's good to be booting a footy, regardless of the permanent pulmonary damage it's costing. "OK, couple of stretches, lads." Sean now leads the group in the final pre-game limbering routine.

There's an older member of the group who has put on a fluorescent singlet and blows his whistle in the middle of the field. It's basically a converted soccer pitch with the goal posts replaced with some miniature replications of Aussie Rules goals instead. As we jog to the middle, I become acutely aware of the fact I've never actually played this game.

"Flynn, you're pretty tall, you go ruckman aye?" Thanks Sean.

"Yeah, sure." What's a ruckman?

The ref blows his whistle and Tom stands in the middle of the pitch near the ref in a Bombers jersey.

Sean yells at me, "Flynn, go ruckman!"

"Yeah, got it." What the fuck is he on about?

"Well get in the fucking middle mate, contest the bounce." Ah, I'm supposed to be the tall gangly bloke who tips the ball at the bounce. The ruckman. Yes. We're in business. I take my spot opposite Tom and the ref hunches over to bounce the ball into contention. Tom and I run towards the centre to tip the ball. I jump forwards, straight on. Tom instead spins ninety degrees, as he jumps up and extends his right arm, his elbow crunches through the base of my sternum like a bony dagger. If I had any hint of abdominal muscles, they might have deflected the hit. Instead I'm winded and useless as the game clock strikes 1 second.

Tom taps the ball to one of his Bomber teammates and they race off down the field. I lurch towards the ground and feel some light rain on my back. It's probably acidic. The whistle blows again in the distance. The Bombers have scored the opening goal and I'm still looking at the dirt, having even more trouble breathing than usual. I stand up fully as the others come back towards the middle for another tip off. I take a deep breath to prepare for the second bounce in sixty seconds and the heavy breathing induces a sickening cough. My lungs are burning like I've just inhaled pure sulfur dioxide, which is extremely likely.

Fuck this. I line up Tom as the ref leans in to bounce the ball. I give my all in the five step lead in to the tip off and jump up, completing the newly tutored ninety degree swivel and smash all my weight into Tom, barely feigning an attempt at the ball. Tom and I collapse to the ground, both missing the ball, Sean yells, "Great work, Flynn!" as he scoops up the ball and races down field. Here we go. I dust off and jump up, running down in support, not too sure of what exactly I'm meant to do. Sean kicks the ball wide to another Eagle who then proceeds to kick the ball to me. Oh shit.

The ball bounces a few metres infront of me into clear space. I haven't sprinted in years, but the knowledge there has to be someone chasing close behind me causes me to run at full pelt. I lunge down to shovel up the ball and continue on to goal scoring glory. Not this time, Flynn. The ball wobbles as I bend to scoop, I lose balance and face plant, missing the ball entirely but sliding along some gravel that somehow found its way on to the oval. My face is covered in dirt and my right leg is covered in blood. For fuck's sake, Shanghai, can you just help a brother out?

A guy from the Bombers sees the blood and runs straight to me, "mate, go get that sorted right now, we have a good first aid kit, clean that cut straightaway." As much as I don't want to play anymore, I don't want to seem like a total pussy, "Nah, she'll be right mate, I'm fine."

"Honestly mate, the turf here is fucking toxic. Another lad lost his leg last year, thanks to a gnarly infection from a cut way smaller than that..."

I don't respond. That's enough for me. I like my legs. I don't like China. I yell out to Sean I need to sub off and get straight to the sideline, coughing, wheezing and bleeding profusely as I rummage through the first aid kit. The emergency training component of my physiotherapy studies comes rushing back with the imminent threat of lower limb amputation. I find the gauze, bandaging, antiseptic creams and don't skimp on the application.

One of the player's wives sees me cleaning up the wound and asks if I need any help. I reply that I'm fine and she follows up with saying that she's quickly going to the shops. If I would like some food or a drink, she can grab it for me. I hand her a few hundred Yuan, "a bottle of baijiu please." She gives me a strange look of accepting disapproval and trudges off.

I continue on with cleaning any fragment of leg removing infection possibilities. I'm all bandaged up and back in the original clothes I set out from home in several hours earlier. My baijiu delivery arrives. I thank the lady, Jen, and gulp the hideous potion under slowly falling rain on the sidelines, becoming rapidly intoxicated as I watch grown men chase an oblong, leather ball around a field of venomous earth in the foreground of a horizon crushing power terminal. Happy New Year, China.

"He's a pisspot through and through, he's a bastard so they say, meant to go to heaven, but he went the other way and down, down, down, down!" The back lounge of the Camel erupts, toasting to Bill, a lad from Perth who won best on ground for the day. There's no award for worst on ground, though it's certain that crown would be mine. Bill is no stranger to this cultured Aussie drinking theme song. He waits for the 'down, down, down' like a seasoned pro and demolishes his pint of Tsing Tao.

I am absolutely off my guts. I stayed warm while watching from the sidelines by polishing off the entire bottle of baijiu. I could barely board the bus, but once I did, I told half of my new mates I loved 'em, and the other half to go get fucked. No one was overly touched or offended. It seems they were mostly impressed at my ability to finish off the bottle solo and all fairly entertained as I pissed out the window on a few occasions during the homeward journey.

The moment we arrived back at the Camel, Sean ordered me a chicken parmagiana and forced me to down a litre of water. Top fella. I'd not eaten any chicken for the past month though, we're in the grips of a nationwide poultry scare campaign. A bird flu epidemic has killed a few hundred people in the outskirts of Shanghai. But when the parma arrived on the table I couldn't resist. If there is one thing I will gladly die for, it's a chicken parma.

It's now around 8pm and the rest of the Tigers have done an excellent job in catching up to my level of drunkenness. The back lounge of the Camel is filled with ice buckets full of beer, wine and champagne bottles. Every minute or so there is a toast to a player for some performance or attribute, everyone sculls their drink and swiftly refills in preparation for the next toast. We're dancing on tables and singing along to whatever 80's classic is booming through the room. This is the happiest I've been in months. I feel temporarily like I'm not actually in China, there's no better way to feel in this country than that. Tom jumps up on the bar, tells everyone to get back on the bus, we're going to do a lap of the city and he's just spent 5,000 Yuan (about $1,000 USD) on fireworks.

"Let's show Shanghai how the Tigers fucking party at New Year's boys!!"

"Yeeahhh!!"

We storm out. Sean waits at the door of the bus with garbage bags full of firecrackers, giving us each all sorts of explosives as we hop on. There's a huge esky with wheels on the aisle, stacked with bottles of baijiu and vodka. Tom stands at the front of the bus once more, telling us to aim the fireworks out the window and light the fuck out of the French Concession. Sean hops in and takes the reins at the driver's seat. The firecracker express is off and blazing.

"Light 'em up!"

Everyone at the window aims their rocket launchers into the outside air and ignites the fuses. The night is alight with out of control Shanghai Tiger Aussie Rules revelers, the rickety bus deafened with shoddy Chinese firecrackers. The half of Shanghai's population which hasn't abandoned the city for the holidays surely now wish they had. Each street we enter, filled with polite Snake worshippers, is instantly obliterated by the Tigers' shenanigans. If we're not lighting up the streets, we're drinking baijiu and vodka like three eyed fish from the Bund.

I'm seated in the row behind the driver. Sean's driving is shocking, but the time spent with Rob in his Range Rover has accustomed me to feeling on my deathbed at all times of engine propulsion. I take a huge swig of baijiu and yell through the blasting for Sean to open the door. I pile some rockets into the back of my jeans, tell Sean to drive a bit slower, walk out the door of the moving bus and climb up to the roof using the side windows as perfect foot holds. Tom joins me on the roof and we fire the rockets into the night sky, laughing with certifiable elation as we dodge low hanging tree branches, power lines and dirty laundry. The street beneath is glowing through the nonstop flashes firing out of the bus' windows.

Sean pulls up with a slam on the brakes, you fucking cunt. We're only moving marginally faster than snail's pace, but Tom and I are still flung forwards and drop over the front of the bus, two metres down to the frosty bitumen of Donghu Street. This is really going to hurt tomorrow. My right leg fires with pain, but I'm otherwise fine and ready to plow on with doing my country anything but proud. Tom is just laughing, screaming at the others to get out of the bus and bring all the booze with them. The 5,000 Yuan of fireworks have evaporated into the New Year's sky.

We reassemble in a park and the twenty or so of us finish off the bottles of hard liquor. Opposite is a huge sign for Club 88. The booze dries up quickly and Tom leads the charge, stumbling across the road and up the brightly lit side steps leading to 88. We walk into the most tackily elaborate nightclub of Chinese decadence. In the far distance is a bar, but the intervening space is a sea of timber stalls, crystal chandeliers, and people, so many people. This is the playground for Chinese trust fund babies. Each booth is full of Shanghai's versions of the Hiltons and Kardashians, the Chinese elite, popping bottles, chugging cigars and playing some weird dice rolling game.

As we walk on through to the bar, the Chinese wannabe superstars look us over with acute hatred. I'd never before been so obviously vilified for the colour of my skin, but it seems clear the barman is avoiding serving us for being Caucasian. We stand at the bar for fifteen minutes while bar staff make purposeful eye contact with us but continue to serve others.

I'm completely over it and not interested in satisfying the barman's joy at being such a cunt. I tell Tom I'm going to shoot through and head home. As I begin my walk out, the barman yells, "yeah that right white boy, get out my club, fuck off!"

"What did you say?" Any intoxication instantly wipes clean.

"I say suck my dick. Fuck off!"

"Listen you little fucktard…" Tom grabs me and pulls me away from the bar, "Just leave it, you fight him, you'll have to fight your way out of the club. Look around mate. This is his turf. Leave it."

Tom's right, dammit. I haven't been in a fight since I was 14, and the first chance I get in almost two decades is against someone an anorexic, teenage girl could beat the shit out of. This just isn't fair. Tom and I shake hands and I continue the walk out, taunted by the fuckwit barman's unrelenting "go home you fucking white boy" as I muster every cell of self control to stop me from smashing the nearest champagne bottle and shoving the shards through the racist pindick's neck.

Walking back down the Club 88 stairs, the pain of the gash on my right leg returns with a vengeance as the alcohol binge starts wearing off. Each step sends fiery pangs through me. A late night BBQ has been set up on the street corner nearest to the park. There's a light drizzle. I take cover under the BBQ's tarpaulin and wait for the guy to grill some kebabs of undetermined meat. I don't know if it's dog, monkey or panda, but it tastes sensational. I order another half dozen kebabs while an irritating cab driver keeps courting my business. I tell him I will get a lift in a few minutes and give him my address, but just leave me the fuck alone as long as I'm under the tarp, can't a man eat in peace. He seems happy enough with this and starts chatting with someone on his mobile.

The rain stops and I throw the kebab sticks in the bin, make eye contact with the cabbie across the street and hobble over, taking as much weight as possible through my left leg with each stride. He opens the back door for me and I hop in. No more than half of my body has entered the cab before I'm shoved in and thrown to the far side of the back seat. Three Chinese girls have crammed in next to me. The driver sets the cab in motion. We're flying through the streets.

"White boy! We come home with you. You pay us, we fuck you!"

"What the fuck? No. Fuck off."

"Come on, we make you feel good. Which one of us you like?"

I should qualify; these girls are horrendous. Jabba the Hutt spent time with girls like this when preparing for his movie debut.

"Well, how much then?" If the price is right…

"How much you fink?"

"Fuck, not much sweetheart. I just want to go to sleep."

"No! We have fun with you, big boy. White man. Big banana. Banana massage for you."

I'm not sure what role the cabbie plays in this whole scam, but he has at least driven me home. We're on Maoming Rd, a few hundred metres short of my place, I tell him to pull up, pay him and get out of the cab while the most ambitious trio of prostitutes on Earth carry on with trying to convince me of their sexual prowess. As soon as girls like this start to look appealing, I'll be sure to chop my dick off. I wave the girls goodnight and start the walk home.

I hobble across the road to a Chinese '7/11' equivalent, grab some two-minute noodles and a tall boy of Tsing Tao. I'm sure I'm drunkenly mistaken, but the girl behind the counter is giving an alluring air. I see her almost everyday on my way home when I pop in for milk, beers and noodles, the diet of champions. I never sense any hint of sexual tension nor have I previously noticed her slender, downtrodden beauty. But having just spent the past fifteen minutes in Shanghai's taxi of unsolicited piggery, I suppose anything looks reasonably spectacular.

"Happy Chinese New Year, sir!" She's never this friendly, maybe she's been sculling baijiu all day in honour of the Snake.

"Thank you, Happy Chinese New Year to you too! You have an excellent English accent, where did you learn?"

She just giggles and playfully says, "Happy Chinese New Year" a few more times, smiling constantly. She unpeels the lid on the noodle box and pours in some hot water from the tap behind the counter.

"Thank you so much…Shay Shay."

She walks the noodles around to the front of the counter and proceeds out of the shop with me. What the fuck? We walk together all the way to my apartment. I'm holding an ice cold Tsing Tao and a boiling hot plastic bowl of noodles. She's stopped giggling and stares intently at her feet, not losing eye contact with the pavement or saying another word. I open my door, immediately turn the heater on and motion Miss 7/11 to take a seat on the couch. I pour half of the Tsing Tao into a glass for her. She refuses the drink but starts undressing out of her blue and white uniform. I place the noodles and her full cup of Tsing Tao on the counter and lead her through to my bed.

We start kissing and undressing each other as the heater whirs away in the corner. She's now completely naked, a flat chest, massive bush of pubes and a nervously smiling young woman look up at me. For a girl who appears every bit a virgin, she reaches across to her pants on the bedside table and grabs a condom from the pocket, astutely unwrapping the Johnny exuding everything but inexperience as she does so. Yep, this is happening.

I'm pounding away hammer and tongs, wishing I'd never turned the fucking heater on as streams of sweat pour down my face and back and my right thigh cut burns in agony. She's lying on her back, her hairy legs wrapped around my pudgy torso. I'm soldiering on stoically, certain that my baijiu bender has numbed my dick and there are far too many flab molecules where muscle should be in my stomach and glutes to produce fast enough pelvic propulsion to have any hope of dropping a load.

I roll on my back content to just let her bob away on my cock like a crazed, communist pole worshipper until she gets fed up with it. She gets frantic, pulling on her hair and slapping my face as she must be hopefully about to climax. I feel something starting to rouse in my

207

loins too. Maybe the slap to the face enraged something deep in the pleasure cortex. I'm gonna blow too. Fucking beauty. She covers her mouth, letting out a final scream as I shudder in unison, my first Asian.

She rolls off and cuddles up next to me. I look down at my heroic little todger, eager to congratulate the tireless trooper. Fuck off. The condom is split in half. My bare knob stands unprotected and covered in muck. The ring of the condom still stuck around the base. My right thigh covered in blood, please by my own. Fuck you, China.

. . . .

A mosquito the size of a small plane lines up for an easy buffet on my forearm. I wait for its safe landing then smack the malaria spreader to kingdom come. A puff of blood stains my skin. I hate this place so much. Easter holidays, like Christmas, are not celebrated in the People's Republic, but I'm taking the piss so royally at work it really isn't an issue, completing the bare minimum of operational tasks and simply hoping the phone rings sooner rather than later with the return to Singapore request.

I'm lying under the shade of a tree in the gardens lining the Bund, sweating out my hangover on this Easter Monday lunch break following a particularly savage Easter Sunday session with the Tigers. I sit up and watch people walking the Bund promenade, smiling and laughing, the stench of the Huangpu River no concern to them. Am I the only person with a functioning olfactory system round here? Who knows? I head back to work wreaking of booze.

The office is empty, lunch hours are two around here and they are taken very seriously. The majority of my workmates like to convene in the dining hall at the base of the building. Imagine an enormous school cafeteria full of an assortment of corporate citizens from each rung of that unifying corporate ladder, all bound together by the common tight arse thread of not wanting to pay for their lunch. Sure, thriftiness is next to Godliness, but lining up for 30 minutes to get a tray full of free rice and chicken, miso soup and green tea…no way, not for me.

It's hard to tell if my workmates think I'm a bit stuck up for not joining them each day for their cafeteria lunch and chin wag. The two times I've joined, it's the same routine. Line up for fucking ages amongst all the other plonkers from the building's various companies, get your meal of barely edible prison food, then sit at a table, quickly finish your tucker then slowly look at the clock until it's the designated time to return to your desk. Corporate citizenship is something I despise enough already without having to undergo that sort of torture. I'm amazed I went twice, but I figured I best sample it two times to be completely certain of the lunacy of my workmates.

It doesn't really matter though, since the wheeling and dealing season with smelter alcoholic sex addicts came to a close, lunchtime usually involves me racing off to the Shangri-la gym to go about a foreign concept to Chinese people, exercise. I hate gyms, but the place is pristine. The pool may be full of chlorine but it is impeccable. Most endearing of all, the gym is always empty. It's my solitary oasis in this overcrowded city.

My phone rings, it's the big cheese.

"You ready to start trading yet?"

"Thought you'd never ask."

"Great. Listen, Paul's all sorted for you to take up the derivs role we spoke about before you took off to China. You haven't had a holiday since you started. How about you take a few weeks, go recharge or whatever it is you stupid Australians do and let's get you started back in Singapore in the last week of April?"

"Perfect."

"Right then, I'll let HR know and they'll send you an email with all the details, blah blah. See you soon sport."

"Thanks so much Joel. See you soon."

I hang up, clench my right fist in a little self-congratulatory pump then update all the communal files with every piece of necessary information about the cargoes I'm taking care of so my cafeteria loving colleagues can carry on fine without me. I take a quick glance of Google maps thinking about where could be best for a quick holiday. I'll work something out. As long as I'm out of China, I'll be euphoric.

I switch on the out of office function on my email, shut down the computer and hurry to the elevators without seeing a soul. I ring my parents from the overhead walkway atop Lujiazui Ring Road, letting them know the great news as I proceed down the stairs to the station, letting fly with spit all over the hand railing and a final shoulder charge into an oncoming pedestrian. Fare thee well, China. Operations 101. Over.

Liam Carroll

5/ A Mexican Pit Stop with a Quick Taste of Sin City

When there's hard work to be done, take a holiday

The road descending from Oaxaca through the mountains to Puerto Escondido is not maintained in a manner designed to be the Rancho Relaxo of bituminous causeways, but after ten hours of clenched fists and heart-infarcting trumpet blasts, you think maybe, just maybe, Pablo, behind the wheel, takes sadistic pleasure in seeing bright eyed tourists fearing for their lives through his rear-vision mirror. He tweaks the cassette player. The Scots have their bagpipes, Hawaiians their ukuleles and these Mexicans have the trumpet. Be damned if you think they'll let you enjoy the brass broadcast at low volume. Pablo tweaks the knob clockwise until it twists no more. Full blare. The trumpets blast on.

Dawn is breaking over a desert so barren only scorpions, stray dogs, and gas station owners survive. The mountains to the right block most of the rising sun's rays, but the odd break between peaks allows the sun to cast cactus shadows hundreds of metres long like giant cowboys shooting guns to the horizon. I'm carrying nothing but a backpack with the bare necessities; boardshorts and t-shirts, sunscreen and Mexican pesos.

Only two days ago I was leaving Scion's Shanghai offices, my trading career confirmed, now I'm chasing surf in Central America with my two best mates. I should be accustomed to good fortune, but timing an impromptu, enforced holiday with the exact same moment as my two best mates from school going on a Mexican surf trip followed by a Las Vegas bender? This is miraculous, even for me.

It has been almost five years since I've seen Mark or Chris, but we'll be making up for lost time with interest, chasing Central American waves and Nevada babes for the next fortnight. Chris is on his way to becoming Australia's Kofi Annan, having just completed 18 months serving with the UN in Sudan and is due to be stationed in Beirut once this holiday is over. Mark is an equally ambitious humanitarian. He studied physiotherapy with me at Sydney University, but his family is from Jakarta, where he now lives, and is busy setting up a full spectrum medical centre, aiming to provide best practice western healthcare for the Indonesian capital.

It's shortly after 7am. Sweat levels are already excessive. It's hot. Fucking hot. The day has barely begun, but southern Mexico is shrouded in a merciless, crazed heat reserved for overweight jockeys on race day morning. We're nearing some form of civilization, the cacti are starting to fatten up and the occasional roadside dog looks almost safe to pat. The chocolate brown water of the Pacific coastline a few hundred kilometers northwest of the Guatemala border is now visible.

Puerto Escondido is the jewel in Mexico's surfing crown. Well, it is a jewel to those of the human race chiseled from Mayan stone, in possession of Orca's lungs, Romanian gymnast balance and relish being pounded into the fine black sand of the ocean floor by mountains of angry almond water. I currently tick none of those boxes. As we pass an increasing number of houses drawing into our eleventh hour of the trumpet concerto, we see what must be the infamous jewel. Even from a kilometer away, I know with absolute certainty, I have no desire to surf Puerto Escondido. Line after line of macking swell marches to shore before fusing into thunderous peaks and exploding forwards to produce freight train barrels almost directly on the shoreline.

Pablo turns off the main highway and we endure the final few dozen potholes to Mexican Pipeline. Sporting a flannel cowboy shirt, tight black jeans, lazy brown eyes and sparse, lengthy facial hairs, he tells us we've arrived and helps carry our boardbags down from the roof as a pair of lithe Swedish girls in bikinis walk out of a hotel across the street.

"Let's stay there hey fellas?"

We perform what should be a simple crossing of the road, but the searing heat means the road-crossing task is accompanied by buckets of sweat. We arrive at the reception, perspiring and breathless, and book a room for three for the night. "With air-con?" "Shit yeah". Once we drop our stuff in the room, there's nothing to do aside from try to figure out a suitable, face-saving excuse for why we shouldn't risk immediate death by surfing this world famous break. We figure we better at least have a proper look at the break from the sand.

We take a seat on the beach, the morning sun blazing our backs. Huge, fluid slabs of ocean are erupting everywhere, there's no order whatsoever. You may as well walk to the beach blindfolded and paddle out wherever your toes end up touching the water.

"Get farrrrrkkkkkkkt!"

Chris is first to spot the feathering top of a gigantic set. The three of us stand immediately. The 30 or so crazed surfers in the water are scratching to the horizon. The first wave of this set is 12 foot and building. Five guys shape up to paddle for it, two commit, paddle full throttle and split the colossal peak. With barely a breath of wind they stroke in to the bomb cleanly, pushing down the face, rising to their feet simultaneously.

At precisely the worst possible moment, the natural-footer taking the left loses his footing. He's mid way down the face of a 15 foot wave, side-lying on his board in a soon to be aborted fetal position. His body weight is completely on the tail, lifting the nose of the board and preventing him nose-diving. He reaches the flat water of the wave's trough milliseconds before a lip, formed from a million Pacific Ocean mega-litres, descends from five metres and thunders through his stomach between his floating ribs and right hip. A wall of whitewash erupts skyward, the front half of his board flies with it. A broken board and a broken man are somewhere in the bedlam of black water.

While watching the carnage going left, I've missed the surfer going right. As he flicks off, his relaxed stance and spread palms by his sides make me think he's probably just had the barrel of his life, his face all smiles. As the second wave of the set approaches I can only assume that smile evaporates. The next wall of water is about to break on his head.

We hurry to the shoreline. A pulverized ghost of a man surfaces face down in the shallows. Three lifeguards run past us, yelling something in Spanish. One motions at me to help. Even in knee-deep water, the sweeping undercurrent force of Puerto Escondido is immense. I dig my toes into the sand and pick the bloke up by the right shoulder while a lifeguard holds his head and neck and the other two hold his legs and left side. We carry him away from the water's edge.

He's a mess, blood streaming from the corners of his mouth. His right foot appears several inches shorter than the left, the impact of the wave on his right side has dislocated his hip, shearing it upwards and back towards his sacrum. Blood oozes from his left side. A jagged laceration runs from atop his left hip to the base of his sternum, shards of fiberglass visible, piercing his stomach. The lifeguards call in an ambulance, bandaging and compressing his wound, telling me to step back.

In moments, he is loaded into an ambulance, blood flowing relentlessly through the bandaging on his side, as well as the corners of his lips. Waves continue their march to shore, the mid morning heat becoming stifling, trumpets blasting from every available speaker, stray dogs trying unsuccessfully to find shade. Welcome to Mexico.

We've seen enough, no surfing today. We head back to the hotel, not to our room, straight to the poolside bar. The first sip of an iced Pacifico beer goes down a treat. The Swedish girls from earlier are setting up for a day of tanning, swimming and being closely watched. Complete attention is now directed at Scandinavian flesh. Images of ocean carnage disappear.

We walk over to some deckchairs by the pool and drop the shirts. Swedes 1 and 2 seem completely unimpressed. They're probably lesbians, or at least blessed with 20/20 vision. Fuck my body is shocking. I quickly put my shirt back on. We decide we best leave them to tan up a little before we introduce ourselves and commence operation swoon. The first Pacifico has gone down far too easily. They're 10 pesos a pop (about $1), that's worth celebrating. We order margaritas to accompany the next round.

Two young guys working at the hotel tell us they can take us to a jump rock thirty minutes drive away. Two American couples, the Swedes, Mark and myself are all keen. We grab some sunscreen and head off with the others, leaving Chris on his lonesome to enjoy a possible nap and a certain wank.

There's a plump Mexican chap at the wheel of a van, waving us in. I jump inside, looking through the window to watch the two local lads advising the Swedes to ride with them on their bikes rather than in the mini-van. Don and fucking Juan let fly with a few thousand revs, the Swedes wrap their arms around our tour guides' waists and squeal as they scream off ahead, leaving behind a cloud of dust and a mini-van empty of nubile Scando skin. Bastards.

Thirty minutes north of Puerto Escondido, Don and Juan have a long way to go to redeem their shameless cutting in on mine and Mark's turf but this jump rock is spectacular. Perched about five metres above the sea, looking out over the Pacific Ocean. I can picture generations of Mayan basket weavers and grass cutters, much like Don and Juan, coming to this spot for thousands of years. This latest generation is blessed with the obvious added benefit of enjoying not only a refreshing swim, but also a high probability of pounding a tanned young tourist with a deep wanderlust.

We take our turns jumping in. Don and Juan ham it up with a *uno, dos, tres* countdown routine for each of us. Gracias muchachos. The water's a crisp few degrees cooler than the hotel pool and an azure blue unlike the brown beach water of Peurto Escondido. I'm treading water at the cliff base, bubbles starting to boil in my alcohol-filled veins. What the fuck are these blokes doing now?

Don and Juan are stripped down to their budgy smugglers, resembling Olympic divers. They stand side by side on the jumping ledge, their backs facing the ocean, rising on the balls of their feet as they simultaneously raise their arms over their heads, bounce through their ankles and launch back-first into the Pacific. Through the descent they complete two perfect forward flips with legs fully extended, elbows by their knees and hands cradling their heels, landing in the water with less splash than most of my visits to the toilet.

You'd think the Swedes have just seen Moses part the Red Sea, screaming, clapping and swimming over to hug the guys. Tall Poppy

Syndrome rages through me, I find little solace in hoping Don and Juan love cock as much as Greg Leganis. The Americans join in, praising the Mexican diving experts too, pleading with them to get a sporting scholarship in a US College. They politely smile away the tribute. Through broken English they explain they couldn't dare leave, their mother is far too ill, their father has passed away and they have three younger sisters to care for. Cry me a river. Only Mark and I can see these two for the Swede-thieving, ridiculously muscle-bound complete cunts they are.

Praise be to Allah, the sermon to Don and Juan eventually comes to an end. We dry off and board the minivan back to the hotel. Don, Juan and the once-were-lesbians drive off on the scooters in the opposite direction. Outplayed by Mexican divers, that stings. We return to the hotel pool and set about drinking to oblivion, passing out in air-conditioned comfort before long.

Mark and I wake the next morning to hangover shattering buckets of ice-cold water in the face. Thanks Chris! He's organized a ride south to one of the finest righthand pointbreaks on Earth, Barra de la Cruz, and is eager for us to hurry up and get moving. We've not really unpacked anything. A few minutes and we're back infront of the hotel. Massive waves are smashing into the Peurto Escondido sand across the street. I'll be glad to never see this place again.

"Hop in guys, please. There will be fine waves past Huatulco. Let's go."

Our driver, Julio, no doubt has a genetically inherited love affair with the blasting trumpet but is considerate of gringo music tastes and pushes Pink Floyd's Dark Side of the Moon cassette into the player. He drives through chaotic traffic littered with cattle, lorries, young children, feral cats, avoiding them all with grace and minimal horn deployment.

As we arrive into Huatulco, Julio suggests we stop for some breakfast, while he gets fuel. We're about 45 minutes from Barra de la Cruz. We pile into huevos rancheros and coffee while Julio fills up the van. Chris notices an old school barber opening up for the day across the street.

"I think I'll get a quick straight razor shave. All right with you guys?"

"Go for it mate."

We walk across the street together, some early morning traffic starting to build. The barber is no more than five feet tall and is aged somewhere between a half to a full century. He's wearing a spotless white coat any professor would be proud of and is, to my seasoned eye, acutely hungover. Chris is committed, only growing cognisant of the mezcal stank on his barber's breath as he leans in to splash the hot towel on Chris's now heavily perspiring face. He reclines in the chair, while the barber gets set up, stumbling about the shop, swinging the razor blade through the air as if he were composing for the Sydney Symphony Orchestra.

I try to be reassuring, "Hawh, this guy is quite the showman. I'll go next." No fucking way will I ever sit in that chair.

221

"You sure Slip? You ever done this before?" These may be Chris' last words.

"Yeah mate, I had the same thing in Peru years ago. They love flashing the blade like that. They all think they're matadors or some shit."

Miraculously, Chris' skin remains cut-free for several strokes. The freshly shorn skin of his cheeks and chin are glistening, the hand of God surely guiding the barber's hands. Here we go, the neck. The barber leans in to clear bristles of neck stubble, millimeters from what we can only pray are billions of platelet rich blood cells raging through Chris' jugular, aware of imminent danger above the surface and ready to clot like they've never clotted before.

The barber uses his left thumb to pull on the underside of Chris' chin, the skin of his neck perfectly taut, his testes somewhere in the vicinity also. Divine intervention is surely involved as the barber's clean razor swipe from the right mandible sets out south towards the sternum with complete control. A split second passes. Jesus, Allah, Buddha and Tom Cruise leave the premises.

"Argh Cheeww!" Chris sneezes. Fuck.

His neck explodes upwards, leaving the blade with no choice. Slit. Shots of bright red launch through the shop, "Fuck, fuck Fuck!!! What happened? Fuck!"

I'm laughing so hard I can't respond. Chris launches from his chair, staring at the mirror as spouts of blood shoot out from his neck.

Slippery

"Shit! Fuck! Fucking fuck!"

The barber puts down the blade and grabs some clinical bandaging. How often does this happen? Through soothing Spanish words we don't understand, he convinces Chris to recline back in the seat and gently applies the bandaging to a fairly small cut, but in a concentrated, blood rich location. A few minutes pass, the blood flow slows.

"Deep breaths bro, deep breaths." Mark's calming words barely match the tears of laughter streaming down his cheeks.

Julio sees us through the shop window and walks in, shaking his head. He speaks with an as yet unseen passion and annoyance with the barber. He then turns to us, "Guys, let's go, please. You should not have come in here without asking me. This man...he is crazy man. Always drunk this man. Please, I hope you are OK. Let's go."

Chris maintains the bandaging in place around his neck as we leave the shop, his cheeks are clean-shaven, his neck is mangled in a confused five o'clock shadow of drying blood and residual bristles. Julio resumes driving in his casual and relaxed way. Within half an hour he takes a right turn off the main highway, the road winding through dusty mountains. Crystal blue ocean glimpses tease us as we drive on. There are occasional green, lush trees, but the cacti dominance prevails. A battered, bullet holed sign welcomes us, 'Barra de la Cruz'. We amble through some final potholes, past a soccer pitch of dust and into Cabanas los Pepes.

"Guys, we are here. Welcome! This hotel, it belongs to my cousin. It is 50 pesos per night, rooms with fan and is closest to the surf break. You will like it here."

"Gracias Julio, thank you so much."

"Hello guys, I'm Pepe. Welcome." The same warm smile of Julio.

"G'day."

The hotel is laid out with eight rooms along the periphery, a large dustbowl car park in the middle and an open-air undercover restaurant in the corner, overlooking a barren field of anorexic cattle. Our room has a latch handle with a padlock, a hammock and three chairs facing onto the dustbowl. There are three single beds inside, a dust floor with besser block walls. A standing fan rotates side to side. Jail chic. Communal toilets are around the corner. 50 pesos also includes breakfast. The surf break is a 15-minute walk through the national park.

We give Julio a few hundred pesos for the long drive south, thank him again and shake hands. He tells us to call when we want to head back north and he can drive us again. Pepe tells us the waves are five foot, the best surf in months, recent rain sculpting the sand perfectly along the length of the point. There's a shop on the beach where you can leave your things, grab lunch and hang out between surfs.

I managed to convince Mark to pack a board for me when I flew direct from Shanghai to meet the boys in LA. It is an absolute gem. I haven't held a board under my arm for way too long. We hurry to put fins in our boards, throw sunscreen, towels and water bottles in a backpack and start the 15-minute walk to the waves.

The dust, the warm, heavy air, the swarming flies, the road's pebbles catching between heal and thong with each step, Chris' freshly half barbered, half butchered face breaking into some awful rash, none of it matters, not one iota. The first view of Barra de la Cruz as we pass over the final crest and down into the bay, you could be facing execution and still be aware of one thing only; how perfect is this place?

Every surfer's cartoon scribbles have transformed to reality, wave paradise is unfolding before us. A beach shack laden with hammocks from every available post spills on to the sand, surfers waxing up in its shade then jogging up the point. To the right, a headland covered in earth brown boulders drops into the sapphire water. A lonesome rock stands tall out of the water a few metres into the sea at the most distant edge of the headland, waves standing up as they approach it, pulses of swell unraveling into endless barrels as they hug the sandbank from the top of the point all the way to shoreline half a kilometer down the line. The wave faces light up in the mid morning sun, a handful of surfers stroking effortlessly into faultless top-to-bottom barrels, forming silhouettes behind the lip, lines of swell stacked to the horizon.

A slight onshore wind is starting to feather at the crests of the waves as we get ready in the beachfront shack, gorgeous barrels becoming playful walls, lips of whitewater fluff begging to be destroyed. An assortment of surfers from each wave-blessed corner of the planet, as well as some poor landlocked guys from Switzerland and Montana, say "ola" as we go about our pre-surf routine. Those lucky enough to have been in the water at first light are now resting, sipping on Fantas, Sprites or Coronas, watching from their hammocks as Barra de la Cruz puts on a show.

"Just run up the point to the very last little bay of sand, then paddle from there and hope no sets clean you up. Then you're out there." A Californian who's been here plenty of times, gives us as much info as we need and we're off. As we start our jog up the point, I see five waves lined up the length of the bay with five guys flying down the line on each of them.

We paddle straight through a lull and into the takeoff zone. There is a spattering of blokes waiting patiently for the next set. There's no hassling thanks to a horizon stacked with perfect waves en route. Mark nabs the first wave of the trip, taking off seamlessly as a wave bounces off the outer rock and flies past me, lining up 500m of fluid ecstasy.

A guy to my inside squanders the second wave of the set, floundering rather than paddling. He looks to double dip and lines up to paddle for the third wave of the set. Fuck that, I paddle straight past him without a hint of remorse, having traveled halfway across the globe to be here, this thing's mine. A bounce of side-wash off the headland wedges the wave a foot bigger as I get to my feet, sling-shotting me across the face. I feel my left foot hugging the deck grip as I drive off the bottom and up the face into the most welcoming piece of lip I've ever seen. I glide back down, taking in the clear view to the ocean floor racing beneath, before driving once more off the bottom. I'm shaky on my feet, far too much time has passed since my last surf, but the waves are insanely perfect, you can't go wrong.

Three hours pass; surf till your legs shake, jog up the point, paddle, hoot, surf, smile, jog back up the point, hoot, paddle, surf, smile, jog. I feel my shoulders aching, retinas baking, guts growling, wet boardshorts tearing away layers of inner thigh skin with every jog round the headland. I ride my last wave to shore and walk back to the shack.

"Beer, Slip?" Chris is lazing in a hammock, a Corona in his hand, an overload of surf stoke shining through his sun-fried eyes.

"Definitely."

Two coronas and three fajitas later, we're asleep in our hammocks, the blazing afternoon sun making it difficult to see guys ripping the afternoon walls to shreds. 4pm and we paddle out for the afternoon session. The setting sun wreaks further havoc on heavily glazed eyes. Surfers, bong-head and non-bong-head variety, can't help redeye syndrome. I've long been accused of smoking the peace pipe, my first physio boss threatening to fire me for persistent red eyes. 'Stop turning up to work stoned!'

It was her fault, giving me the afternoon shift. I've never smoked in my life, but living on Australia's east coast, the rising sun is the harsh mistress that leaves pterygiums in her wake. No surfer can escape. I was 23 at the time, fit, tanned and I'm pretty sure my cougar boss took pleasure in accusing me of being naughty. She was gagging for a young pleasure wand. I really should have just given her a pounding.

Equally gagging were all the neglected middle aged mums I'd been tasked with teaching Pilates two nights a week. 'Great class, Flynn, have you tried that new bar round the corner? I'm heading there now if you're keen?' Gravity had taken hold of these ladies and no amount of poorly instructed Pilates could change that, but again, I should probably have pounded the lot of them. The Toy Boy window closes far too quickly.

We surf till dark, the onshore wind abating to complete glass, barrels throwing wide at the take off, warping uninterrupted all the way to shore. It's pitch black as we stumble up the beach for the final time, pack up, give the shack man a stack of pesos and walk through exhaustion back to Pepes. "How good was that", "How good is this", "Fuck I'm buggered", "Farking starving aye", "This place is fucking sick," modern day philosophers in quite the tete-a-tete.

Twelve days of sand-bottom barrel bliss at Barra de la Cruz pass in a euphoric, overtired, sweat-filled trance. If there is one sacrifice you have to make to enjoy this heavenly piece of south Mexican manna, it is the foregoing of sleep. You cannot sleep here. No chance. It is so fucking hot. We spend each night on sopping wet mattresses filled with litres of sweat. We chat through the night reliving past glory days, and play music or podcasts until pure exhaustion finds us collapsing to the lightest of snoozes around 5am only to be woken within moments by the first rumblings of fellow surfers waxing their boards and gathering their things for the walk to the beach in the pre dawn dark.

After twelve days, having shed several kilos and surfed countless perfect waves, it's time to go. We bid Pepe farewell and shake hands once more with Julio as he arrives at Cabanas Los Pepes. We load boardbags onto his van and begin the journey towards the international terminal at Oaxaca airport.

....

"Ladies and Gentlemen, please ensure your seatbelts are fastened, we will now be commencing our descent into Los Angeles." I'm looking out the window at the urban sprawl of the city of Angels beneath but my thoughts are filled with images of Girls Gone Wild, running amuck along the Vegas strip. We will momentarily be landing in L.A before connecting through to Vegas.

Going about our transit routine in LAX, our three night itinerary in Vegas becomes two. In the age of terror alerts, a bomb threat has grounded all flights for the evening. We can jump on a bus to Vegas, but I've got a better idea. I Facebook message a girl I'd hooked into a few years earlier during her holiday to Sydney. She already has plans to have dinner with her girlfriend, but says I should join, asking to bring my friends from my recent Mexican Facebook posts along. Stalker. Awesome. Chris says he has no interest in joining, Mark's keen though, fingers crossed the friend is hot and desperate. Can always hope.

We make sure our flight to Vegas is booked and confirmed for the following day, as well as back up bus tickets in case the terror hotline stays on red alert. Mark and Chris book rooms in the Standard Hotel. Mark's highly optimistic and locks in the honeymoon suite. Chris takes a simple studio room.

Mark and I are now shaved and spruced and join Chris to sip on Miller's Draughts, ready to embark on 'date night'. We tell Chris not to wait up and cab it to the restaurant. The entrance is appropriately swanky, a fine establishment to commence our US dating careers.

"Hi there, I believe there is a booking for four under the name, Stephanie."

"Yes, follow me gentlemen."

We're led through the restaurant filled with endless tables of yesteryear's Stepford Wives who have now been liberated through lucrative divorces and botox addictions into fixed-faced, bling-laden, uber-cougars.

"Boys!! Boys!! Well hellloooo! So good to see you again." Stephanie looks stunning. She probably chose this place because she wanted to be the youngest woman here by several decades. I'm fine with that.

"You look amazing Steph. I'm so glad my flight was cancelled. This has worked out perfectly. Great to see you." Go for it Slip, lay it on thick, you debonair hound dog, you.

"Thanks handsome."

"This is my friend, Mark."

"Great to meet you. My friend is a few minutes late. She'll be here soon OK."

"Cool, no problem."

I sit next to Steph and she's already getting busy, stroking my leg. I give thanks to the overzealous staff at LAX and scandalous headlines Rupert Murdoch deploys to create a nation of burka fearing paranoids. Smirking at my good fortune, I look up. A spectacular brunette is walking our way.

"Mark, here's Katie." Are you serious? Are you fucking serious?

All smiles, wearing tight black jeans hugging a pair of legs Jessica Alba would envy, a soft grey woolen knitted top that, despite its flowing looseness, clings for life on to breasts of utmost pert, high beaming directly towards us, towards me, surely. A flawless olive skinned face, the perfect combination of angles and curves. Librarian black rimmed spectacles bridging the cutest of button noses. This is Mark's blind date? The flukey fucking bastard. I'm crushed with jealousy, picturing Katie throwing her glasses to the floor, rolling her neck, flinging Goddess hair in tantric circles like the lead groupie backstage at a 1991 Guns and Roses gig, chugging bourbon from the bottle.

"Katie, meet Mark and Flynn." Stephanie and Katie giggle hysterically. Mark and I try to suppress primal grunts. Our brains send all available blood cells in a crotch-al direction.

"Great to meet you, Katie"

"Hi Katie, how you going?"

"Guys, great to meet you. Please, please don't call me Katie, my friends call me Special K."

Special K…Special Fucking K. The sort of girl you would slit your best mate's throat, just to hold her hand, you would gladly drive a dagger through new born Jesus' pure heart in the manger, to grab Special K by the ankles, raise her legs to the sky and drive your shoulders through the back of her calves, roar like a love-starved lion and drive as deep into her being as human anatomy would allow. Baby Jesus deserved it. What good could come from having women like this on Earth?

Mark has struck gold. Special K is lapping up his rubbish chat, throwing her head back laughing at everything he says, reaching across the table to stroke his elbow. Unbelievable. I'm stealing glances under the table to see if footsie shenanigans are taking place, none as yet. I stretch my legs as far as possible in Katie's direction, hoping for a case of mistaken lower limb identity.

Stephanie orders for all of us, I pick out a bottle of red and Mark senses this as a momentous occasion, demanding we grab a bottle of bubbly too. The chancey prick. The girls ask about Mexico. Mark gives a particularly shameless recount of the life-and-death waves of Puerto Escondido. He was now out in the waves that day of course. The girls lap it up, Special K particularly enthralled. Jealousy boils away. The girls excuse themselves to the restrooms.

"They're probably comparing blow job techniques."

"You'd have to think so, Slip. Special K is so fucking hot man. Holy shit."

"It's ridiculous, I've never seen anything like it. And as much as it shits me, she is loving you."

Steph and Miss K arrive back at the table. We stand like the chivalrous gents of a long gone era.

"Guys, do you think after dinner you'd like to come to my place? I'm house-sitting at this amazing mansion in Beverley Hills. There's a huge pool overlooking the whole city. You'll love it." Yes, yes, a million times yes!!!

"Of course, that sounds incredible." Mark replies. I'm speechless, fairly certain a few warning shots have fired off in my pants already. I'm consumed with envy at Mark's imminent Special K conquest and a little distracted by Steph's hands giving my todger a welcome stroke under the table.

Special K's phone starts ringing. She looks disinterested at the screen when she sees the caller ID and places the phone on the table, switches it to silent and leaves it to ring out.

"It's fine Katie, you can answer the call if you like," Mark, such a considerate fourth wheel.

"I'd rather not, it's my stupid boyfriend. He is so annoying." Mark almost chokes on his sip of wine. I can't resist a faint smile.

Katie's phone continues to flash relentlessly on the table, three messages in less than a minute.

"What does he want?" Katie is clearly peeved at this inconvenience. Steph now also seems annoyed at this inconsiderate boyfriend ruining our night. I mean the hide of some people. Who the hell does he think he is?

"He says he's just flown in, wahoo, asking where am I and he'll be on his way soon. Oh great…God, he's so annoying."

Mark should rise above our confusion and snatch his chance. Special K is spectacular and, in possession of a boyfriend or not, she's obviously craving a good ravishing.

"I'm sure he can't be too annoying. I mean, he is your boyfriend and you are such an amazing girl, he must be a great guy." Mark is not only defending this mystery man, he seems to be auditioning to give the best man speech at Special K's wedding to the bloke. I start to kick Mark under the table, he continues on regardless.

"If he calls again, please answer." I'm going to be sick.

"Umm, OK yeah, I guess you're right." Special K is transformed from a giggling Goddess bursting with joy to now looking bored and depressed, wishing she was anywhere else.

Within less than ten minutes, Mr. Special K rolls into the restaurant, a speccy wanker. Special K, how could you? He's flown in on a private jet. What a cunt. His parents live in Moscow, Rio, Sarajevo, Freo, I dunno, some 'o' place. If he's not telling you how much money he has, he's making sure you know how awesome a DJ he is. I seriously consider glassing him with the bottle of bubbles. Do the world a favour and I'll be the one sent to prison. Maybe a conjugal visit from Special K could make it all worthwhile.

The night descends rapidly into a non-event. Dating, what a waste of time. Mr. Special K pays the bill though. Maybe he's not so bad. Special K disappears from our lives forever in the passenger seat of a black Ferrari. Mark returns to the honeymoon suite at the Standard Hotel and promptly runs up a $60 bill ordering porn on the hotel's credit-card-automated-adult-channel. I go home with Stephanie and unleash a couple lonely weeks of Central American buildup in the undercarriage like a milk truck hitting a brick wall, back of the net.

. . . .

Breathing easy knowing the world's terror alertness has been switched back to neutral, we're back in the air, headed to Sin City. The desert gives way to a clearly defined oasis grid of high-rise opulence, Eiffel Towers, Arcs de Triomphe and aqua blues of five-star pools. Disembarking from the plane, we're greeted by a dozen poker machines in the airline lounge. Obese men in pearly white sneakers and oversized T-shirts are playing the 'slots', watching their hard-earned greenbacks disappear while they stroke their goatie beards and seem genuinely surprised when the computer programmed machines don't rain quarters, nickels and dimes.

We're booked in at the Hard Rock Hotel and walk through the terminal. The hotel's mini-van is waiting and we cruise through the early afternoon Nevada traffic humming with tourists and hawkers, Lamborghinis and double-decker buses, circus performers and busty blondes. The iconic jumbo Hard Rock guitar signals our arrival.

$40 per night goes a long way in terms of Las Vegas accommodation currency. Our suite is incredible. The proven theory being, of course, lure the masses in with cheap flights and accommodation, pump the clubs, bars and casinos with neon lighting, zero sunlight and excess oxygen, and watch testosterone, blind hope and free drinks concoct into a sea of splashed cash, credit-card debt and anxiety-filled journeys home; The American Dream.

We each shower, shave, spruce and mentally prepare for minimal sleep over the next 48 hours. Mark and Chris have graced Vegas with their presence before and feel a certain honour in introducing me to the place. "Let's grab a cab to the Palms. You're gonna love it, Slip."

The Palms Hotel stands tall in the Vegas skyline, a monster skyscraper in the Nevada desert. Mark leads the way in as soon as the cab drops us off. We waltz straight past a line of people waiting for the maxi-elevator to take them to the nightclub on the top floor, 53 stories above. We continue on to some private elevator. Chris and Mark are shining as tour guides already.

"Level 52 please, mate."

"Of course."

"Gentlemen, have a tremendous evening."

"You too mate."

The lift doors open, revealing a sleek, chrome bar directly opposite.

A lone barman is serving two Indian men. As we take our first steps forwards towards the bar, a flood of curvaceous flesh, green velvet, soft leather, and fuzzy white fur reveals itself to our right. The Playboy Casino. Playboy bunnies parade the floor, womanly perfection encased in one-piece black leather suits, pokey bunny ears, black stilettos and white furry rabbit tails, serving drinks, dealing black jack, scooping dice at the craps table, spinning the roulette wheel.

The bar is perched a few steps higher than the game floor, a supreme viewing platform. The bartender is far from bunny material. He must surely be the most fortunate, balding, chubby, thirty-something bloke in Vegas.

"Three tequilas, thanks."

"What ya reckon, Slip?"

"You never disappoint."

Mark parks himself at the black jack table, the casino's lone cherry top bunny is dealing cards as Mark goes about his Austin Powers routine, holding on any hand in the early double digits. Chris and I admire the scenery a while longer from the bar, watching the plebs splashing cash and the Goddesses splashing skin. We neck our way through some Heinekens and tequilas then join the craps table.

The rules of the game escape me, I'm guided wholly by the reaction of those around me as to what is happening, amused to see my chip stack building with each roll of the dice. It's my turn to roll and the soft breath from Miss December's lips into my quivering dice-filled fist almost sends me to the floor. The dice hit the back wall. Who cares what numbers come up, but everyone cheers, chips flying all over. Miss December wraps her arms around me, her bunny ears poking into my eyes as she leans up, kissing me on the cheek. I pick her up behind the thighs and shoulder blades, twirling her through the air. She loves it, I assume. The bouncers aren't impressed. I'm politely asked to leave.

We relocate to the nightclub upstairs. A huge rectangle bar forms the epicenter of a pulsating mass of sweating, alcohol-fuelled revelers. Mark muscles in to the bar, his black jack winnings barely accounting for three Heinekens and accompanying Sambucca shots. We down the shots and move outside to an open air balcony overlooking Vegas, sipping beers 53 stories above Sin City, admiring the neon and readying for a dance floor offensive.

We return inside, the scent of North American skank guides us like sonar. Chris instinctively drops a few shirt buttons, allowing his Mexican-induced tan to blaze through chest hairs and sweat beads into the forgiving dim lights. He quickly spots a pair of girls looking vulnerable. Like most female duos, there is a beauty and a beast, a star and a manager, a swan and a pig. Chris eyes off the stunner, while Mark must owe him a favour I'm unaware of, as he goes to work on the manager. I watch on from close-by, keen to get my own slice of tang, but also interested in watching the boys' spading performance.

Mark's not short of good chat, but this manager is proving

particularly protective of her star client. "She has a boyfriend, you know. Brandon. He's at home in Minneapolis. He plays ice hockey." The words sloughing out of her mouth at Mark, slobber oozing down the side of her overfed face and numerous chins. Her name is Mindy or Kimmy or something equally hideous and managerial.

Mark leans in close to her ear, reassuring and composed, "Oh, don't worry, Chris has a girlfriend too, he just loves his dancing. His girlfriend understands. She's in a wheelchair, you know, just terrible. They met when Chris, well Dr Chris to be fair, was completing his medical studies. She'd just been in a car accident and was in intensive care at hospital. We're going to help him pick out an engagement ring tomorrow, he wants to propose when we get home." Yet another stellar performance from a wing-man of the highest pedigree. Chris is single and as far removed from medical practice as possible.

"Wow, that's amazing." The manager's protective shield now shattered, she is close to tears, true love does exist. Not all men are bastards. She watches Chris sweating profusely, another button being dropped, grinding his hips into her friend's arse. He's grinding her like a fucking maniac. Through my eyes, I see a grown man gyrating disgracefully about to blow like Vesuvius at any moment all over a pretty girl in a little green dress. Through the manager's sob story obtunded vision, she sees George Clooney saving lives, a modern superhero armed only with a stethoscope, white coat and winsome smile, full of purpose marching the hospital wards only to find everlasting love with a paraplegic in intensive care. Why wouldn't he like to partake in a little harmless dancing? He's entitled.

"You look so pretty in that dress. Where did you get it? I'd like to buy my sister a present tomorrow. It will be her birthday when I get home. A dress like that would be perfect." Mark is just going to town now. He winks at me as these lies pass his lips. The hideous beastly manager is putty, oblivious to Dr Chris and her two-timing friend walking hand in hand to the stairwell. They open the fire stair door and start groping frantically. The ferocity of their passion finds a brief reprieve when the slightest hint of guilt forces the girl to pull away for a moment.

"I can't do this…" She steps back to the stairwell door, trying to push it open. It's locked shut. She tries again, and again. Not the brightest this one. She tries once more, "I think we're locked in." Chris does well to hide his delight. He pushes her against the door, licking the entirety of her face with everything but sensuality. Having groped most of her body, he settles on her hair, breasts and inner thighs. His long arms and wandering fingers are everywhere. She's breathless. Her pants are now round her ankles, impressive jugs out in the bright lights of the fire stair's fluorescent globes for Chris to rummage and security guards behind CCTV screens to drop spunk to.

"Fuck me, Brandon, fuck me! Fuck me!" Brandon? Chris doesn't correct her. He definitely introduced himself as Chris. She miraculously produces a condom as if from thin air. What sort of loving girlfriend takes condoms with her for a trip to Vegas? Slut. Excellent. Chris unzips his jeans and unwraps the johnny round his cock before any guilt or remorse for this poor Brandon bastard can stop him from finishing the job.

Moments earlier, her emerald green knee length dress was hugging her luscious body in a suggestive and alluring way. It's now wrapped around her waist like an Amazonian tree snake, revealing immaculate bare breasts and a freshly waxed United States of American puss. She wraps her legs around Chris's waist, flinging her laced knickers a few stories below with a well-practiced flick of the heels. Chris's pants are around his ankles now as he runs his fingers through her hair, his knuckles pressed against the fire door behind her head, he thrusts his hips back and forth with the force and precision of Wayne Gretzky.

Despite being very obviously fucked, she continues to yell, "Fuck me, fuck me, fuck me, Brandon!" Chris is pumping and pounding as furiously as he can in a semi squat, his quads sure to fail him soon and the persistent "Brandon" screams starting to wreak havoc on his focus. He summons every ounce of gluteal, quad, calf and abdominal strength for a thunderous finale. With his and her weight completely balanced on the balls of his toes, the door yanks open, a smoker escaping to the stairwell is now lying beneath a human crush of heat and desire, grog and infidelity.

The crash of three humans tumbling to the floor booms through the club. A thousand eyes focus on Chris's bare bum, Brandon's girlfriend's ragged blonde hair and some bloke's lone hand clutching a pack of Marlboros and a lighter underneath the carnage. The music stops, the crowd absorbs the scene and applauds.

Chris tries to stand, hunched over his hard on. His fire-stair companion is crying, racing to the bathroom with one breast still out, her panties long gone. The mystery door opener rises to his feet and admires his work.

"To Chris, the Stair Fucker!" We cheers the great man and are soon making our way back to wherever the Hard Rock Hotel is to pass out.

By midday we find our way to the world famous Hard Rock Hotel pool. In every direction groups of perfectly tanned and proportioned girls with fake hair, fake boobs and fake, impossibly white teeth parade, swim, and lounge. Muscle bound gym junkie Jersey Shore type dudes are equally prevalent, sipping mineral waters while finding innovative ways to flex their steroided bodies or say things to reveal to anyone bored enough to listen, that they are indeed as stupid as they look.

We group three plastic deck chairs in knee-deep water and drink our way steadily through the afternoon. Within a few hours we're pleasantly boozed and fully recharged, ready to hit the tables, the stairwells, anything the night and Sin City has on offer. We quickly freshen up and decide to start the evening off in the Hard Rock casino.

The Hard Rock has the town's second most impressive hiring policy. The Playboy Casino is the obvious clear standout, but the Hard Rock is a distinguished second with an army of part-time models, full-time sharks, manning the tables. Preying on the meek, they deal cards with precision. The hand is faster than the eye, especially when the eye is concentrated wholly and completely on the delightful cleavage of the card dealer, clad suitably in leather, blessed with a disarming smile, an ice-cold heart and lightning quick numeric mastery.

I am impressed and frightened, the fear any bright man should have around girls with the sharpness of intellect that belies the softness of their curves. They are dangerous creatures. They know it. Hard Rock knows it. The only people clueless are in the torrent of overzealous black jack and poker enthusiasts clawing to be on the floor. Money pours forth from their pockets, chips disappearing from their grasp across green felt tables into Hard Rock coffers. It's clinical. I nurse a bottle of Heineken and cruise the casino floor, admiring the velocity of wealth distribution in the house's direction. Mark and Chris are making friends and losing money on one of the many craps tables.

"Let's hit a nightclub hey? Fucking sick of losing money at this place. Let's get some chicks." No shortage of libido for stair-fucker, Chris.

"Suits me mate."

Mark leads the charge to the hotel taxi rank and we take off to MGM Casino, some new nightclub there is all the rage and his mate, Rodney, works the door. With a name like that, he is sure to be a legend.

"Mark! Hi man, glad you made it. Babes everywhere tonight, you'll love this place."

"Cheers Rodney, this is Flynn and Chris."

"Great to have you here fellas. Listen, take this pass and hand it to the girl just inside the door, no cover charge for you guys. And you'll get a bottle of bubbles on the house too. My treat. Go get busy."

The club is called 'Liquid', an arena of flesh and sweat. A huge dance floor is the central focus. It's a jumbling mess of limbs and hair, soft shoulders and bouncing booty. It's surrounded by podiums with bikini-clad dancers, three sleek bars fortifying the dance floor from every angle aside from the entrance.

As I enjoy the first sip of free champagne, I turn to my right. Two gorgeous girls stand awkwardly, looking extremely confused.

"Hi there, would you like a drink?"

"Oh, yes please. Thank you! Where are you from?"

"Hey, no worries, pleasure. I'm from Sydney, here for a few days with a couple of friends."

"That's great! We're here from San Diego. It's Lisa's 21st birthday today."

"No way. Happy Birthday. I think we better get you some champagne, Lisa."

Lisa and Macquenzie. Complete stunners. There is a third girl too, dear oh dear, she must be their kooky Aunt or something. She's horrible. I obviously don't catch her name, but can assume it's Lynne or Susan, something suitably cougar-ish. In the process of introductions, Mark and Chris immediately take Lisa and Macquenzie by the hands and force them on to the dance floor. I'm left all alone with the rubbish litter of the trio, chit-chatting.

I re-visit the bar, grabbing another bottle of bubbles and a cheeky Sambucca shot for myself. Returning to refill everyone's glasses, Mark and Chris are making aggressive plays for their dance partners. I'm cursing myself for making the introductions, all the while trying to deal politely with this cougar's continued unwanted advances. She's stroking my elbow, wrapping her arm around me, trying to do the lean in. On me! That's my move, baby. Back off.

"Are you OK, Flynn? Don't you like me?" Fuck's sake, I only just met you.

"No, you're great." You're rubbish.

"Kiss me." No way.

"Nah, nah, that's OK." Back off, cougar.

"Do you have a girlfriend at home? Is that it?" Perfect way out. Say yes.

"No, no girlfriend." You idiot!

"Well, are you a faggot or something?!" What the fuck?

"Whoah, whoah, calm down." I'm John West and you are just what I reject. Simple.

"You faggot!" Wow. Cougars…so easily upset. Their deductive reasoning for being shunned needs some fine-tuning, or a mirror, at the very least.

I walk away, leaving the homophobic cougar to find fresh meat. She works quickly. I turn around as I reach the bar to see her pashing on with some other dude. You have to admire the ferocity. Mark and Chris are also making out with the girls on the dance-floor. Fuck this, I'm out.

As I'm leaving, I take in the whole scene and lock eyes on one of the podium dancers. I walk straight back to Rodney at the front of the 'Liquid' queue, "mate, what's the best strip joint in town?" I have no idea from where this question has risen. Strip clubs aren't something I enjoy. The Sydney clubs are foul, crack-whore dens, at best.

"Flynn, my man, that's easy, Spearmint Rhino. Spearmint fucking Rhino. Cab it there in about ten minutes brother. The shit there is crazy town man."

"Have a good night, Rodney. You should see the boys soon, they've both picked up some little hotties."

"Oh yeah, boom baby. Adios buddy."

I walk through the MGM lobby, past the lion, straight to the cab rank, "Spearmint Rhino please mate."

"Yes, sir. Excellent choice."

It's closing in on 11pm, the night is still young by any standards, least of all Vegas. I have to be in LA tomorrow night by 5pm for the flight back to Singapore. There's still plenty of time to get rowdy and feel the reassuring touch of fake breasts in a wide-eyed face.

"Here you are sir. Have a great night." The cabbie is all smiles, laughing into the darkness as he drives away. How many blokes just like me has he dropped at this place? He's probably bought his house on these very fares alone.

I walk in, paying the $30 cover charge for the privilege. There are some private rooms to my left as I make my way through a short hallway to the prime showground. It resembles the Qantas lounge, businessmen-looking types seated at couches with small tables nursing their drinks, while they chat to their colleague opposite. Only there's more perfectly sculpted breasts than I had imagined the world possessed gracing the men's faces. Asians, Europeans, Americans, Latinos, Africans. Dazzling tanned skin, impossibly magical lioness hair, outfits revealing essentially every anatomical feature of feminine curvaceousness, while leaving you pleading with the Lord above to reveal just a sliver more.

I take a seat. Within three seconds a scandalously arousing girl asks if I'd like a drink and a lap dance.

"Beer, yep. Lappy…yep."

Twenty bucks for the lap dance and five for the beer. Competitive pricing. I like it. I push any experience of heinous Australian strip clubs to the very back of my thoughts. This is a different world. I brush off countless girls offering further lap dances and sip my Heineken, soaking up the view of this hedonistic strip club in full flight. I decide to swig the last of my beer and head off.

"Would you like to get a private show…?" The voice is all husk and irresistible, a breathless whispered suggestion that may as well have been shouted with a loudspeaker. My ears scream at the rest of me to get the damn private show before I even have a chance to view what I'll be privately seeing. I turn my bewildered glance to look straight into the eyes of a Latino deity.

"Umm, yeah, private show, great. Let's go."

Within an instant, I'm gracefully taken by my quivering hand and led away by this blonde haired, brown eyed, olive skinned supernatural being.

"The private show will be two hundred dollars." She could have said two million, there is no saying no to that voice. The forceful clout of hushed Latino rolls from her lips. If there is a polar opposite audio experience to the Aussie twang, it is indeed the Latino hush.

"No problem."

I'm led into an L-shaped corridor, a sweeping lounge along the entirety of the L-shaped wall, divided about every half a metre by floor to ceiling carpeted columns, providing a certain degree of seclusion. The extremely dim lighting is equally as effective. I'm instructed to sit down. There could be someone next to me, divided by the petition, having boobs rubbed all over his face, I don't know, but safely assume. It may be a private show, but the actual privacy is somewhat debatable

The almond brown skin of this taut Latino is encased in the whitest of bikinis, her muscularly slender curves wanting to fight free of that pure white restraint with every movement. There is a hint of a white skirt too, draping barely a few inches below her waist, essentially non-existent. She sits next to me, the space available on the couch between petitions barely sufficient to accommodate two people, leaving plenty of overlapping thigh. I look down in wonder at the sculpted perfection of her right thigh resting on top of my grey corduroy pants. Absorbed in the study of this leg, I look up to see that barely a few metres away, the corridor of Spearmint Rhino is bustling with bright lights and a stream of bright-eyed visitors, impatient at the ATM, chomping to get to the showroom with their wallets stacked.

"What is your name?" Ah, that voice.

"Flynn"

"I have never heard this name. I like it very much." Yeah, sure you do.

"What's your name?"

"I cannot tell you my real name, I am sorry. But call me Princess. I am from Cuba."

"OK, Princess. That name suits you very well"

Smiling, in one move she transitions from being seated to my right, to straddling me, staring into the depths of my eyes with unnerving concentration.

"I love your eyes, you have beautiful blue eyes." She's laying it on thick now. My eyes are equally as ordinary as every other man on Earth. I have to admire her exuberance for her job, but this is getting silly and as I start to laugh, she leans in, kisses me. I'm in shock. Is this part of the protocol? I've had the odd private show before and no stripper ever started passionately kissing me. I'd become a little over enthused on the Gold Coast once many years ago, letting my fingers stray a tad, and was immediately ordered to vacate that particular premises. Not an easy task when you're raging fit to burst. I hunched my way out of the place quasimodo style, cursing my wandering hands and their heartless enforcing of the no touching policy.

So, what the hell is going on here? She pushes me against the wall, leaning in with full force, her right hand grabbing the roots of my hair, her left arm pushing my right shoulder back firmly into the wall. I wrap both hands through her hair and make out with this Cuban stripper like we we're on the dance floor during a Year 10 high school formal and Dirty Dancing's 'Time of my Life' is filling the airwaves. After a few minutes, she sits back next to me, the corridor lights glaring as though I've just woken from a dream, but here she is, seated to my right, my Cuban stripper in the dove white bikini.

"I just want to suck your dick." The words every man would love to hear, delivered with lustful breathlessness through the fleshy lips of a cock hungry Cuban. Before I can even answer her, or text all my mates, she's unbuttoned the fly of my pants and is nuzzling away downstairs like she's licking a hokey pokey ice cream waffle cone in the harsh summer heat. I thank the heavens above as I look down at this sea of dyed blonde hair flowing up and down.

Despite not wanting this moment to ever stop, I'm a little put off by being conspicuously noshed off with wafer thin petitions either side of me and the glaring lights of the corridor in front. Sensing this, Princess takes a well-earned breather and says there is a more private area in the far corner of the room. She pulls my shirt over the tent pitcher she's erected and leads me to this secluded nook. Being led by her hand, I notice other fellas between petitions, breasts being thrust in their faces, usual lap dance frivolities. I don't witness anyone else's todgers being sucked on though. I swell with pride. I just can't stop swelling.

Princess knows how to find seclusion. This far corner is indeed a step up on the privacy ladder. The corner of the room offers a much larger dividing petition and the space itself is triple the other areas. She pushes at my chest, flinging me down to the seat, as she kneels in front of me, staring into my eyes she claimed were so incredible as her hands sweep from my knees straight to my crotch. She is true to her word. She really does just want to suck that dick. God bless Cuba.

Minutes pass as I mess her perfect hair to straggled knots. I'm absorbed in the absurdity of the moment. What the hell is going on here? Princess crawls up my chest, her breasts yet to break free of the pure white bikini top, she leans in to whisper in my left ear, my eyes eating the bikini, my hands wrapped around her waist.

"I want you to fuck me. Fuck me, Flynn". I can't respond, I grab her by the back of the head and pull her lips to mine, gorging on them while untying her top. She stands up, hazelnut nipples and divine Latino breasts, an hourglass body of taut supple skin. She stares a mischievous smile as she spins to face away from me, my world now consisting of premium Cuban booty veiled in a transparent white skirt and ready to burst through her bikini bottom with the slightest flex. My hands reach and hold these gluteus most maximus, Princess twists her neck, looking down at me with magnificently wicked eyes as she flexes forwards, her upper body disappearing to leave glutes from heaven atop perfect pins. Maintaining her stare while holding her body at ninety degrees to her legs, she reaches her waist, removing the white panties to her ankles. The movement is so fluid, so inviting, her look into my eyes is suggestive of only one thing, devour me. With both hands, I squeeze Princess' regal rump and dive tongue first into her Cuban ring piece, licking like a dehydrated Kalahari bushman on beads of dew on a sole green leaf in the desert dawn. I lick for my life in that delectable cave of Cuban perfection, chocolate fecal heaven in the seedy depths of Sin City.

Glazed and breathless, I retreat from the buffet between Princess' cheeks, resting my back against the couch. Princess, still facing away from me, holds my eyes while backing towards me, slowly, so fluid. Her pants wrapped around her left ankle, white veil of a skirt now a belt around her waist. She slides my pants to my knees. I grab her waist, watching the muscles of her spine arch, her expert and exquisite hips guide my bare backed Down Under todger straight into a clenched Cuban puss so smooth and welcoming, I momentarily don't care less that I'm probably in the process of contracting AIDS.

I'm fucking a Cuban stripper in Las Vegas at midnight on the last day of my surf trip. I'm fucking her no dom. I've just eaten her arsehole. I'm going straight to hell, via Singapore. I'm going to look like Tom Hanks in Philadelphia within months. I am a dead man fucking. I suppress every shred of grey matter in my brain trying to process the situation from a sexual health viewpoint and focus instead on the more urgent task of fucking this Cuban in a manner Castro would be proud of. Viva la Revolucion!

"I want to fuck you all night, Flynn". Yeah Princess, I want to let you. I expel some sort of grunt, it sounds horrendous.

"Let's go to a private room". As she says this, we take a small rest, though my unprotected little fella is still inside her, wriggling madly without any hip and abdominal muscle flexing to assist.

"Yep, awesome. Let's do that."

"It is eight hundred dollars for the private room."

"Wow, really…"

"Yes, but we have champagne and our whole room. We can fuck all night."

"OK" You had me at 'it'.

I still haven't processed any of the preceding 45 minutes. What has just happened? A stripper kissed me. She definitely kissed me. I knew the rules. I didn't want to get kicked out. I didn't touch her, let alone kiss her. She kissed me. Then she sucked my dick. She sucked my dick. Then paraded that immaculate Cuban booty in my face. I had to lick it. For minutes? I had no choice. If perfect Cuban ring piece is thrust towards your face, you lick boy, and you lick good. I licked till my lips were cracked dry. Then I fucked her. No dom. Rough.

We are now walking to some distant room for a more intimate private show, a room to fuck all night...I should run for the hills, with my AIDS covered dick bouncing side to side in my Reg Grundies and HIV-filled blood in my veins. Instead, Princess is leading me back through the corridor, through the showroom, to a region in the back of the complex, reserved for Spearmint Royalty, the big spenders. The VIP end of town, reserved for the particularly stupid and frivolous. I already have a HIV death sentence. Who gives a fuck? Go out all guns blazing.

"Welcome sir, I understand you would like to take advantage of a private room." The gatekeeper is a 6'6 bald headed, smooth scalped, muscle bound, ex navy seal looking character with a black suit, crisp white shirt and polite smile that says, do not fuck with me.

"Ah yeah, please mate."

"We will require some identification and your credit card please, sir."

"No problem, here you are."

"Ah, Australian. Mr. James, welcome to Spearmint Rhino. Please, right this way."

For eight hundred dollars, I am treated to an almost private room. Yes, there are four walls, though the entrance resembles a sort of fish and chips shop inspired drapery affair. The entire room is essentially a U-shaped couch with an ice bucket standing alone, frosted and glistening in the middle of the room holding a bottle of French champagne waiting to be popped. I take hold of the bottle, hold it over Princess and pretend I'm about to pour it all over her. She takes me by the wrist, pouring bubbles all over her pristine naked body. She holds her face angled to the ceiling, French champagne flows past her closed eyes and over the pink tongue on her full brown lips and wide open mouth and down her bare, impeccable breasts. I throw her to the couch and imagine I'm in the back alleys of Havana, pummeling this puss of perfection into a fish taco pulp.

Moving throughout the room for the next two hours, mixing swigs of champagne with robust licking of Cuban curtains and relentless thrusts of overtired hips. Princess says she has to return home and be ready for her 'real job' at 7am. I ask her to marry me, telling her we can move to Cuba. "I love you!" Barely two days in Vegas and I'm a pathetic shell of a man. She graciously declines my proposal and kisses me goodnight. I walk her back to the main bar, watching her wave goodbye as she disappears forever.

It's shortly after 4am. I'm beyond exhausted. I have AIDS. 100%. But it's been worth it. No regrets. I order a beer, scull it, and take off out the door. I grab a taxi back to the Hard Rock while booking an earlier flight back to Singapore, focused more than ever on the sole reason I'm alive, to make big fucking money.

Liam Carroll

6/ Access Granted to the Big Boy Buttons

Oil, money, power, women, yep, beauty, I'll take it

My third home in under twelve months is a one bedroom apartment in a fortified complex on Club St. It's a short stroll to work, an even shorter walk to plenty of wannabe hip bars and obscenely overpriced restaurants. It's also on the cusp of Singapore's Chinatown, filled with sweating, dinner-plate-faced men in stained yellow singlets and fleeting hairlines, slumped in the endless fluorescent, flimsy plastic chairs of food halls packed with bargain hunting, diabetic MSG addicts. It's a far cry from the Manly beachfront where the Tasman Sea stretches out in crystal blue to New Zealand while Scandinavian backpackers scour the promenade for surfing lessons and Aussie cock, the air filled with palpable convict contentment, that, for our forefathers' sins, they were undeservedly shipped to a distant paradise.

My dear Balmain Tigers are playing against the hated South Sydney Rabbitohs on the only TV channel that every fair dinkum Australian expat in Singapore cannot live without, the Setanta Network. I crank the air-conditioning to its lowest possible setting and grab a beanie from my closet to add to my tracksuit and woolen socks. I'm a greenie sympathizer at heart, I suppose, but my lucrative employment is based wholly on man's dependence on oil and my life prior to Scion involved watching rugby league in the bitter cold of winter. The game is simply better when you're holding onto a beer can through the outstretched arms of a jumper. It's science.

Outside, the sun is blazing, obviously, the temperature no doubt somewhere in the mid to high thirties, the humidity its usual three figure percentage. I'm glad the Shanghai days are behind me, and grateful for a Mexican wave buffet to bring my physique back somewhere towards fighting weight, but you'd think these fucking Tigers could help a lifelong supporter out and learn to play with at least a little skill or some remote amount of passion. The Bunnies are whopping my Tigers 24-0. The whistle blows for half time. I slide along the tiled floor to the kitchen to grab another can of tiger beer, the tigers that never disappoint. Tom Waterhouse's ugly mug pops up on screen for a sideline report and an update of gambling odds for all sorts of punting possibilities at his self titled website betting den.

I've spent most of Sunday morning doing two things; unpacking my belongings into the serviced apartment I will now be calling home and reading through online Australian newspaper articles. My possessions are neatly packed and sorted, but I'm still coming to grips with Australia's deep-rooted hatred of Tom Waterhouse. Now, in Tom's defence, I doubt many of these haters actually know him and have simply jumped on the Tom-Waterhouse-Revulsion-Bandwagon. That is not cool. Those people should be ashamed of themselves. Me, however, I went to school with the pompous little slimy turd faced fuckhead. I've known he's a royal cock for many,

many years. My due diligence on this subject was complete almost two decades ago.

All that aside though, why do people hate him so much? Because he is offering live gambling during sporting events. So what? Seriously, so what? Ah, the children, ah problem gambling, ah, ah, fucking ah. Where do these useless, fantasy-world-inhabiting morons think their meager $2 savings go after the government has concocted ever more taxes to shunt them out of every other spare coin at their disposal? It goes into superannuation. That little Paul Keating chestnut designed to save us all.

Once it's gone to a 'super' fund. What a term that is too, by the way. Super. That's like saying you have supernatural powers if you can successfully wipe your own arse. Bravo. No, these 'super' funds 'invest' your money. And how do they 'invest'? They employ legions of anal-ysts to fabricate graphs, mull financial data and eventually, once they realise that is all one complete waste of time, they take a punt. They take your hard earned money and punt it while they're off playing golf on a weekday afternoon and you're busy, slogging your best years away in some degrading task, which is euphemistically described as gainful employment.

Now, investing in any market carries far lower odds of 'winning' than going to the casino and putting it all on black. Markets are full of people; retarded, fearful, greedy people, like you and me. You have to predict what these people are going to think. Good luck. They think they deserve to live well, die rich and work very little. Fair enough. So, you have to second-guess where they're going to park their borrowed, inherited or superannuation-donated investment capital in a roulette wheel of equities, currencies, commodities, whatever else the regulators wrongfully deem to not be gambling.

The gyrations of markets are determined by these people, not by true underlying value, there is no such thing, but by people's perceptions of future value. Are you scared? You should be. At least basic mathematics are involved at a casino. Next time you point the finger at poor little silver spooned Tommy W for his live gambling service, remember, you've been bamboozled the whole way along. Your hard earned enforced savings are being punted all day, everyday.

Tom's half time update is over and his nauseatingly smarmy face smears off the screen. I settle in to watch the second half, keying in a $500 bet on my laptop for the comeback of the century paying $6.85. I like those odds and I love my Tigers. Within the second half's first minute, the Tiger's halfback throws an intercept pass into the waiting arms of a fluky fucker in a Rabbitoh's jersey who races seventy metres for another try. I walk to the nearby booze shop for a case of tiger beers and return home to get completely wasted, yelling at the TV from the couch, feeling homesick, $500 lighter.

I wake up to a message from Paul. He wants to meet at 8am at Dimbulah for a flat white and quick chat. I presume he'll want to talk through plans on how we can quickly become the most profitable desk in the Scion network. I jump in the shower and hope for some half decent, opening day trading ideas to soak in through my pores.

No such luck. I towel off, shave and douse myself in Issey Miyake. Shrewd ideas or not, you should always look and smell the part.

"Welcome back mate."

"Yeah, cheers Paul. It's great to be here. Have you been coping OK without me?"

"Ha, yeah, I've been OK. So today, we'll set you up on all the systems and all those sort of admin tasks. We can trade anything really, oil, metals, equities, foreign exchange. Our only real mandate is to provide option prices for any of the specific oil or metals trading desks when they ask. It doesn't occur too often but we do need to make sure we provide a price for them if we're asked."

"OK, cool. No problem."

"Aside from that, you'll work side by side with me for the first few months and then take progressively bigger positions on your own."

"Awesome, sounds great."

We head into the office around 8.30am. The Singaporean 9am arrival devotion is unchanged. The room is empty. Paul sits at the end of a row of desks. Six blank screens surge to life as he takes his seat to boot his working day into first gear. My new seat, to his right, is endowed with only three screens. This is bullshit. I'm a big swinger now, apparently. Surely noone here can read my thoughts which are screaming I don't belong, I'm a hoax, I'm retarded, I'm hopeless. I'm suppressing that astute inner voice and preparing to give Erwin an earful for not having more screens prepared for me. A trader. I'm a big deal. Ask anyone. Fuck knows what I'll be looking at on all the extra screens, but I'll work that out when I get there. Joel arrives and walks straight over.

"Welcome home son."

"Thank you, good to be back."

"So how was China then?"

"Not what I expected…"

Joel's phone rings and he walks off, insulting whoever happens to be on the line. The expletives increasing as he reaches a glass bubble meeting room in the corner and shuts the door behind him. I see Andrew arrive in the distance, walking straight into the meeting room with Joel.

"Nyess, good to see you Flynn."

"Artem, good morning."

"Rob, he says you were veerry good help for him."

"I'm not too sure about that, but it was a pleasure to meet him and a great experience."

"Nyess, nyess. Oh well, you take job here with Paul then. That's OK. Good luck."

"Thanks, Artem."

My phone rings, "Scion Commodities, Flynn speaking."

"I like that official sounding voice of yours mate. Andrew here, can you come down to the meeting room with Joel and I?"

"One sec."

I proceed down the room and see Pranav scrolling on his Blackberry. Some things never change and we don't make eye contact. I pass by him, "Good morning, Flynn, hope you're well." He literally must have eyes in the top of his head. "Morning Pranav, I'm well, thanks." This is the first I've seen of Mr. Naphtha since my initial interview. Boy wonder has quite a memory. I continue into the 'Michaelangelo' room.

"Flynn, good to see you." Andrew shakes my hand as I walk in and motions me to take a seat.

"Mr. James, we've got a problem." Joel doesn't speak with his formal voice too often, something's far from rosy.

"A problem?"

"Sorry, is there an echo in this room? Now shut up and listen. Andrew's fellow fuel oil trader, Bing Zhao, has just cost us a highly profitable relationship with Powcom. We do almost zero fuel biz with them, but we do a fuckload of gasoline and naphtha deals, all of which are usually highly lucrative. Thanks to Bing Zhao's persistent fuck ups on fuel though, Powcom isn't going to deal with us at all now. One of the biggest traders in the world is going to pretend we don't exist. Now, before I take great joy in firing Bing, Andrew and I wanted to sound you out for a fuel trading role rather than derivatives."

"Umm…"

Andrew takes over, "Flynn, you can trade derivatives at any stage of your career. Physical trading though, it's the learning ground to really cut your teeth in the commodities world. I'll be next to you to teach you every step along the way. I apologize for not putting this option on the table months ago. Obviously, I watched you during your deals desk time here last year and I know you are exceptional. You and Paul will make an amazing duo, no question, but I'd love the chance to welcome you to my team also. Learn the trade properly and there will be derivatives trading roles for you aplenty in the more distant future."

"That all makes sense. I'm fine either way, but my operations training in metals hasn't really prepared me too well to jump straight in to physical oil trading."

"I will teach you everything mate. And Rudy is a brilliant operator. I'll make sure he pays particular attention to you and teaches you everything on the steepest learning curve possible."

"Will Paul be OK with this?"

"Of course. He can carry on solo with his work. You'll only be sitting a couple of chairs away from him. We can change the seating arrangement so you two Aussies can still hold hands all day if you like."

"Fuck off!"

"Haha, good man. So you're in?"

"Yeah, why not hey, let's do it."

"Excellent. OK gents, I see Bing has just arrived to work, the stupid cunt. Please excuse me, Bing Zhao is about to be Bing fucking gone."

Andrew and I walk out together. Bing walks back past us and into the Michaelangelo room with Joel.

"Flynn, best go grab a coffee mate. Get me one too could you. I'll break the news to Paul and get Erwin to reconfigure Bing's workstation for you. Five screens enough for you to compensate for all the knowledge you don't have and at least make the receptionists keen to suck you off?"

"Five should be just fine."

I jump in the elevator and head back to Dimbulah, stopping for a moment in the foyer on the ground floor to say good morning to Jannah. She's well and Marcelo is still going strong at Revlon. I look over her shoulder to see Bing walking out the doors, smashing his Blackberry into the pavement. A cleaning lady scoots over and sweeps the innocent remains of the device into her dustbin. Keith Wang is in the distance, spitting abuse into his Blackberry and sucking down his morning pack of cigarettes. Jannah carries on to the elevators.

I focus back on my coffee errand, knowing all too well, I'm even more out of my depth than usual with this sudden change of events. I return with Andrew's coffee and we grab a seat back in the meeting room for the obligatory pep talk and his verbal illustration to describe the lay of the land.

Fuel oil trading is, quite literally, tantamount to scraping the bottom of the barrel. If you manage to find some crude oil and successfully run it through a refinery, gasoline, kerosene, jet fuel, and of course naphtha, all float upwards, pack of show offs. Meanwhile, the heavy molecules of the crude slate will sink to the bottom of your distillation tower. The shining light at the weighty depth of the barrel is fuel oil.

It's so potent and disgusting, the brains trust at the helm of civilization decided it was wise to power all manner of gargantuan oceangoing vessels with it. It is termed 'marine fuel oil' by some in the business. This highly pollutant sludge of viscosity, sulfur and hydrocarbons is stored in ship's bunkers and accounts for the lion's share of global chartering costs and environmental catastrophes. If it's not powering global shipping, fuel oil also finds its way to electricity generating utilities, forming a valuable component of the energy stack alongside coal, nuclear and natural gas.

Singapore is the world's dumping ground for fuel oil and it is now all that my universe is consumed with. My role all of sudden, far from pricing up options, speaking in 'Greeks' and trading derivatives, as unqualified as I am for doing that, will instead comprise analyzing the tonnage and timing of fuel oil reaching the Singapore basin from every corner of the globe. I will be assisting Andrew in assessing cargoes he is looking to buy and ship into our tanks while simultaneously working with Rudy, our operator, to ensure we profitably sell bunker parcels of fuel oil direct into the domestic bunker market from our storage tanks which are clearly visible in the Singapore harbour from the Michaelangelo room windows.

I have no idea what I'm doing but do have the luxury of being catapulted quite unexpectedly into this role. That should buy me at least 48, maybe 72 hours, to be up to speed with every facet of the fuel oil business before I can expect to be fired for the smallest of mistakes. Andrew and I return to our seats, Paul gives me an approving 'what can you do' shrug of the shoulders and I quickly set about filling up my five screens with spreadsheets, charts, interactive maps, anything at all that might make fellow traders presume I have any idea what I'm doing and the receptionists inclined to fuck me.

....

Andrew hails a cab infront of the office and we jump in. It's Wednesday, 'Lady's Night'. Women receive free champagne at all the major bars every Wednesday in Singapore. It sounds like utopian paradise for sleazing on heavily boozed chicks, high on free bubbly and eager to make bad decisions with their legs spread. Unfortunately, it's not like that at all. It's a total sausage sizzle. Every other grubby bloke transplanted to this sweat hole of a city has the same idea; find drunk tarts and let the magic happen. The ratio of wang to vag is heavily lopsided to the pork swords. The cab passes by countless bars advertising their lady's night deals while scores of horny blokes chat impatiently to each other, sipping on their full priced tiger pints. There's the odd unfuckable expat munter amongst the crowds of blokes, smashing free champers and blaming yellow fever for the lack of attention she's receiving.

One of the fuel oil brokerages has booked a balcony area at Kudeta, the bar atop Marina Bay's floating serpentine. I'm three days in to the new role and obviously without a clue as to what I'm doing or how the hell I'm going to help Andrew complete the necessary alchemy required to ensure ongoing overpaid employment as a trader. As the cab circles Marina Bay, I sincerely hope someone chooses tonight to fulfill the quota of one weekly suicide from the airborne boat, it would really take my thoughts away from how soon I'm going to be fired.

The taxi pulls in at the entrance foyer, we continue through to the elevator and both pinch our noses as we hop out at the 56th floor, neutralizing air pressure after the almost instantaneous 200m skyward journey. We follow the bordello scarlet signage to Kudeta's entrance and endure the stares of condemnation being hurled at us by the steroid-injected eyes of the doorman. *'Do we even lift?'* No. No we don't. Andrew tells the ear-phoned retard our names so he can pretend he can read while he glances down at his bicep cradling a name filled clipboard for a few moments before waving us in.

We are welcomed by a large, empty dancefloor. The doorman's twin brother appears to be lurking in the DJ booth, eyes on the decks, left hand to the ear, right arm raising the roof as he drops some sort of Korean pop song through the airwaves, sending his anabolic body into a writhing seizure. I need a drink. The DJ needs a bullet. There is a massive bar which leads away from the dancefloor and out to a balcony with a mesmerizing view of nocturnal Singapore. Neon stretches out forever in the clear night sky.

Andrew leads the way past the bar and to the balcony. A group of middle aged, overweight blokes are sipping Asahi's and being fawned all over by some extraordinarily high class hookers. Well played, lads. That can't be cheap, enjoy it. The most stunning of the girls sees Andrew and races over, her virtually non-existent black leather skirt riding up her thighs as she paces our way.

"Andrew! So glad you could make it, la." Andrew, the sly bastard, didn't know he was a brass lover.

"Claudia, good evening. It's great to see you. This is Flynn, my new prodigy."

What? These are the brokers?

"Hi Flynn! Welcome. Please, grab yourselves a drink, la."

"Cheers."

Singaporeans and their fucking 'la's'. I'll forgive Claudia though, Jesus, she is forcing me to rethink my anti-yellow fever convictions.

Over the course of the next two hours I am introduced to the other members of Claudia's team; a group of young women who dress like whores, drink like fish, laugh at my every joke and look pensively into the night sky with any quasi-serious statement that passes my lips. In a perfect world, all girls would treat me like this. But I'm wise enough to know this world is far from perfect. They say they're brokers, but I'm unconvinced. Every aspect of their behaviour is screaming 'full service' of a sexual, not commercial, nature.

The other gents all seem OK, I guess. They're an interesting collection, spanning many races and age brackets, all joined together at the hip by fuel oil trading and male gender. I wonder if fuel trading paid the same salary as high school teaching, if any of these blokes would still be here. These girls certainly wouldn't. Andrew is making a special effort to introduce me to the entire group, a wad of business cards now bulging in my pockets, hopefully taking attention away from my raging hard on thanks to Claudia's nonstop stroking of my arm.

It's shortly after 10pm. The dancefloor is now heaving. I'm having serious health concerns for the DJ, the music he spews out of his booth is garbage, but his violent thrashing has continued unabated since I arrived. He must be epileptic. His beats certainly aren't my cup of tea, but there are hundreds of revelers making fools of themselves in the strobe lighting. Three of the brokers have managed to drag a handful of the most lifeless looking of my fellow fuel traders onto the floor. It's a little like watching fathers of the bride stealing a waltz with their daughters before matrimonial bliss ensues, only these newly married young ladies are grinding their papa bears with all the fervour of a Tasmanian only child.

As has become typical over the past year, my surroundings are truly bizarre but everything seems honky dory to those around me. I take a final sip of my Asahi and peruse the full length of the balcony railing with the acute hope of seeing a willing jumper ready to launch into the afterlife. None. Ah well. My fuel knowledge is insufficient to maintain a proper conversation with any of the other traders but I've been closely eavesdropping on everyone's conversations and have picked up plenty of trading ideas to chase up more fully.

Andrew is chatting earnestly with some bloke who looks important, one of the brokerage girls nods on in agreement with everything they say and ensures their drinks are full. I let Andrew know I'm going to head home and slide past the dancefloor without saying goodbye to any of the others and escape to the elevator. It's not actually all that long a walk from Marina Bay Sands back to my Club St home. I decide to walk on through the dense night air. My phone rings as I step out on to the Marina Bay promenade. It's Joel.

"So you met some other fuel traders tonight?"

"Yeah, just heading home now."

"Good. So now you can put faces to the companies we're going to fuck up."

"I guess so."

"Wake up! I want you to get angry, Flynn, really fucking angry. You're a trader now, no more fucking around. I know you pretend to be a nice guy, but I'm certain you're the greedy, crafty cunt I've been waiting for to transform our fuel business."

"I was never pretending to be a nice guy."

"That's what I like to hear. Rest up. Tomorrow, we start fucking this market up."

"Beauty."

"Good work heading home early too, son. All those useless cunts you met tonight are probably still in fantasy world happily believing those whore brokers are at all interested in anything they have to say."

"Ha, yeah, seemed a bit over the top."

"Meet me at the office at 6.30 tomorrow morning and we'll go for a run, talk through the strategy."

"OK, see you then. I'm not too fit though."

"Good, I'll make you sweat you little bitch."

The skies open and a monsoonal storm soaks me a few hundred metres from home. I'm glad for the instant drop in temperature. I turn into Club St and continue the final steps, completely drenched. I immediately switch the air-con into full throttle and jump in an ice cold shower. Ice cold in Singapore translates to about 25 degrees Celsius. I dry off, grab a tiger from the fridge and take a seat on the couch with the living room temperature now a relatively humane 20-ish degrees. I turn on Setanta. Gaelic football pollutes the screen while I scribble away notes from all the conversations I overheard tonight. Joel's right, it's time to fuck shit up. I place my gym gear by my bed and drift off to sleep.

I snooze straight through the night, waking moments before the 6am alarm starts blaring. I switch on the kettle, brew a Nescafe, and watch the Bloomberg headlines. There's nothing really to report unless you're interested in watching Donald Trump's candy-floss-topped head demanding to see original copies of Barrack's birth certificate. What a prize fuckwit. I head to the bathroom, unleash Nestle's top selling product's repucussions into the porcelain, splash my face, don my gym gear, lace up the Nikes, and walk into work carrying my corporate clobber on a hanger.

"Ah, Mr. James, good morning sir." Joel looks extremely fit. This is going to hurt.

"Morning boss."

"Let's hit it."

The early morning light bounces off the bow of Marina Bay Sands. Joel is powering around the bay while I'm too exhausted to concoct a reasonable excuse as to why we should rest a moment. I focus on not face planting and resist the urge to collapse. I'm glad Joel is talking strategy without expecting me to say anything in reply. I'm breathless to the point of wheezing. The dawn heat is intensified by complete stillness, not a single wisp of air exists aside from those pounding through my chest. I consider tripping Joel, but can't think of any plausible way to explain away such action as accidental. We're barely ten minutes into the run, less than 2km through whatever demented course Joel has planned and all I can think of is praying that a splat fucking corpse show itself underneath Marina Bay Sands so that I can take a breather.

"OK, let's stretch here hey?" Thank you, Lord.

"Huuuuhhhh." I slouch, hands to my knees, sucking in the big ones.

"You see, it's all good and well Andrew wanting to persevere with our storage tanks, but they're a massive expense. Unless we can find suitably cheap blendstock and still meet the regulated bunker fuel specifications, I really can't see the point of shelling out a million bucks each month for some fancy tanks out there in the harbour."

"Huuuhhhhh." Suck 'em in, Flynn, suck 'em in.

"No point keeping up appearances and going broke."

"Huuuhhhhh."

"You made any progress on the Arb sheet?"

"Huuuuhhhhh."

"The Arb sheet, Flynn? How's it going with that?"

"Yeah, getting there. Huuuuhhhhh."

"Hurry up with it. That's going to be the platform we'll start trading from."

"Will have it finished today."

"Rightoh, you've finally stopped huffing, let's head back."

The homeward journey seems less painful. We round the bay and I start to jog with a modicum of grace once I can taste the wall of crisp office air-conditioning waiting for me in the distance. We reach the foyer shortly after 7am. Joel heads straight up the elevator and to the office change rooms. A 7.30am conference call with the Panama office beckons. I grab a seat at the ground floor waiting lounge, on the verge of crying with the realization the office air-con doesn't kick off until 8am. I sweat my way through the black leather for fifteen minutes before composing myself for my fourth day of fuel oil trading and head to the change rooms.

. . . .

"Flynn?"

"Yep, who's this?"

"Mate, it's Sean, from the Shanghai Tigers."

"Sean! What's happening mate?"

"You're in Singapore yeah?"

"Yeah, been back here a week now."

"Cool. A bunch of us are in town. The Aussie Rules Footy Asian cup is on today here in Singapore."

"You don't want me to play do you?"

"Course not, you're fucking awful."

"Well..."

"Nah, just seeing if you were keen to catch up afterwards? We'll be heading out for a bit of a session."

"Of course. Just message me when you're heading out."

"Will do."

"Where you playing? Might come watch."

"We'll be at the ovals near the Singapore Cricket Club."

"Too easy, will see you there then."

It's almost midday. There's a lack of construction noise in this part of the city, most of the old buildings in the immediate vicinity are heritage listed and safe from Bangladeshi operated jackhammers. This means I am actually able to wake up leisurely and with a degree of peace. I stay lying in bed, checking my emails on the Blackberry, nothing urgently important in the hundreds of subject titles I scan over amongst the unread list. Week one. Done. Not fired yet. That's better than I'd expected.

I head to the bathroom, catching a quick glimpse of myself in the mirror. I'm still holding on to my Mexican glow and, if I'm not mistaken, I think there could be visible musculature in my shoulders and chest. Back on track, baby! My guts are still laden with cellulite that belongs in a pensioners' aquarobics class, but I'm cool with that. Six packs are for homos anyway. I shower and shave before reading properly through all my unread emails and munching away on a bowl of Weet Bix.

Joel has shot holes through my Arb sheet. 'Arb' is short for 'arbitrage'. And arbitrage is one of the abundant overly used and poorly understood words in the finance industry. The finance industry, some call it 'high' finance, because you no doubt have to be blazed off your head to believe any of the garbage entrenched in the world of finance. The industry is full of these sorts of words, these syllables that roll so effortlessly off the tongue and yet very few of the market participants actually have any real idea of what they're waffling on about.

Crowds of published economists will tell you arbitrage means taking advantage of price differentials for the same product, which are simultaneously available in different markets. So, if you could buy a schooner of Heineken for $5 from the downstairs bar of your favourite pub, then walk upstairs and sell it to your mate for $6, you could make $1 risk free profit provided, of course, you were blessed with a steady hand, the ability to not sneak a cheeky sip of that fresh Heinee the moment it arrived in your grasp downstairs, and, most importantly, able to nonchalantly be a complete cunt.

The economic theory goes that such price differentials close quickly. It's only a matter of time before your mate upstairs realizes you're ripping him off and either undertakes the walk himself for the cheaper groundfloor schooie or just smacks you in the head and glasses you in the jugular. Either way, the price gap won't last long, contrary to popular belief, people aren't that stupid, apparently.

Now, in terms of fuel oil, there are two major global price benchmarks. One in Singapore, the land that fun forgot, and the other in Rotterdam, Holland, the land that fun's had a fucking gutful of. That poor fuel oil molecule that emerges from a three day bender in Rotterdam only to get shunted into the storage tank of an oil tanker and shipped to the most uptight city on Earth must be rightfully pissed off it's been shipped across the planet in the name of arbitrage. But, in Europe, fuel oil is relatively cheap, most power utilities use higher quality inputs and the European shipping industry is a little hamstrung by somewhat stringent environmental regulations. By 'somewhat stringent', I simply mean, 'some'. Demand is weak. While in Southeast Asia, fuel oil is needed for shipping and power plants alike. Ship it in, baby, we'll take it.

The price difference, the 'Arb', between the two locations is usually a simple, direct relation corresponding to the shipping costs. Obviously, fuel oil in Rotterdam can't jump aboard a KLM flight. No, it has to trudge the English Channel, round the Rock of Gibraltar, cruise the Med, snap a few photos of the pyramids on the way through the Suez, pray like hell Somali pirates are bedridden, nursing a HIV or Ebola outbreak as the Arabian Sea flows around the hull, then time the Indian Ocean crossing with a dearth of tectonic silly bugger activity and, finally, slide through the Malacca Strait reflecting on Charles Darwin's *Origin of Species*. It's quite a journey and is usually valued somewhere around $20 per metric tonne. That differential is known as the 'East-West'. Let's say the price per fuel oil metric tonne in Singapore is $610, the price in Rotterdam is $590, fuel oil traders are so efficient with linguistics they'll spit all day the 'east-west is trading 20'.

Now, what I'm charged with providing is an analysis of this east-west Arb. Assuming the quoted east-west price is $20, and let me just qualify, that is a derivative 'paper' price. You know, a price on an exchange. A price which is nice to look at, a quote which newsreaders may include in their daily 'markets summary' and a risk analyst will likely call upon to summarise a trading firm's *Value at Risk*. But it really is quite meaningless. When you do actually stump up to some grouchy cunt in possession of barrels of fuel oil, he won't necessarily deal at that exchange quoted price for real live physical barrels. It's a bit like cash starved battlers pawning their inherited gold jewelry to slimy Indians in suburban shopping centers. The price they may receive for that gold is not going to correlate too closely with any London Metal Exchange sanctioned bid-offer.

The Arb sheet has to include shipping, financing, insurance, the whole kit and kaboodle and provide a specific price we can sell fuel for in Singapore if we buy it in Rotterdam and undertake the journey east. Like all things theoretical, it's piss easy. We're all Einsteins when we can dwell in a theoretical wonderland of fantasy and unicorns. *If I'm traveling in a train at the speed of light…*you're dead, that's the answer, you are dead, your internal organs no longer the required degree of internal thanks to unbearably powerful forces. No, the problem is providing a theoretical basis for physical trading in an eternally practical universe.

My best summary at the moment shows the Arb being closed by $10, meaning, if we buy oil in Rotterdam at $590 per metric tonne, ship it to Singapore, we will spend $30 per ton for the privilege, but the price in Singapore is only $610, so we've expertly burned $10 of God's money, which he will not be happy about, multiplied by a few hundred thousand tonnes. No, entry inside the pearly gates to welcoming arms handing out heavily zero-laden bonus cheques with that approach is mighty ambitious.

I reply to Joel's email that the numbers simply don't stack up for moving an arbitrage cargo right now. He replies back instantly, saying 'other companies are shipping in oil from Europe, I'm certain, something must be wrong with your numbers. But fuck it. It's Saturday. Rest up. We'll fix it Monday'.

Thank God for that. I rinse my Weet Bix bowl in the sink and call a cab. I'm thirsty.

"Singapore Cricket Club."

"No problem sir."

The cab takes off as a message from Mark lights up on my phone. One of his mates, Joe, who works in Jakarta, is in Singapore for the week. He just arrived this morning. We should catch up. He's apparently as retarded as I am. Perfect. I text the number Mark has given me, welcome this Joe fella to Singapore and let him know my movements.

The taxi arrives at the grounds. Temporary Aussie Rules posts are planted at each end of the oval, a bunch of uniform clad grown men prance around the perimeter in the stifling heat with their matching colour ensembles, warming up, I suppose. It seems unnecessary. There's a small stadium constructed on the sideline with a sun-shielding roof and a booze vendor standing infront of an alcohol beverage filled dinghy stranded a long way from the sea and drowning in ice. Game on. I buy an oversized can of Heineken from the dinghy and take a seat.

Joe clearly has very little on his schedule. He joins me within the first fifteen minutes of my arrival and earns some strong brownie points by insisting on buying the beers. He trades palm oil for an Indonesian company and can expense the whole affair as a business meeting. I stupidly make it clear to him that Scion doesn't trade agriculture products. He couldn't give a fuck. What a legend. Thanks Mark for the hook up.

The Shanghai Tigers take the field and proceed to get absolutely punished by the Singapore team that appears filled with actual ex-professional players. This is an absolute shellacking. Sean manages to kick through a behind for Shanghai as the final whistle blows. 137-1. An incredible score considering the game was merely two ten-minute halves. Sean spots me in the crowd and heads over.

"Mate, tough opponents there."

"Yeah, the Singapore team is always strong. They'll win the cup for sure."

"So, all done then?"

"Not yet. It's a round robin. We're still due to play Hong Kong and

Vietnam."

"Two great Aussie Rules footy heavyweights."

"Ha, yeah. I gotta get back out there. See you later on."

"Smash it up mate."

Sean takes off. I'm wasted already. These beers in the heat carry extra clout. Mark was right, Joe is hilarious and, if he did live in Singapore, I'd almost consider myself to have found a friend. Like so many people in this part of the world, he is yet another strange hybrid of ethnicities and cultures. He's just over six foot tall, has the unblemished almond skin tone synonymous with mixed race breeding, and that unique international accent which is only spoken by those who were taught English in the international schools of non-English speaking countries.

He's originally from America, but attended school in Jakarta, where he met Mark. His Father, a Texan with oil exploration skills, is currently working somewhere in Africa, after being based in Jakarta for many years. His Mum, an ex-swimsuit model from Argentina, still lives in the family mansion in Jakarta, accompanied by a personal workforce of maids, beauticians, chefs and drivers. I'm not sure why Joe confides so much info in me, I barely know him, but the thought of his ex-model Latino trophy mum waking each morning at 10am for a mani-pedi-brazilian, followed by a bottle of Grey Goose and a packet of Oxycontin, has me very much aroused.

The beers keep flowing as the afternoon stretches on. The dinghy is rapidly losing its booze filled lustre and the Shanghai Tigers are proving to be equally as pathetic as their Balmain cross code counterparts. Sean, Tom and the precocious Ben are huddled together, singing the Shanghai team war cry. I can't quite hear it, or remember it from my one brief playing near death experience, but Beck's 'Loser' would be fitting. I mean, losing to Vietnam, that really is pathetic.

Joe and I are sweating bullets and completely flogged. Sean trots over to let us know the finals will be tomorrow. The Shanghai squad will clearly not be participating in those. But all the teams who have bowed out today will tonight be meeting at Harry's Bar, the world famous watering hole where Nick Leeson used to top up his alcohol levels when he wasn't front running the collapse of Barings Bank. Nick was the centuries old bank's arbitrage trading expert too, I should add. Arbitrage…is there anything it can't do? Aside from make risk free profit, of course.

I tell Joe we should just head straight to Harry's now. It's almost dark. We walk to the road and hail a cab. I can see Harry's Bar in the distance on the opposite side of Boat Quay. It's barely 500m away, but there's no way I'm walking that far. Streams of perspiration are already sliding down my back straight through my arse crack following the briefest of strolls to the taxi rank. The cab pulls in at Boat Quay. Harry's is empty. Joe buys me yet another beer and we order bangers and mash while the Sydney Swans kick off against the Melbourne Demons on the big screen.

I can understand my Shanghai buddies are keen to look their best for a night out on the town, but it's been almost two hours that Joe and I have been sitting here downing pints and watching even more blasted Aussie Rules. As I pick up the phone to call Sean, he calls me.

"Mate, where are you? I said Harry's Bar, yeah?"

"Yeah mate, I'm here at Harry's Bar. Boat Quay. Where are you at?"

"Harry's Bar at Orchard Towers mate. It's number one Claymore Drive. Jump a cab here, Flynn. It's gonna get loose."

"Cool mate, see you soon."

I let Joe know we're at the wrong bar and we take off. It's nearing 8pm. I wave down a cab, which pulls over on Circular Road behind Harry's. I can see a group of flippers loosening their jaws, getting ready for an evening of smoke shows at the far end of the street. How's Strop, I wonder.

"One Claymore Drive please."

"Harry's, Orchard Towers?"

"Yeah, cheers."

Joe's face lights up.

"Orchard Towers, sensational. The boys back in Jakarta told me I had to check this place out."

"Yeah, why's that?"

"Orchard Towers mate. Four Floors."

"Four Floors is at the Hyatt, isn't it?"

"No mate, that's Bricks."

"OK, so what's Four Floors?"

"Well, you fucking retard, it's Four Floors of Whores. Bricks is only one floor of whores."

"Yeah, that would seem to make a lot of sense."

The cab passes through my old suburb of Somerset and continues on past the Hyatt before completing a huge circle through a series of back streets and finally dropping us in a side alley beneath an overhead walkway connecting two buildings. Huge signs for 'Harry's @ Orchard' make it fairly obvious this must be the place. I recognize a lot of my Shanghai mates on the ground floor balcony area. Joe pays the driver and we hop out.

We grab beers and are soon involved in sculling contests with any number of new mates. When it comes to forming friendships, the expatriate life in a new city is about the closest experience available to reliving your childhood. Remember those glorious times when parents were allowed to let their kids roam the streets each day after school without risking a visit from the Department of Community Services. That time spent exploring the streets on your skateboard or BMX would open up your world and inevitably result in new friendships, working out how to outsmart bullies, maybe blow up the odd letterbox.

These new friends weren't in possession of anything more than merely being of a somewhat similar age and equally keen to not go home till the sun went down. If you had any more than that in common, you quickly became best mates. The only differences in the expat grown up version of that story are that the age brackets considered 'similar' are greatly expanded, and, rather than returning home when the sun goes down, it's more customary to want to hide indoors once the sun comes up.

Harry's Bar is full to the brim with Aussie Rules enthusiasts from all the major Asian cities. Tom, as always, is leading the masses in the 'he's a pisspot through and through' tried and tested, drinking theme song, while Sean mixes gulps of grog with swipes of dating Apps on his phone. He shows me one of the girls who is text messaging him. Dear oh dear, I pray he never meets the girl in the photo. It is surely a police instigated sting operation to entrap paedophiles. Anytime a dating site has 'women' in light pink pajamas with crayons and colouring in books, it would seem wise to proceed with caution.

Across the street, a series of buses pull up. Hundreds of girls, maybe thousands, making absolutely zero effort to conceal their overt whoredness, proceed in an orderly line along the footpath and up the stairs into the building opposite. Orchard Towers, Four Floors of Whores. The girls can barely walk. Their pink high heels and undersized pleather skirts probably aren't designed with graceful cadence at the fore. The girls maintain their place in the line with military precision, a unified, noble army of poorly paid cock suckers.

They're each adorned with the same drag queen sense of makeup application and a clear environmental disregard when using hair spray. These stick figures in wonder bras and every possible variety of leopard print all look the same coat of troll doll as they face away from Harry's to continue up the stairs opposite, clutching their handbags to the hip as their 1960's air hostess bouffants barely pass below the sliding entrance door.

It's 10pm. The arrival of the whore bus convoy seems to be the unofficial closing time for Harry's. Every man is now draining the last of their drink and crossing the road, headed straight into the Towers. Any bank with an immoral grain of entrepreneurial salt has an ATM parked here. The line for the ATM's is 50m deep. I'm waiting with Joe in line, taking in the spectacle of Towers mayhem.

There are girls everywhere. Everywhere. They appear mainly of Thai or Flipper descent, spouting the usual 'love you long time' or 'you very handsome, honey bunny', the typical Southeast Asian mating calls of call girls. You've seen one, you've seen 'em all. None of the girls float my boat. I'm not particularly attracted to girls who look fresh from Rocky Horror Picture Show auditions. I'm more intrigued by the blokes here, the no-nonesense sexual predators who make a crust as postmen or customs officers. The milky white, soft flab of their lazy cheeks and drooping double chins turn a rose shade of crimson as they walk away from the ATM and ready themselves for a night of particularly vile pleasure.

This place is fucked. I'm scoping all angles for a viable smoke bomb opportunity. Ben, our 17 year old expert on eastern European whores, rounds up the troops and we head up some non-functioning escalators to the very top floor. The bar to the right has 'Top 5' written over the entrance. Ben continues in. There's a $10 cover charge, which includes a drink. Our group consists of close to 50 lads, all pissed out of their minds and brimming with ATM withdrawals.

Once the stout entrance lady takes my cash, gives me a drink voucher and stamps my wrist with the Top 5 insignia, I walk through a mirrored hallway into a huge arena. There's a long bar to the left leading to an elevated stage where three Thai girls, a drummer, guitarist and singer, are belting out the Red Hot Chili Peppers song, 'Otherside'. Every time she squeals 'take it on the other side' she spins around and points at her arse.

The boys are hooked in at the end of the bar, a cavalcade of girls heading their way from the far side of the room. The Thai girls follow up 'Otherside' with Britney Spears', 'Baby, one more time'. To the right are four oversized rows of tiered seating, a sort of stadium. The room is huge, empty aside from the Aussie Rules superstars and about 15 ladies competing for their attention. I notice a girl pole dancing on the bar, two of them. I re-scan the room. There are stripper poles stationed all throughout the venue with heroin addict looking Ukrainian girls slow dancing completely out of sync to the Thai girl band's Britney tribute.

Aside from the stage entertainment and the bar staff, all the girls here have a Russian look to them. Ben is chatting away with three of them at the bar. His study buddies, I presume. Sean is on stage, doing single arm pushups with his shirt off. The rest of the lads cheer him on while pole dancers on elevated platforms all throughout the stadium continue to clumsily squat and bend with their eyes closed. The Singaporean guys behind the bar look disinterested as they polish glasses. Joe and I grab our courtesy drink and sit at a table right by the bar.

The unmistakable intro to Men at Work's 'Down Under' fires up. The boys storm the stage and the poles, drowning out the band with their screaming and relieving the Ukrainians of their woeful pole dancing attempts. Tom starts frisking up the lead singer, getting all touchy feely as he joins her at the microphone, "traveling in a fried out kombi". Another bloke takes over the drums, security guards rushing in as the room erupts, "he just smiled and gave me a vegemite sandwich!!!"

There are fights breaking out all over the floor. Girls are bashing everyone with their leopard print handbags, the Singaporean security are no match for the Aussie pissheads. Tom holds off four of the little cretins as he commands the mic to the very end, "you better run, you better take cover." I'm in hysterics, still sitting in my chair, copping the odd handbag belting to the head but not spilling my beer. The boys back at the Round bar in Manly would be so proud.

The Australians are told to leave and never come back. Bothered? Ben leads the way back down stairs a level to 'Club Romeo'. Two Singaporean doormen welcome us warmly, "Have a great night guys." The entrance is a velvet curtain that requires reasonably heavy lifting to fling to the side and get in to Romeo's club. A rectangular room of severely dim red lighting is lit up in the centre by a slightly raised stage. There are two poles at each end of the runway and a peculiar collection of Thai and Russian girls eye us off as they dance with all the rhythm of a down syndrome choreographed special Olympics performance.

We proceed to the bar in the far end of the room. A Thai girl on stage whose head almost touches the roof, her Adam's apple surely visible from a satellite alerts me to the trans nature of the sexual apparatus lurking beneath her skimpy black dress. There is a couched area to the side of the bar. Ben commandeers this space and orders five bottles of champagne. I take a seat but make sure I can still clearly see the runway. Sean is dangling upside down from one of the poles, the security contingent loving it, as too are the onstage girls and lady boy.

Ben's purchase of the champagne seems to imply the girls now talk to you. Much the same as the smoke bars of Circular Rd, you pay top dollar for a grog and it's inclusive of female attention. I'm fine with this. Nadia, my allotted female, is first and foremost, a woman. I'm fairly certain. Secondly, she is smoking hot, oozing an intoxicating Russian assassin chique sense of enthrallment. I'm confident she would have no hesitation in slitting my throat, but even more confident I desperately want to the fuck the shit out of her.

Joe appears equally captivated by his champagne swilling partner. She's of Asian descent. Joe's another yellow fever victim. Her hands are traveling perilously close to my new pal's crotch. He necks the glass of bubbles and goes the lean in, grabbing her by the back of the neck and gorging on her lips. The two of them get busy pashing on as the girl's right hand takes an exploratory journey under Joe's belt, jacking him off with breakneck speed. Fucking hell. Some bloke appears out of nowhere with a towel, handing it to Joe to tidy up his muck explosion. Stock standard hey? What service. The girl pours them another glass of bubbles each and Joe leans back, relaxing fully into the leather couch.

I drain my own glass and quickly pour another. I'm not too sure how comfortable I feel about just seeing Joe being tossed off under the thin veil of his blue jeans, but I'm trying to guide Nadia's hands in a similar direction. She doesn't want a bar of it. Through her almost incomprehensible Russian accent, she tells me I'm a "vaeerry nyice maeeen" and that she would like to go on a date. Huh? Yeah, she would like to get a coffee, maybe watch a movie. We exchange phone numbers and continue sipping away on bubbly in the corner. Does she even know this place is called Four Floors of Whores? Maybe it doesn't translate well into Russian.

I ask her where the toilets are and excuse myself through a back door to a bathroom down a back hallway. Joe's hand-job deliverer walks in, stands next to me at the urinals, hoiks up her skirt and takes a piss from her impressively sizey wang. I vomit into the trough while this lady boy laughs at me, spinning her cock in big circles. I don't care if it's a man or woman, that's one fucking big dick. I vomit a second time and watch on as this thing dolls itself up in the mirror, pushing its dick deep between its legs and applying mascara and lipstick before walking back in to Club Romeo.

I escape to the street, calling Joe once I'm outside. I tell him I have to get home, I've just become violently ill and to make sure not to take any girls home from Club Romeo, a guy just told me the girls from there will definitely rob you, especially the Asian ones. He seems cool with this. I can only hope. If not, I'll gladly drive him to the mental institute tomorrow or to Marina Bay Sands for an appropriate farewell. I see a cab down the street and get moving. A few hundred girls, maybe they're lady boys, beg me to take them home. No way. I need an ice bath and a motherly cuddle.

"Club St, mate"

"Sure."

No Shanghai cab crashers join me. I text Nadia, saying I'd love to go for a date some time. The taxi pulls up at my place. I head in, vomit a couple more times and lay in bed, staring at the ceiling. Images of concentric lady boy dick circles are now plastered to my mind's eye.

I wake up on the couch around 9am. I must have relocated to the living room at some stage through the night. There's an open, full can of tiger beer on the coffee table. The Setanta network is streaming on screen, the volume through the roof, last night's matches being spoken of by a panel of commentators as though the importance of the games is of world changing gravitas. My first thought is, obviously, of that thunderous transgender penis. When will it end? My second thought is of Joe. I text him, 'how'd you pull up bro?' No reply. I put my shorts, t-shirt, cap and sneakers on, and resolve to run through the intensity of Singapore heat until lady boy cock is the last thing on my mind.

I jog past the office and continue around Marina Bay. Alcohol flows from my pores. My lungs are burning. The thudding of my shoes on the scorched concrete surface is matched by the pressure of my pulse beating through my temples against the sweat-laced brim of my New York Yankees baseball cap. A fellow retard, oblivious to the equatorial location, is running with spring and vigour in the opposite direction, dressed in full corporate triathlete regalia. He gives me a nod and a smile as he passes by. I want to punch the prick between the eyes and force him to eat his step-counting, heart-rate-monitoring watch but he's already too far gone. I battle on through overtired delirium. The image of feminine thighs, skirt round the waist, a monstrous oriental dick being flung around like a lasso, ready to ensnare innocent victims into a world of gender ambiguity and crippling sexual self doubt, continues to plague me. I start to sprint.

A large group of Chinese tourists clamour at the entrance to Gardens by the Bay, each of them eager to get the same worthless photo of Marina Bay Sands. Here's an idea, how about one of you takes the shithouse photo and the rest of you get the fuck out of the way. I run full pelt through the congregation of spitters, screaming "fuck off!" as I almost knock one of the oldest and most frail to her death. I continue sprinting another kilometre to the distant end of the Gardens and collapse on a patch of sweltering, prickly grass, roll to my side and vomit.

I lay on my side for at least half an hour. Hungry flies have hit the jackpot, dining out on the thrown up smorgasbord seeping into the lawn. Thoughtful parents lead their children in polite detours around my sprawled body on their morning walks through the park. None bother to help me or ask if I'm OK. I think I hear one particularly useless woman say to her child, "that's what happens if you take drugs." I make the calculation that one of the God fearing fuckwits who's walked past and left me to die has probably called the police. It's best to get moving. I stand up, dust myself off, ensure there's no vomit on me and walk to the nearby road. I can't believe a cab turns up almost instantly.

I'm no longer huddled around a pool of spew and am clearly Caucasian. The taxi driver has no reservations in picking me up. I'm driven home in air-conditioned comfort. So what, I saw a lady boy's cock, big deal. The run has achieved its desired effect. I'm ready to get back to doing what I set out to do over a year ago. Make big money, nothing more, nothing less.

There's a reply text from Joe waiting for me at home, 'cheers for an awesome night mate, let's do it again some time'. It's unclear whether or not his awesome night included continuing on to full fourth base disclosure with Club Romeo's well endowed, preeminent, self taught hand jerker.

I jump in the shower, freshen up and take a seat back on the couch. I let Setanta play on mute, no point listening to the commentary, and read through all the market analysis articles I've accumulated over the past week with a can of tiger to liven it all up and a Super Dad inspired playlist with a hefty dose of Lou Reed and Leonard Cohen buzzing from my laptop.

Three hours pass. I highlight all the info I deem relevant to imminent market price movements and whatever technical words or concepts I need to chase up in order to better understand what the hell it is I'm paid so much to do. Thankfully, not everyone else at Scion is a qualified physiotherapist. Some of them have actually worked in refineries or at least studied chemistry. These guys are well worth sounding out for sage wisdom about important refinery economics concerns. I look over the notes and rest back on the couch to finish off my second beer as the phone rings.

"Joel, what's up?"

"I need you to come with me to Seoul for a meeting."

"Yeah, what time?"

"Be at Changi tonight by 10pm. Call me when you get there and we'll check in together. Pack your jami's if you like. We land in Korea first thing tomorrow then I have meetings with some clients. I don't want you to say anything, but I can't turn up alone, that would look ridiculous."

"Suits me."

"We'll be back by tomorrow night."

"See you tonight then."

I connect the Blackberry to the charger, read back once more over the notes highlighted this afternoon, scan through the entirety of Morgan Downey's *Oil 101*, scoff some leftover pizza from Friday night and make sure my passport is included in my traveling bag before I pinch myself and hop a cab to the airport.

My knowledge of South Korea is fairly limited. I associate the name Seoul with images of Ben Johnson ruining his career while enlightening the planet to just how fast a man can run when ably assisted by steroid abuse. I also have good memories of watching the red army of South Korean soccer supporters. Entire stadiums filled with red jerseys. Men, women and children cheered on their country so passionately as they completely outplayed Spain, Italy and Portugal in the 2002 world cup, giving the limp wristed Fabio's of southern Europe a thorough touch up on their way to the semifinals. There's not much else in my knowledge bank about this part of the world.

"Did you know, South Korea has the highest proportion of plastic surgery in the world?"

"No, I was not aware of that."

"Yep. Fact. Look around. Good luck spotting some A-cups, thin lips or wrinkles round here."

Joel and I are sitting in a restaurant having breakfast. We're in the central business district of Seoul. I suppose. The cardinal signs of capitalism prevail; skyscrapers, smog, beeping horns, depressed suit wearers with grim faces and polished shoes, mustering up the resilience to spend yet another day in a cubicle.

It would appear Joel has been here many times before. He speaks flawless Korean with the waiter. Laid out on the table are noodles, soups, vegetables, whole fish, some sort of multi-layered legume lasagna, who knows. It all tastes pretty good. My first ever job was a kitchen-hand and all I can think is thank fuck I didn't work here. It's only Joel and I eating and there are over twenty ceramic items on the table. Culinary delights care precious little for the dish pig.

"Do you know anything about the Korean War?"

"No."

"Good. Me neither. Don't bring it up in the meeting."

"Yeah, rightoh."

"Now, don't look straight away, but see that man standing over there on the far street corner?"

I wait a few moments, bend down to pull up my socks and look through the window and across the street as I hunch over my chair. A middle aged Korean man in a navy pin stripe suit stands alone on the street corner, staring at his phone. A couple of metres to the right, a street vendor is selling all manner of nondescript food. I do recognize some corn cobs amongst the shelving displays of probable dog mince and tiger testes.

"The fella in the navy suit?"

"Yep, him."

"What about him?"

"In one minute, I want you to take my briefcase, walk over there, stand between him and the street cart, place down this case, buy a corn cob and then walk to the very end of the street."

"You shitting me yeah?"

"Do I look like I'm shitting you? Wipe that confused look off your face and do as I fucking tell you. Once you drop off the bag and buy your corn cob, walk the few hundred metres to the end of the street then get a taxi to this address."

Joel hands me a slip of paper with an address written in Korean, I guess. He slides the briefcase towards my left shoe and walks to the counter to pay the bill. I grab the case, proceed out of the restaurant, look down at my chest, making sure there are no red dots, though I'm not too sure what I'd do if I did indeed see a red laser pin point over my aorta. I check right and left for any traffic, cross over, attempt unsuccessfully to make eye contact with the navy suited briefcase recipient, take a break at the vendor and place down the case.

I motion to the corn and hand the old street merchant 5,000 Won ($5). He hands back the corn and some change, which I wave off. He places the tip in his pocket as his facial features disappear in a million wrinkles of smiling gratitude. I doubt that money will be going towards cosmetic surgery. Mr. navy suit takes the briefcase and walks away, I continue up the street, as instructed, and take my first breath in over two minutes once I'm 50m up the street.

I look back towards the restaurant. Joel has vanished. The street vendor continues spruiking from his street perch. I throw my corn cob to a homeless bloke in a side alley who looks oddly disappointed with the gift. Well fuck you then cunt. I hail down a taxi and show the driver the address. He says something in Korean and we take off, my thoughts blank with the lack of information making me look all types of retarded in the rear vision mirror.

The taxi pulls up infront of an impressive building. Joel's standing in the foyer, speaking on his mobile. He sees me hop out of the taxi and waves me over as he hangs up.

"Well done. All went well from what I saw."

"Yeah, all sorted. Is it a bad idea for me to ask what was in the case?"

"No. But save it for later OK. I'll explain when we fly back to Singapore."

"I'm not going to jail before then am I?"

"If you are, I'll be sure to bake a cake with a file in it for you."

"You bake?"

"Not often. I file though. Every day. Just look at these nails."

Joel's such a smug bastard, but all I can do is hope he's on my side. He leads the way to the elevators and we head up together to the 32nd floor. The lift doors open and, as always, two yellow fever inducers greet us. They're decorated in the prostitute inspired sense of fashion which receptionists throughout Asia appear bound by thanks to some unspoken union agreement. We are asked to take a seat. One of the girls leans over the glass coffee table to rearrange some newspapers and magazines. Joel gives me a knowing wink of carnal intentions as she drops to her knees to more precisely tidy the table. I ask where the bathroom is and head off in the stated direction. The whole bag drop fiasco, I'm way too on edge and have to try and relax somehow. A quick wank should sort me.

I'm sweating in the cool air-conditioning of the bathroom stall, trying to think exclusively about a naked Katie Upton making sand castles on a tropical beach. Some blood starts to circulate away from my overburdened mind and I focus on rubbing one out at Ben Johnson pace. Two men enter the gents, speaking to each other with the clanging, eardrum thumping resonance that Asians have perfected. I've got a full mast in my grip, but the voices instantly send me quivering back to the lady boy cock visual hellhole lurking in my thoughts. Katie's disappeared. The sand castles are ruined. Fuck's sake. I can't do this.

I stand up to take a piss instead. I'm hunched, my torso at ninety degrees to my legs, my left hand's holding the cistern as my right tries to aim my full-fledged hard on down towards the toilet. I reckon they must edit out these aspects of James Bond's life. I manage to dribble into the bowl for a few seconds consecutively without a spurt shooting north into the underside of the seat. After a minute or so, urine has made its way mostly into the bowl and blood has thoughtfully flowed back out of my cock. I wash my hands, splash my face and take a deep breath.

I walk back into the waiting area of the firm whose name I don't even know. Unlike most offices, there are no clichéd logos, company buzzwords or reprehensible phrases of the joyous delights of upstanding corporate citizenship. My throat muscles spasm, Joel is chatting amiably with the navy suit man. What is the stitch up here? I think momentarily about running. Joel calls me over.

"Seung, please meet my associate, Flynn. Flynn, please meet Mr. Seung Kwan."

"Good morning. Pleasure to meet you, Mr. Kwan."

"Gooood morrrning. Ahh please, call me Seung."

"Flynn, I know you had an important call with Andrew about an urgent issue. Seung and I can continue on with our discussions if you need to go and call Andrew right now to resolve that."

"Yes, of course. I will take care of that immediately."

"Excellent."

"Very nice again to meet you, Seung."

"Thank you, Fwynn. Nice to meet you."

"We won't be too long. See you downstairs."

Joel and Seung walk off down a hallway. The briefcase is nowhere to be seen. I hop back in the elevator, there's no mirror to check my facial expression, but there's no doubt whatsoever that I am back to looking completely retarded. Having absolutely no idea what the fuck

301

is going on will do that. I continue into the large ground floor foyer and call Andrew.

"Andrew, Flynn here."
"Morning mate, all sorted over there?"

"Umm, I guess. Joel is now in a meeting with some sketchy fucker, Seung Kwan. Joel said I needed to call you."

"Got it. And you lose a bag this morning?"

"Ah yeah, sort of, well yeah, I did."

"Perfect. OK, I'll sort everything out this end. Just grab a coffee and wait for Joel. I'll see you when you're back."

"OK, see ya mate."

I suddenly feel like a chess piece. A pawn too, of course, a completely expendable pawn. What the hell are these blokes doing with me? Playing all these cryptic games, sending me on unexplained errands. I bet they didn't expect me to have an attempted wank. Who's playing mind games now hey? Nah, they probably anticipated that too, fucking wankers. I grab a coffee at a cart just outside the building, continuing to scan my chest for red laser beams, and return inside to one of the couches. I wait, watching everyone coming and going, double taking all the women, making my own assessment of the silicone content of their chests, the botox concentrations of their lips. This is the Mecca of plastic surgery hey, why not? Mentally undressing all the women at least clears my thoughts of whatever the fuck my boss and Mr. Kwan are orchestrating upstairs.

After thirty or so minutes, Joel walks out of the lift, catching my eye on the couch and motioning me to continue with him straight out of the building.

"All taken care of, Flynn. I've booked us on an earlier flight back to Singapore. You ready to go?"

"Yeah, of course."

A sleek, black car pulls up. Joel opens the back door, "after you sir". I hop in and I'm actually surprised when Joel gets in behind me and I haven't been tazered.

"Thanks for your help today mate."

"No problem. I'm not too sure what I've done to help though."

"Well, that Seung piece of shit is chief inspector for the nuclear safety office. And I know you're only one week in to the world of fuel trading, but what are the feedstock components for power utilities in this part of the world?"

"Fuel oil, coal, nuclear, natural gas."
"Right on. Maybe you aren't retarded."

"Cheers."
"So, old fucker there, he conducts safety inspections of nuclear facilities."

"Got it."

"Some nuclear peddler paid him off to keep quiet about his recent findings that a couple of plants have serious safety faults in their reactors."

"How do you know?"

"I just know. Anyway, I didn't want to spook you earlier, it's best not knowing sometimes when you're being a hero."

"Hero?"

"You actually delivered a bribe to him this morning to actually do his fucking job."

"What?"

"Andrew's been sitting on a shitload of fuel oil we can't sell. Seung, for the princely sum of a quarter million bucks, has finally handed down the fucking safety report his country relies on him to deliver. No more nuclear for this country until they sort their fucking shit out."

"OK. And now Andrew can sell the fuel oil to other power utilities with a spike in energy demand now that nuclear power is off the table."

"See, Flynn, when I explain everything to you, you can regurgitate that info as though you really know what you're talking about. I'm so proud of you."

"Has Andrew already sold the barrels then?"

"Yeah, check your emails. Seung put the news release out a half hour ago when I told you politely to go fuck off and Andrew locked in his trades. Problem solved. Let's fuck off out of here."

"Why did you need me to drop off the bag? You could have just given it straight to Seung."

"Flynn, Flynn, Flynn, you just don't get it do you? You didn't flinch. You took the bag, kept your cool. It was awesome. I know you trust me now. You're smart. I'm sure you don't do exactly what anyone tells you, but you're smart enough to do exactly what I tell you. Good man. You keep doing just that and rest assured, you'll be one of the lucky few on Earth to be blessed with more money than you know what to do with."

We continue in the steady stream of air-conditioned comfort and the swanky black leather of the car's cushioned seating to the airport, then carry on in the lush brown leather of Singapore Airlines business class cushioning with evermore air-con, all the way to our zero latitude homes away from home. I keep the legions of gorgeous flight attendants busy with incessant requests for them to top up my whisky glass. I down the drinks with the unwavering resolve of a man coming to grips with now residing well and truly in another man's pocket.

. . . .

Paul throws a tennis ball at my head. Good shot, bastard. It ricochets off my noggin and knocks over my coffee. My notes and keyboard are drenched in cappuccino. Andrew is bowled over his chair, laughing it up. At least it all takes my attention away from yet another text message from Nadia asking when we're going to catch up. She says she can come to my place and make me dinner. Are these Russian euphemisms for fucking me, robbing me, killing me? Surely there's no way she genuinely wants to bake me a home cooked meal.

Joel laughs at me wiping up the spilt coffee on my desk as he walks past and down the room, sending my thoughts straight back to the Geneva simulation interview when he devastated Kenneth. I hope I get to destroy candidates' hopes and dreams too some day, what a blast. Rudy hangs up his phone and lets out a little yelp. It sounds gayer than a grown man explaining the pros and cons of various hair products. He immediately walks over to my desk.

"The assay report is in. It meets regulations. We nailed it!"

"You fucking ripper!"

I'm three weeks into my fuel oil trading career. That's a fairly lengthy stint in this business. And now, sharing this moment with Rudy, I feel I may have actually discovered the alchemy required for long lasting overpaid employment. Like all great things in my life, it's a total fucking fluke. When Joe returned to Jakarta without ever knowing he'd been flogged off by a lady boy, he emailed me the specifications of a residue which didn't meet the base requirements to be sold as palm oil. He asked me if there was any use I may have for it and was looking forward to his next visit to Club Romeo. Ignorance is bliss.

I obviously had no idea what could be done with the palm oil runoff, but ran the specs by our resident scientific genius, Rudy, the operations guru. He's some sort of Arab. I've never delved too far into it to find an accurate answer as to his specific heritage. When he speaks on the phone with his family back in some Middle East cave, it sounds like he's about to cough up a lung. Whenever the news headlines spray the usual propaganda about terrorist masterminds hell-bent on eradicating infidels, there's usually a Rudy look-a-like on the screen, shooting a machine gun to the sky from the dusty comfort of the Star Wars film set.

The core of Rudy's lifetime in oil operations has centered on creating a *blender*. Not the sort scorned wives threaten to throw unfaithful husband's dicks in, but a blender in which you can place any combination and permutation of individual oil blendstocks and get a read out of the end product you'll create when you mix each component in our storage tanks. As Mother Nature has decreed, it seems when you take a small portion of this palm oil residue and mix it with some of the filthiest fuel oil available you can create bunker acceptable fuel oil. Fucking fuck yeah Mother Nature, you glorious bitch.

We've just run our first batch, mixing two thousand tonnes of the palm oil reject with fifty thousand metric tonnes of utter fuel oil shit from a Russian refinery and a further twenty thousand tonnes of similar garbage that a Saudi refiner offloaded for a price too low to refuse. And voila, bunker fuel oil ready to pump out of the tanks for the current market price of $625 per metric tonne. The concoction set us back $564 per metric tonne to source and stir. $61 clean, blemish free profit, times seventy thousand tonnes…say hello to 4,270,000 of Uncle Sam's Greenbacks! The milky bars are on me, kids.

"Exceptional work." Joel is suitably impressed. As he bloody should be. I am the fucking King.

"My palm oil mate reckons this residue is in pretty consistent supply. We should be able to replicate this on a regular basis. It's like holy water."

"Tell him to not tell anyone he sold it to us."

"OK."

"Tell him right now. We can't have anyone know we're blending with this stuff."

"I'll message him right away."

"Don't message him you useless teenage girl. Call him. Now."

"OK."

"And when that's sorted, come grab me, you're coming to play golf with me this afternoon young man. Can't have you making too much money."

"I don't have any clubs."

"No problem, we'll buy some at the course."

"You buying?"

"No, I have a feeling you'll have some bonus money burning a hole in your pocket son, you're buying."

I get on the phone to Joe and thank him again for the palm oil dregs. I let him know I've managed to mix it with some other components and it turned out OK, but if he can do me the solid of keeping my purchase to himself, I'll gladly relinquish him of future stock and can agree terms today. He's over the moon. He's locked in an added revenue stream and I'm now set to be swimming in two thousand metric tons a month of palm oil I'd gladly take a bath in, I love it so much. He even bases the price off a fuel oil benchmark for me, now I can hedge away any pricing exposure with zero basis risk, unheard of in this industry. It's not what you know, it's who you know indeed, and once you know 'em, fucking milk 'em.

I hang up, throw the tennis ball with my full force back at Paul, miss him entirely and smash the deals desk piece of shit, Darryl, right between the eyes. Not an unlikely shot really, considering there's about a six-foot gap between his pupils. "Fuck you, Flynn!" Yeah, whatever, mate. I look forward to seeing his PNL report for me tomorrow, four million bucks in the black in one day, cuntface, whack that in your option pricing formula, deadshit. I'm Charlie Sheening so heavily.

"All set boss, let's hit it."

"Good man. The course is in Malaysia, you got your passport here?"

"Yep, in my drawer, one sec."

I grab the passport and we take the lift to the basement car park. Joel walks towards a gunmetal, showroom fresh, Aston Martin, throwing me the keys, "you drive buddy." I hop in to the boss mobile. This beast is beyond primo, a far removed, extreme distant relative from the dilapidated Mitsubishi Express van sitting back in Sydney waiting for my tail between the legs return some day. I take the driver's seat and look at the fighter jet controls infront of me, how the hell do you drive this thing?

"Well, start her up then you fucking moron."

"How?"

"You really are a pleb." Joel leans across and presses the start button.

"So just how small is your dick then boss?"

"Just drive. It's auto, no gears for your pea brain to worry about."

I take it nice and slow through the car park, probably not a great idea to scrape the big cheese's car. There are two pods in the back. You could maybe seat a Chihuahua there. Maybe. Why do they even bother? We reach the exit, Joel passing me the swipe card, and we're on the streets. Singaporean soulless consumers watch on as they walk through the midday heat, crushed with jealousy. Two awkward minutes pass, nervously making my way through traffic and simply praying I don't drive into a parked car. But once we hit the freeway, my balls are swinging, my pin dick duly compensated for by the V12 thunder. I'm giving this Aston a beat down and I am fucking loving it.

"I know I talk a lot of shit, but well done with this new blendstock. I mean, really, really well done."

"Thanks a lot, I appreciate that."
"This is a tough business. It takes its toll. I just want you to know, you're doing well. These decisions you're making, connections you're building, you're on the right track son."

"That's great to hear."
"I told you that I knew you were the greedy, crafty cunt the fuel business needed."

The drive takes over an hour, crossing the bridge into Malaysia and completing a quick customs check. We arrive at the Johor Country Club. Joel instructs me to complete a lap of the overly lavish water fountain and pull up at the reception area. We hop out and he hands the keys to a parking attendant who grabs his clubs from the trunk while some other guy in a black suit and white gloves drives the car away to the parking lot.

A male concierge welcomes Joel and leads us through to a dining room and bar overlooking the course. Two men, each with powerful beer bellies, jowl laden jaw lines and bottles of Heineken are standing at the end of the bar, smiling at Joel and I as we head their way.

"Afternoon gents, great to see you again," Joel and the men shake hands, "please meet my new fuel trader, Flynn James."

"Flynn, nice to meet you, I'm Leonard." He's the more rotund of the two, a signet ring adorning his frankfurt sausage pinky and a strong regal voice to match his imperially blood vessel damaged skin.

"Hi Flynn, I'm Charles." Less plump, though the theory of relativity is a wonderful thing for a moderately fat man next to a modestly obese one.

"Great to meet you both. I haven't played golf in a long time, I hope you're ready to win."

"Already foxing hey. Well, we'll wait until the second tee off before I start gambling too heavily on how bad you are."

"No foxing, I'm horrific."

"Flynn, Leonard is Powcom's head of Far East Fuel Trading."

"That I am. Joel tells me you're working with Andrew now, trying to iron out all of Bing's fuck ups."

"Ha, yes indeed, I never properly met Bing, but, for my sins, that's what I'm now doing, working with Andrew to iron out all those creases. We're making progress."

"That's good to hear, I'm sure you've got your work cut out for you."

"And Charles is their Gulf Coast fuel trader, based in the Houston office."

"Excellent. How long are you in this part of the world for?"

"Just this week, head home tomorrow."

"OK gentlemen, if you'll excuse us, we'll get ready and see you on the first tee off in twenty minutes."

Joel shows me to the Pro Shop and takes great pleasure in forcing me to purchase golf attire that was surely salvaged from Payne Stewart's plane wreckage. I look flamboyantly gay and am putting the rage in raging homosexual. He then asks the Pro to hook me up with the latest Callaway set of clubs. The bonus I'm yet to be paid will barely cover this one afternoon of golf. The bill comes close to $5,000 SGD for some clubs which have more advanced technology than most satellites and a set of clothes in which even George Michael would blush. Fuck it. Let's play.

Joel takes my work clothes with him and heads to the change rooms, reappearing a few minutes later in perfectly acceptable golfing attire. We head to the first tee. The Pro says the new clubs will be brought to the first tee by our caddies. Caddies? Joel jumps in a cart and tells me to hop in. He floors it to the opening hole. Charles and Leonard are twisting their portly physiques through some sort of feeble warm up attempt as we pull up.

We join them at the tee off and look back at the path with our mouths on the turf. Two more golf carts comprising four Malay girls head our way. Our clubs are on the back of their carts while their schoolgirl smiles beam out from beneath Nike visors. Our caddies. They park at the tee off and each walk to their assigned player. Luckily, my almost criminally homosexual outfit inspires the most striking of the foursome to head my way. Each girl is sporting a pink cheerleader skirt, white sleeveless top and thigh high plaid socks. My temperature soars with an almost immediate dose of fatal yellow fever. My caddy's name is Carmen. Of course it is.

"You hit off first, Flynn."

"Rightoh."

I conceal my boner under my belt and step forward. Carmen hands me the biggest of Big Berthas and gives me a quick neck and shoulder massage before placing my ball on a tee with an added degree of bent over verve in the process. This is exceptional. I line up the shot, taking a slow back swing and then belting the fuck out of the pure white Titleist. Whack. I've well and truly thumped the first shot, straight down the middle of a par 4. It's shimmering in the middle of the fairway.

Carmen's ecstatic, clapping her hands together and squealing in delight. She takes the club back, places it in my new bag and hands me an ice cold Heineken before continuing to massage my shoulders. This is next level. I take a healthy sip and watch the others take their shots. Charles and Joel hit respectable drives, no match for my wonder shot though, Leonard shanks one deep into the woods.

We jet off in the carts, now paired out in boy-girl duos. Carmen speaks very little, but giggles nonstop. I let her take the wheel. She seems to think this is amazing. We pull up at my ball and wait for the others to take their shots. Joel and Charles follow up their drives with impressive iron shots. Joel is on the green for two, Charles is in a bunker just to the right of the dancefloor. Carmen hands me a six iron, that's actually a very good club choice, well done.

I go through a warm up swing, taking a look into the rough where Leonard's ball is somewhere. The big fella's deep in the tropical bushland with his pants round his ankles while his caddy uses her right arm to hold off his huge guts and is busy sucking away on the Powcom's head of Far East Trading's cock. Jesus Christ! I look on in amazement and horror. Joel and Charles are completely unfazed. What world am I living in? I try to refocus and take my shot, the tropical birdlife no match for the slurping in the rough.

Leonard emerges back on to the fairway after a few more minutes. He's sweating profusely but looking thoroughly relaxed. He lets us know he couldn't find his drive and will take a drop. Yeah, please, do what you like. He strikes his shot on to the green. Charles escapes the sand trap with his first effort and we each putt out the hole. I win with a par.

At the second tee off, Leonard scrolls through his Blackberry to show me a photo of his wife and kids. Why? Why do that? I say how lovely they all look and enjoy Joel's approving stare from his safely eavesdropping distance. This is a business relationship requiring delicate mending thanks to whatever Bing did to ruin it. Maybe he simply had a moral compass that wasn't completely fucked up. That can happen to the best of us.

I hook my drive deep into the rough and scoot off with Carmen. She doesn't even pretend to draw out the task at hand or feign an interest in trying to find the miss-hit tee off. She dives straight for my crotch and gets nuzzling feverishly. I pull her back upright and quickly feel her up to make sure there's not some huge dick under her skirt. Phew. Please, carry on. I don't care what the membership cost is, I'm sold. We head back to the fairway and I hit a dropped ball.

The others are nowhere to be seen, all exploring the rough with their shirts on and their slacks off. Carmen hands me a five iron and I play a conservative shot straight up the middle. We continue up the fairway as the others slowly return from their wanderings. There's all sorts of wrong going on right here, but I've been in Asia long enough now to have given up chastising myself for being at the top of the food chain. Fuck it all, if I'm going to hell, I may as well go full throttle.

We carry on for a few more holes. We're no superannuation fund managers here. Despite being on the golf course, we have serious business concerns to attend to meaning there is no shortage of Blackberry scrolling between drives, putts and blowjobs. Charles and Leonard excuse themselves for a moment, as we are about to tee off on the fifth hole. They return after a five-minute discussion and look deflated. Not surprising though really, at least for Leonard, he's had three blowjobs already. I mean fucking hell, that's impressive.

"I'm sorry to be a downer gents, but we've got a fairly urgent issue to fix. We may need to call it quits early sorry." The gloom on Leonard's face as he says this makes me think he was definitely planning on several more wayward drives this afternoon.

"Apologies for being nosey, but is there anything we can assist with." My Charlie Sheening hasn't worn off yet. Joel looks nervously angry as I say this.

"Umm, well maybe you can actually. That former colleague of yours, this Huan bloke that seems to think he's invincible, he's fucked us." Leonard and Keith would get along great.

"Really? He's trading crude isn't he?" At least he was trying to do that when I was his deals desker.

"He can't trade anything, he's a piece of shit. He told us he had a stream of fuel oil and sent over the specs. It looked legit. We've now run the assay report with the vessel parked at our terminals. The oil's completely useless. How the fuck he has a job in this industry is beyond me."

"Yeah, noone knows, but, depending on how much you need, maybe I can help you out. I'm assuming you've got some Singaporean bunker buyers screaming at you for deliveries."

"If you can muster 20,000 tonnes over the next three days you would be a lifesaver."

"Let me quickly call Andrew."

I walk away from the tee off. Carmen follows close behind. Some blood starts to race south, but I focus instead on business and tell her to leave me alone, the consummate professional.

"Andrew. Mate. The new shipment with the palm oil blend, you haven't committed that to anyone yet have you?"

"I've got a few buyers circling, but was going to wait until the window this afternoon and sell it out piecemeal."

"Great, can you hold off? The Powcom boys have a supply problem. If we can sell it to them, at least 20,000 tonnes between today and Friday, I reckon Bing's fuck ups will be a distant memory."

"Fuck yeah. Lock it in. And tell them we'll deal at a $3 discount to market. We can try to make up for Bing's shit. Fucking result though, with this palm oil blend, we'll still be making fucking shitloads."

"Perfect mate. Let me lock it in. Call you back in five."

I return to the fifth tee. The girls look so bored. Maybe they do sincerely love sucking sweaty Anglo dick. Women, who knows what they want?

"20,000 tonnes, no problem. We'll give you a $3 discount to market too. It's the least we can do."

"You're a lifesaver!"

"No problem. Please, hopefully the Bing nightmares will be somewhere close to buried soon."

"Of course! Joel, how'd you find this young man? Keep an eye on him. He'll be getting money thrown at him left, right and centre. From me at least."

I message Andrew to lock in the trade and step forward to smash my drive down the middle. Carmen hands me a fresh Heineken. Ice cold, tasty goodness. The others hit errant tee shots into no man's lands, better known in Malaysia as gob stops. Joel's caddy hands him a Heineken as he walks back from his tee shot. He takes a seat on the cart next to me, "your bonus has just doubled now thanks to that quick thinking. Excellent work."

. . . .

Joel kicks off the weekly trader meeting, "let's start with crude oil. Keith, any news to report?"

"So, this week in crude, we've seen..."

I'm already nodding off as Keith Wang launches in to some inane market commentary. I'm filling in the blah blah blah's in my own head rather than bothering to contaminate my thoughts with any of Keith's talk.

Every Tuesday morning, Joel leads the traders through our weekly meeting: The Tuesday Trader Meeting, a completely pointless exercise. The well-intentioned genesis for the gathering is obviously a sharing of ideas so that the collection of Scion's Singapore traders spanning the full barrel of oil products can band together to generate the most astute possible trading initiatives. We'll all bask in the glow of shared success and coalesced wisdom.

There's one glaring fault with that plan. People, on the whole, are selfish, thieving, two-faced, backstabbing cunts. And that's normal people, let alone the money-obsessed, wholly immoral, hyper achievers in this room. We're all paid the big bucks to be smart here, to make shrewd trading decisions and avoid the inevitable pitfalls of believing the typical bullshit each day is filled with when you're forever bombarded with misinformation overload.

Lesson number one, once you do manage to have a half decent trading idea, the rarest of commodities in the commodities trading business, whatever the fuck you do, do not tell anyone. Only once the trade is sealed and the profit is locked in, then and only then, is it prudent to enlighten others as to what you were thinking. Even then, there's no real upside in sharing your thoughts, but inviting others into your thought process at any earlier stage is immensely flawed.

Unfortunately, trades will always need to be run past the big boss before the trigger can be ultimately pulled, so you do have to explain your trading logic to at least one person, the big cheese. Luckily though, the he's a manager not a trader, he can't easily steal your idea and get in first. Privately, I've let Joel know my thoughts as to the idea-thieving ways of all the traders in the room. He's happy for me to say whatever the hell I want in these meetings, as long as I fill up a few minutes of everyone's precious time with something reasonably meaningful about the fuel oil world and don't say anything too ridiculous. That seems a fair deal. Andrew takes care of it all anyway. He's one of those people rather enthralled with the sound of his own voice.

Keith is a phenomenally intelligent, albeit autistic, trading mastermind. I'm sure he's clued on to the would-be intellectual property thieves in the room and fills his dialogue with misleading non-pearls of insight. He's ten million in the black for the year so, unless he's as fluky a prick as me, he must be doing something right.

He stops talking and Pranav takes over, impressing noone with technical jargon and biblical references in his wrap up of all things naphtha. His PNL is twelve million in the wrong direction, so he feels the need to make particularly employment saving statements as to the current chaos in the market as his discussion meanders on. The Indian once-upon-a-time-whiz-kid concludes his worthless drivel by introducing his new sidekick.

Mr. Nakahiro Tagasan, another fucking naphtha trader. He has been poached from some Japanese refiner, no doubt for some ludicrous sign on bonus. He spits and stutters his way through a lengthy opening monologue. The words are apparently English. The meeting room's air-conditioning is robust, but Nakahiro's woolen scarf and double breasted suit do little more than ensure we all wish his grandfather could have been considerate enough to kamikaze into Pearl Harbour before impregnating Mr. Tagasan's grandmother. I mean seriously, someone shut this bloke up.

Next, it's time for the fuel oil summary. Andrew handles this, informing the room of trends in Chinese teapot refineries switching from crude to fuel oil feedstock, debatable, Russian refinery turnarounds affecting European premiums, common knowledge to everyone, and ongoing civil unrest in Libya wreaking havoc on oil shipments through the Suez, a more obvious statement has never been uttered to a collection of oil traders. Great speech.

I don't say a word and pray noone asks me a question. I'm late for a coffee date with Nadia. I suppose you could say she's my girlfriend. She eventually did come round to my house, cooked an inedible Russian dish and then fucked my brains out. I'm no foodie and she seems enamoured with my puny Aussie dick. A match made in heaven.

Four months into my trading career and I'm up twenty million big ones. Yeah people, that's how it's fucking done. Everyone in this room, myself included, thinks I'm a complete cunt. That's understandable. All these parasites have no idea how it is that I'm making so much damn money selling bunkers. Joel, Andrew and myself have stayed strong to the cause and kept our blending sources top secret. Rudy too.

Everyone knows I'm up twenty million but can't for the life of them figure out what the hell I'm up to. If any of them knew, they couldn't really steal the idea per se, but they're liable to go shooting their mouths off to other traders and brokers all over town, letting the cat out of the bag and bringing the show to an end for my dizzying profits.

I never utter a word at these meetings. If Andrew is traveling on business or away on holidays, I simply don't turn up, staying at my desk and pretending I'm insanely busy while the other troopers amble past to waste the next half hour of their lives. All my communications from my desk are via emails and messenger chat rooms. I never speak a word of trading significance in the office. It's the smartest thing I've ever done.

I just keep my head down, mouth shut, and watch on each month as I book another bumper profit thanks to the palm oil manna. I spend most nights drinking heavily at Club Romeo, watching uninformed yellow fever riddled men getting felt up by Thai lady boys while I chat away with Nadia and the platoon of dazzling Russians. It's the best entertainment in Singapore.

The meeting concludes with Paul's recount of the week in derivative markets. Noone has a clue what he's talking about, but all nod, stroke their chins and adjust their cufflinks as he plows on discussing the 'VIX' (volatility index) and trading out his gamma while his delta doesn't give a fuck about his theta. I'm paraphrasing. One day before I'm fired, I sincerely hope someone just stops and says, 'Oi, what the fuck are you talking about?'

Joel calls the meeting to a close and we continue back to our desks. Darryl watches me with total contempt as I joke around with Joel, trying to trip him over. I stop at Darryl's desk and place down my apple juice popper, "put that in the bin mate, I'm too busy making money."

I proceed down the room and take my seat, firing up the latest screen addition. I've got six now. I could honestly do the job from my Blackberry I reckon, but that's not the point, is it. The newest screen is a live video feed to all the offices in the Scion network. Shanghai, Beijing, Moscow, Cape Town, Athens, Geneva, Houston, Panama, every office is now blessed with my hideous face on the screen of any trader who has similar access to excess technology and is part of the 'fuel trader chat room'.

It's 11am in Singapore, the same in Beijing, and our Chinese fuel expert, Cheng Bo, is in the communist capital. I have no questions for him, but he doesn't know how to mute his speaker so I can crank the screen to full volume and fill the Singapore office with all the 'nigger' sound bytes of the Beijing rabble. It actually means 'this', but such knowledge eludes the new recruit from Mozambique who sits across from me. Mr. Mozambique is fuming, forced to listen to the mundane Mandarin conversations going on a thousand miles away. I'm going straight to hell. That's fine. Mr. Mozambique will be happy.

I enjoy my African colleague's death stares and focus on the new hobby I've taken to over the past few weeks, writing letters. Not emails or text messages or whatsapps, no, letters. I scope people's names and addresses from Google and write them very thoughtful and articulate letters, stories of love and woe, betrayal and triumph, cryptic anecdotes, nonsensical poetry, dinner recipes. I write all sorts of trollop and am always sure to add in something spicy, 'I slept with the boss' or 'stole money from the fund'. I then seal it, stamp it and send it off. I make sure to put a return address on the back of the envelope, Darryl's.

I put the finishing touches to my latest letter, 'by the time this reaches you, I fear it will be too late. My love for you knows no bounds. Even the frontiers of your bitter cold heart will perish at the tender crush of my lips. Yours, always, Darryl.' I really have lost my mind.

I take off for the door to post the letter and grab a coffee with Nadia, wondering what shade of figure clamping leopard print she'll be wearing today.

7/ Fight or Flight, Hide or Seek

Searching for the sweet spot between a rock and a hard place

"Come on, pick which ever one you like, go big."

"Honestly, Joel, this is too much."

"I'll give you a few more minutes to pick one, otherwise I'll choose for you."

"Yeah, rightoh, how about that?"

"Flynn, I've got a two hundred grand budget for you on this mate. Don't skimp out when someone else wants to shout you. Didn't your parents teach you anything?"

"OK, OK."

Joel's taken me to a boutique jewelry store which requires an appointment before trotting along to throw your money away, or in my case, my employer's money. I'm trying to decide on an absurdly overpriced watch to adorn my womanly wrist. I'll probably have to get a female strap put on one of the men's timepieces. The saleswoman is drooling at the commission she'll soon be receiving.

As soon as she hears Joel mention the two hundred grand budget, she shifts into fifth gear of overzealous watch whore. I wish she'd just fuck off, but I suppose someone has to unlock the glass cases full of Swiss crafted ingenuity.

My first APPEC week with authentic trader credentials is one day away. I've managed to get through five months of trading super fluke-dom that has been mistaken by my countless superiors for superstardom. If I had even the slightest hint of talent to praise for my incredible success, I'd be more than happy to accept the gift of an insanely expensive watch as due gratitude for all the money I've swung into Scion coffers, but the callous truth only I seem to be aware of is, I'm a total impostor. I've got one golden goose, one lone client who continues to provide the palm oil residue straight from heaven. Andrew sources the globe for suitable concoctions of fuel oil to mesh with Joe's Indonesian palm oil stream, we run the likely outcomes through Rudy's blender, ship it all in, stir it all up, sell it all out, and laugh merrily to the bank every single month.

Joel, Andrew and many more take credit for their expert judgement in selecting me out of the thousands of candidates to groom into a trading powerhouse. Darryl's daily email fires out with the PNL summary. Every single day I'm sure it's all a joke and someone is going to point out the candid camera in the room somewhere. As of Friday, it's 'Flynn James 2013 PNL: +$24.6mio.' The biggest of big wigs in Geneva don't seem too concerned that my client concentration risk is dire. Those 'don't put all your eggs in one basket' words of wisdom everyone's heard at some stage seem to

326

have skipped the top brass at Scion. I suppose it all depends on the basket and the eggs.

When offering out bunker parcels of fuel oil each day, I make sure never to undercut the market, even though our profit margins are incredible and I could easily cope with a hefty haircut. I have the discipline to hold firm and talk up how much we're struggling to compete with market prices. Lies, beautiful lies.

Joel's aware of my concern that I am the epitome of a one trick pony. He and Andrew have set up a full schedule of meetings with oil refiners, producers, traders and anyone else he can think of for the APPEC week of back slapping and ego rubbing so that I can attempt to add some other revenue tributaries to the palm oil torrent. And a glitzy timekeeper on my wrist is just the ticket to show the oil trading world I know what I'm doing, so he tells me.

"This one here please." There's a Batman appropriate device amongst the Hublot watches, black banded, black dialed, black cased.

"Excellent choice sir."

"Just to be clear, how much is it?"

"The Hublot Big Bang King is $185,000 Singapore Dollars."

"How's that then Joel?"

"Perfect."

She places a pair of white gloves on before opening the case and handing me the Big Bang King. It sounds pornographic, which is appropriate, I'm sure it will get me plenty of gold digging vagina. It has a rubber bracelet. My Granddad would be ropeable to think of how expensive this thing is and they don't even have the common decency to provide a leather strap. Swiss cunts. The rubber bracelet is apparently Hublot's signature for their *sportswatch* collection. Spare me. It's Casio's signature too, but their watches are available at most supermarkets and often include a calculator.

All my bitching aside though, this Big Bang King feels incredible. It's hugging my feminine wrist with precision, the flawless black face of ceramic and sapphire beams up at me. Joel pats me on the shoulder, the lady continues to smile and congratulate me on such an astute decision. I admire the latest luxury in my life but realize I better sign up for boxing lessons, I've just given would be muggers 185,000 reasons to beat the fuck out of me at any given moment.

Joel sorts out the payment at the counter while I'm being watched by five other sales staff, all ruing the cursed hand they were dealt, not blessed with the good fortune to be serving a clueless Aussie with a practically bottomless disposal of cash. There are some other customers in the store. They're the usual middle class, middle aged, ultra conservative consumers who wouldn't dare spend over a thousand dollars on a watch without scrupulous research and passionate devotion from their sales staff. Joel finishes off the transaction and we walk out into the stifling warmth of Sunday afternoon.

"That's one impressive watch you've got mate."

"Thanks again. Honestly, this wasn't necessary, but I have to say, it's grown on me already. It looks sensational."

"Good man. You've earned it. Get some rest, lots of meetings this week. Add some more clients and keep making plenty of money, you'll be due for an upgrade on that watch in no time."

"Ha, fair enough."

"Oh, one more thing."

Joel hands me a cheque.

'The sum of one million five hundred thousand dollars payable to Flynn James. $1,500,000.'

Fuck off! Seriously, just fuck off.

"Spend it wisely. So, you know, fast cars, slow women, strong liquor."

"The holy trinity."

"Indeed. See you tomorrow."

I can't stop looking at the piece of paper. I don't say goodbye. I just stand on the street corner in the mid afternoon tropical heat with my Bruce Wayne watch, looking down at the cheque. I read and re-read it again and again and again. I'm a millionaire. I better wait till it actually clears before calling my parents to let them know how incredible I am.

I hail a cab to take me home for an afternoon on the couch watching Setanta, stopping at the bottle shop to grab a case of tigers. Before enlightenment, sink piss, watch footy. After enlightenment, sink piss, watch footy.

It's finals time now, September, the month the boof-heads train all year so diligently for. My Tigers ended up second last for the season. The finals will gladly carry on without them. They are probably in Bali anyway, getting flogged off their heads and putting groupies on the spit, standard post-season frivolities. I'm watching the Bulldogs take on the Knights, Tom Waterhouse has been banned from the sidelines now, his website still works a treat though. I grab my laptop and key in a $1,000 bet on the Knights for the win. Make it $2,000. Wait, I've got a $1,500,000 cheque in my pocket, fuck it, make it $5,000.

I don't watch the game too closely. From what I do see though, my money's safe, the Bulldogs are having a shocker and the Knights are ahead 12-6 at halftime. My attention is focused on completing mandatory KYC training before all the APPEC meetings kick off tomorrow. I've managed to delay completing this compulsory training for a couple of months now, but Scion's legal eagle fucktard had a big song and dance on Friday about risking the firm's Singapore Trading Licence if everyone didn't complete this pointless crap by Monday. It's an empty threat, without doubt, but I may as well assist the poor bastard. He is a lawyer after all. His life must be filled with suicidal thoughts in between cross checking the fine print of million word contracts.

KYC stands for Know Your Client. There's a sub species of particularly useless solicitors who specialize in this crap. When they're not spitting garbage about the importance of KYC, they're equally adept at thieving oxygen while rattling on about their CAML credentials, Certified Anti-Money Laundering. They believe, in some demented way, that finding ever new and more innovative ways of preventing traders from trading is somehow worth adulation, respect and bulky bonuses.

The traders, the men and women who actually make money to feed the corporation juggernaut should be assisted in that pursuit, not handcuffed and anchored by these racist legal jump-ropes. Black money is real money, the real money that pays your distended wages.

I complete the training module on my laptop with the requisite level of disgust and finish off my fourth beer as the Knights jog a victory lap of ANZ Stadium, 22-6, you beauty, paying $1.90, my $5,000 is now worth $9,500. Just throw it in the pile with all the other cash. I should have bet more, way more, fucking pussy.

Nadia messages, letting me know it's going to be a busy night at the Floors. Her English is still minimal, as is my Russian, but the bits and pieces of information I'm able to glean about the mechanics of the Southeast Asian sex trade are truly fascinating. Apparently a huge shipment of whores has been ferried in specifically for APPEC week, three thousand extra girls. The Four Floors ATM's have been fitted with quadruple the capacity of cash to dispose of for the evening ahead and an especially intense week of withdrawals thereafter.

She's told me many times, the Russian girls aren't whores, rather, they're just paid handsomely to dress in a bare minimum and bring out the overpriced novelty, firecracker coated bottles of vodka and champagne and then to talk with the guys. Just talk. I guess I believe her. I've never paid her for anything. Even the ingredients for the atrocious meals she likes to cook up are bought at her own expense. Apparently the Asian girls are the actual whores. And the lady boys, you can never forget the lady boys. I reply, 'the spare key will be in the hiding spot, see you later on xo', and drift off to sleep.

I waltz into the office foyer, lathered in the usual amount of Singapore daybreak sweat, grasping a coffee, sporting a tie and brimming with the confidence of a man who is paid so extortionately well, you simply can't help but believe that maybe your mum was right and you are extremely special. My sleeves are rolled up to highlight a watch capable of being valued in terms of GDP percentages rather than specific dollars and cents.

Nakahiro is in the elevator, taking a brief reprieve from scrolling on his Blackberry to survey my Hublot, then straight back to the berry. These naphtha cunts and their fucking Blackberries, they're not fooling anyone. Joel was right to invite me along to an afternoon of golf and head jobs months earlier with Powcom's traders. We're now back doing more business than ever with the behemoth of oil trading. Bing Zhao's fuck ups are a distant memory but are sure to be replaced by this Japanese piece of shit in the elevator before too long.

We continue out of the lift and to our respective seats. I wish him a good day in Italian as he takes his place infront of a wall of nine computer screens. Yeah, that's right, nine. It's ridiculous. I told the person on the opposite side of Mr. Tagasan's desk to sue him for radiation poisoning. I even wrote up the legal paperwork. The weak pussy never followed through with the claim. Where's the justice? And Italian, well, Nakahiro decided it was a prudent idea to go on holidays for two weeks almost immediately after signing up with the company. He barely had time to update his out of office email message, but he did.

'I am currently on annual leave. If you need to contact me, I will be available on Sicilian business hours'. Sicilian? Nakahiro Tagasan, the definition of fuckwit. He's more Japanese than a karaoke machine or Mount Fuji, but for some unfathomable reason has decided he's Italian. I mean really, what the fuck? Maybe he watched a little too much Godfather in his manically depressed teens, stoned out of his brain, cursing his Japanese parents, sipping a Lavazza espresso, eating Quattro Fromaggio pizza, watching Inter Milan versus Juventus from the comfort of a Tokyo high rise shoe box. Who knows? But his love affair with Italia is utter insanity.

Ever since I first noticed his wank-infused sense of fashion at his introduction to us all in a trader meeting, he has continued to strut through Singapore in full suit and tie at all times, a woolen scarf too, of course. How much sweat can a man endure? He has perfected the art of intentional mumbling. I assume. Noone ever has any idea what the hell he is saying. The trader meetings are hilarious. He'll pontificate and gesticulate his way through many minutes of incomprehensible stuttering, heavy exhaling and profuse spitting. If someone pretends to have understood anything he's said and asks a question, his agitation levels spike sharply. It's the pinnacle of my Tuesday. I usually ask a few questions.

Mutterings of his pathetic trading ability are becoming more abundant. I've spread a couple of unflattering rumours myself, let's be honest. Some people defend him, saying he struggles with English, he's a good chap, an excellent trader. If trading excellence is defined by the amount of computer screens you require, the number of heart attacks you've had before forty and the magnitude of money you spend on your Italian wardrobe and Swiss watches, then yes, he is indeed one supreme trader.

If, however, trading excellence is determined by how much money you make and opportunities you create by communicating market-moving information with your fellow traders, well then, my dear Japanese blooded, Italian clobbered, Swiss watched colleague is woefully appalling. He'll soon be fired, perhaps today. God's in town after all, and loves nothing more than relieving staff of their overpaid employment.

I check my meeting schedule for the day ahead and prepare some background information that might endear me to the Chinese, Taiwanese, Japanese, Bangladeshi, Indian, Saudi, and Kenyan clients I will be seeing today. Multiculturalism is alive and well in the Hydrocarbon World. KYC alright, I know my potential clients are motivated by nothing but greed, hindered by everything but ethics and are to be anything but trusted.

God enters the room from the elevator well and the entire floor takes a hush. He continues down the floor, his bushy eyebrows masking the intense focus of a lifetime spent sniffing through bullshit to unearth dizzying profits that non-cunts would be blissfully unaware of. Joel stands to greet him and they walk away to a meeting room. Da Vinci, Michaelangelo, Darwin, who gives a fuck what it's called, it belongs to God. I refocus on my multicultural background information to hopefully assist with all the meetings ahead today.

Joel and God exit the meeting room after a few more minutes. God walks back out to the elevators while Joel strides down the room, stopping at Nakahiro's wall of screens. Joel waits patiently for the Japanese fuckwit to acknowledge the big cheese's presence. Joel is not known for his patience. This is going to be awesome.

"Oi, fuckhead!!!" Joel leans in to a whisker from Nakahiro's face, yelling with explosive venom while the room of spineless Singaporeans watch on with complete fear. I wish I had some popcorn. This is sensational.

"Yeah, you fucking piece of shit naphtha boy. Do I have your attention now mate?" Joel smashes his fist through the top left of the nine computer screens. Nakahiro is crying and cowering, covering his useless face with his quivering hands. Joel pushes Nakahiro and his seat away from the desk, shoving all the keyboards and watch catalogues clear in one perfect Ari Gold sweep.

"Give me your access pass!! Give it to me you fucking stupid cunt!!"

Nakahiro hands over the pass with his right hand while his left arm is still pathetically shielding his crying eyes.

"Now get out of my fucking office and never come back!" Nakahiro tries to clear his drawers of whatever garbage is in there. "Get the fuck out now!!" Joel grabs him by the collar and shoves him towards the elevator well.

What a fantastic start to the day, absolutely fantastic. Joel walks past me, smiling and continues to the stairwell. What a legend. Mr. Tagasan whimpers out of the room in the other direction. Arrivederci, Sensei.

I drain my coffee, put on my jacket, adjust my tie and head upstairs for the opening meeting of the day, asking Darryl if he's lost his virginity yet as I make a particularly graceless show of checking the time on my new watch as I pass by him towards the stairwell. Somewhere along the way, I've learnt to really enjoy the feeling of being an outright cunt, an occupational hazard.

"Flynn, wait, Flynn." Rudy yells out from the doors leading into the room from the elevators and runs towards me.

"Rudy, what's up mate? I'm late for a meeting." He's already breathless from the 20m sprint. I thought I was unfit. Rudy doesn't say anything as he catches his breath and leads the way into the stairwell.

"We've got a problem." Nothing good ever starts with that.

"What is it? Fuck mate, you look like you just saw Darryl's dick."

"Flynn, there's big trouble in the terminals. The police stormed our tanks this morning. My friend at the terminal, he just called me…"

"Yeah, what did he say?"

"Our tanks…police scuba divers have found drugs."
"Drugs?"

"Drugs, Flynn. Cocaine in some sort of storage devices."

"What the fuck?!"

"Joe's palm oil delivery arrived yesterday. That's all we have in the tanks right now. We're still waiting for the Russian shipment to blend it."

"Joe has shipped drugs into our tanks?"

"I don't know. I think so."

"Who knows about this? Who?!"

"Noone, just you and me, and my friend at the terminal."

"Fuck, fuck, fuck!!"

"Call Joe."

"Yep."

What the fuck has happened here? My hands are shaking. The

$185,000 watch is little comfort for the potential execution I'm facing after a short stay at Changi prison if any of what Rudy has just said is correct. Fuck. Fuck. Fuck.

"Pick the fucking phone up, Joe!!!" It rings out.

I call him three more times. Nothing. Rudy and I are still alone in the stairwell. He must be as shit scared as I am. I make all the money but he handles these shipments, if I didn't like him so much I'd be figuring out some way to blame him for everything, but my little Arab coworker is an absolute legend. Fuck. I ring one more time and stare into the cement stairwell wall as it rings out.

"Faarrrrrrkkkkkkkk!!!!"

I'm about to throw the phone into the wall and it vibrates with a text message. It's from Joe. Phew. Thank God.

'Run'

This cannot be happening. What the fuck has Joe stitched me up with? I call him straight away. It doesn't even ring out now. It just goes direct to voicemail. I'm a dead man.

"Rudy, go back to your desk, this conversation never happened. I'm going to sort this out."

I reach out to shake his hand in a bizarre farewell gesture. His palms are ice cold, his face completely drained of blood, tears in his eyes. He leaves the stairwell and I slap my face with both hands. Fuck! I sprint to the next floor where the meetings are taking place, opening the door as slowly as possible, channeling all my Jedi training from a lifetime spent watching Die Hard reruns.

Joel is entertaining some clients I don't recognize at the lavish front desk. I try to catch his eye, praying like hell one of the prostitute dressed receptionists doesn't spot me and call me over. It can't be Baby Jesus, but some divine being is on my side temporarily, Joel spots me, excuses himself from whatever conversation he's filling with bullshit and walks over to the stairwell door and I motion him in.

"Flynn, what's the matter sport? You OK?"

"I'm fucked. Rudy tells me the customs police have just stormed our fuel tanks and found some shipment of cocaine."

"What?"

"Apparently they had scuba divers pick out a stash of coke from the fucking tanks. There's only Joe's palm oil in there at the moment. I messaged the cunt in Jakarta and he just said, 'run'." I show Joel the message and break down crying.

"Calm down, calm down."

"I don't care what the fuck has happened mate, I need to get out of Singapore. Now."

Joel mulls on this thought for about fifteen seconds. I'm having flashbacks of kicking a football with my Dad as a young lad, eating Nana's apple pies covered in Sara Lee ice cream and home brand custard. That'll be my last meal if Singapore prisons work anything like those in US TV dramas.

"Let's go," Joel sprints down the stairs and yells again, "let's fucking go!" We're 25 floors into the sky, racing down the concrete steps. After about 15 flights I can literally feel my heart about to beat through my chest, I stumble on a step and fly head first into the wall, smashing the side of my face, blood instantly streams down onto my right shoulder. "Don't fucking stop, Flynn. Run!"

We get to the basement car park. Joel races across the bitumen to his Aston. I whip my jacket off and apply pressure to the cut on the side of my head as he clicks the unlock button and we jump in. He speeds out of the car space at full pelt, slowing down as we approach the exit, swiping his card and proceeding past the building's entrance foyer with the refined elegance of a seasoned criminal.

There's a squadron of police officers inside at the reception desk. Holy fuck. He continues with grace past the entrance, thankfully not putting the pedal through the floor, as would be the case if the accelerator were under my foot right now. We proceed into the morning peak hour traffic.

"Give me your ATM card."

"What?"

"Your keycard, give it to me."

"Rightoh."

Slippery

"What's the pin?"

"1-6-7-5"

I hand Joel my keycard and he pulls over infront of the Citibank building on Church St. There's a street cleaner sweeping the curb, hoping to find some chewing gum and score a bonus from the neat freak government.

"Sir, yes, you. Hi there. Good morning. Please, can you do me a favour? I'm in a spot of bother, would you mind seeing if my keycard works over there at that ATM? The pin is 1675. And here's a hundred dollars for the trouble."

The elderly cleaner looks at him with the bemused astonishment you'd expect. I'm holding my suit coat to the side of my head. Joel smiles with the polite charm of a dictator as he passes the old cobber the card and the cash. He places down his broom and dustbin, and proceeds to the ATM booth. A few moments pass. A police car flashes by, sirens blaring.

"Fuck! Yep, you're in big trouble mate."

Joel speeds off as I look back at the ATM. The old man is already handcuffed, his face plastered to the marble flooring by the branch's security guard as the police storm the building. This cannot be happening. I'm frozen. For once, I'm not fucking sweating. After ten minutes of driving out of the inner city traffic, my thoughts completely blank with fear, we pull over into an empty street and hop out.

"OK, so they've already suspended your account. Fuck knows what you've got us into with this palm oil shit. Fucking agribusiness, I've never trusted it."

"I need to get out of here mate."

"OK, I've got it. This is how this is going to work. I'm going to get you to Malaysia, wave you goodbye then come back to try to explain to the world that you've been wrongfully accused and hope like fuck that Andrew, Rudy and myself aren't executed in the meantime."

"You don't need to…"

"Shut the fuck up!" He opens the trunk of the car and grabs his golf clubs, and picks out some nail scissors from the side pocket. "Cut this in half. I'll smuggle you out of Malaysia in my golf bag. I'm going to race round the corner and buy you a prepaid mobile. That bag better be perfectly split in half when I get back."

I'm sweating again. My body hasn't gone completely into breakdown mode just yet. That's good, I suppose. The scissors are designed for nail trimming, not Callaway leather golf bags, but I truck on as best I can. The taste of blood fills my mouth as the gash on the side of my head fires up with full force now that I can't apply any jacket pressure to it. I furiously cut the bag down the side and rip away at the seams on the base, yanking out the club dividers at the top. This is my fourth new home since jetting out of Australia, please don't be my last. Joel jogs back.

"Sorted?"

"Yep."

"Well, hop in."

I lay down on my side in the boot. Joel places the re-crafted bag over my fetal positioned body, the driver socks providing some camouflage for my head, the irons are pressed into my face, reminding me of the undersized overhead bars of the Shanghai train commute.

"Rest up, son. Once I get you to Malaysia, you're on your own."

He shuts the boot and here I am, compressed inside a set of posh golf clubs in the miniature trunk of the finest luxury car known to man, unable to even look at my exorbitantly priced watch in the pitch black darkness, pressing my right hand into my temple trying to stop the bleeding and hoping I don't hyperventilate. A childhood fear of confined spaces is the least of my concerns, death row a far more pressing issue.

After the initial couple of minutes of struggling to find some comfortable way to lie in the boot, the realization that I am well and truly fucked hits me. If I do manage to get to Malaysia, then what the fuck am I going to do? My money is frozen in the Citibank account, the only account I have. I've got a null and void $1,500,000 cheque in my pocket, a $185,000 watch on my wrist and a face that is probably plastered all over the news with a "Most Wanted" sub title. I think of my parents, my family and friends. I sob so uncontrollably I think it might stop the V12 engine.

My weeping subsides with thoughts of Joe's betrayal. His palm oil residue must have been a set up from the outset. Like all things too good to be true, they usually are. Bargain basement palm oil laced with narcotics. Fucking beauty, top bloke. I'm nothing more than an oblivious drug mule. Ignorance and bliss…they're far from the bum chums everyone assumes they must be.

The car stops. I can hear muffled voices. We must be at the border checkpoint. I close my eyes, cradle my hands around my mouth and nose and try to focus solely on the hot air hitting my palms, and breathing it back in slowly through my nose as quietly as possible. A couple of minutes pass. I've reached fifty breaths but feel I could break out into some sort of seizure soon if we don't start moving again. I focus my attention completely on breathing, feeling my chest rise and fall, my index and middle fingers massaging the bridge of my nose, my left hip numb against the trunk flooring.

We start moving again. Maybe we're in Malaysia, maybe Joel's been instructed by a customs official to park in a holding bay and I'm about to be imprisoned or maybe we're both about to bypass many more years of misery and enjoy a fiery car crash to bid this life adieu. The driving continues unabated. We must be safely into Malaysia. I'm a fugitive. That'll look mighty impressive on the resume next to physiotherapist, gold trader, oil baron, and drug mule.

Knowing I must be out of Singapore sets my thoughts racing through a pragmatic chain of ideas. I've never been to Malaysia, that's not ideal. Well I have been sucked off on the golf course, that's not really going to help now though, but it'd sure be nice. First things first, I'll need to grab some grubby traveler's clothes, Birkenstocks and a backpack immediately. A friendship band too. Thanks Kristian for reminding me of that core essential of every Eurotrash backpacker. Where are the touristy places in Malaysia though? Fuck, I've got no clue.

I really have only one shot at survival, aside from Joe emerging out of the woodwork and telling the world I am an innocent man. I need to call Mark and hope to high heaven he isn't in cahoots with Joe. If that wish is somehow granted, I need his expertise more than ever. He and his family are incredibly well connected throughout Southeast Asia. They're my only hope.

But Mark's the sole reason I'm in this nightmare predicament in the first place. Thanks for the intro buddy, thanks heaps. Fuck. No, it's my only shot. If my best mate did indeed stab me in the back and is ready to turn me in, I'll gladly die execution style, paying the price for being a horrible judge of character. The car pulls over. This is it. The boot opens. It's Joel, not a carjacker or a police officer. I'm off to a promising start with the latest career move.

"Right mate, all clear, out you get."

I push the clubs away and edge forwards. The heat overwhelms me. I'm so sick of the equator. We're a short way down a dirt road in the shade of some tropical overgrowth. I hop out and feel the side of my head, the cut seems to have healed over somewhat and the bleeding has at least stopped.

"Flynn, there's a train station around the corner. Get a train north, hide out and keep as low a profile as you can." He hands me his business card, the prepaid mobile phone package with two $100 credit vouchers, a recharge cord and all the Singapore dollars in his wallet.

"Joel, I want you to do me one last favour. Can you write a new cheque for me? Make it out to Mark Rassad and please get it to him in Jakarta, here's his phone number." I hand him the $1,500,000 bonus cheque he gave me only yesterday, the piece of paper I thought had confirmed me once and for all as the supreme package of success and brilliance.

"I'll try my best mate."

"Please, it's my only hope."

"We're going to get you out of this mate. Lay low, keep your eyes on the news and contact me whatever way you can. You'll be back in the office as soon as possible."

"Yeah. Well just in case that's not the way this story ends, give me a hug ya big poofter."

"Good luck mate."

Joel hops back in the Aston and takes off. It really is a magnificent stack of metal. I check my Hublot. It looks impeccable. 10.27am. I hold back more tears. Get it together, fuck's sake. I walk the short distance across the dust to the bitumen road as I put my jacket back on. If global warming could just hurry up and bring about a new ice age, that'd be great. I'm sweating heavily.

There's the dreariest of train stations a couple hundred metres down the road. A collection of clapped up beige, blue and gray Honda Civics, Mitsubishi Colts, Nissan Pulsars and dozens of scooters are parked on the street. There's a sign for an ATM, but the clothing and nick-nack outlets to fully stock up on my well thought out Eurotrash costume are not going to be found in this backwater train stop. Fuck that plan, dress for the job you want, not the job you have. I'll stick it out with the James Bond garb.

I turn away from the street to face the trees and do a quick count of the money Joel's given me, $3,455 SGD. I've got $925 SGD myself. OK then, well that's going to have to last me a lifetime. I walk up the station stairs and check the maps and timetables. I'm at Kempas Baru. Have you been? I wouldn't bother. I see a sign for the toilets and head in. It wreaks, as you'd imagine, of dank piss and steamy shit.

There's a cracked mirror above a plastic hand basin. I wash my face and tidy up the cut to the side of my head as best I can. I take a piss at the urinal, shooting off a lengthy splash to the floor for no sane reason and return to the basin to wash my hands and face again. I take the mobile out of the packaging and my own Blackberry from my pocket. Fuck, can they track me on this thing? I quickly scroll the contacts and transfer the numbers for Joe, Mark, Mum, Dad and Joel into the new phone, before removing the battery.

I call Mark on my new prepaid. Pick up!! What is with these fucking bastards and screening my calls today? It's a new number, so he doesn't know it's me, I'll give him that, but I can't risk sending him a message in case that can be tracked as well. Can they even track you like that? All this CSI, NYPD, Police Academy, Hollywood junk, fuck knows what cops are truly capable of. They always seem blessed with an incredible flair for finding semen, but aside from that, does anyone know what detective talents are actually at their disposal in the real world?

I head to the counter to buy a one-way fare to Kuala Lumpur. I pass a $50 SGD note to the inert, glasses wearing, frizzy haired old lady in the clear plastic booth. She hands me a ticket through one of those prison cell meal dispenser trays, as well as some change in Malay Ringgit. I've got no idea what the exchange rate is or how much the ticket actually costs, but now I have 200 MYR, $4,330 SGD and a watch that could see me comfortably retire in basically any Asian nation if only there were a way to sell it for its supposed market value. I already know I'm going to be handing it to some chancy prick for a pittance, probably before today is over, in exchange for a bowl of rice or a promise not to inform the police of my whereabouts.

There is a bookshelf type case to the side of the ticket booth with all the usual handouts and pamphlets about touristy shit. I grab a bunch of brochures and continue through the turnstiles, up to the platform. Walking tours, scuba diving, sailing, yada, yada, fucking yada, all the usual tropical endeavours. There's zero mention of cock sucking golf caddies. Black markets always have the premium produce. I take a seat at the far end of the platform and find a brochure with a map of the train network overlying a map of Malaysia, now we're talking.

A train arrives within a few minutes. A handful of Malaysian battlers disembark, carrying their sweaty, stunted bodies and waddling off to whatever wretchedness the rest of their lives have in store for them. I don't see any police officers or notice anything non-routine about the setting. It starts to rain as I jump into an empty carriage, take a seat and refocus on the maps. How the fuck am I going to get out of this?

This train line looks to pass through Malaysia basically from south to north. Aside from KL, I don't recognize any of the names of the various train stations. I call Mark again. Fucking hell, still no answer. No pick up. Nothing. Fuck. Noone is going to help me here. It hits me, I have to get to the coast. Indonesia is my only chance. I speak the language, bits of it at least after countless surf trips to the most wave-blessed destination on the planet. Most importantly, it is the ultimate land of opportunity. If I can barter with this watch somehow, I'm sorted for a lifetime.

There's just a little Malacca Strait crossing to worry about. How hard can it be? There'll be fishermen who can ferry me over. Yep, this is how I'll live to fight another day. I take a close look at the map. Malacca. That's my launching pad. I have to get to Malacca.

The resolution of how I'm going to survive puts me immediately on edge. Why the fuck am I on a train? I'm a sitting duck. Joel has probably returned to the office by now and has had to explain himself to authorities. God would also be demanding an explanation as to what's happened to me. Plenty of people saw me in the office this morning, it's not as though I just vanished into thin air. The police will be able to check Joel's passport and know he passed into Malaysia this morning. They'll be straight on my tail.

The train arrives at the next stop. I don't even notice the name of the place. I get straight out, run through the turnstiles and race to the first taxi I see.

"Malacca?"

"Malacca long way boss."

"Yes, long way, that's fine, let's go."

"Much money. You pay now."

I have no idea how much it should cost, no idea if this is the last cab I'll ever catch. I hand him $200 SGD. He has a whinge, huffing something in Malaysian. I hand him another $100 SGD. He doesn't smile, but he stops looking like his daughter just blew me and gets driving. I let out a long, slow breath, take off my jacket and wrap it over my head and sink into the synthetic leather seat. We're no more than a few hundred metres into the journey when I see a bookstand on the side of the street and the title 'Malaysian/Indonesian Phrase Book.' Fuck yeah.

"Stop, stop!" The driver lets out another agitated wheeze, turns his head to face me, but his eyes are rolling so far back in his head, we don't actually make eye contact. I'm a supposed drug lord, I should smash his face in, but I was raised far too well for such behaviour.

"One minute, I'll be right back."

The curbside bookstall not only has the phrase book, there's also a proper map of the region. Done and done. The stall proprietor is a young girl who can't be older than ten. She says something in Malaysian and holds out her hand. I pass her $50 SGD. I'm assuming this is way too much, but motion for her to keep the change and walk away. As I open the cab door I hear the innocence of her kindhearted voice, "thank you, mister." She'll do well at Four Floors in the not too distant future.

The cab shoots off. I open up the map first of all, asking the prick driver to point out where exactly we are. Kulai. OK then. He tells me it will take about three hours, maybe more, to Malacca. It's 11.15am. Rightoh. I find the patch of seating with the least amount of scratches and focus on learning Malaysian, brushing up on my Indonesian and becoming as best acquainted as possible with every nook, cranny and potential hiding cave in the Bermuda triangle between Chennai, Manila and Darwin.

The drive takes us through pouring rains and overcrowded roads. Somehow, we've not passed a single roadblock or police officer. I'm focused intently on the phrase book. Malaysian and Indonesian are essentially the same language. I'm going to need some reasonably smooth talking to get my way across the Malacca Straits. I read again and again through the phrases, not wanting to practice speaking them aloud with the driver in case the conversation gives away my fugitive status.

It's 3pm. We've made it to Malacca. If I weren't on the run for my life, I'd be sure to stay a while, the place looks stunning. But fuck all that floozy shit, I've got an escape plan to bring to fruition.

"Take me to the fishmarkets." Gee, what sort of a pompous cunt talks like that? Old mate behind the wheel lets out his usual huff, fair enough, can't blame him. After a few minutes, he pulls up infront of a huge series of tarpaulins connected between two old red brick buildings.

"Fish market here."

"Cheers mate."

Well, that's that then, here we go.

I hop out, folding the map of Southeast Asia into my coat pocket and handing the phrase book to a beggar on the footpath. She looks equally as impressed with the gift as the corn cob recipient back in Seoul. There's just no pleasing some people. I walk through to the tarpaulin markets, great timing, rain starts pouring the moment I step under cover.

The market peddlers scan me without suspicion. CNN headlines haven't reached this place. Stingrays hang from crucifixes, plastic sheets are covered with squids and sardines, old ladies with worn aprons and kitchen gloves shout their sales pitches at me. Old blokes are sitting at the back of the stalls playing some sort of checkers game, sweating fish cakes while they make their move and scoop up rice and curried prawns from banana leaves with their bare hands.

I approach one of the fishmonger ladies. She gives me a toothless smile as I approach. Her aged leather skin belongs in a Marlboro commercial.

"Di mana kapten ikan?" I've hopefully just asked, 'where is the fishing captain?'

Pterygiums fill her colourless eyes. She yells something to the group of old men gambling away their afternoon out the back. The waft of deceased marine life no concern. A rake of a man stumbles towards me, cigarette to his lips, oversized sandals on his muscular feet, in a pair of military cargo pants rolled up above the knees and a torn black shirt drenched in sweat or fish guts, probably both.

"Membawa saya ke bandar Dumai?" I hope I've asked if he can take me to Dumai City. It's the nearest port in Sumatra, a hop, skip and jump across the Malacca Strait away. He takes a break from puffing his cigarette to have a laugh at me. I'm hoping he's finding my accent funny, rather than the idea being too far fetched or the words having an entirely unintended meaning. I say it again, "membawa saya ke bandar Dumai?"

Like all Asian businessmen at every level of commercial success, the reaction to an offer by a white man is always followed by the obligatory few minutes of shock and bewilderment. He continues laughing at me, but I'm certain he understands what I'm asking.

I step forward, pressed up as close as possible to his aged face, "satu ribu dolar. Membawa saya ke bandar Dumai?" I hold his eye with the deathly serious stare I will hold now until the day I die. I've told him

I have $1,000 for him if he can take me to Dumai.

I don't flinch. He can't help breaking into a laugh. My unwavering resolve brings his expression back to deadpan. I place the money in my pocket and turn to walk away. Fuck. He better change his mind or my bluff is ruined. I take three steps and pray he speaks.

"Sir, yes sir. I take you. Dumai city. No problem." Thank fuck. I turn back and hand him the money. I'll be broke soon at this rate.

"We leave two in morning, boss."

"OK, where from?"

He points to the group of boats across the street, bobbing up and down in the harbour, looking unfit to cross an Olympic pool, let alone the busiest shipping route on the planet.

"OK, see you at two. Terima Kasih."

"You crazy man, boss."

I smile and wave him goodbye, walking out of the fish markets and into the rain. No turning back now. In less than twelve hours, we're going to cross the Straits of Malacca, the global shipping super highway. Jesus, Joseph and bloody Mary, I need a drink. There's a scummy looking bar a short distance down the road. It has a sign for 'Ice Cold Carlsberg'. That'll do.

There are some older looking European alcoholics, khakis, lobster tans, pelican necks, yeah, your typical sex tourists. They're joined, as always, by some barely pubescent Asian whores who could be studying medicine if they'd be born in some other patch of planetary dirt. Asia is so fucking depressing.

"Beer, boss?"

"Carlsberg, terima kasih."

I take a stool at the bar and avoid eye contact with anyone but the barkeep and the mounted television on the wall. There's a game of English Premier League on. A multicultural bunch of overpaid prima donnas frolic around on screen, passing the ball back and forth with their own goalkeeper while their fans belt the living fuck out of each other in the stands. Soccer, the world game, God help us all.

I drain the pint in two sips. I can feel the thirst from way down deep and order another, with a couple of tequilas to wash it down. Why not hey? One of the whores decides to approach me. "Hello, handsome man." She's just trying to make a living I suppose. You could drive a truck through the gap in her teeth and I can smell the rampant STD's festering between her legs. "No thanks, young lady." A few more tequilas and she'll no doubt look somewhat less disgusting, so, you know, doable.

I refocus on the game, smashing my grogs and numbing the fear that I may never see my family again. I suppress the tears, but know full well I could cry for the next day and still have plenty left in the tank.

The game carries on, ending nil-nil. The players shake hands and walk off. I'm five pints and seven tequilas deep. It's only 5pm. I've got another nine hours to kill before I can board the leaking boat out of here. My drink is empty and I'm gagging for another.

The barkeep is setting up for an evening of karaoke. Nightmare. The world would be a better place if they somehow took a global survey of who likes karaoke and who doesn't. Answers in. Lovely. Then go and execute all those in favour. Stage one complete of Operation Human Cleanse.

Old mate returns behind the bar. I order another Carlsberg and tequila while one of the Euros takes the stage with a teenage Malay girl. He picks out 'Gangnam Style.' What a cunt. I yearn for the Premier League's prancing excuse for male athletes to return on screen. It's now replaced with this fuckwit sunglass wearing, overweight Korean knob jockey giving deranged cowboy riding impersonations throughout abandoned warehouses, train stations and horse stables. The ageing sex pest on stage has replaced the lyrics, screaming out "Gang Bang Style, Sexy Ladies", laughing it up as a little whore backs her arse up on him.

I leave $100 SGD on the counter, shot my tequila and turn towards the stage, hurling the full pint at the fuckhead's oversized melon. I miss, dammit. The glass smashes on the back wall. What a shame. I cop abuse from all and sundry for being such a rude bastard. Yeah, save it, I know. I tell them all to go fuck themselves and walk outside. I'll wait somewhere else.

Luckily, the rain has stopped. I walk far enough away to not hear the shithouse karaoke renditions and take a seat by the harbour a short distance from my trusty fishing vessel. It looks like a high school woodwork project you'd be ashamed to hand in to the teacher. I'm screwed.

I look up at the full moon, making sure to not drop my head down, I'll break into a sobbing wreck the moment my eyes catch a glimpse of the shimmering water. No, it's just you and me, man in the moon. We'll have a staring contest until it's go time.

I'm woken from my grog-induced slumber by the captain's rushed Malay gibberish. He stops talking as he pulls the boat around to where I'm lying on the concrete wall. I sit up, rub sleep from my eyes and try not to whiff my rancid breath. I step down onto the boat, brushing off his outstretched hand to help me aboard, saying what any Aussie lamb to the slaughter would, "she'll be right, mate."

I'm no historian, but I'm fairly certain these words passed the lips of every doomed Anzac battler as they stepped onto the shores of Gallipoli, sensing the impossibility of the task at hand, just climb a sheer cliff with a heavily armed battalion of Turks firing nonstop at you from up top. No problem. She'll be right mate.

I complete a quick father, son and holy ghost as I'm directed to my place to sit, a tiny plastic chair in the undercover engine room, first class spot. Jesus. My face is basically a snorkel for the boat's lawnmower engine's toxic fumes. Two deckhands jump aboard. They seem to be the captain's sons. They look to be in their early teens and are each carrying four jerry cans. They give me a smile. One offers me a cigarette as he places the jerry cans under my seat. I wave off the smoke but return the smile as a splash of petrol hits my shoe from a lidless jerry can. Here goes then.

The boat is probably 5m long with a timber hull. You could call it a dinghy, I suppose, but to say it's many rungs north of raft status would be a stretch. The deck is already a couple of inches beset with water. We've barely set off. Fuck me dead. Both of the boys are busily scooping out water with plastic bottles cut in half. They're sitting on a plank in the middle of the deck. I've got haemorrhoids just watching them. The plank seating design looks more inclined towards torture than comfort, covered in splinters and drenched in grime. The boys are sliding all over the thing as they scoop out water and prepare fishing gear.

The hull slopes skyward from back to front. The pointy peak of the bow is at least 2m higher than my spot in the stern's engine room. I'm under the shelter of a plywood cabin, designed to keep the engine out of the elements I guess. The skipper is sitting atop the thing, only God possibly knows how. I reckon I could push the whole contraption over with the force of a few fingers, yet here the old cobber is, sitting up there chain smoking, barking instructions at his deckhand sons and expertly steering the ship with one bare foot on the tiller.

We seem to have stopped taking on water. It must have simply been from the afternoon rain. The boys are holding out hand reels with makeshift lures. The captain sings Malaysian lullabies to the moon in perfect time with the sputtering engine, the fumes drift untouched into the wake. Galactic vessels abound in the greater distance, the piercing glow of oil tanker lights filling the sea salt heavy horizon. There's virtually no wind, even less swell, the flat seas allowing for the most tranquil of Strait crossings.

I'm using my scrunched up jacket as a pillow, resting my exhausted thoughts on my coat pressed up against the plywood cabin. This, to my amazement, is the most serene moment of my life. I drift off to sleep, watching the moon play hide and seek behind the bow, grateful to my inner demons for always giving me the misplaced arrogance to fuck the system and just have a red hot crack at life, regardless of the odds. The ending's inevitable. We're all dealt the same losing hand in the womb, but you can bluff and raise or fold and crack, your only choice is to go out swinging.

I'm wakened by the gentle shade of a pre dawn hazel glow enveloping the Strait. The boy to the right yells, the captain stops the engine. He's hooked a fish, the slack in his hand reel flying away in a heartbeat. His brother jumps over, grabbing his twin around the waist before the force of the hooked fish almost catapults him into the ocean. The captain jumps down, helping his one son pull in the catch of the day while the other holds both of them by the belt, wrapping his thighs around the splintered plank, grafting the three of them aboard via the anchor of extreme groin strength and splinter resistance.

I watch on in awe at the teamwork display before assisting with pulling in the catch. Six hands work together to fight the marine beast. Four anorexic Malay hands do the lion's share. The milky soft

Anglo hands achieve little more than bleed into the Malacca. The struggle lasts at least thirty minutes. The sun is shining brightly on my second day as a fugitive before we finally outmuscle this monster Spanish mackerel. I'm assuming that's what it is, that's the only fish name I know.

The guys pull it aboard and lay it in the front compartment of the tiny boat, scooping in some extra water with the plastic jars to keep it as fresh as possible and covering the compartment with a green tarpaulin. We all smile and hug. I'm not sure exactly what they're saying, but it seems obvious this big catch will sell handsomely.

"You are good luck, boss." I'm absorbed in the captain's embrace, tears welling in my eyes. His wiry frame reminds me of my Grandmother. He can't weigh more than forty kilograms.

He returns to his perch, the boys take their spots again, re-jigging their lines and lighting up cigarettes. They motion me back to the cabin, the only refuge from the blistering heat that will shortly engulf the Strait. They implore me to rest. I grab my coat and resume my seated sleeping posture, watching on as the rising sun turns the water a shimmering blue, the shipping super highway's gargantuan vessels the only blemish on this tropical paradise.

"Please, boss, sleep. Long way. Ten hours. Sleep."

The journey carries on. The fresh ocean breeze drowns out the otherwise unbearable heat. Some more impressive fish are brought aboard without the full contingent needed to complete the job. Contrary to populist mythology, we're not required even once to fight off machete toting pirates. As the day plows on, I make my way through some masked Leonardo Decaprio Coachella ball tripping impersonations, thoroughly dehydrated, deadly certain a Bengal Tiger and Indian zookeeper are chasing us down on an inflatable igloo.

I'm positive it must be a hallucination, but after a full day of chasing the horizon, there is a clear stretch of palm trees separating the sea from the sky.

"Indonesia, boss."

I've made it. I look out through the cabin's back window, the captain's toes clamping the tiller, an endless abyss of water beyond, flowing all the way to Malaysia somewhere out there. I turn back to the palm tree dock a short distance off. The joy of this Strait crossing triumph is quickly subdued by the fact that now, yet again, I have to work out what the fuck I'm going to do next.

I can't just turn myself in. I've already come so far. What's the worst part of being imprisoned? Get all your meals, a dry place to sleep, a bit of arse raping…how bad can it be? Apparently one in ten blokes love it up the crapper anyway. Maybe I'm in that poo-pumping minority. There is, however, one absolute certainty of Southeast Asian imprisonment when drugs are involved, it will end in execution.

"OK, you swim now, boss."

"Swim?"

"Yes boss. We must go fish market. You swim, yes?"

"Yeah, I swim. Where's Dumai?"

"Dumai City, one hour, you walk OK?"

"You can't take me to Dumai?"

"Dumai. No. Many police, boss. You bad man, yes?"

"Umm"

"You bad man, that's OK. But no police. Bad for you. Bad for me. Police very bad. You swim."

"Thank you so much. I'll never forget this."

I take out the Blackberry and prepaid phones from my pocket, quickly looking at the important phone numbers one more time and hoping Alzheimer's doesn't hit me now. I hand him the phones, a pathetic gift, but better that than a watery grave. I shake the boys' hands, hop to the edge of the boat and dive fully clothed into the final 50m of the Malacca Strait. The warm, salty water passes through my greasy hair, cracked lips, Zegna suit. It's pure bliss. I hold my breath and continue underwater for as long as I can, eventually rising to the surface to wave my travel companions goodbye for the last time.

I make it to shore, stumbling my way to dry land. I'm all alone on a desolate stretch of soft white sand and crab shells, palm trees and fallen coconuts, a setting sun and drenched clothes. I'd stay forever if only I knew how to fish, or make a fire with fast hands and dry wood, or, most importantly, stave off the mosquitoes preparing for a malaria ambush. Every step of the way there's always some blood-sucking parasite cunt just licking his lips, waiting for you.

I can hear engines in the distance. There must be a road nearby. I take a final glimpse of the Malacca Strait and begin the walk through the jungle, stepping extra loudly to scare off snakes and vengeful orangutans who've heard about Chinese menus.

Within ten minutes I'm the best-dressed, sopping wet hitchhiker in Sumatra. A road like any other throughout Indonesia runs the length of the coastline. Potholes, goats, scooters, chickens, cows, what any seasoned Indo traveler should expect. I hail down a scooter almost as soon as I reach the road. There are two twelve year olds who can barely believe their eyes.

"Bule! Bule!" Indonesian for 'white man, white man!!'

"Saya mau ke Dumai." Please take me to Dumai.

"Bule!!"

They don't reply with a yes, they just point out once again that I am a white man. Yes, very clever. But their eyes light up and they both shift forwards on the seat, opening up room for me on the back of the prehistoric Honda. I hop on, hang my feet out and hold them up to avoid contact with the road while balancing my upper body as best I can without holding onto the boys, much to the chagrin of my baptizing priest. The young driver isn't accustomed to a grown western man weighing down his scooter. He almost sends the three of us off the road as he rounds the first bend, overtaking a donkey drawn cart of dried seaweed and yelling out to his buddies, "Bule, Bule!!"

I'm cold for the first time in recent memory. The wind chill is heavenly. There's a gradual increase in shanty houses and rabies riddled dogs as we arrive into the town of Dumai. You know when you sweep the house, clearing out behind the fridge, under the couch, absolutely everywhere, and you take a final look in the dustpan at the dead skin flakes, abandoned body hair and rotted food crumbs before dropping the contents into the bin. You imagine, 'I wonder if I could shrink down to microscopic size and walk around that filth, what would it look like?' It would look like Dumai.

We pass by a medical center and I ask the boys to stop. They pull over to the side of the road, yelling out to absolutely everyone they can, "Bule! Bule!" These little cunts are just what the doctor didn't order when you're trying to be as low fucking profile as possible.

"Berapa harganya? Saya mau membeli sepedanya?" How much for the bike?

There's no way on Earth it is theirs to sell. They look at each other, unsure what to do. I pull out my wallet, handing the slightly bigger of the pair $500 SGD, the notes still wet from the swim ashore. Their side-by-side faces are joined ear to ear by the biggest of conjoined smiles. I'm handed the keys and take off.

Slippery

"Selamat malam." Good evening.

Their 'bule' screams are no more. Dusk is over. It's now properly dark. I continue through town for five minutes on my postman's bike, the wind blowing over my Hublot watch and salt encrusted face, not once questioning my first impression, this place is a right fucking shit hole.

I pull over at a service station. For those unfamiliar with Indonesia, a service station is a hut by the side of the road. Outdoor bamboo shelves are stocked with once upon a time vodka and rum bottles now filled with gasoline. A Yoda look-a-like Hermaphrodite with heavily sagging titts, a thick beard and a hooded hessian mumu grabs a bottle from the shelves as I pop the tank. He/She/It empties the petrol through a red plastic funnel into my two-stroke getaway vehicle.

The smallest note of currency I have is $20 SGD. The fuel refill would have cost no more than a few bucks. Yoda turns her nose up at the Malay Ringgit I try to pass over, but accepts the twenty Sing and motions to a container filled with chocolates and soft drink. I grab as much as I can to fill my pockets, my last meal was a shot of tequila at Malacca's premium karaoke whorehouse. I'm starving.

All smiles, happy days, transaction complete, I'm off again with a full tank, unwrapping a chocolate bar as I see a sign, 'Jakarta 1,478km.' There may be a few more stops along the way, but I'm headed to Mark's medical centre, he's not ignoring any more calls.

There is simply no way I can twist the throttle a moment longer. My hands and wrists are completely numb. Fatigue through the night of endless driving has not been an issue. Potholes the size of houses and signs warning of Sumatran Tiger attacks have kept me on my toes without a problem. There were plenty of enforced rest stops too. The tank on this piddly bike doesn't buy you many miles before you have to hope another stocked bamboo shelf appears roadside. Thankfully, insomnia seems to be plaguing Indonesia and I found no shortage of petrol stands along the way.

But now, with dawn imminent, I just need to take a break. I pull over, stretch my hands, arms, shoulders and neck, and take a piss into the roadside jungle. I look down, catching a glimpse of the rank attempt at urine passing from my little fella. There's no burning sensation, but whatever this sickly fluid passing from my cock is, it belongs in a vegan's health shake, not my bladder. I flick out the final drops of green-brown sludge and look down with genuine medical concern as the piss makes its way into the jungle like algae filled molten lava.

I get back on the bike as the first rays of sunlight break through the storm clouds. My third day as a fugitive begins. I need to find a place to rest my head, drink a few litres of water, eat some rice and prepare to continue the drive as soon as any hint of physical strength returns. I pass a sign for Kota Jambi. It's only five kilometres further. I can make it.

The city of Jambi is yet another dustpan replicating Indonesian metropolis. These people really have perfected poverty. There is a river flowing through the town that makes Shanghai's Huangpu look like Switzerland's Lake Geneva. I continue over the bridge and through town until a sign for 'Hotel Sekana Putri' catches my eye. I pull the scooter up 50m down the road in a side alley and walk back to the three-storey complex of mustard yellow concrete cancer.

Two women are standing at the reception desk, immaculately well presented in red and white flowing uniforms. I step inside, my clothes thankfully dry, still a slight squish in my stride with each step though. The leather shoes weren't designed for the journey they've just been through.

"Selamat pagi. Ada kamar?" Good morning, one room please.

"Kasih paspor anda?" Fuck. They need my passport. Just give me a room, God dammit.

"Sebentar – itu di dalam mobil saya." One moment, it's in my car.

I walk outside and back to the alley, wiping the sleep that didn't have a chance to fill my eyes, start the scooter back up and continue on my way. Fuck it. Shove the passport requirement up your arse. I'll sleep when I'm dead. That can't be far off. I need to eat something though, and drink some form of water that has not been anywhere near the town's river.

It's early in the day, but Jambi's *Masterchef* is riding his tricycle food cart through the streets. There's a large display cabinet, filled with steaming pots of orange, green and red curries and stews. It's a superb breeding ground for salmonella, giardia and dysentery, all packaged up conveniently onto a three-wheel death trap. My stomach overrides my brain. I drive up next to the man, asking him to pull over. He smiles and comes to a halt.

I don't ask what the differences are between the contents of the various coloured pots. Let's face it, they'll all taste incredible, I haven't eaten properly for days. I point to all three varieties and the rice container as well. He loads it all up on a banana leaf, folding it together like a burrito, and asking me for 25,000 Rupiah ($2). The roller shutter doors of a shop across the street open up; a combination travel agent, foreign exchange dealer, jewelry hawker, garment specialist and wood carving peddler.

I head over to exchange the Malay Ringgit and $300 SGD. He rips me off, I presume, but I'm too tired to haggle, and walk back to my burrito stew, now with 2,500,000 Rupiah in my wallet. Indonesia's *Who Wants to be a Millionaire* is not an overly enthralling show.

The tricyclist restauranteur also sells bottled water. I buy three litres and sit in the gutter, eating with my bare hands and guzzling the water down in a few gulps. I buy another bottle, but wash it entirely through my face, and hair, the fugitive shower, inches of caked on dirt and salt flake off my face. I hop back on the bike and turn my back on Jambi, hopefully never to return.

Driving through the day is not wise. I'm barely a few minutes out of town when it's obvious that I'm sure to run into police before too long. What the fuck is a passport-less white man in a flash business suit doing on a shitty bike in the middle of Sumatra? I need my

Slippery

Eurotrash intrepid traveler outfit. I turn straight back.

The garment specialist is excited to see me again. He looks more Indian than Indonesian, black jeans, an oversized yellow t-shirt and wispy facial hairs that pop out of random locations on his face and nose. He speaks but I'm not listening. There are all sorts of hideous hippy pants and reprehensible rainbow shirts. Jackpot.

I grab myself an emerald green pair of pants, the crotch at the knees, and a purple and yellow button shirt that John Lennon was deservedly shot in. I undress into my new digs and buy a dainty pink backpack, folding up my suit, shirt and shoes into it. There's even a rice farmer straw hat. Its poor aerodynamic design shouldn't impede too drastically on the Honda's top speed.

I take a look in the mirror. Fucking sensational. I look like one of those 'namaste' preaching cunts who thinks four days in a yoga retreat entitles you to speak with authority about diet, relationships, healthcare and the universe. I can do all that and I've never even wasted the four days of miso soup and stretching to achieve Zen-level self-importance. I put the Hublot in my backpack. The insanely expensive watch is looking way out of place.

I hand over $50 SGD, grateful that his shop doubles as a foreign exchange desk, and smile off the rotund little man's attempts to add a wood carving or silver necklace to the purchase. I grab a pair of double-plugger flip flops and, just as I'm about to leave, I see an earth brown friendship band on the table, the perfect final touch. I wave farewell and take my spot back on the bike, refueling fully at the

Liam Carroll

first petrol stop I see. I notice a pay phone and decide it's time to make some calls.

No pick up from Mark, God dammit. I decide to ring Joel. If they can trace a phone call from this Allah forsaken city, then I deserve to be caught. It rings and rings. I'm about to hang up.

"Hello, Joel Ryan speaking." His voice shoots flames through me. I can't speak, transported straight through time to a moment when I had the world in my hands, not the other way round.

"Hello? Hello. Who's there?"

"Joel, it's Flynn." I start crying as soon as the words hit the receiver. I shield myself from any pedestrians, my face millimeters from the dial pad.

"Mate, you're quite the global sensation."

"What?"

"You've not seen a newspaper?"

"No mate."

"Australian drug lord fugitive, presumed dead."

"Fucking hell."

"Your dear pal Joe has stitched you right up. He's in prison in Indonesia somewhere, busy telling every policeman and journalist that you're some criminal mastermind."

"Perfect."

"I'm sure you're a criminal. Who isn't? But mastermind? You're the dimmest cunt I've ever met. Meanwhile a bunch of crazy hot Russian girls are telling everyone that you're a very nice man. Fucking hell mate. You're a surprise package. Times are tough when you've got the Russians supporting you. Are you a spy for Putin or something?"

"Great pep talk, as always."

"Sorry. Sorry. Mate, it's great to hear from you. You OK?"

"I'm alright mate."

"Listen, I just got back from Jakarta. I ripped up your cheque but took a truckload of money to your mate, Mark. Get to Jakarta, son, he's got all the money in the world for you. I added a severance bonus."

"What? You serious?"

"Serious as a heart attack. I can't help you wherever you are. Don't tell me anything. But just work out some way to get to Jakarta, your mate has $3,000,000 USD for you. You just vanish and have a nice life somewhere OK."

"Joel, listen and listen fucking closely, I will take great pleasure in killing you if any of what you've just said is your usual load of shit. Are you serious? Deadly serious?"

"Three million mate. US Dollars. Least I can do. Get to Jakarta. Get the money. Live happily ever after."

"Will do mate."

"Keep your eyes on the news, we're trying to get you off this thing."

"Just one thing mate, what number did you call Mark on?"

"The number you gave me. I flew down last night. Horrible timing, it is fucking APPEC week after all. Not everyone can be a fugitive like you."

"And you gave him the cash."

"Yeah, a hell of a lot of cash. I met him at his physio clinic."

"Thanks Joel. I gotta go."

I grab the bike, tears gone, rev the fuck out of it and set off. I won't be resting again until that money is in my hands. Joel...if there is anyone on Earth I wish the fate of my life didn't rest in, it would be Joel. He's a superstar oil trader. He's scum, but three million bucks. He smuggled me to Malaysia. That has to count for something, right?

And Nadia, shit, I forgot all about her. But Jesus, it can't look too good having the Four Floors star performers making righteous claims as to the soundness of my moral standing. What a fucking debacle.

I'd love to call my parents, but a crying wreck is the last thing central Sumatra needs right now. I press the rice farmer hat down hard into my skull, focus on the worn out bitumen below and pin every possible hope on Mark.

Slippery

It's mid afternoon, Thursday. I managed to lay my head to rest for an hour on a spare patch of grime during the overcrowded Sumatra to Java ferry ride. As we pulled into port, I almost couldn't lift the side of my face from the metal flooring, decades of spilt cola welding itself to my ear and cheek in the midday heat. My Yogi outfit had been endearing me a little too strongly to some similarly dressed fuckwits from California who wanted to pick my brain on my travels. Assuming the fetal position on the deck for a nap seemed a reasonable way to non-verbally tell them to get fucked. I was asleep instantly.

Ripping my face from the floor as we pulled into port proved an invigorating way to start the final leg of the marathon journey. Four days of trunks, trains, taxis, fishing boats, ferries and this blessed scooter and I've almost made it. I am so fucking tired. I caught a glimpse of myself on some polished metal on the ship's staircase. Fuck, I look about as healthy as Keith Richards at the base of a palm tree.

I've run and rerun thousands of times through the predicament I'm about to face. I have no clear conclusion. Joel could easily have lied to me about bringing the money to Mark. Mark could justifiably be screening calls from unknown numbers. As always, all I have is hope, well hope and a bottle of highly concentrated sulfuric acid. It caught my eye during a petrol stop last night after yet another unsuccessful attempt to call Mark.

The acid's commercial use is for cleaning metal. Scooter lovers throughout Indonesia apparently like to have the metal on their bike engines positively beaming. Whatever. I'm hoping I won't need to deploy the concentrated sulfur for a more meaningful purpose. Best mate or not, there's no telling what people are capable of when huge wads of cash are guiding their moral compass.

Entering the final stage of the journey, fully taking in the horror of Jakarta, I'm certain of one absolute truth, mankind does not belong on Earth. The Indonesian capital is the pinnacle of man's antipathy toward nature. Skyscrapers sprawl in every direction. Concrete is so entrenched it grows aggressively in the omnipresent smog and aggressive equatorial heat. Ten lane roads are saturated, any gaps between stationary, horn blaring cars is filled with motorbikes carrying five or more people each. I feel spoilt, all alone on my very own scooter, rich prick.

Clouds of pure toxicity spew heavy rain and vicious lightning as I pull over opposite the Pondok Indah Physiotherapy Clinic. According to the sign, Mr. Mark Rassad is the Head Physiotherapist, and Thursday's closing time is 6.30pm, three minutes away. I cross the road, torrents of discarded two-minute noodle packets and cigarettes clog overburdened drains after a mere sixty-second deluge.

I reach the footpath infront of the clinic as a middle-aged woman walks out, locking the door behind her. Fuck. I race around the block to the back of the building. Physiotherapists don't leave the moment their last patient appointment is over. There are always notes to catch up on. There's a small car park with a lone sedan. I push the exit door. I'm in.

A vacant hallway leads through to the reception area. I can see my scooter through the glass doors across the street, the rice farmer hat over the handles lit up by the headlights of endless traffic. I proceed past the reception. There is a large open area with three treatment plinths spread along the right wall, beige towels stacked neatly on top, starched white medical bedding draping to the floor, backless roller stools at each. The left wall forms the framework for all manner of resistive rehab and strengthening equipment. At the far end, a solitary desk, my best mate seated with his back to me, a pen in his right hand, left hand scratching his brow, patient files spread across the mahogany, waiting to be scribbled on.

"Is that Mexico's greatest ever barrel rider?"

"Flynn!! Fuck man, you're alive!!"

"I couldn't let a little drug smuggling charge bury me."

"The headlines are crazy!"

"Yeah, so I hear. I haven't seen them, been a bit busy."

"Yeah, of course. What are you wearing? Nice backpack. Jesus Christ, that's crook."

"New style I'm rocking now bro."

"Shit man, you smell like arse."

"Easy hey, I'm on the run you know, not prowling for chicks."

"Yeah, of course. How are ya?"

"You mind if I take a seat? I'm fucking rooted."

"Here mate, sit down."

Call me old fashioned, but if my best mate was on the run for his life and turned up on my doorstep, the first thing I'd do is give him a hug, a big fucking hug. The strangeness of this interaction so far leads me to grab my backpack and place it on the floor at my feet. I feel for the acid bottle inside as I place the bag down, making sure the sulfur is within easy reach.

"The old Leuko sports tape is still in use hey?" I grab a roll of sports tape from the desk and unroll a length of it between my hands.

"It's the only thing that works, you know that, or all that oil trading make you forget your physio roots?"

"I used to love this stuff. I'd get so excited when a patient needed an ankle or shoulder strapped."

"Yeah, it's still my favourite thing too."

"Now, excuse me for getting straight to the point here mate, but I'm in a bit of a rush and a little birdie has told me you have a big wad of cash that belongs to me."

"Fuck, what? I wish, mate. I wish. I'd love to have millions of dollars to give you."

Millions…I never mentioned millions.

"Just wishful thinking then maybe hey?"

"Fuck yeah mate, I don't know what you're talking about."

"Really? You see, we go back a long way, but the last time you contacted me, it was to ask me to meet up with a bloke who has since gone on to completely ruin my life, so I'm sorry if I don't outright believe you like I would have once upon a time."

"Flynn, honestly mate, I don't know what money you're talking about."

Please Joel, please be telling the truth. Mark senses me on edge and flinches in his seat. I lunge forward, pinning the length of tape over his eyes and head butting his forehead, hoping to inflict some damage without knocking either of us out. He's rocked back in his chair. My skull hates me. I gouge his right eyeball with my left thumb, through the tape, fucking retard. I make zero impact other than to tear the tape a little and alleviate his blocked vision. Get it together, fucking hell.

Mark bounces back from the head clash to sit bolt upright, shaping his pen into a dagger hold. I kick his right arm with my left foot, knocking away the pen and smash his face with my left fist, a weak punch but my knuckle definitely cocked him fair in the temple. I think I've fractured my hand. Hopefully Mark's in as much pain as I am.

The tape's in my right hand, I manage to wrap it completely round his head, covering up the patch I made, as I stomp into his guts with my left foot and knee him in the face with my right leg. I feel the crunch through my kneecap of his nose breaking. He collapses forwards to the floor. I grab both wrists, dragging them behind his back and taping them together as he lays prostrate and still.

I'm so exhausted, I feel I could collapse right on top of him. I shake my head back and forth, trying to wake myself as best as possible considering this is my fourth day on almost zero sleep.

I reach for the backpack on the floor next to his head, grabbing the acid with my right hand while my left arm holds Mark's head to the floor, blood oozing from his nose. I hold my left shin across his upper back and neck, my right shin over the back of his hips, pressing him into the floor.

"You've got one more chance to tell me the truth."

"Please mate, I've got no idea what you're fucking talking about."

"I picked up a little acid on my way here. We've watched Fight Club together, many years ago. I'm sure you still remember the chemical burn being a tad painful."

"Flynn…"

Please Joel, I've gone too far already, you have to be right. As Mark quivers my name I break down in tears. What the fuck have I become? This is my best mate here I'm stomping. I weaken my hold, losing my grip. Mark tries to squirm free. My right knee drops down past his hip to the floor, his mobile phone brushing my leg. Perfect. I grab straight for it.

"What's the pin? What's the fucking pin?!"

"Flynn, I don't have any money for you mate."

His voice is muffled and sobbing. I wipe tears from my eyes, careful not to bring the acid anywhere near my face. Mark relaxes completely into the floor. I strap his wrists together far more tightly and his ankles as well. I run the last of the tape around his head a few more times.

"What is the pin on your fucking phone!?"

"Mate."

"Pin or acid?" I pop the lid.

"7-9-6-2"

I scroll through the call log. I'm heartbroken but relieved.

"Would you like to explain why you spoke with my boss for seven minutes on Monday at 12.53pm?"

"He wanted to make sure you were OK, to see if I'd heard from you."

"OK, and another call Tuesday. He's your new best mate is he? And then another call last night. Mate, that's a lot of chin wagging with someone you don't even know."

"Again, he was just checking in. He said you'd given him my number, that you and I go way back."

"Open up your left palm."

"What?"

"You heard me. It's time for a little chemistry."

"Flynn. You've gone crazy mate. Just calm down, if I had millions of dollars for you, I'd give it straight to you."

"Noone said anything about millions. Now open your palm, you lying cunt."

I'm on the run for my life and my best mate thinks he can hold me for ransom. I've got no choice, the money's here somewhere and the money's fucking mine. It has to be. I'm certain. I let pour. Purple-black toxic liquid spills forth. Mark's left fist is still clenched. The backs of his fingers disintegrate instantaneously, a boiling broth of smoldering flesh, the stench of fingernails and sinew meshed in one sordid fluid of purple and red.

Acid drops spray onto the back of his right hip, his body spasms wildly. I'm flung across the room. He rolls frantically onto his back, but there's no stopping the sulfur. The acid simmers on. His breathing rapid shallow breaths but screaming in agony. I've broken him.

Joel, please mate, this better work otherwise you're next.

"Where is it?! Where's my fucking money?!"

"The money's in the safe you fucking psycho."

"Where?"

"Under the middle plinth just there. There's a safe."

I raise the sheets covering the mid section of the plinth. A length of weak plywood covers the safe. I throw it out of the way.

"What's the code? The code! What is it?"

"You're fucked in the head."

"The code. Now!"

"4-2-7-3-Enter"

I key in the pin. The lock's release deafens me to Mark's relentless sobbing. The fetid stink of decomposing flesh is replaced by stacks upon stacks of crisp, green US Dollars, breathing in their new owner. My superannuation in one generous lump sum, it's gorgeous.

I race to Mark, pull him to his feet and drag him to the sink, dousing his hand in water for minutes and soaking the back of his right hip, "it's gonna be OK mate. Just breathe."

Mark lies back down on the floor, the burn neutralized but the residual pain must be severe. Good. It's well deserved, the greedy piece of shit. I return to the safe and fill my backpack to the brim. This is so much fucking money. Mark's whimpering continues, his breathing a more relaxed rhythm though.

There's way too much cash for the one bag. I grab a Leuko case full of sports tape and first aid gear. Fuck that off. I empty the useless physio shit onto the floor and fill another bag to the brim with cash.

I've got no idea if this is $3,000,000 or not, but it's more money than I could have ever imagined. If Mark does have another stash somewhere else then good luck to him. I have to get moving. I'll need a decent head start to find somewhere to live happily ever after at one of the 18,000-odd islands of this archipelago.

"You're a dead man, Flynn."

"Calm down sunshine. This wasn't your money to begin with."

I bend down to pick him up, noticing his car keys on the desk. I'll lock him in the trunk. Boots aren't so bad. Someone can find him tomorrow.

"Fuck you, Flynn! Why couldn't you go and just die somewhere."

"Trust me, some day I will."

"Know this, you arrogant piece of shit, you're fucking dead. My family, we're everywhere. Every customs officer and policeman, they're all friends with my family. We'll find you, we'll kill you."

Fuck, he's got a point. Shit. Lying here tied up in Leuko tape on his clinic floor, you'd think he'd be smart enough to just shut the fuck up. This sulfuric acid must have some sort of spiteful truth serum additives.

"And not only you, your family, dead."

"What the fuck did you say?"

"Your parents, brothers and sisters, dead. What are you going to do?

You stranded cunt. You can't go anywhere, you're stuck here, waiting to trip up and my family or the cops to find you. Meanwhile, I'll fly straight to Sydney, console your family and arrange their deaths. Do not fuck with me, Flynn."

My eyes fill with tears, my fists are clenched and sure to burst, a fury rages through my chest and neck, the shit storm of everyone else's creation that I'm somehow fucked with completely overcomes me. I grab Mark by his ears, lifting him to his feet, ripping the tape from his eyes.

"I am the last thing you will ever see you useless fucking cunt!" I dig my fingers into the back of his neck and headbutt straight through his broken nose. He crumples to the ground.

"You will never touch my family!!" I kick him one more time in the nose. It's plastered completely sideways to his face. "Where's your family now?!" I pick him back up, bend him at the waist and drive my knee through his face one final time. He's covered in blood as he collapses back to the floor, lying on his back, struggling to breathe.

I lift him up so he's sitting and dig my body in behind him to prop him up, pulling his head back by the hair to raise his mouth to the ceiling. I grab the acid, pouring it straight down his mouth, holding his head back, fully emptying the bottle into his eyes, throat and down his chest, pushing his convulsing body to the floor and sliding away.

A haze of fried flesh, torched skin and flamed organs, rises through the room, my five senses each completely horrified. Mark's body writhes slower and slower until he's perfectly still. I stand over him, afraid to touch him, the popping bubbles of unyielding sulfur, cooking and killing below.

He's dead. There's no question. I'm a murderer. I'm numb, devoid of any sympathy for the bloke before me. What's wrong with me? I look at my hands, dead still. Shit, if God does exist, I can only hope he doesn't hold grudges. I'm a complete psychopath. My family's safe, I'm still fucked, but I've got $3,000,000, I'll cope. I think back to my religion lessons during a strict Catholic primary schooling, maybe there's more to Cain's story than we've been told.

I lay some plinth bedding over Mark's corpse, crying as I remember our every shared moment until this. Money…flimsy paper printed with ugly faces and arbitrary numbers. It fucks everything. I wash down every surface I've touched, making extra sure not to have a quick wank, the cops don't stand a chance.

I cross the road, the steam of overcrowded concrete in the tropics always feels awful, you never get used to it. The trusty Honda is drenched in rain, but starts first time. I don my straw hat, place the Leuko bag in my lap and pull on the pink backpack straps, solid as a rock. The peak hour traffic has relented. There's plenty of open road in between deep puddles filled with sewerage. Fuck you, Jakarta.

I take off, four days into my fugitive life, ready to retire. I think I'll live in Sumatra, massive coastline of perfect surf, maybe buy a little fishing boat, pay the locals to drop me at the outer reefs each day, I'll surf, they can catch my tucker. Symbiosis is a beautiful thing. I can feign devotion to Islam, that'll keep everyone off my back. No passport, no problem, I'll just never leave, they only hassle you when you try to escape. I'll have to check the headlines from time to time, see if Joe comes clean or Joel works some magic to clear my name. I am guilty of murder though, it wouldn't seem right to live without ongoing fear of the law.

I pull over at a small shop roadside to grab some water and chocolates for the night ahead of ever more scootering. Every imaginable product from mops to televisions covers any spare inch of floor and wall space. A lone man stands smoking behind the cramped counter, looking far too relaxed considering an entire Walmart's inventory is crammed into his retail cube. His young son is holding a toy gun, laughing as he follows me through the shop, shooting me over and over with imaginary bullets.

There are all manner of clothes, shoes, hats and sunglasses. I grab a Billabang t-shirt and a pair of Quiksliver shorts. I add some Nike shoes and a hat. The logo's spelling is correct, but the swoosh looks completely wrong. I take off my murder evidence collection of hippy clothing drenched in blood and dirt. I reach inside my backpack to grab some cash and see the Hublot. It still looks flawless. I place it back on and proceed to the counter, adding some water bottles and chocolate bars to my clothing purchase.

The old bloke notices my watch, "very nice boss." I take it off and hand it to him. Big Bang King, it's too flashy for me anyway.

"All yours."

He smiles, looking down at the fine specimen hanging loosely from his malnourished wrist. His son throws the toy gun to the floor to join his father looking over the watch.

"You very good man." Maybe I am.

I walk outside, taking a moment to sit on the scooter, breathe in the hot rain and drink a few gulps of water. I look back at the poor old bloke, mesmerized by the Hublot. He can't take his eyes off it. When he eventually checks on-line to see what that thing's worth, he'll probably die of a heart attack. What a way to go. His son now stands at the shop entrance, watching me without blinking.

There's a payphone by the side of the road. I want nothing more than to call home, hear the voices of my family and friends. I stare at the payphone for five minutes, my head tilted to the side, rain running down my face, Dad's warm voice in my ear, 'when life gets tricky, son, just look at it this way…'

I'm beyond exhausted but I'm alive and all of a sudden blessed with more cash than most people will ever know exists. I can picture mum crying at the kitchen table, waiting by the phone, my family and friends scratching their heads, completely lost as to what may have happened to the smiling larrikin who left their world only a year and a half ago.

Presumed dead? For the time being that is the best possible scenario. I've fluked my way through yet again.

I turn away from the payphone, rev the engine and drive off into the night, as always, completely uncertain of whatever's waiting next. Tears flow down my cheeks, Super Dad's voice steers me straight, wouldn't be dead for quids....not a chance.

ABOUT THE AUTHOR

I grew up in the Sydney suburb of Balmain. I completed a Physiotherapy Degree at Sydney University and worked in that capacity for a few years. With age and independence, I realised cash was of extreme fundamental importance, having somehow missed the memo during my first quarter century on Earth. I was drawn to financial markets and completed a Postgraduate Masters of Applied Finance. I scored a role trading precious metals derivatives with an investment bank before continuing on to trade oil and metals for a commodities trading firm. This is my first novel. I hope you like it.

www.slipperyscribbler.com

Made in the USA
Columbia, SC
01 May 2017